ENTER THE EDGAR RICE BURROUGHS UNIVERSE™

A century before the term "crossover" became a buzzword in popular culture, Edgar Rice Burroughs created the first expansive, fully cohesive literary universe. Coexisting in this vast cosmos was a pantheon of immortal heroes and heroines—Tarzan of the Apes™, Jane Porter®, John Carter®, Dejah Thoris®, Carson Napier™, and David Innes™ being only the best known among them. In Burroughs' 80-plus novels, their epic adventures transported them to the strange and exotic worlds of Barsoom®, Amtor™, Pellucidar®, Caspak™, and Va-nah™, as well as the lost civilizations of Earth and even realms beyond the farthest star. Now the Edgar Rice Burroughs Universe expands in an all-new series of canonical novels written by today's talented authors!

JOHN CARTER OF MARS: GODS OF THE FORGOTTEN

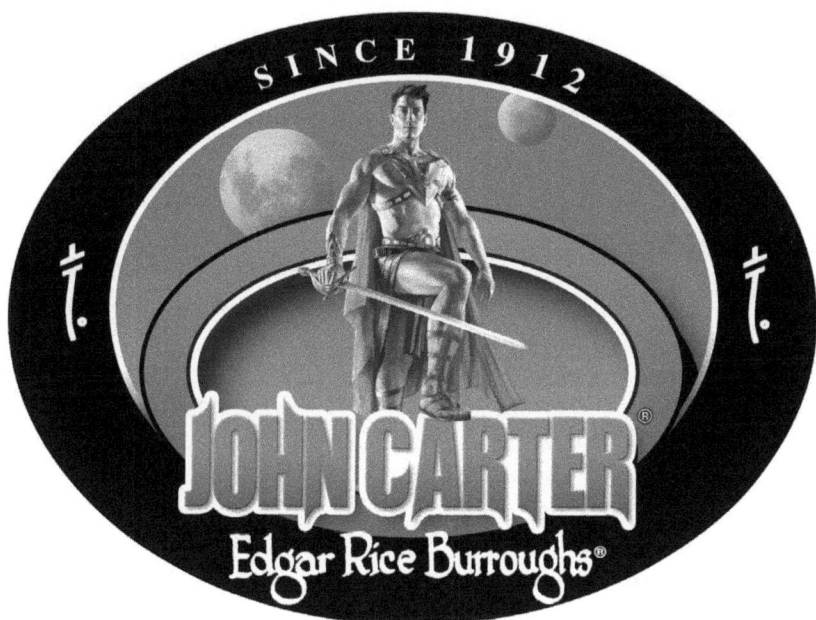

SINCE 1912

JOHN CARTER®

Edgar Rice Burroughs®

EDGAR RICE BURROUGHS UNIVERSE™

The Edgar Rice Burroughs Universe is the interconnected and cohesive literary cosmos created by the Master of Adventure and continued in new canonical works authorized by Edgar Rice Burroughs, Inc., the corporation based in Tarzana, California, that was founded by Burroughs in 1923. Unravel the mysteries and explore the wonders of the Edgar Rice Burroughs Universe alongside the pantheon of heroes and heroines that inhabit it in both classic tales of adventure penned by Burroughs and brand-new epics from today's talented authors.

TARZAN® SERIES
Tarzan of the Apes
The Return of Tarzan
The Beasts of Tarzan
The Son of Tarzan
Tarzan and the Jewels of Opar
Jungle Tales of Tarzan
Tarzan the Untamed
Tarzan the Terrible
Tarzan and the Golden Lion
Tarzan and the Ant Men
Tarzan, Lord of the Jungle
Tarzan and the Lost Empire
Tarzan at the Earth's Core
Tarzan the Invincible
Tarzan Triumphant
Tarzan and the City of Gold
Tarzan and the Lion Man
Tarzan and the Leopard Men
Tarzan's Quest
Tarzan the Magnificent
Tarzan and the Forbidden City
Tarzan and the Foreign Legion
Tarzan and the Madman
Tarzan and the Castaways
Tarzan and the Tarzan Twins
Tarzan: The Lost Adventure (with Joe R. Lansdale)

BARSOOM® SERIES
A Princess of Mars
The Gods of Mars
The Warlord of Mars
Thuvia, Maid of Mars
The Chessmen of Mars
The Master Mind of Mars
A Fighting Man of Mars
Swords of Mars
Synthetic Men of Mars
Llana of Gathol
John Carter of Mars

PELLUCIDAR® SERIES
At the Earth's Core
Pellucidar
Tanar of Pellucidar
Tarzan at the Earth's Core
Back to the Stone Age
Land of Terror
Savage Pellucidar

AMTOR™ SERIES
Pirates of Venus
Lost on Venus
Carson of Venus
Escape on Venus
The Wizard of Venus

When a mysterious force catapults inventors Jason Gridley and Victory Harben from their home in Pellucidar, separating them from each other and flinging them across space and time, they embark on a grand tour of strange, wondrous worlds. As their search for one another leads them to the realms of Amtor, Barsoom, and other worlds even more distant and outlandish, Jason and Victory will meet heroes and heroines of unparalleled courage and ability: Carson Napier, Tarzan, John Carter, and more. With the help of their intrepid allies, Jason and Victory will uncover a plot both insidious and unthinkable—one that threatens to tear apart the very fabric of the universe…

SWORDS OF ETERNITY SUPER-ARC

Carson of Venus: The Edge of All Worlds
by Matt Betts

Tarzan: Battle for Pellucidar
by Win Scott Eckert

John Carter of Mars: Gods of the Forgotten
by Geary Gravel

Victory Harben: Fires of Halos
by Christopher Paul Carey

CLASSIC ERB UNIVERSE

Tarzan and the Valley of Gold
by Fritz Leiber

Tarzan and the Dark Heart of Time
by Philip José Farmer

EDGAR RICE BURROUGHS UNIVERSE™

JOHN CARTER®
OF MARS®
GODS OF THE FORGOTTEN

GEARY GRAVEL

Includes the bonus novelette

VICTORY HARBEN™
STORMWINDS OF VA-NAH™

BY
ANN TONSOR ZEDDIES

EDGAR RICE BURROUGHS, INC.
Publishers
TARZANA   CALIFORNIA

JOHN CARTER OF MARS: GODS OF THE FORGOTTEN

© 2021 Edgar Rice Burroughs, Inc.

VICTORY HARBEN: STORMWINDS OF VA-NAH

© 2021 Edgar Rice Burroughs, Inc.

Cover art by Chris Peuler © 2021 Edgar Rice Burroughs, Inc.
Map of Barsoom by Cortney Skinner © 2021 Edgar Rice Burroughs, Inc.
Quantum Interlude © 2021 Edgar Rice Burroughs, Inc.

ERB Universe Creative Director: Christopher Paul Carey

Special thanks to Matt Betts, Win Scott Eckert, Dana Calvert Gravel, Janet Mann, Chris Peuler, Dale Russell, Cortney Skinner, James Sullos, Jess Terrell, Cathy Wilbanks, Charlotte Wilbanks, Mike Wolfer, and Ann Tonsor Zeddies for their valuable assistance in producing this book.

First paperback edition

Published by Edgar Rice Burroughs, Inc.
Tarzana, California
EdgarRiceBurroughs.com

ISBN-13: 978-1-945462-33-7

- 9 8 7 6 5 4 3 2 1 -

DEDICATION

For
Gabe Gill   Sophie Gill
with much love

And in loving memory of
"W3UIP"
who always enjoyed a good story

CONTENTS

FOREWORD

Director of Publishing
Edgar Rice Burroughs, Inc.
Tarzana, CA

Dear Sir:

As per your request, I am pleased to provide a little background information on how I came to be in possession of the unusual narrative I am enclosing with this letter.

My earliest years were spent in the Pocono Mountains of Pennsylvania, where my parents were the owners and proprietors of a summer resort. Located on a hundred and twenty-five acres of spruce and pine not far from East Stroudsburg, the town where I was born, The Pinehurst had been in our family for generations, the main structure having been erected as a boardinghouse in the mid-1800s. It was a wonderful place to be a child, with forests, lakes, and, in the complete absence of streetlamps and city lights, a night sky whose vast display of brilliant stars never failed to captivate my youthful imagination.

For most of his long life, my father was an avid amateur radio operator, the sort of devoted hobbyist that members of the commercial radio community initially referred to with disdain as a "ham"—a term that amateurs eventually adopted with pride for their own use. Familiar to his many contacts as "W3UIP," he had his own radio room in the basement of the cottage where we lived from October through May, while the hotel was closed for the season. I believe he was happiest during the hours he spent sitting at his radio rig, for he was a great lover of words and stories, and liked nothing better than to while away the evenings in lively conversation with people he had never met, throughout the United States and in countries all over the globe.

Running a seasonal resort was an unreliable source of income at best, and required year-round upkeep, not to mention round-the-clock work during the months when it was open to the public. When I was just shy of ten years old, my parents made the momentous decision to sell the property, and we departed the mountains for a more conventional life in a small apartment in a bustling suburb of Boston, Massachusetts—a place so unlike my familiar surroundings that it might as well have been the planet Mars.

My father brought his radio equipment to New England with him, as well as the meticulous records he had kept of each of his contacts over the years. Gaining a new call-sign with his new location, he continued his passion for ham radio until shortly before his key fell silent forever. After his death, his electronic gear was given to his closest friends in the amateur community, as he had desired. Never a radio enthusiast myself—but always sentimental and a pack rat at heart—I retained his boxes of records, hoping to someday gain some nostalgic pleasure by reviewing the contents before eventually disposing of them.

Many years passed before curiosity and the need to free up storage space prompted me to finally begin the process of sorting and discarding. It was only recently, while going through a file folder labeled "JC/1951," that I discovered what appeared to be a manuscript of sorts: a thick sheaf of pages written in longhand, which, according to my father's notes, he had transcribed from transmissions he received over a series of several days from an unknown source. Skilled in electronics and an inveterate tinkerer, he was always recording his experiments with this or that new modification to his transceivers in an attempt to improve the strength and quality of his communications. To that end, he had scrawled on the topmost page various cryptic notations of frequency and equipment settings in a shorthand that was unfortunately fully meaningful only to himself—but that seemed to indicate he had intercepted these signals after making a particularly novel series of adjustments to his apparatus.

At first riffling idly through the pages of this stack, just as I had perused many other records of my father's radio contacts reaching back over the decades, I soon came to realize that this was no perfunctory report of signal clarity data or friendly exchange of local weather conditions. Gripped by a strange fascination, I settled back into my chair and read the tale from start to finish, the day fading into deep night around me.

As I stated in my initial letter, I make no claims as to the actual origins, or, for that matter, the veracity of the enclosed narrative, and offer it only in the same spirit of wonder that I myself experienced as I turned the pages. That said, I should very much like to believe that every word of it is true.

Yours sincerely,
Geary Gravel
Greenfield, Massachusetts
November 2020

BARSOOM®

Eastern Hemisphere

Okar ◉
Great Ice Barrier
• Ghostly City
Duhor ◉
Artolian Hills
Phundahl ◉
Ptarth ◉

Greater Helium ◉◉ Lesser Helium
Hastor ◉
Zodanga ◉

Otz Mountains
Valley Dor

Dry Sea Bed
Marsh
Water
Heavily Forested

Western Hemisphere

Panar ◉
Great Ice Barrier
Toonol ◉

Gathol ◉
Kaol ◉
Exum ◉
Bantoom ◉
Xanator ◉

The Nine Circles
Otz Mountains
Lost Sea of Korus

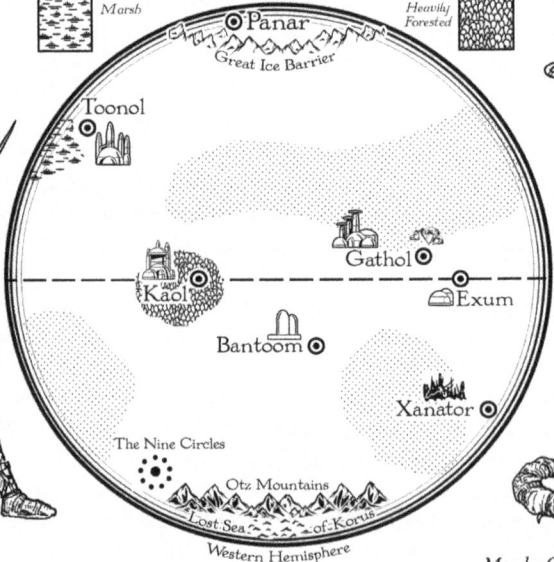

Map by Cortney Skinner

1

OF LIFE AND DEATH

I AM A VERY OLD MAN; how old I do not know. Possibly I am the oldest man who ever trod the green hills of Earth, possibly not. I have little doubt that there are some here upon the planet Mars who are far older, for the life spans of those who throng the ancient cities or roam the dead sea bottoms of my adopted world may easily surpass a thousand years—when they are not cut short, as is so often the case, by war or assassination.

I have long believed myself more naturally suited to the unfolding of age and time here on my beloved Barsoom—the name by which its inhabitants refer to the Red Planet—than I ever was on Earth. Once achieving a youthful maturity, the average Barsoomian lives out the remainder of his life with little or no evidence of physical deterioration, while I myself look much the same as I did a decade or a century ago, remaining to all outward appearances a clean-limbed fighting man of about thirty years.

On Earth I had been a soldier of fortune, a hired sword with allegiance to whichever master I found deserving of my service. Thus I was an advocate of individuals rather than causes, though one with few deep ties of friendship or family. In the former regard, there had been a handful of trusted comrades-in-arms, not to mention certain members of high rank in government and royalty scattered across the globe. Of the latter, there was in the great Commonwealth of Virginia a close-knit clan of worthy individuals by the last name of Carter that considered me their blood relation—though as I passed virtually unchanged through their succeeding generations this claim eventually acquired, at least to my ears, the ring of absurdity. To hear

1

me addressed as "Grand-uncle Jack" by a wizened gentleman leaning upon his cane must have been as disconcerting an experience for those who styled themselves my kin as it was for me. Yet they loved me sincerely, whatever our true connection, and I felt an equal affection for them; and whether the child I dandled upon my knee during those times of laughter and fellowship in the great hall of the Carters was my nephew or my great-nephew's grandson mattered little to any of us.

So it was that for many years I had a home in which to plant my boots whenever I desired respite from fighting and adventure; yet still I roamed the Earth with an unappeased wanderlust, as if in endless quest for something more, and it was not until my advent upon another world entirely that I would come to discover the one place my soul was destined to take root, and thenceforth devote myself to she who bore the mate to that soul, and to the ever-growing family of our own for which I had unconsciously yearned for time without reckoning.

To this day I remember nothing of my long-ago childhood, nor of any youthful years lived in Virginia or anywhere else. There are, of course, both advantages and drawbacks to having no recollection of one's early life. Fewer memories mean fewer regrets, and the absence of a true past may encourage a man to dwell more profoundly in the present instant. When from time to time his eyes stray to a far horizon, then it must needs be that of an unknown future, replete with all the mystery and thrilling promise that entails.

But still some questions have persisted, and with them certain doubts. In my darker moments I have found myself wondering if the emptiness that defines my early life would be confined to those years alone, or if it might not continue to spread forward in time like a destructive wave, devouring an ever larger swath of my experience. Yet while it is true that much of the record of my life on Earth has faded and lost its luster since first I found myself inexplicably transported to Barsoom, nearly every moment that I have lived here remains as sharply etched in my mind as upon the hour on which it occurred—and for that I am supremely grateful.

Even now I need but cast my thoughts backward and I am again opening my eyes, naked and alone, beneath a sky at once alien and strangely familiar. Once more I may stand wonderstruck amid the ruined splendor of a world-old city, transfixed by my first glimpse of the incomparable woman with whom I have gone on to spend these many years—already a lifetime to those I left behind on Earth—yet whose matchless beauty and shining spirit remain eternally undimmed. If I so choose I can call to mind each detail of the unimaginable horrors that greeted me upon my second crossing to Barsoom, there in the Valley Dor, that purported Heaven to which countless billions of believers had made their way down the River Iss over the ages, only to be thrust into the depths of Hell itself upon their arrival at those grim shores. Again may I relive the battles without number that I have waged and won against men and not-men of every hue and conformation, against monstrous beasts roused from their ancient lairs, and artificial monstrosities newly spawned in laboratories, all in devotion to the princess who claimed my heart and the dying planet I have come to cherish as my own.

I arrived on Mars a simple soldier—albeit one who has since been hailed by friend and foe alike as the best swordsman on two worlds—with no broader ambition than to test my mettle against a worthy opponent in the next campaign and the hundred after that. Over the long years that followed I was propelled by my fighting ability, by an unquenchable thirst for justice, and by plain good fortune to stations of ever higher authority, until the restless warrior who once lived and expected to die solely by the sword now commands the twin titles of Prince of Helium and Warlord of Barsoom, and meets regularly with heads of state from a score of disparate nations, to deliberate on matters that like as not will have profound consequences in the daily life of every inhabitant of this ancient world.

It was at the conclusion of a protracted series of such assemblies, this round dragging on for weeks and involving, as they all too often did, heated discussions, dry scientific lectures, and declamations that were by turns obsequious and bombastic, that I found myself longing for escape from what had become the stifling boundaries of my own beloved city—and aching for the opportunity to exercise muscles beyond those select few that were required to perch for hours on end on a hard slab of cold ersite.

I had overseen the departure of the last of the visiting dignitaries from the palace landing stage with what attention to decorum I could muster, and then made my way almost at a run back to my apartments, feeling in that moment more like a schoolboy released from a long day of hated examinations than a responsible bureaucrat. As the door slid shut behind me I flung myself down upon the nearest couch with a heartfelt cry of relief. I reached out for a waiting goblet, into which I poured a few inches of the cold, clear water that here on parched Barsoom is often more prized than the finest wine.

I had taken only a few cooling sips when I felt delicate fingers caress my shoulders from behind.

"Has my indomitable Virginian at last won his way to freedom?"

Turning at the sound of that treasured voice, I beheld my Princess of Mars.

For a moment I sat in silence, the goblet forgotten as I drank in the vision of my beloved Dejah Thoris. Her unlined face was beautiful in the extreme beneath its complicated coiffure of coal-black hair, her dark eyes set above cheeks of a smooth reddish copper, and her smile as radiant as on that long-ago evening when I first realized that I loved her and, moreover, that I would continue to love her with all of my heart for however many years the Fates saw fit to allot me.

I have habitually described the attire favored by members of both sexes among virtually all the civilized peoples of latter-day Barsoom as a simple harness of leather, but where that characterization might be sufficient for the humble garb of the average soldier or laborer, for whom it serves chiefly as a utilitarian arrangement of straps and fasteners designed for the holding of tools or weaponry, it could not begin to do justice to the elaborately ornamented trappings upon which I now gazed.

On this occasion, the artfully intertwined bands that framed my mate's slim form were all but hidden beneath rubies and opals in fanciful settings of pale gold, while clasped about her upper arms, wrists and slender ankles were intricately figured bracelets of the same metal, the combined effect at once exotic and regal. The heat of midday was beginning to dissipate, and Dejah Thoris had wound a length of gossamer crimson silk several turns about her body, fastening it at one shoulder and again at the opposite thigh with golden clasps, in anticipation of the chill that inevitably follows the brief Martian sunset.

Motionless, the Princess of Helium was a master sculptor's personification of beauty and grace. When she rounded the couch and took a step toward me my breath caught in my throat.

With a grateful smile, I drew my princess down onto the couch by my side and took her into my arms. Dejah Thoris kissed my cheeks and then my lips, and I returned the gifts with interest.

At length she leaned back to regard me with a look of earnest appraisal.

"From the grim set of your mouth when you departed for the Hall of Jeddaks this morning, I half feared you would spring like a cornered banth before the day was done, slaughtering with a single blow that unlucky scientist or head of state who dared prolong the session with another speech," Dejah Thoris said, the roguish dimples at the corners of her mouth belying her solemn tone. "May I assume the meetings have concluded with neither international incident nor excessive loss of life?"

"Your assumption is correct, though just barely, on both counts," I acknowledged with a wry grin. "As the hours plodded by, your Virginian banth felt less cornered and more like one caught in an iron trap, to escape from which he must finally resort to gnawing off one or more of his several legs." I gave my head a mournful shake. "I am not suited for politics and the endless bandying of subtle words. Let someone else be Prince and Warlord for a time, while I don the plain leather of a warrior and resume my rightful place with longsword raised in the front ranks."

Clasping my face in her hands, Dejah Thoris rested her smooth brow gently against my own.

"Sadly, John Carter, your people have long since come to recognize your great prowess in both arenas. If you had truly set your heart on devoting your days solely to cutting down foes on the field of battle, you should never have exhibited an equal facility in diplomacy and governance."

"It was a grave error," I agreed, and kissed her again.

Late afternoon gave way to dusk and evening came on with its usual swiftness. After I had scratched out a few notes on the day's dubious accomplishments and indulged in a long hot bath to cleanse myself of the grime of statecraft, Dejah Thoris and I sat down to a quiet supper on the upper terrace of our palace overlooking the main plaza of Greater Helium. We had been dining by ourselves often of late, many of the friends and relations that had once gathered in our spacious halls now occupied increasingly with their own pursuits. Though I savored every moment spent alone with my peerless princess, I had grown happily accustomed to the company of those cherished others.

My great friend Tars Tarkas, the giant Jeddak or emperor of the Thark nation, still joined us in Helium when he was able, but lately much of his time was taken up in the continued consolidation beneath a single flag of peaceful coexistence of the many hordes of savage green men that ranged the dead sea bottoms—a laudable but arduous campaign, given their millennia-spanning tradition of bloody mutual enmity.

Ulysses Paxton, my fellow Earthman now known more commonly as Vad Varo, had recently returned to his own princess in their home in Duhor, high in the snow-capped Artolian Hills, following a prolonged stay as our guest.* While here, he had assisted in the tutelage of a group of Heliumite scientists in the transmission and reception, via the miraculous Gridley Wave, of those dispatches that were from time to time lobbed back and forth through the ether between Barsoom and the small town in California where resided my friend of longest standing on any world—that member of my reputed kinfolk whom I regarded in many ways as my one remaining link to a world grown increasingly foreign.

As to my immediate family, our son Carthoris had been spending

* See *The Master Mind of Mars* by Edgar Rice Burroughs for the account of Vad Varo's first adventure on Barsoom.

much time of late in the navy yards of Hastor, where he worked with engineers aboard Helium's great fleet of air vessels to improve the electronic navigation and control systems that were his particular passion. For the past month his mate Thuvia and their young son had also been away, off visiting at the court of her father, Thuvan Dihn, in the friendly nation of Ptarth where the latter ruled as Jeddak.

Since her marriage to its sovereign, Tara, our younger child, had dwelled in the far distant land of Gathol; she had her own burgeoning family there, and her sojourns in Helium had lately been few and far between, owing partly to duties of state and partly to persistent unrest in the lands that lay between Helium and that isolated kingdom.

Over dinner Dejah Thoris and I discussed the topics of the day, she apprising me of interesting news reports that had surfaced while I was sequestered in my meetings, while I in turn offered a summary of various items that had been discussed on the last days of the conference. Occasionally the two lines of discourse dovetailed, as when our conversation settled upon the latest updates on the progress of the five principal air centers of the planet whose conversion to fully functioning auxiliary atmosphere plants had been decreed nearly a decade earlier by Tardos Mors, Jeddak of the Empire of Helium and my wife's grandfather.

This was a subject of close personal interest to both myself and my wife.

My first meeting with Dejah Thoris had occurred when we were fellow captives of the green men, I a newly arrived visitor from another world and she the only survivor of a devastating attack on a mighty Heliumetic airship. The vanguard of a strictly scientific expedition, the ill-fated vessel had been in the midst of performing atmospheric density tests and charting the currents of the life-giving air emitted by the advanced machinery of what was at that time the sole atmosphere plant on dying Mars, when it strayed above enemy territory and was blasted from the sky by the deadly accuracy of Thark sharpshooters.

Ten years later, I myself was instrumental in saving the entire planet from swift extinction when a still mysterious set of circumstances resulted in the death of both the atmosphere keeper and his sole replacement, immediately followed by the unexplained failure of the great pumps responsible for the continuous replenishment of Barsoom's inadequate atmosphere.

Now almost nearing completion at locations deliberately scattered around the globe, this massive project spearheaded by the red race was meant to ensure that no such catastrophe could ever again bring us to the brink of doom. An accomplished student of the physical sciences in her early years, Dejah Thoris maintained a long-standing interest in the artificial generation of a breathable atmosphere for our fragile planet, and her understanding of the scientific principles behind this miraculous accomplishment far surpassed my own.

By the end of our repast the conversation had turned to a fond discussion of our absent loved ones. Dejah Thoris had paid tribute to our children and their mates by concluding the meal with a rare wine from the celebrated vineyards of Ptarth, served in a pair of extravagant goblets, each hand-carved from one of the massive diamonds for which Gathol is renowned.

Neither of the moons had yet risen to begin its hurtling course across the darkened sky by the time we lapsed into a pleasant silence, our eyes drinking in the magnificent cityscape before us. Greater Helium at dusk was a panoply of brilliant lights, which gleamed in a myriad of hues from the white marble domes and gilded spires, and scintillated in golden flickers and bursts from the personal aircraft that darted like fireflies among them. In the middle distance the great scarlet tower that marked the city's center thrust into the gathering shadows like an upraised sword, a fitting symbol for the mightiest nation upon warlike Barsoom.

The view from our lofty terrace included one of the soaring walkways that each day brought visitors to and from the Warlord's palace, and as we sipped our wine my attention was drawn to a lone figure making its way in our direction. Aware that it was well past the time when state business was normally conducted, I suppressed a faint qualm of foreboding.

Minutes later there came a tap on the door in the chamber at our back, which slid open at my command to admit a single individual flanked by the pair of warriors who served that evening as guards for our private quarters. A short cape of black silk trimmed with silver identified the newcomer as a member of that cadre of scientists Vad Varo had lately trained, whose charge it was to oversee the communications conducted between here and the Earth, while also preparing for the activation of a network of Gridley Wave stations on this planet, pursuant to the establishment of no less than eight additional communication centers across Barsoom. Already equipment had been delivered to several of the nations whose rulers were bound to Helium by ties of friendship and, in some cases, kinship. Thuvan Dihn of Ptarth, Kulan Tith of Kaol, Kor San of Duhor, and Talu of Okar had all accepted Gridley Wave transceivers, as had Tars Tarkas, Jeddak of Thark, and Xodar of the First Born, who since the fall of the discredited goddess Issus had ruled a patchwork nation comprising what remained of the inhabitants of the Valley Dor at the south pole. Two more sets remained to be delivered, one destined for the court of my son-in-law Gahan, Jed of Gathol, and another to be based in the scientific installation at Exum, on Barsoom's equator, after which the great network would finally be activated.

Although preparations for the realization of the latter mission proceeded apace, there had been a puzzling suspension of communications with Earth of late, with Vad Varo determining before his departure that the fault seemed to lie not with our equipment, but in the very functioning of the Gridley Wave itself. The presence of the technician on our doorstep at this unlikely hour had me wondering if that situation had changed.

I rose to my feet and crossed the room to meet her, my eyes fixing on the single scroll of white paper she held in one hand.

"Communication with Jasoom has been reestablished, John Carter," she announced without preamble. "This message was transcribed scant minutes ago, and I thought it best to deliver it at once."

Handing me the scroll, she bowed and took her leave. I sank into a chair and sat frowning at the narrow cylinder.

Dejah Thoris had come to stand by my side. She laid a hand on my arm, her dark eyes on my face as I unrolled the paper and read the single sentence within.

"Is it . . . ?"

I nodded. "The message is from one of his sons," I told her. "He is gone."

I sat in silence for a little while, then rose and strode back to the balcony to stand with my hands resting heavily on the iron railing.

"Of course, it is hardly unexpected after so many years," I said, feeling the warmth of my wife's presence at my shoulder. I gazed up into the night to where a brilliant star shone like a sapphire among the lesser lights that had begun to appear in the firmament.

"Yet he was dear to you, both as a young child and an old man," said Dejah Thoris. "And throughout his whole life your devoted friend."

I nodded again. "More than that, he was my last true connection to that world."

Dejah Thoris rested her head upon my shoulder for a moment. "Ties still exist upon both sides," she reminded me gently. "Are there not his children? And ours, who may one day wish to know more about the world of their father?"

"Perhaps so," I said. "Or perhaps there comes a time when one must bid a final farewell to the past. Can any man really live in two worlds?"

I am not by nature given to bouts of melancholy, and the wave of deep sadness that had stolen over me as I stood there was as unfamiliar as it was unsettling. A faint mist blurred my vision when I lowered my eyes from the night. Gazing down, I saw the hands of a strong young man clasped tight around the iron railing, and I found myself feeling both weary and very old.

2
PARTS UNKNOWN

I HAVE FOUND there is no surer way for me to lift the shadows from my heart or clear the cobwebs from my brain than to take my swiftest one-man flier from the royal hangar and range as far afield from the haunts of Martian civilization as possible. Absenting myself for a time in this fashion from society not only buoys my spirits, but also serves as a surefire cure for any feelings of indispensability that may on occasion creep into my mind. In my experience there is nothing more effective for deflating an overblown ego than to race home from time away only to find that the mighty Empire of Helium has not crumbled into dust without John Carter there to keep it whole.

Thus it was that the very next morning found me some thousand feet above the ocher mosslike vegetation that now carpets those great expanses of Martian territory where once great oceans rolled, loitering along at a trifling two hundred miles per hour. I had made my escape aboard the *Tarkim*, a recently acquired vessel somewhat larger than my usual selection, due to my last-minute decision not to venture out in complete solitude. Over the decades my mate has become well accustomed to, if not delighted by, my penchant for unaccompanied excursions. It is a measure of her confidence in my ability to successfully navigate whatever exigent circumstance in which I may find myself, that she is able to bid me a fond good-bye without allowing any trepidations she might harbor in her heart of hearts to make themselves known. Still, I know that it afforded her an additional measure of reassurance when I elected to bring along for the trip he who is my oldest and without a doubt most faithful friend upon the planet.

For all of that, I almost changed my mind as I stood beside the flier with my arms about my wife. Was I indulging a childish whim to once again run off chasing adventure? Would I not be happier here at home at the side of my beloved princess?

Dejah Thoris was looking up into my eyes. "You know that I would much prefer to have my prince always here beside me rather than roaming this perilous world," she said, as if divining my thoughts—not an unreasonable assumption, had I been native to this world. All forms of sentient life on Barsoom, from the most highly evolved human to all but the lowest orders of beast, are to one degree or another telepathic, yet for reasons unexplained no one has ever been able to access the contents of my own mind, nor that of my fellow Earthman, Vad Varo. She smiled at my look of surprise. "I do not need to read your thoughts to know your heart, John Carter. But I also understand that you crave your own company on occasion, and that traversing the world in search of new corners to investigate is as vital to you as is food and drink to an ordinary man." She gave me a warm kiss and nodded to the trim craft behind me. "Go and enjoy your feast! All I ask is that you return to me, as you always have."

I was on the verge of releasing her and springing to the deck of the *Tarkim* when I spied an earnest-looking fellow, no doubt some civic functionary in search of my approval for a new species of ornamental shrub to be planted alongside the palace walkways, making his way with deliberate speed across the platform in our direction. Dejah Thoris turned to follow my gaze. "Go!" she repeated firmly, and kissed me again.

Looking back as I climbed aboard the flier, I saw her interpose her slim form squarely into the man's path. With an impatient gesture in my direction, he made as if to step around her. Though she was shorter than the unlucky fellow by half a foot, the Princess of Helium seemed suddenly to tower imperiously above him. I could not hear the words she uttered, but saw him halt in his tracks as if cold water had been dashed into his face, and then execute a trembling bow that dipped lower than I would have imagined possible. With a smile, I engaged the engine and the flier lifted from the landing stage.

Those familiar with my adventures on Barsoom will not be surprised to hear that there is no dearth of interesting destinations upon the Red Planet, whose dry land surface area, now that the five great oceans of antiquity have dissipated, is roughly equal to that of the Earth. There were many regions I could have chosen to visit in my official capacity, pursuant to matters decided in the conference just concluded. However, nothing was so urgent that it could not wait a few days for my attention, and so I resolved to scamp my duties, and set out not as John Carter, Prince of Helium, Jeddak of Jeddaks and Warlord of Barsoom, but as a simple explorer with a yearning for parts unknown, and seek the satisfaction I often find in those vast stretches of Barsoom which remain as yet unrecorded by the modern cartographer.

It was still necessary to depart the city with the *Tarkim*'s sleek prow pointed in a particular direction, and in this I allowed myself to be guided by whim rather than practicality. Over the past centuries, occasional reports had reached Helium of strange lights glimpsed dancing in the sky at certain times of the year, above the largely unexplored lands lying far to the north and west, just below the vast ice barrier that rings the northern polar regions of the planet. I had long wondered if this phenomenon might be analogous to the spectacular Aurora Borealis of Earth, which I myself had first witnessed long ago, while skulking through the Yukon Territory on a mission to retrieve some treasured baubles poached from a royal friend of mine who lived across the Atlantic. On that occasion I had lain in my bedroll staring upward for hours, fascinated by the shifting veils of green and rose that hung like diaphanous curtains over the night sky. It pleased me to think that I might see their like again, here on this far distant world, and so I departed Helium in the direction of the coordinates at which the phenomenon had been most persistently observed.

I had decided to forgo use of the controlling destination compass my son had personally installed on the *Tarkim*, an ingenious device by means of which I could travel at my leisure, more passenger than pilot—and even asleep if I should so choose—while the mechanism shepherded my craft safely and unerringly to its target through the thin air of Barsoom. But I was hungry for distraction and eager for the unexpected. On my last visit to Earth I had been introduced to the expression "flying by the seat of one's pants," and while the phrase was not strictly applicable to Barsoomian apparel, its underlying meaning greatly appealed to my present state of mind. And so I remained alert at the flier's controls, my eyes peeled for anything out of the ordinary in the landscape below, traveling only by daylight and anchoring my ship where it might float on its buoyancy tanks securely out of danger at night, while my companion and I tucked into our simple rations and then took our rest beneath the hurtling moons.

A day passed in such fashion and then two more, our flight interrupted only by the occasional brief landing to stretch our legs and take stock of the local terrain.

The air was growing noticeably cooler as we made our way north, though the flier's engine generated sufficient heat to keep us comfortable while we were aloft. I had taken care to choose my supplies for the journey with a nod to the rigorous northern climate, and actually found myself anticipating the coming change with some pleasure. While my beloved Barsoom is host to innumerable wonders not found on Earth, this dying world does lack one feature that was such a commonplace during the years of my previous life as to have become unremarkable: weather. Between the ice-clad north and the ice-clad south, nearly all of latter-day Barsoom shares the same unvarying pattern of clear, hot days and cold, cloudless nights, with windstorms being rare events and precipitation virtually nonexistent, the whole making for a predictable, if unexciting, natural environment for one used to the vagaries of Earth's climate. With this in mind, I was looking forward to experiencing a good old-fashioned snowstorm or two once I reached my goal.

In addition to cold weather gear, I had laid in a variety of foodstuff, including the nutritious fruit known as usa, that oft-derided staple of the Barsoomian military which I, in contrast to many of my comrades, have always found eminently palatable, and enough preserved meat to feed a small regiment.

While the northern reaches of Barsoom have their own diverse representatives of both the animal and plant kingdoms, I did not expect to encounter many inhabitants of the two-legged variety, as my planned travels would bring me to a region that lay about a hundred miles above the northernmost known settlements of the red race at that longitude, yet still well below the ice barrier that separates the hothouse cities of Okar from the rest of the planet. I therefore limited my arsenal to my everyday armament: a modest selection consisting of shortsword, longsword, dagger, and radium pistol.

It was late in the morning of the third day when I spied something below that I reckoned might qualify as out of the ordinary. We were passing over an area where the ubiquitous moss had taken on a rumpled appearance, due to the presence of a multitude of small knolls clustered at the base of a handful of taller elevations. These had doubtless been foothills a million years ago, with the larger ones genuine mountains, but Barsoom is an ancient world and time's scythe had long since cut them down to size. Now, in a relatively flat area between two such aggregations, I spotted what appeared to be the scene of a devastating crash. Unsure as to whether anyone remained alive—and armed—I eased up on the throttle and brought the *Tarkim* down to hover just behind some towering granite boulders, where I might further inspect the situation while hopefully evading discovery by anyone below.

All around the downed flier I saw what looked to be the aftermath of a fierce battle—or more probably massacre, given the number of human corpses sprawled in close quarters. I nosed the *Tarkim* a few feet past the outcropping and took out my spyglass for a closer look at the victims. What I saw was startling. Those bodies nearest to the ship had been driven down into the earth, as if pounded by some enormous sledgehammer. Many of those farther away were also crushed—but only partially, on the lower half of the torso, looking for all the world as if they had been stamped beneath a giant's bootheel as they raced to flee the area. As I continued to examine the gruesome scene I became suddenly aware of a peculiar pattern: the flattened portions of the corpses all lay within a rough circle on the barren terrain, as if that same colossus had paused to trace out a disk some hundred yards in diameter before carrying out his acts of mayhem.

I decided at that point that I had indeed chanced upon something worthy of further investigation. As I was swinging the ship around to seek a safe landing, I thought I saw some flickers of movement here and there around the edge of the circle, but when I returned the spyglass to my eye all was still.

Knowing that ambush was always a possibility, no matter how devoid of life the scene might currently appear, I retreated to the other side of the westernmost foothills before bringing the *Tarkim* down in a spot where a natural fold in the land would provide it with some measure of concealment. Instructing my faithful companion to guard the flier until my return, I struck out for the area I had glimpsed from the air.

A small flock of gorgeously plumed birds—mute, as are all of their ilk on this planet—trailed me for the latter part of my trek, watching me with curious black eyes as they swooped from branch to boulder in my wake.

Due to the rough terrain, it took me the better part of half an hour prowling through the foothills to reach my destination. A stiff breeze had begun to blow in my direction, and the rank odor of corruption that assailed my nostrils—mixed in this case with some unfamiliar but equally appalling aroma—confirmed that I had arrived at the site of devastation.

I stepped cautiously out into the open and moved toward the edge of the crater—for now that I was at ground level I could see the entire interior of the circle was at a level two or three feet below the surrounding land. No living thing beyond me and my silent avian escort was in evidence, but as I approached I began to be conscious of an uncanny sensation, a premonitory warning that great peril lay just up ahead.

Shaking it off as an instinctive reaction to the grim surroundings, I strode forward; yet the closer I got, the more intense became the conviction of imminent danger, until I stopped in my tracks some dozen feet away and stood scanning the vicinity for its source.

It was admittedly a ghastly display, this great circle marked out by human heads and skeletal torsos still tenuously attached to the crushed and rotting remnants of their lower limbs; yet I have seen—and smelled—corpses beyond counting in my life, and this struck me as an odd time for an old soldier to fall prey to squeamishness. At the very center of the crater sat the flattened and rusting remnants of a sizable craft, perhaps a military cruiser by its conformation, though any identifying markings had been obliterated by whatever force had visited such extreme damage upon it. From what I could discern as I hovered at the edge of the circle, the ship was of a design employed almost exclusively by the red nations, suggesting that its former occupants had made their fatal journey to this place up from the south, rather than down from the cloistered lands of the yellow race to the north.

Examining the interior from just outside the circumference of the circle, I became conscious of an additional curious feature of the grim tableau: the heads and torsos of the corpses at my feet were for the most part picked clean of harness and ornaments—not to mention skin and hair, some of the exposed skulls and ribs showing narrow, spadelike tooth marks. However, the crushed bodies that lay closer to the center of the crater, as well as those nearby portions of the deceased that had been bisected by whatever force had smashed their lower halves into the ground, still retained a goodly amount of both the trappings and the flesh they had worn in life. Indeed, the condition of the remains closest to me indicated that their former owners had been dead for some time, while the still-decomposing portions of the bodies within the circle argued for a much more recent demise. An odd possibility occurred to me: could whichever scavengers had been making free with those delicacies located beyond the crater's perimeter have received the same warning I had and prudently declined to cross the invisible line?

Though I have never been a superstitious man, I have encountered sufficient eerie phenomena in my time on Barsoom to give me a healthy respect for unseen powers. The wind had shifted direction, affording me some respite from the peculiar stench, and I withdrew to a flattish ridge of rock, where I sat like any seasoned warrior who has learned to satisfy his hunger under less than ideal conditions, and gnawed on the portion of dried meat I had brought along for my lunch.

I turned away from the circle as I ate and surveyed the surrounding countryside. As my feelings of disquiet receded, my thoughts took their own course. Something in the lay of the land sparked a memory, and I found myself thinking back fondly to those times, now so many years ago, when I had been wont to range the acres of meadowland and forest that composed the Carter estate. Though it was my stated intention during these walks to seek out solitude, I was often trailed by one or two of the little ones from the house. These children professed to adore my taciturn company, though I suspect a desire to procrastinate their chores was an equally compelling motivation for accompanying Uncle Jack on his wanderings.

Many times we would take our own noon meal by the shores of the small, stream-fed lake that lay to the east of the main house, lounging on mossy logs and competing at skipping stones out onto the placid water between bites of the bread and cheese I had packed with just such an occasion in mind.

My gaze returned to the enigmatic circle. Still smiling at the long-ago memory, I absentmindedly plucked a shard of rock from the ground by my sandals and skimmed it over the site of carnage that lay before me.

My reverie was interrupted when the stone's graceful arc abruptly terminated just past the perimeter and it dove into the ground with a sharp cracking sound, as if swatted violently from the air by an unseen hand. Frowning, I chose another fragment of stone and repeated the exercise, only to observe the same odd result: a few inches inside the margin of the grisly circle, the missile ceased all forward motion and slammed into the earth.

Rising to my feet, I approached the crater again, stopping at the very edge, my nerves once again jangling like alarm bells. I had brought another stone with me. I tossed it lightly before me and for a third time the small projectile dove to the ground like a sparrow felled by a slingshot.

Long decades ago, the Jeddak of Ptarth and I had made our

tortuous way through the Carrion Caves of the great ice barrier in search of our abducted loved ones, and infiltrated the hitherto hidden polar realm of Okar. Arriving at the capital of Kadabra, we had been mystified as to the significance of a sinister shaft of black iron that reared like an ebon talon several hundred feet above the frozen ground just outside the domed metropolis. We soon discovered to our horror that the so-called Guardian of the North was in fact a mighty electromagnet, constructed explicitly for the purpose of drawing in and destroying any airborne explorers from the outside world who dared penetrate the Okarians' secret stronghold. Now, as I pondered the devastation before me, my mind was filled with the stark images of scores of proud Heliumetic warships crashing with awesome force against the shaft and then sliding down like crumpled insects to its base, where ruthless Okarian warriors waited to range among them, slaughtering those poor souls who had not already perished in the collision yet were too badly injured to take as slaves.

I gazed thoughtfully at the hooks and clasps and bits of ornamental metal that studded my leather harness, the several figured bracelets on my biceps and forearms. Was it possible the shards of rock I had cast into the circle contained metallic ores? If another powerful magnetic nexus lay buried beneath the surface of the crater, might I not also be thrust from my feet and perhaps even pinioned to the ground by my own harness and ornamentation once I entered its sphere of influence?

There was one sure way to find out. I stripped off my leather and stepped back to drape it over the ridge of rock. Then I removed the various ornaments from my body, pausing only over a treasured ring Dejah Thoris had gifted me before slipping that off as well. I surveyed the gleaming pile with rueful amusement, pondering what comments I might have received from my fellow fighting men back on Earth, had they borne witness to the assortment of barbaric embellishments with which their erstwhile comrade-in-arms would one day adorn himself!

I hesitated for another moment. Discarding my longsword would make me feel truly naked, yet I laid it on the rock along with the rest of my arms. At last, with only my worn sandals and a few scraps of silk on my person, I overmastered the warnings that still raced like an electric current along my nerves and stepped forward.

At the very edge of the circle of ruin I paused once again, now frankly baffled by my own reticence. Many was the time I had faced an army of savage green warriors without shrinking, yet now I feared to put my foot inside an imaginary circle, populated, so far as the eye could see, solely by the shattered remnants of corpses! I looked down to find that I still held the chunk of dried meat I had been worrying. On impulse I peeled off a strip and flung it out in a high arc in front of me.

My sudden motion attracted the attention of one of the mute birds that had come to perch in the nearby scrub. Instantly it darted out on a course of interception, closing its beak on the scrap with a triumphant snap, its trajectory carrying it just across the border of the circle. To my astonishment, both bird and morsel suffered the same fate as the stones I had cast, plummeting downward as if struck by an invisible force to end in a splatter of blood and multihued feathers amid the rubble of human remains.

I stood in puzzlement for but a moment. I am no zoologist, yet I knew the odds that the doomed bird had been carrying any metal upon his person were slim indeed!

There is intelligent curiosity and then there is rank foolhardiness. Wondering if I had finally attained that stage in my long life where I was able to discern the line of demarcation between the two, I marched back to the rock and slowly donned my discarded harness and various accoutrements, while I pondered the dual questions of what had been responsible for the strange circle of destruction and who in turn had alerted me to the danger that lay within.

Though my investigation of the gruesome circle had evoked more mysteries than it had solved, contemplation of the baffling phenomenon during my tramp back through the foothills provided a welcome respite from the melancholic thoughts I had been trying to elude since my departure from Helium. Still, my step grew steadily heavier as I made for the shallow defile in which I had concealed my flier, and before long my mind had drifted once more into rumination on such airy matters as Friendship, Life, and Death. Thus doubly preoccupied, I was not as attuned to my surroundings as I am wont to be. In my defense, the mosslike vegetation that covers much of the surface of Barsoom provides a yielding cushion that muffles even the heaviest tread of man or beast, and so I was caught quite off guard a few dozen yards from my goal when a great mass of muscle and sinew sprang upon me like a thunderbolt from out of the undergrowth and bore me to the ground.

I wrestled with the heaving body, straining frantically to keep its massive jaws from my face as I choked and gasped for air.

Prolonged exposure to the breath of even the most abstemious calot can be enough to make one long for asphyxiation, while I knew for a fact that this particular example of that noble species had devoured an entire haunch of dried thoat before I bade him remain on guard duty at the flier an hour earlier while I set off on my fruitless exploration.

I put up a mighty struggle, until the strong affection I bore for the brute and the undeniable humor of the situation at last overcame my fastidiousness. Then I fell back in abject defeat as my beloved Woola, crouching upon my chest like a grinning gargoyle, set to lashing his great tongue back and forth across my face in the manner of a malodorous washrag, all the while emitting such a cacophony of wild cries that any passerby in these lonely hills would surely have deemed one of us not long for this world.

At length I called a halt to my old friend's enthusiastic greeting and pushed to my feet, damper, yet considerably more cheerful, than I had been scant minutes before. My hulking companion trotting like a Brobdingnagian spaniel at my heel, I dragged the flier out from its concealment and we both clambered aboard. I took a few moments to note on my destination compass the precise location of the mysterious crater, so that a scientific team might be dispatched at a future date to unravel the conundrum, and we returned to the skies.

Two days later the afternoon sun glinted off the mighty ice barrier in the far distance before us. Rising hundreds of feet into the air, this forbidding natural formation rings the entire northern polar region of Barsoom, as one effusive Zodangan poet put it, like a diamond choker designed for a goddess.

We flew on through a sky of gathering storm clouds, finally putting down in the early evening, still a good distance south of the coordinates of the last reported sighting of the mysterious lights, just as the first few desultory flakes began to fall. We had settled atop a flat, mesa-like plateau some thirty feet above a rock-strewn plain that stretched off for miles in all directions; I did not bother to search for a place to tether the ship in this barren wilderness, trusting that either Woola or myself would be alerted by the approach of anyone who wished us harm.

Like most vessels of its class, the flier had no cabin, and with the possibility that snow might fall more vigorously overnight, I cast about for some means of shelter. The *Tarkim* was fresh from the shipyards of Hastor, and new enough that it lacked the standard insignia blazoned on its prow, where a large pennon bearing the Warlord's crest had been fixed instead. Unhooking the several yards of stiff cloth, I dragged them onto the deck and fastened them to hang shield-like above myself and Woola.

I awoke the next morning to excited cries from my companion and light, feathery touches along my face and body. I opened my eyes to find clouds of white flakes swirling in at each end of our makeshift tent. I had my snowstorm.

After we breakfasted, I wrapped myself in a cloak of my sleeping silks and furs, then climbed down from the *Tarkim* and called to Woola to join me for a brief excursion in the wintry landscape. The average calot is about the size of a well-fed Shetland pony, and his leap from the flier raised a great plume of white flakes from the ankle-deep snow, through which he padded cautiously toward me on his ten short legs, his misgivings concerning this peculiar turn of events writ large upon his homely countenance. Finding my own morale lifting under the well-remembered experience, I busied myself in the snow for a minute, waited until Woola's broad back was turned, and then pelted him in rapid succession with half a dozen expertly formed snowballs. It was a novel circumstance for the old calot;

although he had tramped dutifully by my side through the frozen wastes at the foot of the great ice barrier more than six decades ago, the skies had been innocent of precipitation at that time, and his grim master far too preoccupied with his urgent errand to pause for the production of snowballs. Now Woola halted in his tracks and stared at me as if utterly dumbfounded. He licked experimentally at some of the white granules that had adhered to his snout and then fell to lapping up all the snow about his feet with such gusto that you might have believed it the sweetest baked apple pudding to ever grace a Virginia sideboard. In no time he had joined me in the spirit of things, and I soon had him romping about me like a pup, as the two of us skidded and flailed on patches of hoarfrost beneath the new-fallen snow.

That night the skies were clear as crystal and ablaze with stars. Between the swift setting of one moon and the slow rising of the second, I had my first sighting of the aerial lights, which throbbed in sheets of gleaming color to the north—like yet unlike the terrestrial aurora I remembered, as they seemed rooted in a single area on the ground from which they fanned upward into the heavens. I checked the destination compass to find that we were less than fifty miles from our journey's end.

We rose shortly after dawn and arrived at the designated coordinates in the light of early morning. I will admit to a small pang of disappointment when we looked down from the *Tarkim* over a vast and nearly featureless plain of white. While I had not been expecting anything in particular, there was a part of me that would have been unsurprised to discover the lair of a mad scientist bent on conquering the planet, or perhaps a lost city or two to be explored. Then, as I cruised out across the plain in search of a suitable landing place, I caught sight of something of possible interest in the otherwise monotonous vista.

Swooping low, I found myself gazing down upon a shallow, roughly circular basin some five hundred feet in diameter. I took care not to fly above the area, my mind instantly hearkening back to the crash site that lay to the south and its foreboding circle of corpses.

The thick snow that blanketed everything made it difficult to discern details, yet I was fairly certain that, with its asymmetrical outline and steep walls, this basin was a natural formation of the land; what lay within its bounds, however, was just as obviously not. There were no bodies in evidence here, crushed or whole, yet my attention was drawn at once to the unique topography of the depression, for the floor of the basin was dotted with thirty or more rounded, snow-covered hillocks. Beginning well inside the perimeter, the mounds were spaced roughly twenty feet from one another in a semiregular pattern, almost as if someone had arrayed the depression with carefully placed boulders to form a gigantic game board. My daughter Tara had once encountered half a world away a monumental game of jetan, or Martian chess, played to deadly effect with human pieces, but I felt fairly confident that such was not the case here.

As always, I preferred a landing spot that would provide some concealment for the flier. The farther afield I strayed from home, the less eager I was to fall prey to a hijacker and thus find myself taxed with making my way back to Helium on foot. I put down half a mile west of the basin, where a great outcropping of purple-gray stone had split apart in some bygone age to form a narrow hollow.

Since our arrival, a chill wind had begun to whip across the plain, above a fresh coating of snow that I judged to be at least a foot in depth. The time had come to break out my cold weather wardrobe.

Modeled after the garb worn by those who have long made their homes in the far northern regions, my snowsuit consisted of a hooded jacket and breeches faced with the pristine white fur of the fearsome arctic monster known as the apt. As light and elastic as the suit was, it felt cumbersome to me, unused as I was to going about clad in anything but the sketchiest of garments. I suspected the boots would feel especially confining, even though crafted of supple zitidar hide, but I had no desire to lose a toe to frostbite and so I tugged them on over my sandals. The landscape I had glimpsed from the air was free of any signs of life, and after a moment's consideration I decided to avoid further encumbrance by leaving my pistol and shortsword behind, buckling only a dagger and my trusty longsword atop the fur about my waist.

Thus well prepared for a wintry stroll, I instructed my traveling companion to remain on guard until my return and clambered down from the *Tarkim*. Woola grumbled his disappointment at my decision to go off larking in the tasty snow without him, but I reassured him that I should be back well before nightfall, and granted him leave to prowl the near environs for game if he were so inclined. Tightening my hood against the wind's icy bluster, I struck off toward the basin.

It was an even more imposing sight close up, the broad floor sunk a good thirty feet into the earth and bordered by a natural wall that reared up in irregular serrations an additional ten to twenty feet above the surrounding terrain. Standing on the rim, I was relieved to feel none of the strange disquiet I had experienced when approaching the deadly crater around the crashed flier. The rows of hillocks, however, looked just as unnatural from this vantage as they had from the sky.

As a final test before descending, I scooped up a handful of snow, packed it into a tight sphere, and hurled it out over the basin. It enjoyed a long, graceful arc before impacting against the surface between two of the great mounds. Thus reassured that I would not be pummeled to the ground if I entered the basin myself, and hoping that a closer inspection of the mounds might yield some clue as to their origin, I scrambled down the slope.

The snow was deeper down here where the winds had not blown as fiercely. As I trudged through knee-high drifts toward the nearest mound, I could see that it had a more irregular silhouette than I had noticed from above. Like its fellows, the mound towered some ten feet into the air and was perhaps twice that size in diameter. I wondered if I had come upon a collection of ancient statuary out here in the wilderness, perhaps the remnant of some long abandoned temple of the yellow race. Though the strong feeling of impending peril was absent from this site, an eerie sense that I was not entirely alone down here had me giving a wide berth to the silent mounds as I threaded my way among them toward the heart of the basin, determined to inspect as many as I could from a respectful distance before I resorted to scraping away the snowy mantle which obscured their outlines.

I was nearing the center of the white maze when I was startled to feel a brief tremor disturb the ground beneath me. Seemingly centered somewhere outside the basin, it was yet strong enough that I swayed in my boots.

Though not entirely unknown on Barsoom, such occurrences are uncommon enough to be remarkable. Naturally, we do not call them earthquakes on Mars—nor even marsquakes—the Barsoomian term for such events translating to "sole-shaker." Having heard sufficient tragic tales of unwary travelers in the polar regions of two worlds being swallowed whole by the yawning of sudden crevasses at their feet, I began to feel unsure of what was solid earth beneath my own soles and what might turn out to be a mere crust of snow, and resolved to start back through the maze of hillocks toward the closest exit to higher ground. As I turned to go, I heard a series of low noises, sounding almost like muffled voices muttering in peevish reaction to the tremor, and these, at least, did seem to be emanating from somewhere within the basin. Drawing my dagger, I surveyed the immediate area, my view still largely blocked by the rows of mounds, but could discern no signs of life. I had taken half a dozen steps toward the nearest slope when the ground trembled again. My boot slipped on a patch of ice concealed beneath the coating of fresh snow and I felt myself pitching awkwardly to one side. Instinctively, I thrust out an arm to steady myself, my unsheathed dagger sinking to the hilt into the side of the nearest mound.

At once a thunderous bellow pierced the air. A second later, the cry was repeated again and again throughout the basin, the combined effect resounding like a hundred trumpets blaring simultaneously at earsplitting volume.

3
INTO THE ABYSS

I GAZED ABOUT IN ASTONISHMENT as the white and silent crater erupted into furious life all around me, the rows of great mounds rising ponderously from the ground on thick, columnar legs. The clamorous noise was matched with blazing color when the colossi began to shake the snow from their backs in wild gyrations, and in short order I was surrounded by a veritable legion of snorting, trumpeting mountains, each covered in black fur vividly striped with yellow.

In an instant I understood where my curiosity had landed me.

Found exclusively in the arctic regions of Barsoom, the elephantine beast known as the orluk does not deign to camouflage itself in the white fur so common to many of those other creatures, both on Mars and on Earth, who dwell in the snowy lands above a certain latitude. Standing fully fifteen feet tall at the shoulder, with a pair of wicked tusks curving downward from its lower jaw and a sinewy, bifurcated trunk that can squeeze a lesser animal to pulp as easily as we might shell a pea, the orluk has little need to conceal its presence from its fellow denizens of the far north. Even the fearsome apt cowers before the charge of these gigantic animals, whose only true nemesis across the icy wastes is diminutive man, with his clever brain and the ability to work in deadly concert with his fellows.

It was while paging through a treatise on extinct fauna during one of my visits to London's Royal Academy some years ago that I came across an artist's rendering of an imposing creature from Earth's prehistory known as a *Deinotherium*, whose appearance at once

27

struck me as not dissimilar to that of the orluk—except in the matter of the latter's dexterous double trunk, additional pair of legs, and unmistakable coat of black-and-yellow-striped fur. A possible added distinction lay in the use to which the animals put those massive, downward pointing tusks, which in the orluk are employed not only in hunting and internecine combat, but also after the fashion of a giant steam shovel, to scoop out the shallow concavities inside the tundra basins which then become their communal nests. This is where the females deposit their eggs, which they then must warm with their enormous bulk, barely leaving the nesting bowl for months on end while the males range the vicinity in search of food. Indeed, this is the one time when the mighty beasts can be seen to practice concealment, albeit unwittingly, often remaining in a state of near torpor for days beneath a thick blanket of snow. (If the image of an elephant hatching an egg seems outlandish, I must remind you that all examples of Barsoomian fauna are oviparous, save for one small and peculiar creature whose mammalian tendencies seem completely at odds with its reptilian appearance.)

Thus it became clear to me moments after chaos erupted in the basin that I had blundered upon an orluk hatchery, and inadvertently roused nearly three dozen of the monstrous creatures into paroxysms of maternal rage.

As I attempted to make my way through the knee-deep snow with renewed vigor to the nearest wall of the basin I suddenly found myself grasped firmly from behind and lifted into the air by a pair of flexible trunks, one of which commenced to squeeze me about the waist after the manner of a South American water boa, even as its mate wrapped like a steel band around my chest. Had I been a typical Barsoomian I should surely have been crushed to death on the instant, but after a few well-placed jabs of my dagger into each rubbery appendage, the combined grip loosened just enough that my earthly muscles prevailed and I was able to extricate myself and hop to the broad nape of a neighboring beast, which then nearly broke its own neck in a frantic attempt to snatch me from its shoulders. From there I went leaping and bounding from one gigantic back to another, not unlike a flea in a kennel—and unfortunately unable to inflict more than a flea's bite with my inadequate dagger through the orluks' fur and tough hide.

At length I found myself at the foot of the basin wall. Here the slope was of a steeper angle, and the wall a good ten feet higher than the area in which I had entered. I sheathed my weapon and proceeded to scramble upward, eager to be free of this madhouse as quickly as possible, while serpentine trunks lashed at my back and six-foot tusks slashed the air below my heels. Luckily, the lower portion of the wall was much too steep to allow the ponderous orluks to follow me very far, though they made every effort to do so, taking turns charging up the slope with screams of rage.

I was a few yards from the summit when I caught a flash of color from above and found myself suddenly face-to-face with another human being. He was clothed in similar fashion to myself, in a suit of white apt fur from head to toe, with the addition of tinted glass goggles over his eyes and an incongruous tassel of multicolored ribbons, which I took to be an identifier of rank or status, affixed to the crown of his hood. The small patch of lemon-colored skin bordered by a bristle of black beard that was visible on the lower half of the man's face was sufficient to tell me that here was a representative of the Okarian race, inhabitants of that far northern nation whose existence had only been revealed to the vast majority of Barsoomians during the period of turmoil immediately following my overthrow of the cruel religion promulgated by the Holy Therns and, unbeknownst to them, the First Born. Though the citizens of Okar were once secretive to the point of mania, with little interest in intercourse with the rest of Barsoom, apparently not all of them were confining themselves nowadays solely to the regions above the great ice barrier.

I had scarcely an instant in which to register the fellow's garb and probable national origins before he had performed a similar exercise and, evidently finding me wanting in Okarian bona fides, launched himself upon me with a howl of outrage. My longsword already leaping into my grasp, I nonetheless stumbled a few steps back down the incline under the force of the sudden attack. It took me a moment to regain my footing and another to adapt myself to the unique nature of his assault. Many a year had passed since I had faced any warrior of the far north in combat, let alone one wielding the Okarian's preferred armament: a straight, two edged-sword grasped in one hand and a long, wickedly curving metal hook in the other. The man clearly felt me outmatched with but a single slender blade to his two implements, for his lips widened in an ugly grin as he advanced down the slope, no doubt with the anticipation of cutting me down at his leisure.

His fierce demeanor indicated that this was no time to attempt to reassure him that I had wandered onto his hunting grounds purely by chance. Indeed, I felt a rush of exhilaration as we engaged, for he was a capable swordsman and I had been craving such an outlet for the past while, the mad press of gigantic beasts at my back affording no real opportunity to release what was by now several weeks' worth of pent-up energy.

It was a quick matter, for all of that; my opponent, as practiced as he proved himself to be with both his weapons, would have been no match for me at my most languorous, and now, with the fury of the trumpeting beasts just below us adding to my desire to climb swiftly beyond their grasp and exit their domain, the duel was soon decided and my foe lay face down on the slope before me, his life's blood staining the snow with crimson.

Stepping over his recumbent form, I resumed my scramble for the rim, only to be halted once again within a few feet of my goal. It appeared that my assailant had not been a solitary hunter, as I had first assumed, but merely the unfortunate individual assigned to reconnoiter the interior of the basin while the half dozen of his fellows now streaming over the summit brought up the rear. All were identically clad in snow-white fur, the tassels of their rank fluttering colorfully in the breeze.

My brief set-to with the scout had only whetted my appetite for a proper engagement. Noting that the newcomers all bore the dual weaponry of my first opponent, I skipped back down the slope to retrieve his discarded hooklike implement, then turned back to face them armed like a true warrior of the north.

This encounter lasted longer than the first one. Two of the men were highly skilled swordsmen and no one of the remaining four was incompetent. The last and most talented of them stared at me wild-eyed, the point of my sword having neatly relieved him of his tinted goggles but a moment before. He was a brave man and stood his ground even as he took in the corpse-littered snow around us. "Who are you?" he cried, eyes fixed on the lightly tanned skin of my face visible beneath my own hood. "Surely no thern has ever fought so well!"

"Indeed, I am no thern," I replied. I tugged my hood back for a moment to reveal my shock of black hair. "Perhaps you know the name of John Carter?"

Recognition dawned in his face then, as well as terror, for both my name and my prowess with a sword are well known by now throughout much of civilized Barsoom. To his credit he did not turn and run, though I saw the shadow of probable doom cross his features.

"We need not fight, if you will simply let me pass," I told him. "I am a friend and ally of your noble jeddak Talu, and I have ventured into your territory by mischance. I would as lief depart without spilling more Okarian blood."

For a second he wavered. Then he pulled himself up and raised his weapons. "No! We are hunters out of Illall and no followers of the usurper Talu. If I do not slay you now, then the others will in a few moments, and I would rather be known as the man who died trying to cut down the Warlord than the coward who let him trespass unchallenged."

"Others?" I asked, my eyes lifting once again to the rim of the basin. He took my averted gaze for carelessness and charged at me with hook and sword slashing in a vicious crosscut. With a nod for his courage, I stepped under the hook, parried the sword, and turned back to drive my own blade neatly through his breast.

The orluks had quieted some during our battle, perhaps recognizing that the instigator of their frenzy was a lone and puny individual and that any further incursion into their territory had now been dealt with, as evidenced by the blood and bodies that adorned the slope. The ground upon which I stood to catch my breath was far too steep for them to ascend, and most stood silently watching below, perhaps hoping that I would lose my footing and afford them another chance to destroy me, or at the very least send a few of the deceased warriors that lay about my feet tumbling down to make their supper. There was no other way for me to exit but up. I looked skeptically to the summit, but no more warriors had appeared, and so I continued my twice-interrupted ascent. Perhaps bidding me never to return, the orluks broke into another round of fevered trumpeting as it became plain that I was departing their great nest for good.

Gaining the crest of the wall, I at once sighted those others of whom my latest opponent had spoken. Approaching the basin with measured caution were fully a hundred white-clad warriors, their deliberate pace quickening to a trot when they saw my unfamiliar form appear on the rim in place of their gaudily crested companions.

A glance informed me that these newcomers were armed not with sword and hook in the fashion of their slain fellows, but with bundles of long, slender spears stained a dark purple at the tip. The sight at once awoke in my memory tales I had heard at the court of my friend Talu, formerly Jed of the city of Marentina, and for years now Jeddak of all Okar, of great hunting parties organized about the prospect of searching out these communal hatcheries of the orluks. Once a nest was located, the hunters would establish their camp a short distance upwind and out of sight, waiting patiently, sometimes for days, until the males departed on one of their periodic quests for sustenance. The hunters would then approach in stealth, ring the rim of the basin, and bombard the inhabitants with a relentless hail of spears dipped in a lethal and fast-acting poison that obligingly vanished from the beasts' bodies within seconds of achieving its goal, thus leaving the meat safe to consume. The adult orluks were quickly slain, their carcasses butchered on the spot and stripped of their distinctive pelts, while those of the massive eggs which had not been trampled during the encounter were hauled off to be tended for future consumption, newly hatched orluk being considered a delicacy among the northerners, much as is veal or lamb on Earth. I had never indulged in one of these forays, despite multiple invitations during my visits to the Okarian domed cities. While I found facing a full-grown orluk of either sex to be a fair contest, I could work up little enthusiasm for the alleged sport of surprising and slaughtering from afar the females of any species while they were occupied in protecting their unborn offspring.

Now I faced a party of men who I surmised had been lying in wait not far from the hatchery, only to have their leisurely preparations for ambush disrupted by the din resulting from the unexpected presence of an arctic fox in their frozen henhouse.

Swordplay with a worthy opponent often affords me an enjoyable pastime, and I am never one to flee an honest contest of arms. However, the prospect of dodging spears that may maim or kill over a great distance presented a diversion of an entirely different character. Without a pistol or radium rifle to even the odds, I foresaw being taken down in a matter of minutes should I choose to stand my ground, with little or no opportunity to bring any of my assailants with me. Accordingly, I opted for the better part of valor and, the mad trumpeting of the enraged orluk females to my rear still ringing in my ears, took advantage of my lofty position upon the basin's rim to leap out over the oncoming horde propelled by the full force of my earthly muscles, deriving in the process no little pleasure from the faces upturned in astonishment that flashed beneath me.

I landed on my boots and began at once to bound over the snow, determined to circle quickly back around the hatchery and thus place it between myself and my pursuers while I set off for the flier. They were a well-organized bunch, however, and at a shouted command from one of their leaders the body of men divided into two groups, the larger of which swarmed up the slope to the hatchery, most likely to rain their deadly missiles down upon the aroused orluks in an attempt to salvage what they could of their expedition, while the other, a force of about forty, raced pell-mell to intercept me, their voices raised above the bellowing of the beasts in a peculiar ululating cry. I had no choice but to head off across the tundra in the opposite direction.

It was then that the earth chose to tremble again, just as it had shortly before the unlucky swipe of my dagger had set the monsters stampeding in the basin—but this time with far greater force.

At a distance of some hundred feet directly before me, a great section of what I had previously taken to be solid ground suddenly sloughed away and disappeared downward amid a veritable geyser of upflung snow, confronting me with a rapidly expanding trench that in a matter of moments stretched a good fifty yards to either side and an ever-growing distance in front of me.

My pursuers had witnessed the opening of the crevasse as well; for a moment they slowed their headlong rush, no doubt fearing the broadening line of collapse would spread backward and eventually engulf them, just as it threatened to do more immediately to me. As they shouted strategies back and forth, the tremors abruptly ceased and the mist of snow began to settle back to earth. Emboldened, the warriors spread themselves out in an extending arc clearly designed to trap their prey between the yawning chasm before him and a broad semicircle of spear-wielding warriors at his back. I had to admit it was a clever plan; they kept their distance, half the party with their spears leveled in my direction and half poised to fling them skyward should I attempt to repeat my parlor trick of leaping over their heads to freedom. At a hoarse command from their captain, the dozen nearest sent shafts hurtling at me to drive home my new predicament, and I was obliged to spring back and forth like a jackrabbit to avoid them, while the hurlers' steady approach had me inching ever closer to the lip of the great crevasse.

Upon reaching the precipice, I leaped and dodged along the edge as a second volley of spears fell all about me. It was quite evident that my pursuers had no intention of taking me prisoner. Had there been any form of cover in the vicinity, a stout boulder or a narrow declivity into which I could have ducked, I would have turned and made a good accounting of myself against my adversaries, for thus have I battled foes by the score and still prevailed. But there was naught but the freshly formed canyon yawning to an unknown depth in one direction and the implacable tide of lancers—opponents that did not need to come within a sword's length in order to finish me—in the other. They flung their spears with practiced accuracy, nor could I hope to avoid the hail of deadly weapons for very much longer. Indeed, for all my undignified dodging and feinting, I had already had a half-dozen close calls, and it was clear that in another moment one of the razor-sharp missiles would find its way beneath the fur of my flimsy coat, and that would be that for the much vaunted Warlord of Barsoom.

Daring a glance over my shoulder, I could make out only unrelieved darkness below. Still, I reasoned there was at least a chance that the walls of the chasm might angle inward not too far past the rim, and that some natural ledge or outcropping would afford me the opportunity to safely halt my descent and, once hidden from view, make my way back up to eventual freedom. Of course, it was equally probable that the crevasse plunged directly downward for hundreds, if not thousands, of feet.

I have always considered myself to be a reasonable man, yet I am a confirmed contrarian when it comes to matters of my own impending mortality. Electing to swallow my last breath on my own terms rather than those of my would-be executioners, I saluted them with a grim smile and leaped into the abyss.

4

THROUGH THE VEILS

THOUGH I HAVE COME CLOSE enough to meeting death to catch
its disagreeable odor in my nostrils on more occasions than I
can count, I have never once experienced that singular phenomenon reported by many who claim to have narrowly evaded
their own imminent demise, wherein a condensed accounting of
one's entire life gallops past the inward eye as if displayed on some
mental zoetrope.

In truth, I have always been quite relieved that this is the case,
preferring my brain to be fully engaged in securing my immediate
salvation, rather than conducting a tour through the dusty halls of
memory—especially when I contemplate the dizzying speed at which
images of my own life must be presented in order to encompass even
a small part of the as yet unmeasured span of my existence.

Thus, as I plummeted toward imminent doom upon the unseen
floor far below, my thoughts were occupied with little more than a
rueful acknowledgment that I had at last surpassed the maximum
number of miraculous escapes allotted me by an overgenerous
providence. Contrary to my hope, the walls of the chasm slanted
abruptly away to an unknown distance rather than inward, while
below me lay only a void of utter blackness, unrelieved by the thin
shaft of cold light admitted through the jagged opening above.
Indeed, there appeared to be no alternative to having my atoms
spread across the chasm's floor in a matter of moments, unless the
rocky surface that must lie somewhere below should be transmuted
in the nick of time into a bed of feathers several yards deep.

It was then that something equally improbable occurred.

36

It seemed that I had been falling for only a few seconds when my body was racked by a spasm of severe nausea. While this was not altogether surprising given the situation, the weird burst of multi-colored light that accompanied the sensation, very like the heavenly curtain I had seen draped across the sky on the previous two nights, was wholly unexpected. In this case, however, the vast pale shimmer surrounded me as if I had dropped onto the surface of a glowing sea, then spread outward in a horizontal wave that for a moment seemed to fill the entire chasm with a wan illumination. At the same time, I felt my hurtling descent begin to *slow*.

It was the latter phenomenon that was the most remarkable, for it was as though I had plunged into a depth of water, or perhaps some more viscous substance, while my tactile senses told me I traversed the same clear, icy air as before. After a few moments the eerie light vanished and the strange conviction of moving through a thicker medium also ceased, as I fell unimpeded once more. Before I had a chance to question whether this had been a mere trick of my imagination, the fantastic episode recurred, and I blinked at another spreading burst of the pale, prismatic light and once more experienced the unmistakable feeling that I was passing through some unseen veil into an atmosphere much denser than air. The sensation occurred several more times, stronger now and with a marked regularity, as if there were close-packed layers of gathering resistance through which I traveled, each one serving to slow my descent for a time until I dropped below an unseen boundary, sped up momentarily, and then, with yet another flash and another stomach-churning shock, encountered the next barrier.

So it was that I continued my remarkable descent until at last I sank like a pebble in a gluepot through a final shimmering veil and then dropped without hindrance a distance of some dozen feet to land sprawling upon the rocky floor.

The light had vanished completely with the final veil, and I lay for a few moments in nearly total darkness. Rising slowly to my feet, I ran my hands over a dozen new bruises, thankful that these appeared to be the extent of my injuries, and craned my neck to peer at the opening of the crevasse, so distant now as to appear only as a narrow vein of bluish light against the black shadows of the cavern's roof. I shook my head in wonderment, with no clue as to how I had survived the strange ordeal, yet profoundly grateful that I stood more or less unharmed upon solid earth, my wits seemingly intact and my longsword still at my side.

Fishing inside my snowsuit, I withdrew the small radium torch from my pocket pouch and flicked back its cap to release a broad beam of cool white light. I turned clockwise in a slow circle in an attempt to get my bearings. The exercise was inconclusive: I stood about a quarter of a mile from one wall in a vast chasm that extended for an unknown distance in all other directions, for the brilliant beam disappeared into blackness no matter where else I aimed it.

I did not care to attempt the arduous task of scaling the almost perpendicular wall of rock to my rear at this time; even should it eventually bring me back to the cleft in the roof, there was a possibility my pursuers now squatted there awaiting my return, in hopes of spitting me on their poisoned spears the moment I levered myself from the opening.

The fissure of light above my head extended before me until it faded into dimness. It seemed logical that somewhere, lost in shadow across the plain beneath it, must stand another wall and atop that perhaps another means of egress from the crevasse. Unlike the rest of my battered body, my bump of curiosity had emerged unscathed from my fantastic fall, and so it was with some eagerness that I determined to embark upon a trek of unguessable duration through an unknown region.

At least, I noted as I lowered my torch to better survey my immediate surroundings, I should not have to slog through snow as I searched for a means of escape. What little had drifted down when the tremors opened the earth above was already melting and the plain of black rock that stretched out before me was quite bare of the stuff. In fact, I felt unexpected currents of warmth in the air around my face and hair as I again thrust back my white-furred hood.

I removed my trousers and jacket with a sense of relief, knowing I would have need of them again if ever I were to find my way out of the chasm, but confident that in the meantime they would serve me well as a substitute for sleeping silks and furs, should my quest extend beyond a single day. Bulky as the garments appeared when worn, they were, like most Barsoomian textiles, marvelously light and compressible, so I was easily able to fold them into a short length that I then wrapped twice about my waist in an improvised cummerbund, before setting out along the bottom of the crevasse.

At first the underground world through which I tramped offered little in the way of variety. Mounds of scree, boulders great and small, all no doubt dislodged over the ages from the cavern's walls and roof, alternated with patches of chest-high plants shaped like furled parasols, whose glossy leaves shone a deep maroon or purplish hue that lingered with a ghostly glow once touched by my beam, their presence further evidence that it was far warmer down here than I would have expected.

The life span of the typical Barsoomian hand torch, utilizing radium bulbs devised and manufactured in the dim recesses of antiquity, is for all intents and purposes infinite. I have heard tell of lights that have burned for ten thousand years without flickering. Yet I soon grew weary of holding the device trained before me as I walked, not least because its cone of radiance consigned all objects beyond its scope—including all potential threats—to near invisibility. Replacing the cap, I found that my eyes adjusted in short order to the dimness, and I began to pick out large patches of wan illumination here and there on the surface of the plain about me. When investigated, these were revealed to be glowing horizontal fans of some sort of scabrous fungoid growth. In addition to the eerie light provided by the fungus, the slight seam of daylight shone like a crack in the world high above, and, lacking any other road signs, I made a point of maintaining its position directly over my head, noticing that it was becoming perceptibly wider as I forged on, to the extent that showers of snow drifted down occasionally.

I kept a sharp lookout for anything that might qualify as edible, and especially for a reliable source of water. Though I was able to slake my thirst at the occasional small drifts of snow I encountered, I knew the relative warmth of the cavern and the sunlight now beating down through the fissure would melt them into puddles that would be absorbed by the porous ground sooner rather than later. As for food, the parasol plants emitted a cloyingly sweet odor I found off-putting, while I was not yet at such a stage of hunger as to test out the fans of glowing fungus—though I realized that at some point I might of necessity start viewing them as prospective ingredients in a hearty mushroom stew.

Soon I fell into a cautious rhythm, my eyes and my thoughts focused on wending my way through the litter of stones that strewed the black rock, the little hummocks and deceptive valleys that lay too often hidden in my path, and the patches of slippery snow I knew might easily lead to a barked shin or far worse. After several hours of mechanical walking, I found myself suddenly slowing, not so much from weariness as from the queer sensation that the very air before me had begun to resist my efforts at forward motion. At the same time I became conscious of a faintly pungent odor and, bringing forth my torch, made out the swirls of a tenuous vapor in the ruddy glow it elicited from a nearby stand of parasols.

Fatigued and half-befuddled, I strove onward for a few paces, until I finally ground to a halt and raised my eyes from the black rock to see a vast sheet of mingled blue and purple light stretching out to left and right before me. Alarmed, I pushed forward with renewed vigor, but it was as if I strained against a thick wall of elasticized rubber, which yielded slightly, only to rebound a second later with even greater force than that I had applied to it. With each effort I made to pass through the shining veil, quivering bands of color pulsed outward from my splayed hands, to be lost in the shadows on either side.

I had come too far to be deterred by a wall of light. Determined to find a way around the mystifying barrier, I thought to take a few steps back that I might search with my eyes for some gap or an area where it seemed less firm, only to find I was now unable to move more than an inch or two in that direction as well—nor could I take more than a single step to either side! Panic surged in my breast, along with an odd yet undeniably familiar sensation that began in the very core of my being and spread outward through my body like a mounting wave of electrical current, as I struggled fiercely to break through the intangible bonds that held me in near paralysis.

There came a sudden sharp sound, as of a metal wire snapped in two, followed by an instant of bitter cold, and a wave of utter darkness.

5
THE GHOSTLY CITY

THE DARKNESS LIFTED as quickly as it had fallen, and I found myself standing stock-still, staring in consternation at a sight that made no sense to me. Unlike the outcome of previous experiences that had commenced in similar fashion, on this occasion I had not been spirited through the void to some unfathomably remote and alien destination.

The veils of streaming color had completely vanished, yet I stood exactly where I had been seconds ago—or so I believed—surrounded by what could only be the same vast hollow in the earth. But instead of an endless floor of snow-crusted black rock and great patches of glowing fungus stretching out before me, I now beheld a sweeping plain of breeze-blown scarlet grass, in the middle distance of which I could make out the lambent outlines of what appeared to be an enormous city. A glance over my shoulder assured me that the softly moving field extended as far behind me as I could see.

I took a step forward, and the scarlet blades brushed softly against my legs, feeling fully as real as the snow that had crunched beneath my boots scant moments before. Here and there in the distance I could see scattered groves of towering trees. Lacking a clear reference point, it was difficult to judge their height, but I guessed the tallest thrust up their leafy crowns no less than five hundred feet into the air.

Turning my gaze upward, I saw that the widened crevice had instantaneously become a much broader opening. The distant walls of rock had vanished and I stood in a great valley rather than a chasm. The sun now beat down far more vigorously against my exposed

42

skin—yet somehow I had no doubt that the sky in which it sat was still that of my beloved Barsoom.

The glowing city beckoned to me and I took another step, and then another.

I had walked on for only a few minutes, head swirling with wild conjecture, when the scarlet sward and the city beyond it began to glimmer and fade out of clarity, as if I were viewing it suddenly through a great depth of water—before the entire scene vanished completely, to be replaced by the return of the familiar windswept plain of black rock.

I stopped, once again dumbfounded. The world had clearly gone mad.

There was nothing for it, however: mad or sane, it was the world I currently inhabited, and I had little choice but to make my way through it. With a shrug of my shoulders, I set out again for the distant wall I hoped still lay somewhere in the formless darkness up ahead.

Half a minute later, the rocky plain vanished, the glowing city reappeared on the horizon, and I strode once more through tall blades of waving scarlet grass.

And so it went, the alternation between the two worlds bringing me to one or the other reality, sometimes for a few seconds, sometimes for a quarter of an hour or more.

How long it took to make my way across that weirdly divided plain, I cannot say. It was tedious work, for all its dreamlike quality, as the floor of the cavern in which I had originally found myself was quite uneven and still dotted with mounds of snow-slick rubble. Now alternating without warning with the gently undulating scarlet savanna, it presented me with the constant danger of stumbling over rocks or pitching headlong into a shallow ravine to crack my skull.

I made my way past a stand of perhaps twenty of the giant trees as I traversed the world of the meadow and the city. The smooth trunks were of varied colors, with boles of gleaming lavender next to deep blue, vivid magenta, and the purest white, the branches heavy with foliage and many-hued blossoms of fantastic design. Viewing them up close, I realized I had seen their like in only one other location on Barsoom—and that was far away, at the other end of the world.

The day had darkened into the rapid Martian dusk well before I drew near to that great city that seemed to exist solely in the secondary world, and stars were becoming visible in the heavens far above me. In one of the dual heavens, I should say—for as the landscape about me continued to fade and re-form at its whim, the stars also changed in their courses.

In one reality it was a narrow slice of the familiar sky of latter-day Barsoom I saw, the stars the same bright pinpoints piercing through the thin atmosphere that I had always known, while in the other, great silver masses of cloud scudded by overhead, their contours lit by a gradually shifting interplay of fiery reds, brilliant purples, and blazing gold, in a gorgeously unfolding display I wagered had not been seen on this ancient globe for eons.

I soldiered on in the eccentric rhythm I had adopted of careful steps and pauses, now squinting under the starlight, now striding more confidently as the city itself glowed like a tantalizing beacon to guide my way through the dimming expanse of scarlet grass. After a time the long, slow sunset of the secondary world melted into a velvet blue evening, as the fleet of clouds sailed grandly out of view and stars like scattered jewels appeared there as well.

In the more familiar reality, one of the moons rose to pass over the opening above: Thuria, by the size of it, to be succeeded as the world dissolved and re-created itself around me a few minutes later by a different, more distant Thuria, the unlikely pair following separate arcs that at one point intersected to produce the uncanny spectacle of moon overlaid upon moon for just an instant, before the two hurtled along on their divergent paths.

By the time I reached the outskirts of the luminous city, the periods in which I trekked across a desolate plain had become markedly less frequent and of shorter duration. With more time spent gazing upon a single reality—if reality it was—I was able to discern a few more salient details of the looming city.

The softly glowing towers, domes, and great edifices were of a teasingly familiar outline. However, unlike the case with the vast majority of Barsoomian cities, ancient or modern, no great outer wall encircled this luminous metropolis to provide a bulwark against the inevitable marauding armies; nor did I see any evidence of the hydraulically raised sleeping apartments favored by Barsoom's more technologically advanced nations as a guard against the ever-present threat of nocturnal assassination. Perhaps the city's location at the bottom of a giant valley—or was it in the far corner of my own dreaming mind?—afforded it a measure of protection from the myriad dangers that stalked the outer world. The fact that no fliers were visible flitting among the glowing towers reinforced the impression that this was a place of limited access to technology—or at least to that form of modern Barsoomian technology with which I was familiar.

And then I had arrived.

Rising directly from the edge of the scarlet field itself, a sweeping staircase of white quartz threaded with gold and silver fronted the gateless city. Some five hundred feet wide at its base and bracketed on either side by another fifty of gently sloping ramps, which I assumed were for the convenience of wheeled vehicles and animals, it narrowed to a mere hundred feet at its apex, where it terminated in a series of grand silver archways that I supposed must lead into the heart of the metropolis. Stairways of any size are a rarity on modern Barsoom, where the ramp has for millennia been the favored means of traveling between levels.

Swaying on my feet at the base of the magnificent staircase, I found myself truly exhausted. Night had fully descended, though the various structures that composed the city continued to glow softly by some unknown artifice from within. Yawning, I conducted a brief internal debate as to the relative merits of making my way stealthily into the sleeping city to take stock of the situation, or waiting until morning to make my presence known as a proper visitor. In the end, fatigue won out over caution.

No one seemed to have noticed my approach as yet, and I cast about for some place of comparative concealment, where I might pass the hours until morning without being apprehended by whatever force of guards patrolled the nighttime environs, and then awake reinvigorated and more ready to present myself to my prospective hosts.

Not far from the stairs, I located a small stand of ornamental trees that were strikingly reminiscent of the little parasols that had dotted the plain of black rock; yet these sat in an artfully arranged pattern, their tops, nodding in the breeze between ten and fifteen feet above the scarlet sward, unfurled to form a canopy of delicate limbs bedecked with tiny leaves in shades of lavender and rose. I shouldered my way in past the outermost trunks, curled up at the base of the tallest tree, and promptly fell asleep.

I awoke feeling much refreshed. Sunlight streamed down warm and golden from above. Creeping out from my nest among the trees, I returned to the foot of the grand stairway and examined the city by daylight. It had lost none of its arresting beauty. Brilliant pennons embroidered with intricate designs rippled in the breeze among the towers, while swaths of deep maroon and crimson flora intermingled in pleasing fashion with the nearest structures, as if a deliberate effort had been made to maintain the architecture in graceful harmony with the natural world.

My hand resting lightly on the hilt of my longsword, I mounted the white stair.

No guards stood at the top of the staircase to challenge me, nor under the trio of high silver arches that framed the entranceway to the thoroughfare beyond. I passed through them into the city.

The broad central avenue was paved with gleaming gemstones in elaborate mosaics depicting various fanciful plants, animals, and—most unusual on arid Barsoom—creatures of the sea. Arcades and pleasant galleries lined the boulevard, though not one of the marble benches or carved and polished chairs bore a single occupant. Making my way with caution, I was struck at once by the complete absence of noise and activity. I wondered idly if the inhabitants of such a majestic metropolis could be so lethargic as to be accustomed to wait until midmorning before they ventured from their beds and went abroad for the day.

Glimpses of sunlit plazas and gorgeously appointed garden parks were visible down the numerous side streets that curved off from the main way. I resisted the urge to explore each one and strolled on, eager to reach what I felt sure would be the bustling core of the metropolis.

It was a long walk, only to discover that silence reigned there as well. What I took to be the center of the city was laid out in a series of great intersecting circles dotted with sparkling fountains and pools amid arbors of cunningly arranged flowering vines; the whole was surrounded by monumental halls, massive in construction yet somehow managing to convey a sense of airy lightness, all of a creamy white marble shot with veins of tourmaline and ruby, and inlaid with other precious materials. Beyond them soared translucent towers, minarets, and domes that glowed, each with a different rich hue. Nowhere did I spy a single person.

There was an undeniable aura of great antiquity about the city, even though the halls and galleries I passed shone as if but recently created. I found it awe-inspiring to wander along the broad thoroughfares, the faces of the buildings all agleam with pristine marble and the myriad of gemstones, wrought metals, and rare woods that adorned them. With no real evidence, I nonetheless surmised I was seeing these magnificent edifices just as they had appeared in the lost youth of the world—perhaps already centuries old, but as yet untouched by the millennia that had passed between their building and my own relatively recent advent upon an aged Barsoom.

Passing through the outermost circle of what I had assumed to be the city's center, I found myself in another collection of interwoven rings. Beyond that lay yet another, until I realized the entire city must be laid out as a giant maze of circles within circles, which were themselves arranged in vaster rounds. It occurred to my dazzled brain that without an endless supply of breadcrumbs to scatter in my wake, I might soon become helplessly lost in this fascinating place.

At length I came to an immense plaza ringed by a dozen domed structures, each with a different elaborate device emblazoned on the marble above its doorway of gold and silver filigree. Were they museums? Temples? Municipal buildings? I paused to seat myself on an ingeniously carved bench of polished ersite so that I might better take in my surroundings, experiencing an instant of vertigo when the surface of the bench seemed to yield momentarily to the pressure of my body before resuming its state of solidity. Puzzling over the strange occurrence, I took my rest there for a few minutes, curious to see if the bench would retain its solid form for the duration, or grow tired of the imposition and deposit me unceremoniously upon the ground.

Moving on in my exploration, I soon made another queer discovery: the marble, the polished metals, the scintillant gems, and most of the other materials used in the construction of the city were palpable to my touch—though, like the bench of ersite, there was often a moment's uncertainty upon first contact with my flesh, during which they seemed almost permeable. Yet anything that had recently been alive, or was living still, might as well have been constructed of colored smoke when I attempted to lay my hands on it. This included the gorgeous plants that filled the gardens and lined the avenues, the foodstuff so invitingly arrayed in the outdoor shops and markets. The ground itself was solid, but the various grasses and flowering moss with which it was carpeted were not. Fascinated, I made my way deeper into the city, experimenting as I went to discover what might shy away beneath my touch and what would stand firm.

Having despaired of ever encountering another living creature within the city's confines, I was startled when I caught a hint of motion from above and saw for the first time several flocks of majestic birdlike creatures gliding serenely among the upper reaches of the towers.

These were no more eager to feel my caress than were the plants that filled the gardens, as I learned when I chanced upon one perching docilely atop a filigreed screen and reached out to stroke its gorgeously plumed head, only to find my palm falling through the insubstantial body to rest against the cool metal upon which it sat.

I had been aware for some time that other than the sound of my own footfalls on the avenues, the city was not only untenanted, but virtually silent. Neither could I smell any fragrance from the ubiquitous flowers and plants, or—strangest of all—feel the water that filled the ornamental pools in which I was now beginning to descry the darting flicker of bright-scaled fish. It seemed that, although I was allowed to walk the boulevards and gardens of this eerily beautiful place unmolested, I had not yet been granted permission to fully experience its wonders.

Having not encountered a single soul since entering the city, I had naturally continued to speculate on the whereabouts of its occupants, wondering at first if I might have arrived during the enactment of some grand ceremony or other civic occasion that had gathered all the residents into one area—or if perhaps they had recently departed the city en masse, in flight from the threat of a mighty host of belligerents that had preceded me into the cavern and come knocking with swords drawn at their unfortified gates.

Yet the buildings were in fine repair and the walkways and gem-strewn avenues immaculate. The luxurious gardens showed signs of recent tending. I wandered in and out of numerous open-air marketplaces, as splendid and beautifully appointed as every other aspect of the city, where displays of fresh fruit and vegetables—all intangible to my eager fingers—sat in plenty.

It was then that I commenced to notice brief flashes of bright shapes here and there that lingered in the corners of my vision, until I began to discern that they were beings of manlike conformation, golden-glowing and half-transparent, but demonstrably alive nonetheless. I wondered if, like the birds that soared among the spires and the fish that darted in the ornamental pools, they had been here all along, and were only just now becoming apparent to my eyes.

These airy phantoms soon began to approach me, as if they had registered my own presence at the same time I had become aware of theirs. At first my hand strayed instinctively to the hilt of my sword each time one flitted toward me; but they advanced in what I perceived to be an attitude of curiosity rather than menace, and before long I had an increasing number of them striding alongside me or following in my wake, until I moved through the city like a comet with a glowing tail of silver-gold.

For a long while I could not see them clearly enough to make out individual details of face or form, but I did note that they were all clad alike in flowing raiment of rich colors and purest white, while what I took to be their exposed skin glowed, like much of their architecture, as if illuminated in some inexplicable fashion from within.

I became conscious after a brief while of a phenomenon among the inhabitants that would have aroused little notice on Earth, but was definitely far from ordinary here on Barsoom: a number of very small children, either carried in someone's arms or toddling along among the graceful adults that composed my entourage.

As I have often mentioned before, the most striking of those features that distinguish the human inhabitants of our two worlds, aside from the placement of certain internal organs and the Martian talent for mind-reading, is the manner in which we bring forth new members of our respective species. All Barsoomians, be they red, yellow, black, white, or even green, are oviparous rather than mammalian—though in all other respects the first four races, at least, appear identical in physical construction to their counterparts on Earth. (This includes the presence of a navel, which, as in the case with some terrestrial egg-laying species, on Barsoom bespeaks the necessary connection within the egg between the developing child and its source of nourishment). As to oviparity, it has always been a mystery to me that my Martian brethren should share this one peculiar characteristic with the six-limbed, white-tusked, fifteen-foot-tall green men—as well as with ninety-nine percent of all the other creatures that walk, soar, or slither their way across the planet. Of course, to the savants of Barsoom, the peculiarity is that the dominant species of their sister planet has evolved to give birth to helpless and pathetic offspring that must be carefully tended and protected for long years before finally acquiring the means to fend for themselves! Here, a more practically minded Martian Mother Nature has ordained that the child who emerges from an egg that has steadily increased in size over the five years of its incubation is fundamentally identical to a young adult in nearly all aspects but dimension, and quickly able to speak and walk and defend itself.

Despite having no more ability to physically interact with them than I had with the birds above or the fish below, I soon grew used to the sight of my newfound acquaintances, and even derived a pleasant sense of companionship from their presence as I continued my exploration of their city.

For the most part the members of my ghostly entourage maintained a respectful distance. At first they followed me by the dozens wherever I wandered. Inexplicably, the growing pangs of hunger that had begun to afflict me on the plain of black rock, as well as any thirst for water, had vanished shortly after I entered the city. I did, however, still feel the need for occasional periods of rest. When I stopped to take my ease upon an exquisitely crafted bench or stretched myself out on the ground beneath a vine-draped arbor in one of the parks, my glowing retinue would politely disperse for a time, gathering round again only after I had roused myself. Sometimes I discovered by my side carefully arranged offerings of food and drink that I could not consume—though they seemed to be growing steadily more perceptible in both appearance and substance, until I swore I was beginning to catch the tantalizing scent of the viands.

As time passed, my ghostly attendants grew fewer and fewer. I suspected that the mystery of my phantom presence, intriguing as it might be, had lost much of its hold upon them—though there were a few steadfast individuals who lingered with me almost constantly, some of whom I eventually became able to recognize.

One lively and inquisitive person habitually clad in a robe of azure blue, whom I had identified from the style and grace of its movements as a youthful woman, paced alone at my side for a considerable while one morning before impulsively reaching out delicate fingers to pluck at my garments. Her mouth opened in surprise as her hand passed right through one of the straps of leather harness that crossed my back—and then continued on until it protruded from my chest, whereupon she snatched it back with a faint cry of amused wonder.

I halted in my tracks then, more startled by the fact that I had heard her exclamation than that I had experienced an arm passing painlessly through my flesh, for up until that moment the city had been silent as a sepulcher beyond the hollow sound of my own boots on marble. Thinking to finally gain some answers to my ever-mounting store of questions, I posed an excited query to her. She responded by cupping her hand to her ear and leaning closer, to indicate that she had heard me as well, but only just barely. Thus encouraged, we took turns addressing one another in raised voices, and from time to time I caught snatches of her musical utterances, quickly realizing with disappointment that she was speaking something other than the common tongue I had grown used to encountering in all corners of Barsoom. Nor, as she confirmed with a mournful shake of her radiant head, did she appear able to decipher any of the questions I bellowed at her. As a last resort, I tried to read some of her thoughts, but attempting to probe the mind behind her glowing face was the equivalent of staring into the noonday sun to discover its heart, and soon I desisted.

Other sounds were becoming audible to me now. I often thought I heard the ringing of far-off bells, sometimes deep and sonorous, as one would expect from an earthly cathedral, more often the light clashing that harness bells might produce.

As I moved in my meandering way from the city's central precincts toward its outer reaches, I began to be aware of a low, steady rushing that I recognized after a time as the sound of a considerable body of moving water. A river? It seemed to emanate from the far periphery of the city, an area I had not yet attained in my leisurely explorations. I never did gain its banks, though I glimpsed it once from a lofty hilltop garden. It was a broad and curving waterway, bordered by tall trees with lavender trunks whose wispy foliage, which dipped down almost to the water, made them reminiscent of weeping willows. Moored on the opposite shore I thought to see a score of graceful, ivory-colored vessels. I wondered if the river made connection with any of the man-made waterways that for millennia have carried life-giving moisture down from the polar regions to irrigate the rest of Barsoom. For all I knew, it might be one of the many subterranean watercourses scattered over the planet that eventually wend their way to some larger tributary of the enigmatic Iss, that storied river that for millennia bore untold legions of deluded and life-sick Barsoomians on their final voluntary pilgrimage to, as they supposed, eternal bliss in the Valley Dor.

There were still vast areas of the city that I had not visited at all.

On the whole, it was as much a place of parklands and gardens as it was a metropolis, for the skillful blending of the natural surroundings with human habitation had been carried on throughout. Since my arrival, I had confined myself mostly to the outdoor spaces, feeling unwilling to venture inside buildings whose purpose I did not know—especially once the inhabitants of the city had started to become apparent to me, and I to them. Though the citizens seemed to have no objection to my tramping along their boulevards or relaxing in their parks, I had no idea how they would react to waking up one morning to discover an insubstantial stranger prowling through their bedchambers.

Their own glowing shapes grew more substantial by the hour—or was it by the week? My sense of time had been hopelessly upended, though I felt little urgency in my languid quest, surrounded as I was by such beauty—not to mention the persistent mystery of who and what these strange folk were, and the still unfolding question of whether we would eventually exist on the same plane or forever remain nothing more to one another than animated phantoms. How could I think of leaving when there was still so much to learn?

As I had expected, over the course of time I began to lose track of which portions of the city I had already visited, and at intervals found myself retracing my route. On one of these occasions, I allowed my curiosity concerning the contents of the various buildings to bring me inside for the first time. I had found my way back to the grand plaza surrounded by a ring of domed buildings that had earlier attracted my attention. Each of these structures was marked by an insignia above its doorway, and this time as I strolled through the plaza I saw that one pair of ornate doors was now open to the sunlight. I made my way up the stairway and after a brief hesitation walked inside.

It took my eyes a few moments to adjust to the relative dimness inside the entrance hall. As I moved farther into the interior a sourceless warm light grew all around me as if reacting courteously to my presence.

The interior of the building was considerably larger than I had expected, dipping gradually downward into halls and galleries that must have been at least partially underground. In contrast to the decorative parkways and gardens of the city outside, this edifice seemed to combine the aspects of a natural history museum and a biological laboratory. Many of the exhibits were of variations on a specific organism. I came to an immense room where scores of crystalline vats filled with clear water were recessed into the floor. Pictograms set in plaques above the tanks showed a gradual alteration of the inhabitants from one tank to the next, while metal walkways crossed the room several yards above, so that one could observe the aquatic beasts that swam or floated below. I became fascinated by a succession of aquaria showcasing the transformation of a particular species of hauntingly familiar aspect, which began as a four-foot-long insectile creature of olive-green coloration, propelling itself about the tank at great speed with its six long limbs, and turned gradually through a score of phases into a greatly elongated, semi-aquatic form in the farther enclosures that was now capable of climbing from the depths to squat upon rocks. Other rooms held different classes of creatures, from small crawling things to great lumbering beasts, each of them apparently in transition from their original form into something else, though whether the different stages represented the natural evolution of these species accomplished over the ages or a deliberate manipulation of their conformation by the savants who dwelled here, I could not discern.

I am sure I could have lost myself in endless hours prowling through the building, had not my mind been so saturated with the dreamlike detachment that had pervaded much of my stay in the city, as well as the conviction that there would be time enough to explore everything. Eventually I made my way back to the entrance hall and then once more outside into the sun to continue my order-less wanderings.

In a few instances I was surprised to find myself within sight once again of the vaulting silver archways through which I had passed when I first entered the metropolis. On one such occasion I was accompanying the blue-clad individual—who seemed to have ap-pointed herself my guide and companion ever since she had intro-duced her slender arm into my torso—in a long stroll beside a stream of clear water that wandered through a garden of fantastic foliage, while the fragrance of flowers came faintly to my nostrils. As I said, I had remained immune to the urgings of hunger and thirst since my arrival in the city, yet the flowing water looked so cool and invit-ing on that warm afternoon that at one point I hunkered down on the flower-strewn bank with the intention of helping myself to a refreshing draft. Some things were still beyond my grasp, however, and I only succeeded in coating my cupped hands with the faintest sheen of moisture before giving up in mild frustration.

Rising, I felt a fleeting touch of warm flesh upon my arm, and looked down in startlement. My companion, who was also visibly taken aback by the brief shared sensation, hastily withdrew her hand, in which she held a goblet of chased bronze, perhaps with the intention of offering me some of the refreshment I so obviously craved.

The evidence was clear: our worlds were merging. Or rather, I thought with hazy detachment, my own half-remembered former world would soon be subsumed by this glorious new one.

I gazed at the gorgeous scene about me with a surge of eager anticipation—only to feel it overtaken almost immediately by one of equally profound dismay. As if sensing my warring sentiments, my host peered searchingly into my eyes, her arms raised as though she would grasp my hands with her own if I allowed it, and I thought to see an expression of troubled concern upon her glowing features. Looking at her now, I saw her with a new clarity that confirmed the hints of delicate beauty I had only glimpsed before. I leaned forward, yearning for the touch of something solid and real.

Then slowly, slowly into my drifting consciousness came the image of another woman: not golden-glowing and ethereal, but also hauntingly beautiful, with copper-red skin and dark eyes. I heard the familiar tones of her cherished voice as from a great distance: *All I ask is that you return to me, as you always have.*

"Dejah Thoris . . ." I gasped, my placid acceptance of the ap-proaching transformation dissolving into bewildered alarm. I looked around wildly as the serene garden, the great metropolis beyond, and the exquisite creature by my side all melted away in an instant and I stood solitary again in the chill gloom of a rock-strewn plain deep in the earth. Panic clutched at my vitals. How long had I lingered in this city of dreams, wandering like a lotus-eater, while the outside world—my own beloved world—grew dimmer and more distant?

A moment later there came another shimmering pulse and the veiled city returned to me in all its tantalizing glory, though subtly less substantial now in outline. My golden-glowing host was there by my side again, her slender arms extended in an attitude of entreaty, her murmured words imploring me to some action I could not comprehend.

I turned from her at once and hastened back to the main thoroughfare, upon which I fairly raced toward the unguarded entrance to the city. Bright shapes flashed past and voices rang out, but I ignored them all. It seemed to take an eternity, but at last I reached the silver archways. I stood at the top of the grand stairway, my heart pounding and my lungs afire. Then I rushed to descend.

Yet after but a handful of steps I skidded to a halt, overcome by a great wave of nausea and discomfiture. I looked up to see bright bands of purple and blue streaming in a living web before me, insubstantial yet unyielding.

I took another step down, my jaw clenching with the effort. If the pressure that had opposed me earlier as I strove to break through the veil that hung between the dark plain and the luminous city had been strong, that which I now encountered as I fought my agonizing way down the white stairway was many times more powerful.

Colors roiled in shimmering curtains before me, and every step was contested, as if I were leaning into a savage gale: a relentless, unseen force of nature that strove to drive me backward up the great stair.

A chorus of bells clashed behind me. I glanced back over my shoulder to see a host of glowing individuals come pouring out beneath the silver arches, a slender figure in azure blue robes in their midst, her arms outstretched. I turned away from them all and pressed desperately forward, but the barrier before me held fast.

For a moment I gave in to despair, believing for the first time that my will might be unequal to the task of breaking free. It was then I heard what sounded like a voice rising in exhortation above the clashing bells—or was it merely sounding in my own mind? It was the impassioned voice of a youth, strange in this moment yet somehow familiar to me, and it cried out: "Come *on*, Uncle Jack—you can do it! *Fight!*"

At this, the old fighting spirit rose in me and a red mist floated before my eyes. Lacking a foe of flesh and blood against which to direct my sword, I marshaled my will and hurled it against the pulsing barrier with all my might. There came a sharp snapping sound, a great wave of intense cold that chilled me to the marrow, and all went black. And then—

Then I was free of the glorious city and back again in the dreary confines of the crevasse.

Without a single backward glance, I stepped forward into the gloom and began steadfastly to retrace my steps beneath the narrow line of light streaming down from the world above.

6

AN UNSEEN HAND

I HAD NO WAY TO GAUGE the duration of my grim march back across that desolate plain—nor any knowledge of how much time I had squandered while I roamed the ghostly city. Apparently my innate comprehension of time's passage had been cast out of equilibrium when I fell into the chasm, and now it struggled to find its way back.

For the first half of the trek I could glimpse what I surmised was the bright glow of the city behind me from the corners of my eyes, though I refused to look back even once for fear of being snared again by that other realm. At some point I became aware that the uncanny light had vanished, but whether this was because the city itself had retreated forever back into that other world, or I had simply gone far enough that it was no longer visible, I did not know. I walked with my gaze alternating between the rubble at my feet and the seam of pale light above me, so powerfully were my thoughts bent upon leaving this buried realm. Eventually—though I could not have said whether days or mere hours had elapsed as I forced myself to stumble along—I realized I had reached the end of the guiding fissure that had become my obsession, and found myself within sight of the wall of black rock that rose not far from the place where I had begun my fantastic underground odyssey.

Here I was surprised to find that others had joined me in the crevasse: the white-clad bodies of two men lay sprawled on the rocky floor, not far from the spot where I had concluded my own bizarre descent. It was evident that no veils of otherworldly light had appeared to slow their falls, for the corpses were twisted and broken—as mine should have been had not a preternatural force intervened. I presumed they were members of the orluk hunting party who had been delegated to investigate the lip of the cleft in case their elusive quarry had somehow survived to secrete himself below the rim, and that they had lost their footing on the icy rock with deadly results. At this point they were beyond any help I might have wished to offer, and I left them there.

I quickly covered the last quarter mile to stand at the base of the wall, where I stared upward in a near daze. After the wonders I had already witnessed, I was only a little surprised when my torch picked out what looked to be a series of ancient steps carved into the black rock itself. Shining my light upward, I could see that the rough staircase ascended in zigzag fashion far up the side of the chasm until it was lost in shadow several hundred feet above the floor. I could only hope that it continued all the way to the surface.

I mounted the first timeworn ledge and began to climb. After fifty steps angling upward to the right, the stairway reversed course to the left for another fifty, and so it continued back and forth. For the first time in an unknown while I was feeling the pangs of hunger and thirst. It occurred to me that if I had chosen this path to begin with, I would never have found my way to the city of the glowing people and might have been back on the surface in mere hours, instead of . . . My mind supplied no number and I wondered for the hundredth time how long I had dallied in this hidden land. My head swimming with exhaustion, my ascent soon became a mere mechanical exercise of placing one foot a few inches above the other as I toiled upward.

At some point I became aware of golden light slowly increasing above me. Switching off the torch, I raised my eyes and examined the cleft, realizing it must have been well into morning when I had started up the stairs, for the bright noonday sun was now clearly visible at the center of the opening. I plodded onward.

At last I arrived at the final stair. It was then I discovered that the carved steps left off some fifty or sixty feet below the lip of the fissure, the final section perhaps sheared away in some previous troubling of the earth. Gauging the distance through bleary eyes, I decided that one powerful jump—accompanied by a hefty dose of luck—might just be sufficient to carry me to the edge of the opening. Though I had barely noticed due to the exertion of the climb, the temperature had been steadily dropping as I scaled the wall, and an icy wind blew down in gusts through the fissure. I paused to detach from my harness the folds of fur and fabric that constituted my snowsuit, shook them out until they once again approximated the form of a hooded jacket and a pair of trousers, and then, balancing precariously on the topmost step, girded myself against the harsh world above that I so longed to reach.

There had been no further evidence of glowing veils or viscous air as I ascended the stair, nor any renewed manifestation of that other powerful resistance I had fought against, once on the plain below, and then again in the glowing city before I made my final supreme effort to break free. Still I hesitated, wondering if there might not be some last barrier set as a trap to catch me in midair as I leaped upward, and then hurl me back down to the cavern floor. I racked my brain for an alternative, but found none.

I leaped.

A long moment later I was clinging by my fingertips to the jagged edge of the opening. I scrabbled up and over the rocky lip, hoping none of the surly hunters from Illall had lingered beyond the loss of their two fellows, poison-tipped spears in hand, to await my return.

The landscape all about the fissure was covered in a carpet of freshly fallen snow and empty of any signs of life. Squinting against the glare the sun struck from the carpet of unrelieved white, I breathed in deep lungfuls of the cold arctic air, a welcome balm after the dank atmosphere of the chasm. I took a moment to scoop up a few handfuls of snow to slake my thirst. Thus partially reinvigorated, I left the fissure and slogged through the drifts to the orluk hatchery half a mile away, where I crept cautiously up the outer slope and peered down into the basin. This was also devoid of inhabitants, the latest snowfall having obliterated all traces of any carnage that might have ensued after my departure, save for a few unidentifiable lumps and mounds I elected not to investigate. I raised my eyes to the west where I had stowed my flier.

The *Tarkim* was even less visible than when I had left it, the remnants of several snowfalls having covered the sleek outlines with a crust of white. Woola was nowhere in evidence as I climbed aboard. I had assumed the Okarian hunters had headed off in the opposite direction toward their hidden camp upon the conclusion of their grisly business with the orluk mothers in the basin. I felt a stab of anxiety as I contemplated what might have happened if they had instead decided to follow my tracks and thus come upon the flier and its noble protector. Woola was a mighty fighter, yet even he possessed no immunity to poison-tipped spears.

I sensed his presence before I heard his wild cries, whirling about to see him bounding through the snow toward the ship, one of the small creatures that frequent the snowy wastes clamped between his powerful jaws. He leaped onto the snowy deck and danced about in joy, spattering us both with purple blood from his breakfast.

I crouched down to embrace him, gleaning from his primitive thoughts a confused recounting of how he had waited upon my return until his hunger became unbearable, and only then left the *Tarkim* an hour or so ago on a brief hunting expedition. Other than that, he had remained with the flier, crawling under the pennon for a few hours each night to shield him from the chill, before resuming his post near the bow when the sun rose. He had seen no sign of the men from Illall.

Detaching the stiff cloth, I used it to scoop most of the snow from the deck and then broached the storage locker to procure myself a much-needed meal and provide Woola with some augmentation for his dainty catch. Once we were both sated, I returned to the locker and withdrew my chronometer, eager to learn how many weeks I had been absent. To my great surprise, I found that I had been gone from the flier for a grand total of three days! While I could tell from Woola's thoughts that this had seemed like an eternity to him—as it certainly had to me—the brief tally of days only reinforced my supposition that time had conducted itself in a most unnatural fashion during the period I had spent underground.

However long I had really been away, I could not wait to return to my home and the arms of the woman whose undying presence in my memory had saved me from spending the rest of my days in that ghostly city. My climb up the cavern wall had left me thoroughly fatigued, and I forced myself to indulge in a few hours of rest, Woola by my side—though my desire to get airborne again was such that I never managed to do more than doze. I rose at sundown to conduct a cursory inspection of the ship before buckling both myself and the calot securely to the deck and then setting the controlling destination compass to precisely retrace the path of our flight from Helium. Still exceedingly tired, I had decided to eschew the controls, settling down with the intention of drowsing away as much of the return flight as I could, and once we had lifted into the night sky, I placed the *Tarkim* under automatic guidance, my head resting comfortably against the warm expanse of Woola's great flank.

It seemed I had been asleep for mere moments when I was thrust rudely back into full wakefulness by an appalling compound of sensations. All destination compasses are equipped with an automated alarm designed to alert passengers in the event of any unscheduled deviation from course or altitude. A shrill siren that seemed to be located an inch from my ear had commenced to blare just as the *Tarkim* itself rocked violently back and forth, and we were flung down toward the earth by what felt like nothing so much as a giant, unseen hand that pressed the two of us hard against the deck while it bore the hapless vessel rapidly toward the ground hundreds of feet below.

I do not boast when I say that a native-born Barsoomian could not have survived the ordeal. Even I, with muscles conditioned for many years by the heavier gravity and thicker atmosphere of my previous life on Earth, struggled mightily against the oppressive force, feeling as if I moved through molasses as I strove to free the hooks that bound Woola and myself to the deck and then, my arms tight around the neck of my poor companion, who whimpered and panted beneath the frightful pressure, dragged both of us to the railing of the doomed ship. Foremost in my racing mind was the need to win free of the flier. Then, though we might ultimately be smashed upon some rocky surface below, at least we would not be pinned beneath tons of metal or consumed in the fiery blast that would result should the flier's engines explode upon impact.

Gathering the brute in my arms, I marshaled all my strength and bent my legs close to the deck. Then, with a great cry and the inane thought that I seemed to have recently acquired a regrettable habit of leaping blindly into unknown darkness, I propelled the two of us up and out over the railing to sail in an arc toward whatever destiny awaited us below.

I have never doubted for a moment that someday I shall die, for such is the doom that awaits every living creature, be he fighting man or flitting insect. Yet the idea that I should meet my final end under such chaotic circumstances, never knowing what brutal enemy attack or perverse natural phenomenon was behind my death, struck me in that instant as wholly unacceptable. Starry-eyed as the notion may seem, I am convinced that most human beings wish their demise to have some shred of meaning, and I am no exception.

So often capricious, fate was apparently of a mind to respect my delicate sensibilities upon that night, for a few breathless moments later Woola and I tumbled onto a low hillside of soft earth upon which lay an exceptionally thick carpet of ocher moss, and though we were both left battered and dazed, at least we were alive. A second later the *Tarkim* drove into the ground fifty yards from us. Covering my eyes with an upflung arm, I threw my body across Woola's broad head, acting instinctively to shield him from any fiery explosion that might eventuate. But again fate relented and the night remained silent aside from our own stertorous gasps and the protracted creak of metal as the craft executed a ponderous turn and came to rest heavily on its side.

I rubbed the calot's furrowed brow for some moments, impressing upon him with words and mental reassurances that we were out of immediate danger, then rose to my feet and began a cautious approach to the crash site with the aim of examining the extent of the damage to the flier.

I was about twenty feet from the battered craft when I felt a sudden wave of utter dread, followed by a heaviness in my limbs and a simultaneous strange prickling sensation on my skin. I came to an abrupt halt, while Woola, who had been keeping close by my side, eager not to be caught far from his master in these uncertain circumstances, bounded on past me toward the *Tarkim*. To my consternation, I saw him collapse onto his belly an instant later and, uttering piteous cries, turn his head back toward me, eyes rolling in obvious distress.

Ignoring the all too familiar warnings racing along my nerves, I stepped forward at once, only to lurch backward as I felt again the great invisible force that had assailed us on the flier pressing down like a tremendous weight across my shoulders—now with visible results, as I watched my sandals sink half an inch into the soil with each step. My reflexive backward stumble was accompanied by an instant lifting of the pressure.

With dogged determination I shuffled forward again, each dragging step an effort, until I stood once more by Woola's side. Kneeling, I encircled the massive torso with my arms, determined to drag my old friend back beyond the influence of the unseen force. But as I gave my first mighty heave upward, the formidable pressure suddenly vanished altogether and the pair of us went sailing up and back, twisting and flailing through the air.

Rising to my feet with yet another complement of fresh aches and bruises, I retrieved my torch, then squared my shoulders with a grim smile and marched back toward the flier. Woola followed along after a snort of exasperation, this time prudently trailing several yards to my rear. I approached the site with care, sliding a single foot gingerly over the invisible line to find no resistance. That it had been there was undeniable, for the ground itself had sunk an inch or two, resulting in a familiar area of odd concavity I knew had not been caused by the crash. But unlike the case of the deadly circle I had encountered days earlier, whatever unseen force had sent us and our ship hurtling to the earth in this spot had mercifully desisted shortly thereafter.

Moving with an abundance of caution, lest the phenomenon reappear suddenly and catch me off guard, I was able to make my way to the side of the craft without incident, and I began my assessment of the damage. Perhaps because my desperate leap from the deck had carried Woola and myself quickly beyond the radius of the effect, the *Tarkim* had sustained far worse injury than had its occupants. To my relief, both buoyancy tanks were intact; in fact, had the impact not left the ship partially wedged beneath the edge of a great flat rock, it might have floated upward as soon as the downward pressure ceased, leaving us stranded below. The essential portions of the craft's superstructure also appeared to be sound, which told me that we should eventually be able to become safely airborne again. The fore and aft propellers necessary to prevent us from drifting helplessly hither and yon once we left the ground were a different story. I crawled aboard and pried open the storage locker. Then, using a hefty spanner from the flier's repair kit, I did my best to straighten them out against a nearby outcropping. Both of the fittings that bound them to the ship were irreparably deformed. The restored blades now turned at but a fraction of their normal speed, indicating that we would have to limp back to Helium, accomplishing the remainder of our return flight in thrice the time it would normally have taken. My inspection also revealed that there had been some damage to the engine itself. Thankfully, I judged it to be of minor consequence, so long as I was stinting with the throttle and did not demand a level of speed the motor could no longer safely deliver.

The swift Martian dawn had commenced while I was making my inspection. Having judged the bulk of the damage, while disfiguring, to be superficial in terms of the ship's function, I set aside my torch and soon accomplished the few other repairs I deemed necessary to ensure the flier was once again airworthy. Though it was no longer the sleek flying machine in which I had departed Greater Helium, I felt sure that the *Tarkim*—whose name, which translates into English as "Swiftly," now seemed touched with irony—would provide us with a safe, if plodding, return across the many miles separating us from our home and loved ones.

Finally we climbed aboard and I took the flier aloft once more, this time vowing to remain awake and alert for the balance of our journey, despite my fatigue.

Acting on a hunch, I raised the ship high enough into the air to give me a broad view of the area in which we had gone down. Not far to the northwest, I glimpsed a familiar flash of metal on the ground. Sure enough, we were only a mile or two from the scene of the crash site I had investigated on my flight north. Knowing that the controlling destination compass had carried us back along the same course we had taken days ago, it had naturally occurred to me that the force that had brought down the *Tarkim* might easily have been responsible for the destruction of that other ship. The fact that our own crash site was practically adjacent to this one did little to dispel the mystery that now encompassed not one, but two downed fliers. Was there a malignant intelligence behind the attacks, or some natural aberration in the very terrain that was wont to reach up and bat flying objects from the sky?

I could not resist another pass over that earlier and far deadlier wreckage site, making sure not to venture directly above the haunted circle. Then I turned the nose of my flier about and resumed our interrupted journey home.

The return flight lasted eight days and nights, punctuated by half a dozen brief stops due to the need for frequent rest imposed by the pilot's own diminished capacity. At midmorning of the ninth day we caught sight of the gleaming scarlet tower of Greater Helium. Elated, I gunned the engine, using a trick of the gearing to urge the *Tarkim* to whatever remained of its former speed, and flew like a battered arrow toward the palace where I knew I would find my princess, secure in the belief that I had put the baffling events of the past few weeks forever behind me.

I could not have been more wrong.

7
FAMILY MATTERS

I **WAS BOTH SURPRISED** and pleased to see my son there to meet us when at last the *Tarkim* settled creaking and groaning on the landing stage of the palace. Carthoris stood before the hangars with his hands clasped behind his back, a look of mild disapproval on his handsome face as he watched the wounded flier shudder to a stop. His first greeting was of necessity for Woola, who would have propelled his massive bulk directly from the deck into Carthoris' arms, his entire body wagging joyfully, had not my son stepped adroitly to one side, and then knelt quickly to the floor and stroked the beast's hideous head until he quieted.

As always, I saw much of his mother in the carriage and noble features of my firstborn; he was a true son of Barsoom, his gray eyes and the lighter copper of his skin the sole indication that but one of his parents had been a red Martian. Watching him laugh and murmur endearments to the delighted old calot, I reflected that to me he would always be a fresh-faced youth, even though, now in the midst of his eighth decade, he would most likely be nearing the conclusion of a respectable life span had he been born on Earth.

Giving Woola a final embrace, he rose to his feet and approached me, flashing a wry smile at the battered appearance of both his sire and the craft at my back.

"It is good to see you again, Father," Carthoris said with a respectful inclination of his head. We each placed a right hand on the other's left shoulder in the formal Barsoomian greeting.

Then he snatched back his hand to suspend it open-palmed in

the air between us. "Put 'er there, Jack!" he drawled in comically accented English.

Over the years, both my children had evinced a sporadic interest in their father's otherworldly heritage. Each had acquired a smattering of words and phrases in Earthly languages, and both had some rudimentary understanding of English, though neither had mastered the tongue; nor did I expect them to, given the limited opportunity for practice on a world many millions of miles from where it was in daily use.

With an indulgent shake of my head, I allowed my son to lead us through the complicated exchange of slaps and handclasps that Vad Varo had taught us one evening over dinner, claiming it to be the secret greeting of the Royal Order of Mukluks, or some such folderol that he had learned in his college days in Delaware.

We were both grinning by the time the ritual was complete. I gave Carthoris an abbreviated recounting of my most recent adventures and he promised to go over the *Tarkim* from stem to stern for any clues as to the nature of the unseen power that had swatted us out of the sky. I asked him also to take charge of Woola and to procure some decent vittles for the deserving creature.

"Now tell me where I may find your mother, lad! I have missed her greatly, though it appears I have been gone for a far shorter period than my heart would have me believe."

"She is in her Gold Room preparing for today's special luncheon," he said, with a dubious glance at my disheveled state. "I am sure she will be overjoyed at your return, though I think you would be wise to take a few moments to get yourself in order before you seek her out."

I looked down with a chuckle at the grease and machine oil that streaked my body, and the smears of muck caked on my harness. "Nonsense!" I said. "Dejah Thoris has seen her mate dripping with the blood of great white apes, bearded like a warrior of the north, and crowned with the false yellow hair and diadem of a Holy Thern. I imagine she will forgive a little dirt and disarray in one who is so eager to take her in his arms again."

I clapped him on the shoulder before he could reply and sprang down the ramp to the palace, my eagerness to be reunited with my princess carrying me in prodigious strides. Carthoris called something after me, but whether it was a word of farewell or further commentary on my unkempt appearance I could not make out.

It was at times like this that I occasionally wished Dejah Thoris and I lived in a two-room cottage by a peaceful waterway, rather than the grand and labyrinthine palace deemed proper for a member of the royal family of Helium. I had another one like it in Lesser Helium, and there were times when I confused the two great piles to my chagrin, taking a right turn down a corridor that existed only in the other palace and almost flattening my royal nose against a blank wall.

At length I penetrated to the floor upon which was situated the Gold Room, a chamber wherein my wife kept a collection of antique literature and art in lavish volumes, some of which were many thousands of years old. As I hurried down the corridor I could see her beloved figure, perfectly framed by the archway that led into the room so that it resembled a work of highly skilled portraiture.

Dejah Thoris stood between the curving arms of two embroidered couches, her head bent over the sheaf of gilt-edged sheets she held in her slender hands. Before she could look up at my approach, I let out a quiet laugh of triumph and burst through the doorway like any young swain desperate to be reunited with his lady love—only to skid to a halt when the rest of the room came into view and I realized that she was far from alone. In fact, as I noted with sinking heart, she was far from the only representative of Heliumetic royalty in the room.

I have noted before that while there are few beasts and even fewer men that have caused me over the course of a long life to momentarily consider turning tail and running, I have too often found myself inexplicably cowed when in the company of certain women. This feeling is compounded when the individuals in question are highly cultured and schooled in the intricacies of polite society, a daunting labyrinth in its own right that has ever been beyond my ability to thread. In fact, the only women that have made my stout heart quail more piteously than those skilled in verbal fencing and innuendo are the ones who have seen fit over the years to openly express their romantic interest in me. At least, I thought as I stumbled forward toward my mate, there was but one princess in this chamber who had any such designs on me, and those I heartily reciprocated.

As for her companions, I was outnumbered three to one—though in truth, only a single member of this elegant ambush party held the power to reduce me to the stammering bumpkin I must have been long ago in my thankfully forgotten early years.

As Dejah Thoris rushed into my arms I momentarily forgot all about the other occupants of the Gold Room, and we traded kisses and exchanged words of affection as if we were quite alone. At length I lifted my face from hers and nodded a fond hello to the two who sat on the cushioned divan to our left. The nearest of these was Thuvia, my son's wife and our treasured friend. Daughter of the Jeddak of Ptarth, Thuvia had once been my fellow prisoner in the Valley Dor. She had gone on to be my savior on more than one occasion, as we battled to free ourselves from the clutches of the false gods that ruled there.

Next to her sat Thoria, my beloved's mother and mate to Mors Kajak, Jed of Lesser Helium. There was no more gracious woman in all Barsoom than Thoria, and none more joyful of spirit—though I had sometimes glimpsed her lovely face tinged with sadness when she thought no one was watching her. More than a century past, before my own advent upon Barsoom, Kajan Dan, brother to Dejah Thoris and Thoria's only son, had departed Helium on an expedition to gather scientific information related to the planet's artificially generated atmosphere, and never returned. It was Kajan Dan's disappearance and presumed death that had persuaded Dejah Thoris to embark upon her own tutelage in the atmospheric sciences, a pursuit that had ultimately led to the two of us meeting as captives of the Tharks.

With my mate still nestled in my embrace, I exchanged warm words of greeting with these two—until a small cough bade me turn my attention to the personage who sat ramrod straight on the right-hand couch, a plump sorak sprawled languidly across her silk-draped lap.

Much beloved as a symbol of wealth and status among the upper classes of red Martians, the sorak has always struck me as an exceedingly unattractive creature, both in disposition and appearance. Picture an Earthly weasel gifted with three pairs of legs and a double row of needle-sharp fangs, completely hairless but for a single tuft of yellow fur in the center of its forehead and another at the tip of its long tail, with the balance of the naked, glossy hide a grayish lavender brindled with streaks of deep purple—a combination which has always reminded me of a skinned rabbit. The temperament of the average sorak is evident in its name, which may be literally translated from the eloquent common tongue of Barsoom as "answers with claws."

This particular representative of that unlovely species was currently reposing like a feline empress in the lap of a very human one. I bowed my head to Vara Martis, the revered mate to the Jeddak of all Helium, whose imperial beauty was said to be equaled (and to my own discerning mind eclipsed) only by that of her granddaughter, the radiant woman who stood at my side.

To say that adult Barsoomians show no signs of age over their long lives is not entirely accurate. One does not face grim death daily on the battlefield or rule as a tyrant for centuries on end without accruing some visible record that may be interpreted by the perceptive eye. Wisdom acquired, suffering endured, avarice, lust for power, the blessings of joy and fulfillment: all these inscribe the tale of years upon the face and body. To be fair, Vara Martis had never shown me a moment of true discourtesy, in spite of my sometimes rough and unpolished warrior's ways, yet one does not pass close to nine hundred years as empress of the most powerful nation on all Barsoom without acquiring a certain aura of formidability.

Dejah Thoris had not failed to notice the object of my gaze as she urged me forward into this unexpected arena with her hand pressed discreetly to the small of my back. With an impish smile she said softly into my ear, "Here is your chance, John Carter. But comport yourself correctly in the presence of my grandmother this morning, and she may deem you fit to polish her darling Sompa's teeth, after all."

Relaxing just a bit, I could not resist a chuckle at this reference to one of our earliest misunderstandings, back when we were both captives of the Tharks in the dead city of Korad, and I, a blundering newcomer to this world, was already thoroughly besotted by her charms—and then just as thoroughly crestfallen when I learned that I was held in such low opinion by the object of my devotion as to be deemed unworthy of applying a toothbrush to her grandmother's cat!

Reluctantly leaving the haven of my wife's arms, I stepped forward to meet my doom and raised the hand of Vara Martis to my lips. "Jeddara," I greeted her. "I am pleased to find you here."

"So it would appear, Warlord," replied the empress. "I can see that you have taken great pains to prepare yourself for my visit."

Thus reminded of my disheveled and unsightly state, it was all I could do to keep myself from digging the toe of my sandal into the sumptuous carpet like a servant who has overturned the sweetmeats tray. I glanced at Dejah Thoris for assistance, but before she could intercede on behalf of her abashed husband, I was granted succor from a wholly unanticipated quarter.

"Finally!" proclaimed a musical voice behind me, as I felt slim fingers reach up to further tousle my already disarranged hair. "I was sure I had somehow offended the sensitive disposition of my proper old American, and thus caused him to deny me even a moment of his time."

I whirled about in amazement to see a most unexpected and welcome sight: my daughter.

"Tara!" I exclaimed. She grasped my hands in hers and drew me firmly back through the archway with her. I am not ashamed to admit that I felt the gratitude of a drowning man saved at the very last moment from a deadly undertow. Once we were in the corridor and out of sight of those in the chamber she threw herself into my arms.

"But I had no idea you were here," I told her. "When did you arrive from far Gathol?"

"Barely half a day after you departed on your solitary jaunt," she said, eyeing me with mock severity. "It was rather thoughtless of you to spoil my clever surprise."

"If I had but known—" She touched a slender finger to my lips.

"Then where would have been the surprise? Really, John Carter, one expects more common sense from such a vaunted strategist as the acknowledged Warlord of all Barsoom and at least one of her moons."

I gave a shrug of defeat. "While I should have learned long since not to look for ordinary logic from the girl who once dropped a dozen darseens into her bath in hopes that she might swim in colored water. Your maids did not enjoy chasing a chamber full of slippery lizards on their hands and knees while you laughed at the spectacle."

"If you recall, I had to round up most of the fugitives myself, since no one else could bear to touch them," Tara retorted. She leaned back, her fingers still entwined about my neck, and favored me with a scowl that looked all the more forbidding due to the loveliness of the face upon which it reposed. "At any rate, it is indecorous for a Heliumite to speak so of the mate of the Jed of Gathol," she added solemnly. "It might well mean war."

I laughed. "Well, it would not be the first time swords were drawn in your name," I said. "And I am here at this moment, anyway, and so are you." Her radiant mother had followed us out into the corridor and I extended my arm to draw her into our embrace. "Your brother is lurking somewhere on the premises, as well, and now that all are gathered we shall have plenty of time for a proper family reunion."

Tara's face fell as Dejah Thoris shook her head.

"I am afraid not," said the latter. "Just this morning word reached us that Gahan has been called to quell an incursion on the western border of his kingdom, and so Tara must return at once to Gathol to manage affairs of state in his absence."

"I depart tomorrow," Tara confirmed with regret. "If, that is, you will be good enough to loan me one of your swift one-man fliers, since my royal mate will now be unable to retrieve me himself as originally planned."

"Surely you do not propose to make the journey alone?" I exclaimed. "Gahan would hardly expect us to allow that!"

"*Al-low?*" Tara repeated the word as if she had never heard it before, her face blank with bewilderment. "It may astound you to learn, John Carter, that the Jed of Gathol gave up any attempts to instruct me in what I might and might not do long before I deigned to wed him. Furthermore, you are well aware that I am perfectly capable of piloting a flier on a par with my husband—or, for that matter, my esteemed sire."

"Yet the last time you elected to depart Helium on your own—" I began.

"Yes, yes." Tara surveyed me coolly, her brows arched high. "The great scarlet tower itself toppled over and I ended up being considered for the main course in a kaldane's banquet. Are you going to claim that my momentary lapse in judgment was to blame for the single most powerful storm to ravage Barsoom in all of recorded history?" She leaned forward suddenly and sniffed the air by my face. "And why do you smell of engine grease? Mother, look at your husband! How can you allow the Prince of Helium to dine with us in this disreputable state?"

I was formulating a rejoinder involving a renewed examination of the word "allow," when Dejah Thoris said simply: "He is John Carter."

With a cluck of her tongue, Tara drew a finger along my begrimed cheek and wiped it carefully on the underside of one of her silks. "Indeed. And I suspect he is attempting to use his rough appearance to alter the course of the conversation. The fact remains that I am no longer a child with eggshell in her hair who needs her father to take her hand and guide her down the twisting path of life."

"I have had a fatiguing several weeks," I told my daughter firmly. "Yet I should not be able to sleep this night nor any other if I knew you were truly set on making your way unaccompanied back to Gathol."

"Here is a solution that should displease neither of you," my wife interposed smoothly as Tara parted her lips to reply. Dejah Thoris turned first to me. "Though I would much prefer not to relinquish your company so soon after your return, I am aware that you have been aiming to deliver the final sets of Gridley Wave equipment to both Gathol and the scientific installation at Exum before the communication network is activated." She shifted her attention to Tara. "For your part, Daughter, have you not been lamenting the circumstances that now threaten to prevent you from spending time with your father as you had planned? If John Carter accompanies you to Gathol, the two of you will have ample time to reacquaint yourselves. Once he has seen you home, he may continue on the journey he would soon be undertaking in any event."

Tara mulled over the compromise. "Well . . . when presented from that perspective . . ."

"The suggestion is eminently reasonable," I said.

"Perfect," said my wife, slipping her arm through mine. "And now let us join the others in the dining hall, motor oil and all. Vara Martis has some further questions for Tara regarding Llana, of whom she claims to have seen far too little of late."

Taking my other arm, Tara cast me a stricken look as we headed down the corridor toward the great dining hall. "I fear Great-grandmother does not approve of the approach I have taken to child-rearing. Since my arrival in Helium she has made it clear that she believes Gahan and I have been much too permissive with our daughter, who now, to quote Vara Martis, 'acts just as she pleases.'"

"Shocking," I said with a glance toward Dejah Thoris, who seemed to be struggling to maintain her composure. "Though, as I think of it, I am sure the Jeddara occasionally expressed similar concerns about the unwise degree of latitude that your mother and I granted our own daughter."

As we neared the ramp that sloped upward into the hall, we were suddenly accosted by none other than Carthoris, who emerged from a side door and, with a wink for his mother and sister, whisked me off into a small chamber where two male servants awaited, armed with towels and ewers of steaming water.

A short time later I buckled myself into fresh leather and a formal cloak of crimson silk figured with the device of the House of Tardos Mors.

"You are a good son," I told Carthoris, rubbing the palm of my hand along my freshly shaven cheek.

"Say rather that I am a loyal subject of the Prince of Helium, who has an image to maintain, even if it is only for certain exacting members of his own family," he told me with a smile. "Now let us present ourselves for inspection and hope we are deemed fit to be seated at a civilized table and not forced to crouch on the floor and beg for scraps."

Carthoris had reminded me during my last-minute ablutions that the occasion for this special gathering was one of several holidays observed among the red Martians in veneration of deceased family members. Ancestor worship is an almost universally common practice on Barsoom, perhaps even more prevalent now that the cult surrounding the holy person of Issus—revered for millennia as the Goddess of Death and Life Eternal, until her once-faithful followers had seen fit to tear her apart with their bare hands—had been thoroughly debunked.

Tardos Mors and his son Mors Kajak were off on inspection tours of the northern and southern borders of the empire respectively, while Carthoris and Thuvia's son, Djon Dihn, had elected to remain for a while at the court of his grandfather in Ptarth, leaving my own son and myself the only male representatives of the royal family in attendance.

The luncheon proceeded amicably enough. Though the food was far too rich for my warrior's palate, I managed to choose the correct utensil for the various courses, and by the end of the meal even Vara Martis was behaving more like a woman surrounded by family members whom she held dear and less like someone who had ruled by her husband's side for nine centuries and showed every intention of continuing to do so for another ten. Stories were told of the departed that illustrated their sterling qualities, often with the addition of affectionately humorous anecdotes. I listened with interest, but did not contribute, since all of them had met their ends before my introduction into the family. I learned that one of Vara Martis' uncles had been obsessed with the idea that there were hidden doorways to other worlds on one or both moons, that Dejah Thoris' brother Kajan Dan had burst from the shell with an insatiable appetite for gambling, and that Carthoris was apparently the spit and image of his thrice-great-grandfather on the maternal side.

Dejah Thoris and Tara had committed themselves to spending the next few hours following the meal with the gathered relatives, while Carthoris begged off in order to return to work on the *Tarkim*.

After announcing that I had several pressing affairs of state to which I must attend, I devoted the afternoon to avoiding them, preferring instead to catch up on a personal project that was much more dear to my heart.

At least that had been my plan.

Though curiosity has often been my friend, it occasionally plays me for a fool, leaving me vowing ruefully to never again give in to its many temptations.

8

THE EYES IN THE DARK

YEARS AGO I HAD EMBARKED on a one-man crusade to eliminate paid assassination as an acceptable global pastime among the civilized nations of Barsoom. Resulting first in the kidnapping of Dejah Thoris, and later in an improbable journey to rescue her in an interplanetary flier controlled by an artificial brain, my earnest efforts had ended as a resounding failure. Since then I had narrowed my focus to undertakings that seemed more prone to success.

Beneath every Martian city worthy of the name stretches a vast network of pits and catacombs, a dismal underworld forever hidden from the light of day, which has been utilized since time immemorial to house dungeons and sites of torture. I myself had languished for what seemed like grim eternities in not a few of them, my cellmates often the skeletal remains of unknown previous inmates still affixed to the wall by the chains in which they had perished. I daresay most of the upstanding citizens of Barsoom gave little thought to what lay beneath their feet—yet to my mind, these twisting tunnels and forgotten cells were not only a mark of shameful barbarity, but dangerous warrens inhabited by a veritable zoological garden of vermin that ranged from the merely foul to the deadly, and every year an untold number of curious citizens wandered off to go missing in their labyrinthine depths. Gambling that it would be less liable to spark controversy among the good folk of Barsoom than my rash attempt to halt killings for hire, I had quietly initiated a public works project to open up and cleanse the pits of Helium, with the hope that this civilizing gesture might eventually spread beyond our borders.

Work had begun beneath my own palace in Greater Helium months ago and was reportedly proceeding at a satisfactory pace—despite the loss of no less than three of the workers, who had apparently strayed unaccompanied into the less explored sections of the pits, never to be seen again. Feeling that a personal inspection was long overdue, I made my way down to the lowest stories of the palace, then descended deep into the ground by means of an ancient spiraling ramp.

Eventually, radium bulbs would be permanently installed at regular intervals along each corridor, but for the present time all was still in darkness. My pocket pouch containing my own hand torch was many levels above with the discarded harness I had worn on my recent trip. I plucked a flambeau from a sconce by the entrance to the web of tunnels that composed the pits proper, ignited it with a flint hanging on a chain from the base, and ventured forth among the flickering shadows. Here the air was dank and chill and smelled of mold, the ancient stone walls of the narrow passageways clammy with moisture. It was still difficult for me to accept that gloomy places such as this lurked just beneath the soaring towers and stately edifices of Barsoom's most advanced nation of the red race—a people of contradictions on a planet of enigmas.

It had not occurred to me that due to the holiday there would be no workers present to guide me. I walked alone through many twists and turns, the echoing scrape of my sandals the only exception to the silence that closed about me like a muffling cloak. I could see that the laborers had made a decent start: the stone floors of the first areas I explored, worn smooth by the sandals of untold thousands of jailers and their charges, had been swept clean and washed, while the empty cells I passed in the flickering torchlight had finally been cleared of centuries-old bones and other grim detritus. In an effort to prevent any more lost souls among the workers, each corridor was marked as it was explored with a bold horizontal stripe of luminous pigment, along with a letter-numeral code every twenty feet to keep the wanderer apprised of his current location.

I eventually found myself at the limit of the marked areas, standing poised at a crossing of several different unidentified passageways.

Ever curious as to what lay beyond the next turn, I decided to continue on for a bit. My thoughts found their way back to Earth, as they had lately been wont to do. In the back of my mind were the excited tales told by several generations of youngsters who had ventured with lanterns into the less extensive—and decidedly less perilous—cellars beneath the main buildings of the Virginia homestead of the Carters, always hoping they might chance upon a treasure chest spilling over with gold doubloons, or perhaps the mummified remains of the black-hearted pirate who had crept down there to retrieve his spoils and then lost his way.

There were five tunnels before me from which to choose. Peering into the openings, I saw that the corridors ran at crazy angles to one another, not only veering off unexpectedly to left or right, but slanting steeply upward or downward as well. On a whim I selected the one on the far right and pressed on, fascinated by its byzantine convolutions and wondering if this had been a deliberate tactic to keep any prisoner who somehow managed to throw off his chains from escaping to the outside world until such time as his recapture might be effected.

I was making my way along a corridor that alternated sharply upward and to the right with downward and to the left every ten paces or so, like some nightmare serpent frozen in its death throes, when I became aware of low, intermittent noises that resembled whispered voices, first sounding as if they issued from just beyond the nearest turn ahead, then a moment later as if they originated some distance to my rear. Hand on my sword hilt, I moved quietly onward, and a few minutes later found myself at the end of the contorted corridor. The whispers had ceased.

I stood in an opening perpendicular to a new passageway, a much wider tunnel where I now had the choice of striking out to either side. I leaned cautiously forward into the tunnel, peering first down the right-hand branch, my torch held high above my head to provide the maximum illumination. The way seemed clear for as far as the light penetrated, which was perhaps seventy-five feet. I turned and repeated the exercise to the left, where I was startled to make out a dark form on the floor just at the edge of the far shadows. Could this be one of the missing laborers? As I studied the mass, I became aware of a pair of red orbs burning like coals about eight or ten feet above the floor in the shadows beyond the sprawled shape. The hairs rising at the base of my skull, I thought to discern the dim outline of a vaguely humanlike form.

It was not one of the fearsome great white apes as I had first expected, for it appeared to have only four limbs—yet there was an odd glimmer emanating from its flesh, which allowed me to discern that the arms depending from its massive shoulders were abnormally long in proportion to those of a typical human being, appearing to almost scrape the floor of the tunnel. The thing neither moved nor made any noise as I drew my longsword and took a step toward it. I heard a series of rapid footfalls behind me, and as I turned to investigate, a monstrous gust of wind blew out of the twisted corridor at my back and extinguished the flambeau, instantly plunging everything into absolute blackness. A second later the torch was wrenched from my hand and I heard the sound of footsteps diminishing at great speed away from me in the corridor.

I peered back down the tunnel, but the burning crimson eyes had disappeared with the light.

As much as I longed to investigate whatever lay on the floor, it made little sense to approach it—or the thing which had seemed to loom above it—in the absence of all light. Reluctantly, I turned and reentered the twisting corridor with the aim of swiftly tracking down my stolen torch or at the least procuring another one, lest I be set upon in the darkness.

Distances are more difficult to measure in the dark. I moved along as quickly as I could, trying to anticipate the alternation of rising and falling, left- and right-twisting angles, but still found myself scraping my arms and legs against the rough walls in my eagerness, and once I almost fell when I stepped up at a spot where the corridor abruptly descended. I halted then and proceeded more carefully, one hand on the wall to guide my way and my sword at the ready in the other. Half a dozen zigzagging turns later, my sandal encountered something on the floor, and there was the flambeau, still warm and with a few small embers burning minutely in the darkness. I quickly stooped and retrieved it, then tried my best to coax it back to life with gentle breaths, my flesh crawling as I once again heard the susurration of faint whispers. Finally it flared and warm light bloomed once again. I turned in a slow circle in the dank corridor, ears straining for any noise that might betray the location of the thing or things, but the slightest sound I made reverberated in crazy echoes before and behind me.

It stood to reason that whatever had rushed me earlier was somewhere up ahead in the direction I had been moving. I was torn between attempting to pursue the fire thief and returning to the large tunnel where I had glimpsed both the mysterious dark mass and whatever bore the pair of staring red eyes that towered above it. Reckoning that whoever had made off with my torch could be almost anywhere in the mad labyrinth of interconnecting passageways by now, I retraced my steps back to the tunnel. As I approached the opening, I thought to hear a faint retreating noise, as of something heavy and metallic being dragged along the floor. I slipped from the corridor, quickly moved several paces to the left, and placed my back against the wall to prevent another sneak attack. Once more I raised my torch to illuminate that end of the tunnel. No crimson eyes stared back at me this time, nor could I see the dark mass I had previously glimpsed on the floor. When I reached the place where I believed it to have lain, I found only a few scraps of ancient rags. Several paces beyond, a trail of deeply scored marks shone in the torchlight on the stone floor. Kneeling to examine them, I noted inside the tracks a peculiar glistening substance like a thin coating of slime which emitted a strong and fetid odor.

I followed the trail for several paces, after which it faded into nothingness. I continued on for a few minutes, but saw no more marks. The tunnel itself seemed to stretch on endlessly in the torchlight, and finally I turned back and returned to the corridor opening. From there I made my way once more through the tortuous corridors, my sword at the ready, until at last I sighted the first of the glowing bands marking the tunnels that had already been explored. Not long after I found myself at the base of the ancient runway, which I bounded up, and soon I had emerged from the clammy depths and into the welcoming daylight of the upper levels of the palace.

I issued strict orders that guards be posted at the top of the runway and all work in the pits be suspended until I returned from accompanying Tara to Gathol—at which time I was resolved to foray back into the depths with a cadre of well-armed warriors bearing radium torches. The sooner Helium was cleansed of these ancient gathering places of mystery and evil beneath her feet, the better.

9
TALO THORAN

THAT EVENING MY WIFE and children joined me for our first dinner alone together in some time. Thuvia had returned to Lesser Helium, ostensibly to get her own house in order, though I suspected this was merely an excuse to graciously grant the four of us the all-too-infrequent opportunity to dine again as we once had long ago.

Still pondering the meaning of the afternoon's strange encounter, I did not immediately mention it to the others. Naturally, they had many questions concerning my most recent excursion to the north and the deleterious effects it had had on my new flier, but at my insistence we limited our mealtime discussion to the general topics of the day.

Once dinner was finished, I acceded to the entreaties of the others and regaled them with the tale of the several odd experiences that had befallen me on my journey. They were a rapt and appreciative audience, asking cogent questions and reacting with gasps of amazement or horror at the appropriate moments.

I became aware that my descriptions of the events that had transpired before and after my sojourn in the ghostly city were framed in much more elaborate detail than what had occurred in between. Indeed, the unmeasured time I spent there had seemed increasingly dreamlike in retrospect, and, like a dream, much of it had receded into hazy vagueness.

After I concluded the tale of my northern adventures, I appended an account of the afternoon's encounter with further mystery in the form of the theft of my torch and the sight of those glowing eyes in the pits below the palace. This elicited further expressions of surprise.

"Well, Father, you departed Helium hungering for excitement," Carthoris declared. "It seems your First Ancestor was in a generous mood and decided to gift you with an extra helping."

"Do you believe there is any connection among these various occurrences?" Dejah Thoris asked me.

"I have been racking my brain in that regard," I told her. "Try as I might, I have found no common thread among these odd events."

"Each episode involved your being brought low, in one way or another—either down to the earth or beneath it," ventured Tara. "I have it! You told us once that there is supposed to be another world hidden at the core of Jasoom. Do you suppose that Barsoom could be hollow, as well, and some of its denizens are attempting to make contact?"

Carthoris took up the thread before I could respond: "Yes! Perhaps there are creatures from the dawn of time lurking down there. Having recently discovered that there is a civilization clinging to the outer shell of their world, they are trying to establish relations with its most famous inhabitant. Of course, now that they have stolen fire from you, they are bound to progress rapidly." With eyes wide, he continued in sepulchral tones: *"Beware, John Carter, the monsters from below!"*

We concluded the night with a discussion of our plans for the next day, when Tara and I would depart on our trip to Gathol. With my daughter's assent, I had decided to head east from Helium on a somewhat roundabout route that would afford us a day or two of additional time together.

Carthoris, who had discovered during his cursory inspection of the *Tarkim* no clues as to the nature of the strange force that had compelled us out of the sky, wished to retain the craft for further study. This suited me fine, as there was no way the battered flier could have been made ready for another journey in less than several days. In its stead, my son had promised to personally deliver me another, equally suitable ship. Though I am not in the habit of allowing others to choose my fliers for me, I gladly indulged him in this. I count aircraft as one of my strong interests, yet they are an absolute passion for my son.

As we finished exchanging our good-nights with the children, I thought for a second that I spied a shadow lurking outside one of the tall window arches on the far side of the room. When I went to investigate I saw no one—unsurprising, as the chamber was located some five hundred feet above the ground, though that would not have prevented a determined man in an equilibrimotor from rising through the darkness to hover near the window. The fine wire netting that is used to prevent the ingress of nocturnal assassins even here in the Warlord's palace had not yet been deployed, and I leaned out as far as I could to make sure the area was completely empty, before chalking up the incident to an overstimulated imagination. I gave it no further thought, for Tara and Carthoris had departed for their own apartments and my princess and I were finally alone.

The next morning Dejah Thoris and I parted after breakfast; she had some matters to attend to and promised to join me within the half hour on the rooftop landing stage.

I escorted Tara to the roof, where we met my son, who had risen early to make sure the *Kantim* was not only shipshape but had been outfitted with the latest in equipment and amenities. This flier was even larger than its predecessor, and boasted a small cabin amidship for the convenience of Tara, though she had assured us with some indignation that she was quite capable of roughing it on deck. Carthoris was wiping his hands on a rag as we approached the hangars. "If you break this one, Father, we may have to suspend your piloting privileges." Nodding at Tara, he added in a stage whisper: "And if you value your life, do not let my sister at the controls!"

"And to think, I once considered you my favorite brother," Tara said wistfully. They drew aside arm in arm to say their farewells as I looked about for Dejah Thoris. I saw her emerging onto the landing stage, accompanied by a familiar-looking man who was weighed down by an armload of cumbersome parcels and trailed by a similarly burdened servant.

As they approached, I recognized her companion as the earnest young man who would have accosted me when I took off on my previous journey, had not Dejah Thoris intervened.

They stopped alongside the *Kantim*, where the two men staggered aboard the ship and proceeded off in the direction of the cargo hold. Dejah Thoris caught sight of me and came over.

"What is all that?" I asked. "I thought we were well provisioned."

"That is Talo Thoran, a scholar of comparative linguistics who has become an expert in the operation of the new communications devices you have been scattering around the globe in pursuit of your network, and those are his belongings. A few weeks ago one of your own representatives promised him that he might accompany you when you went to deliver the final batch of Gridley Wave equipment. He is bringing with him the master transceiver necessary to activate the network, and is most eager to settle into his new capacity as officer in charge of communications at the Exum station."

"Accompany us?" I frowned. "Upon my return I shall have to have a few choice words with a certain presumptuous representative. And why does the man not simply fly there himself?"

"Reports have come in that a sizable swarm of green men has lately broken away from the Torquasian horde and migrated east to take up residence not far from Exum, thus rendering the area perilous to air travel. They have been amusing themselves with target practice and have come close to shooting down several one-man fliers that have ventured near. Talo Thoran would have to wait until my father and grandfather return from their own expeditions to obtain a military escort, by which time he fears some sort of approaching solar activity might make it more difficult to calibrate the instruments," Dejah Thoris said, before adding in a low voice: "Also, he apparently does not know how to pilot a flier."

"You're joking." I eyed the man in a new light. I am always amazed to be reminded that individuals who claim possession of the most rarefied learning can at the same time be blithely ignorant of what strikes me as utterly basic knowledge. "Does he know how to lace his own sandals, or will he also require assistance in that area?"

"I am sure he will soon be thanking his first ancestor for putting him into the care of someone as understanding and forbearing as yourself," Dejah Thoris told me. "I should let you know that, although a talkative man by nature, he has been made to understand that he is to keep to himself until you deliver him to his station. Fortunately, the ship is large enough that you and Tara should be able to enjoy each other's company without interference."

"He had better understand that," I said. "Otherwise, I shall hang him by his harness from the bow for the duration of the trip."

Tara joined us and was informed by her mother of the existence of our additional passenger. Before she could pose the questions I felt sure were coming, I observed in solemn tones that the scholar's advanced studies had evidently not included a seminar on how to operate a flier. Tara gave a snort of amazement. "Shall we have to cut up his meat for him, as well?"

Dejah Thoris shook her head. "The poor man," she said.

We exchanged final embraces with my wife and son, and climbed onto the deck of the *Kantim*, where Talo Thoran awaited us with lowered eyes and a diffident expression.

"You are looking especially fierce this morning, John Carter," Tara whispered to me as the scholar crossed the deck and began to fasten his harness to the hooks that would keep him securely bound to the flier during our flight. "With any luck the man will soon be so intimidated that he will choose to leap over the side rather than bear your stern gaze."

"At which time I shall applaud his perspicacity and wish him a very pleasant landing," I said, and made my own preparations for departure.

Though she had made no such requests of me, I had assured Dejah Thoris that I would return as soon as possible after delivering my passengers to their destinations, and resist at every turn the temptation to indulge in further excitement. "While I am certain that is your intention," she replied with a smile, "I have my doubts that the universe will honor it. We both know that adventure follows at your heel as faithfully as does Woola." As the *Kantim* lifted from the landing stage, I exchanged with my peerless princess the sign made by lovers on Barsoom. At my side, my daughter noticed and beamed her approval.

The first day passed agreeably enough. Talo Thoran, who turned out to be a much younger man than his scholarly mien would suggest, had evidently been sufficiently chastened by my wife's cautions that he maintained a respectful distance from Tara and myself. I believe he was genuinely afraid of me for a while—and I was frankly in no mood to convince him of my general good nature, especially if it meant unloosing the floodgates of his purported loquacity. Tara's presence seemed to evoke an entirely different response from the fellow, leaving him a bit tongue-tied, and I was not surprised when I noticed him stealing worshipful glances at my daughter when he thought neither of us was aware.

Late in the afternoon, I engaged the destination compass and turned from the controls to find the young man gazing at me with a strange intensity, almost as if he were trying to bore into my very skull with his eyes. So intent was he that he failed to notice for a minute that I now returned his close inspection, and when realization finally dawned, his face flushed crimson beneath the copper and he averted his gaze at once.

I inquired as to what had caused such an interest in my forehead.

"I do beg your pardon, Warlord," he stammered. "It is only that as a student of all forms of communication, I was curious to see if it were true that your mind could not be read." When I raised my brows at the notion of someone attempting to play safecracker with my brain, he added swiftly, "I swear by my ancestors that I was not trying to pry! As you are no doubt aware, almost all civilized folk and even some of the higher animals here on Barsoom naturally evolve the ability to shield their minds as they attain adulthood. In those cases, however, the presence of the shield itself can always be detected, even if it cannot be penetrated. Yet in your case, it is truly as if there is nothing there at all!"

There came a peal of silvery laughter from the stern of the flier as my daughter raised her head from the songbook she had been perusing.

"I fear Talo Thoran has discovered your secret, John Carter," Tara said earnestly. "Incredible, is it not, that a man could rise to such heights while lacking a mind!"

The scholar looked back and forth between the two of us, his initial expression of bewilderment twisting into a grimace of stricken horror. "Oh no!" he exclaimed, "Princess! Warlord! This was never my implication!"

Tara nodded thoughtfully from her perch. "So you are instead implying that my father has not yet attained adulthood? Or is it your contention that he belongs neither to the category of civilized folk nor to that of the higher animals? A bold thesis, indeed!"

The young man's cheeks were swiftly becoming ashen as all blood drained from them.

"When she was younger we had considered appointing the princess to the post of Royal Torturer," I told Talo Thoran. "As you can see, she still possesses an innate aptitude in that regard. But I am also somewhat interested in the subject. Have you any theories to explain why my brain remains invisible to this sort of scrutiny, through no conscious effort on my part?"

"Not theories as such—not yet." Talo Thoran leaned forward on his bench, the eager scholar quickly triumphing over the panicked youth. "We know from those examinations by experts in the biological and psychological sciences to which you and Vad Varo have graciously submitted, that the conformation of your brain differs in certain minor respects from that of the average Barsoomian. Yet you present to all outward appearances as a normal human being."

I gave Tara a warning glance as she looked up from her book again with lips half parted to speak. Oblivious, Talo Thoran continued.

"I have long been intrigued by the ancient hypothesis that our telepathic faculties are produced, or at the least encouraged, by a cocoon of energy waves that exists around Barsoom in much the same way as once did the various levels of natural atmosphere. Lacking a material component, this blanketing energy (here he used a Barsoomian term that translates most closely into English as "world-mind") has not deteriorated in concert with the actual atmosphere that once surrounded our dying world and is now maintained only by artificial means. Consider this: on your own planet,

you have over a relatively short period of time raised wireless communication to a height of sophistication that we have yet to equal
here. It is this lack of reliable intercommunication between the
far-flung nations of Barsoom that we hope to remedy with the
distribution of Gridley Wave devices to key areas of the world. Some
theorists suggest that the invisible aura generated by this world-mind
interferes with the efficient transmission of radio waves here on
Barsoom, while simultaneously allowing our brains to share and
receive information, both among individuals and in a global sense,
much more freely than is the case on Jasoom. How else to explain
the fact that our common tongue has persisted virtually unchanged
for millennia all over Barsoom—even including those isolated areas
that have had no intercourse with the rest of the world for many
thousands of years?"

"But then why is it that Vad Varo and myself were both able to
read minds soon after we arrived on this planet, while our own brains
remain opaque to outside scrutiny?" I was truly becoming interested
in spite of myself.

"It has been posited that from the moment we break the shell—
and even, perhaps, for the five years previous when we lie developing
in the egg—we of Barsoom are being bathed in these invisible rays,
a process that may well serve to open the mind to the ability to
radiate and perceive thoughts. Having experienced no such early
exposure on Jasoom, your own minds may have passed the devel-
opmental threshold by which they were no longer susceptible to
such alteration. It is possible that upon your advent here you were
immediately immersed in the thought-sphere and able to catch the
thoughts of others—especially the beasts, who have little or no
conscious control over their mental workings—though still unable
to project your own."

"But John Carter is not mute when it comes to telepathic communications," Tara interjected from her seat in the stern. She had
laid aside her songbook and was leaning forward in the same pose
of fascination that Talo Thoran displayed. "If that were the case, he
could never have hurled the nine thought waves that unlocked the
massive doors of the Atmosphere Plant, lo these many years ago,

thus allowing the engineers ingress to the stalled pumps and thereby saving all life upon the planet!"

"The Okarians in their domed cities to the far north have their own atmosphere generator, located in Marentina," I reminded her in the interest of accuracy, "and so they would not have perished, regardless of my actions."

"I am sure that point is of great comfort to the yellow race," she said with a small quirk of her lips, "and I am thankful that you omitted any reference to the red folk of Pankor, who also rely on their own generator, and whose detestable former leader kidnapped my daughter on more than one occasion years ago—yet I for one am gratified that your own quick thinking delivered salvation to the remaining millions below the ice barrier."

"As am I," said Talo Thoran sincerely. "However, I believe that the Warlord has demonstrated—please correct me if I err—the ability to communicate his impressions and wishes to the lower forms of life, as well as to operate the various mind-controlled mechanisms of our contrivance, but never the capability of clearly transmitting his thoughts to another human being."

I turned to my daughter and thought a thought at her, creasing my brow with evident effort, until she laughed and threw her hands up. "You may cease laboring away ere you incur an injury to your brain, for I can detect nothing—though I am sure you were endeavoring to tell me that I am your most beloved offspring."

It was evident from his animated expression that Talo Thoran would willingly have continued the discussion until the next morning, but dusk was descending and so I suggested they break out our stores and prepare dinner, while I turned my attention toward finding us a suitable anchorage for the night.

For all her cutting wit, my daughter has been blessed with a most generous heart. Perhaps gambling that he would have difficulty propounding his theories with a mouth full of food, she invited the scholar to join us in the forward area of the deck as we supped. To his credit, the man was a quick learner, and he excused himself to retire to the other end of the ship on some errand as soon as he had cleaned his plate.

"Speaking of atmosphere plants, Mother told me that the new installations are nearing completion," Tara commented when we were alone. "What a relief it shall be when there is finally more than a single one of them in operation! It seems a year does not pass without some madman attempting to destroy the current plant in the name of 'natural living'—an act that, if successful, would quickly result in an unnatural death for himself and all the rest of us—while just last month three of the great pumps malfunctioned simultaneously on the same day."

"Yes," I agreed. "That was very curious. Of course, nowadays nothing that affects such a huge percentage of the planet's population ever happens without prolonged wrangling among the civilized nations. The new network of plants was one of the major topics of the conference that concluded just prior to your arrival in Helium. Unsurprisingly, there is still a general unwillingness to discuss who will be responsible for the maintenance and protection of the new installations."

Tara sighed. "Indeed, this is no surprise. I am certain everyone agrees in principle that the burden must be shared equally," she said, "while privately vowing that Helium should take care of it all—though not one among them will dare say as much openly." She gave a disapproving shake of her head. "Worm-hopping, as usual! Why do you laugh, John Carter?"

"I laugh because such irreverent language is more often employed by laborers and shopkeepers than by one as purportedly well-bred and refined as the daughter of ten thousand jeddaks."

"Ten thousand and one," she corrected me primly. "Remember, my own illustrious sire bears the title Jeddak of Jeddaks."

Referring to the practice of tiptoeing around delicate issues, the expression "worm-hopping" derives from the millennia-old custom of Barsoomians of all stripes, who allow their cellars to be veritable playgrounds for a particularly obnoxious variety of vermin. The sarovan, a sixteen-legged worm that can attain a length of twenty inches or more as an adult, is found almost universally in the aforementioned dank pits that typically lie beneath Martian domiciles both grand and humble. I myself first encountered the species while languishing in a Warhoon dungeon some months after my initial arrival on the planet. I will confess that as I lay chained alone in absolute darkness, feeling a multitude of slimy bodies crawling over me, I soon became obsessed with the notion of annihilating as many of my tormentors as possible.

My solitary perdition came to an end when another prisoner was chained beside me. This was Kantos Kan, a padwar in the navy of Helium who would later become one of my closest friends, and his mere presence diverted me for a time from what had been near mania, while our animated conversation had the happy by-product of sending the sarovans scuttling off into the darkness. The obsession returned when we left off our discussion and agreed to an interval of rest, the better to prepare ourselves for whatever ordeal might lie ahead. Not long after we fell silent, I felt the resumption of cold and sinuous bodies slithering across my own, and went back with a vengeance to my habit of crushing them beneath my chains, all unmindful of the racket I was raising.

After a few moments of this activity, my cellmate grumbled out of the darkness: "What is causing you to thrash about so, man? Surely you can be dreaming of no worse circumstances than our present situation!"

My simple explanation that I had declared all-out war upon the worms and was now doing my best to squash the life out of as many of the little devils as possible was met with a horrified gasp.

"Truly can I believe you are from another world!" Kantos Kan told me. He proceeded to enlighten me concerning the widely held belief among the civilized peoples of Barsoom that the sarovans were direct descendants of one of the quartet of original beings that had burst forth from pods borne by the sacred Tree of Life some twenty-three million years ago, and subsequently gone on to populate the entire planet. "Along with a great white ape, a plant man, and a human being," he told me earnestly, "these worms are the oldest creatures upon Barsoom, and so considered sacrosanct."

I had long since ceased to be astonished by the multifarious notions given credence in human religions. In this case, I was re-minded at once of the cows deemed holy in certain regions of the

Indian subcontinent, while I myself had been personally acquainted with several folks on Earth who fairly worshipped their dogs. But a many-legged worm?

Something else occurred to me. "I mean no disrespect to your faith, Kantos Kan, and I know not what a plant man may be, yet I have seen men both red and green hack the fearsome white apes to pieces with scarcely a second thought—and for that matter, both races slaughter one another with great abandon! How is it that alone of the primary descendants of the Tree of Life, the lowly worm has been accorded this godlike status?"

To this my fellow captive could only shrug with a clash of his chains and offer the explanation I have since heard repeated on innumerable occasions here on this planet of paradoxes: "It is the custom of Barsoom."

Thus alerted to the sacred regard afforded these noxious creatures, I soon noted on those occasions when we were provided food and water by torch-bearing guards, that the prohibition against their harm often produced extensive and elaborate gyrations on the part of our giant Warhoon captors. Having gone on to enjoy the hospitality of other Martian dungeons over the succeeding years and marveled more than once at the spectacle of brawny warriors conducting enemy prisoners through the pits, while both jailers and captives skipped here and there like children at hopscotch as they tried to avoid crushing one of these paragons beneath a sandal, it was with some amusement that I later heard the term "worm-hopping" used to describe the act of dancing around a sensitive issue.

My own conversation with my daughter hopped from topic to topic, much as it had when Tara was still a young girl with a head full of questions, until the two of us were left smiling fondly at one another in shared remembrance.

"Now what subject shall we wrestle to the ground?" she asked me.

"I am tired of mental exertion. Perhaps you might sing something," I suggested. "You have a lovely voice and it has been far too long since I've heard it raised in song."

Tara protested that she was out of practice, but I could tell that she was pleased by my request and at last she agreed to regale me with one of the tunes currently popular in her adopted nation. "In spite of what our enemies contend, not every Gatholian song involves thoat herders lamenting their stolen calves," she said.

The song she chose was in fact a haunting ballad about the lost days when the ancient city of Gathol occupied an island on the bosom of Throxus, also known as The Boundless Water, largest of the five great oceans that once filled the dead seabeds that cover so much of latter-day Barsoom. As the sea receded, the city pursued it down the slopes of what would become a forbidding mountain, where to this day its citizens still wrest a seemingly inexhaustible supply of diamonds from the rich mines that honeycomb its interior.

I closed my eyes and leaned back against the flier's railing as she began to sing, her matchless voice a crystalline vehicle that transported me back over the millennia, while also reminding me of the ancient dreaming city I had only recently visited. Or had I? The more time that passed, the more the whole episode had taken on the semblance of a dream itself.

I was wrenched from my pleasant reverie by a strangled cry from the third member of our party, who had been politely busying himself at the other end of the deck while Tara and I conversed. A single leap was sufficient to bring me, dagger drawn, to Talo Thoran's side, where I found him crouched before the half-opened cargo locker with an expression of shocked horror on his face.

10
THE STOWAWAY

I HEARD AN ODD NOISE from inside the compartment," croaked Talo Thoran. "I thought one of the parcels must have come loose, yet when I investigated . . ."

Additional words failed him, which I found to be a somewhat shocking turn of events in itself.

I squinted into the shadowed interior of the hold, my weapon at the ready. I had scarce laid eyes upon the source of the scholar's consternation before a pair of slender hands fell upon our shoulders and my daughter pressed forward between the two of us. Talo Thoran was still fumbling at his scabbard in an attempt to extricate his shortsword when Tara bade him cease with a gesture.

"My dear friend!" she exclaimed, extending a graceful arm to the hideous apparition that squatted in the doorway. "Whatever are you doing here?"

At her words the stowaway emerged from the hold with a clicking of chitinous limbs and crawled out onto the moonlit deck. From the corner of my eye I saw Talo Thoran lean forward, sword forgotten, to study the newcomer with an almost unwilling fascination, his thirst for knowledge obviously warring with an instinctive fear of the unknown. In truth I did not think any the less of him for his initial reaction; the kaldanes of Bantoom present a fearsome spectacle to those not already acquainted with their ghastly appearance.

Sitting now fully exposed, the hurtling moons endowing it with a wavering dual shadow that only underscored its uncanny nature, was what looked for all the world like a disembodied head, humanlike in basic conformation, though half again as large and tinged a

97

cadaverous bluish gray. A pair of bulging, lidless eyes peered out at us above the two vertical slits that served it as a nose and a purplish, sphincter-like mouth that seemed pursed in perpetual disapproval. Below the head's soft sphere were half a dozen short, jointed legs resembling those of a terrestrial spider, with the addition of two powerful grasping chelae in the front.

In marked contrast to the scholar's trembling crouch, Tara had sunk to her knees to greet the creature, her slim arms outstretched in warm welcome.

"Dearest Ghek," she said, "I visited your apartments several times while I was in Helium, yet you were never at home! Naturally I am delighted to see you—but what has prompted this strange behavior?"

Flexing his legs, the kaldane bowed his massive head forward, first to my daughter and then to myself. "My profound apologies, Princess, Prince," he said in his toneless voice. "In truth, I had not intended to make my presence known; yet I could not prevent myself from starting in delight, and thus dislodging a crate, when I heard the melodious modulations of your voice.

"I must apologize to you, as well, sir," Ghek added, turning his saucer eyes on Talo Thoran.

"Quite all right," said the latter, who had regained most of his composure and now also lowered himself to his knees before the kaldane. He began to extend his right hand in the typical Barsoomian greeting, realized that Ghek possessed no shoulder upon which to lay it, and drew back his arm. "I am . . ." He paused beneath the moonlit gaze of those gleaming, lidless orbs, blinked twice, and gave himself a small shake. "Talo Thoran. Yes—that is my name. *Kaor* to you!"

Kaor is the universal term of Barsoomian greeting. As Talo Thoran himself had seen fit to enlighten us over the dinner just past, the word derived from an ancient phrase once used to wish another safe harborage, back in those far distant times when most of Barsoom was covered in water.

After we had settled ourselves on the aft benches, Ghek launched into an explanation of his unannounced presence aboard the flier. While I listened, I found myself wondering privately if there were to be any more surprise additions to what had begun as an uneventful, two-person voyage.

"You may have noticed that I am here without the rykor I was riding the last time you saw me," began the kaldane. This was all too evident, at least to Tara and myself, who had rarely seen Ghek without his surrogate body. At first sight, a rykor appears to be a human being of flawless proportions, a prime example of the beautiful red race of Martians, lacking only in one rather important detail: its head. In actuality, it is an almost brainless, humanlike creature bred over the ages by the kaldanes to serve them in a mutually beneficial relationship. Alone, a rykor is an aimless, stumbling thing without eyes or ears or consciousness, unable to even procure food for the oral cavity that lies at the top of its neck; yet when a kaldane mounts its shoulders and inserts the small bundle of tentacular organs at the rear of his great head into an aperture behind the rykor's gullet, he is able to seize its spinal cord, thus gaining complete control of the creature. Thenceforth, he may utilize the body as if it were an extension of his own flesh—even to perceiving the various physical sensations that the rykor undergoes.

"Not long ago," Ghek told us, "the finest medical savants of Helium informed me that even their advanced knowledge could do no more to prolong the vitality of my superannuated rykor, which currently lies upon a slab in a vault in Helium, what remains of its life in a state of chemical suspension until such time as I bid them reawaken the feeble thing. As you know, we kaldanes are so long-lived as to be virtually immortal, whereas the life spans of even the most superior of the beasts that serve us are pitifully fleeting. Were I still a welcome resident of the burrows of my people this would be no inconvenience, for the Valley of Bantoom abounded in fine rykors at the time of my hasty departure, and I would need only to discard my worn-out mount for a fresh one of my choosing. Alas, such is not the case in Helium, nor in any other human habitation.

"Therefore, rather than face an eternity of scuttling shamefaced among the shins of my gracious hosts, a brilliant brain forever denied the variegated capabilities and sensations afforded me by a sturdy body, I secreted myself upon your vessel that I might go in search of a replacement. The air route you are pursuing to Gathol passes not far from the valley of my hatching, where the monarchs of Bantoom ride magnificent rykors specially bred for the traits of strength, vitality, and extended life spans. Such a sterling creature did I purloin from my former master Luud these many years ago, and well it served me for many a year thereafter." Ghek leaped agilely to the flier's narrow railing and stared pensively into the darkness. "It was my simple plan to drop silently from the craft one night as it passed above the treetops and make my way thence to the hives of my people. Were I to obtain another royal rykor—or, better yet, a breeding pair of these unparalleled specimens—I would be assured many more years, if not centuries, of agreeable and productive life."

"Making off with two bodies in a land where all hands will be turned against you seems an extremely risky undertaking for a lone, exiled kaldane," I remarked once I had digested the import of his statement. "Had you not considered recruiting accomplices to your cause?"

Gripping the railing deftly with his spider legs, Ghek executed the complicated gesture with his front claws that I had come to interpret over the years of his residency in Helium as the kaldane equivalent of a shrug.

"I have no wish to inconvenience others in pursuit of a goal that, if accomplished, would serve to benefit only myself. As for the risk, should I fail in my attempt, then perhaps it were better I end my existence there in Bantoom where it began, as sustenance for the voracious banths that prowl the nearby hillsides."

"It is mighty thoughtful of you to consider the dietary needs of the local predators," I said solemnly. "Do you suppose they will pause for a moment to acknowledge your noble sacrifice as they vie for the choicest portions of your remains?"

"Father!" Tara favored me with a look of mild reproof before turning back to address the kaldane. "Dear Ghek," she said, "have your many years among the red race not taught you that true friends may ask anything of one another?" She returned to me with a beseeching look. "I am sure that John Carter will consent to make a small detour from our path to aid you in your quest."

I had been about to make the suggestion myself. I had never visited the valley of the kaldanes, and it would mean another day or two with my daughter. A thought entered my mind. "Speaking of our path, how did you come to know we were leaving on this voyage—or for that matter that the course we had charted would bring us near Bantoom?"

Ghek dropped back onto the deck, where he proceeded to sway gently from side to side. Though kaldanes possess no flexible facial musculature in common with human beings, I could have sworn he wore an expression of acute embarrassment.

"By mere chance I found myself taking some fresh air in the vicinity on the previous night, when you discussed over dinner your route and the time of your departure," he confessed in his characteristic monotone, his spider legs drumming with a nervous *tat-tat-tat* on the wood.

"In the vicinity?" Tara said in puzzlement.

"Ah, so that was you I glimpsed skulking outside our window!" I said. "When I went to investigate, there was no one there."

"It seemed discourteous to intrude on your family gathering, so I continued my climb to the rooftop and then exited down the other side of the palace."

Talo Thoran had ducked into the cargo locker while we continued to converse with Ghek, switching on his radium torch as he worked to refasten the netting around the crate the kaldane had dislodged. Now he uttered an exclamation of puzzlement. He came forth cradling in his arms a peculiar object in the shape of a sphere some fifteen inches in diameter, fashioned of blue and silver metal, its surface etched with intersecting lines. "I do not recall seeing this among the communications equipment we brought onboard, John Carter. Perhaps it is an art object of some sort, belonging to yourself or to the Princess?"

"That is mine," Ghek said. "Though I detest it."

Instructing the scholar to deposit the object on the deck before him, the kaldane used his anterior claws to deftly rotate the sphere until it sat with a certain circular design facing upward. He hopped atop the metal globe and tapped the circle twice with one of his legs, whereupon it retracted instantly to reveal an opening into the interior of the sphere. Suspending a narrow braid of pale tentacles from his posterior directly above the hole, Ghek then lowered himself gingerly onto the sphere's upper surface. Muffled clicking sounds emanated from somewhere within.

"You have brought your own seat along?" Tara inquired, eyeing the contraption dubiously. "Is it comfortable?"

"Alas, it is not," Ghek replied, making small adjustments to his position. Narrow channels had appeared to radiate outward from the central opening, and into these he fitted his six spider legs. "It is cold and hard to the touch. However, it has the potential to be somewhat serviceable."

A mechanical humming sound began to swell from within the object, followed by a series of sharp clicks as the sphere suddenly sprouted several cylindrical extensions. Elongating in the manner of the sliding tubes of a jointed telescope, two flexible silver pipes extruded from the bottom of the device, slowly raising it a good four feet into the air, while four more shot out from apertures evenly spaced about the upper curve of the sphere. Then the sphere itself split into two halves, the top hemisphere rising an additional foot or so on a thicker central pipe.

Tara and Talo Thoran had risen to their feet with exclamations of wonder as the startling transformation commenced. Now I joined them as we three stepped forward to examine the finished product, which resembled an abstracted human frame sculpted from blue and silver metal, with an extra pair of arms facing fore and aft. Both the upper and lower limbs seemed to be composed of flexible rings, which allowed them to bend with more suppleness than human joints.

"It is a mechanical rykor," Tara breathed.

"Ingenious!" said Talo Thoran by her side.

Small alterations were still occurring on the clicking and humming device. Narrow panels of metal slid protectively over the kaldane's spider legs, and a circular blue band rose on the upper hemisphere to form an ornamental collar about the base of his head into which he tucked his claws, while from the ends of each of the four upper limbs emerged half a dozen writhing, fingerlike feelers. The two extensions which served the mechanism as legs had slightly convex disks affixed to the bottoms; as we watched, Ghek effected some unseen adjustment within the device and the metal body took a lurching step forward.

"By the shell of my first ancestor!" Tara exclaimed. "Ghek, this is marvelous." Extending a slender hand, she grasped the metal fingers at the end of one of the mechanical arms, only to release them a moment later with a sharp cry. "Ow!"

"My apologies," said Ghek. "A marvelous achievement it may be, but there is much left to be desired in its operation. I have practiced with the device for hours, yet I still have considerable difficulty in gauging the pressure exerted by these unfeeling manipulators, nor have I mastered locomotion to my satisfaction." He assumed a look of intense concentration, and the machine took another halting step across the deck before swiveling awkwardly to face me. "Please do not think me ungrateful for the efforts of the Heliumetic scientists who devised this thing, John Carter, yet I am sure you will agree that it is a poor substitute for a living, sensing body."

"You have no sensation in the mechanical limbs or elsewhere, then?" I asked. "Does this present a great hindrance in operating the thing?"

"None. And yes," Ghek confirmed. "I know that you are renowned for your ability to become as one with the thoats that you train and ride. Imagine if your favorite mount had been taken from you and replaced with one of gears and metal pipes, so that you must manually control the action of each of its eight legs, its speed and the direction of its movement."

I nodded. "I take your point."

Ghek turned the mechanical body around and after some effort was able to guide it to the side of the flier and lower it to a rather lopsided sitting position on one of the benches. He pulled himself free of the opening at the top and sprang to the railing.

"So long as I remain within close proximity, I can control the device's activity to a certain extent without the need for direct contact." He trained his great saucer eyes on the headless construct. After half a minute it raised and lowered each of its four upper appendages in clockwise order. "I brought it with me because I thought it might be useful for managing the two rykors I am hoping to obtain. Unfortunately, after much practice I am still unable to execute any but the most rudimentary of actions, whether I am beside the thing or astride it."

"We have a few days before we reach Bantoom. We shall help you practice, and perhaps by the time we arrive you will have perfected your control," Tara said resolutely. "If not, we three will be there to assist you in carrying off your new bodies."

"These are gracious offers," said the kaldane. "Though I confess that as the hour approaches, I find myself with very little confidence that my quest will succeed."

"Come, come, Ghek," chided my daughter. "You have studied the varied emotions of human beings for years now. Have you learned naught of optimism?"

"Optimism? Ah, yes. The practice of imagining a positive outcome in those situations where the facts portend the opposite. It has never struck me as a productive approach, though I confess to experiencing a similar feeling myself in reaction to certain stimuli." The grotesque head tilted to one side on its spider legs in what looked very much like a hopeful stance. "I have always felt a completely irrational sensation of well-being while listening to you sing, for example . . ."

11
DEVASTATION

OVER THE NEXT two days, my daughter and Talo Thoran took turns helping Ghek improve his control over his recalcitrant clockwork body, setting up a variety of small obstacle courses on the deck of the flier for the mounted kaldane to negotiate, and calling out rapid sequences of movements to see how quickly he might respond. Even when he was not atop the thing, Ghek kept it nearby in an effort to increase his mental control, and soon I got used to the sight of the blue-and-silver metal sphere rolling along before him as he traversed the deck, in a display that reminded me disconcertingly of an African dung beetle and its prize.

Talo Thoran had become quite fascinated with our new companion and the two spent much time conversing. Kaldanes have the rare gift of recalling the memories of all the forebears in their line—right back, so it seems, to the first individuals to gain consciousness, and the scholar plied Ghek with endless questions concerning Barsoom's distant past. His enthusiasm cooled somewhat when he realized that a species that spends most of its time in burrows beneath the ground—convinced of its utter superiority to all other living beings and thus feeling no need to learn any more about them than in what way they might be of service—will pass along to its descendants a rather constricted view of the world. Still, Ghek himself possessed a highly logical and sophisticated mind, and the pair found much else to discuss, this further increasing the amount of time Tara and I were granted to spend by ourselves. I did not fail to notice that both of the unanticipated additions to our passenger roster practically idolized my daughter, though she seemed oblivious to the adoring glances each turned on her from time to time.

With a day left before we reached Bantoom, I took Ghek aside to discuss our strategy and to learn from him what we might expect to encounter in the way of interference. He assured me that if we entered the valley after dark, it should be a relatively simple task to pluck a pair of superior rykors from the high-walled courtyard surrounding one of the kaldane towers that dotted the land. Those rykors not in use at night were penned there to afford them protection from the aforementioned banths, fierce leonine predators that confined themselves to the surrounding woods by day, but came forth after dark to prowl among the towers in search of easy prey—it being the logic-driven practice of the kaldanes to rid themselves of injured or senescent rykors by merely setting them outside the boundary of the walls. According to Ghek, we need simply hover silently in the *Kantim* above the courtyard for so long as it took us to descend on a rope ladder and make our selection by torchlight from among the gathered livestock.

I could tell that Talo Thoran, more used to frequenting lecture halls and the salons of the intelligentsia in the Twin Cities of Helium than to setting off on unplanned adventures, had been taken aback by our decision to aid Ghek; however, after some time communing with our stowaway, the scholar had professed himself extremely eager to observe both kaldanes and rykors in their natural habitat. Being of the same mind in that regard—and also believing that we would be well served by the opportunity to reconnoiter before we enacted our plan—I decided we would make our cautious approach to Bantoom during daylight, in a manner that would guarantee us some concealment while we observed the valley for a few hours before dusk.

Ghek and Talo Thoran were deep in conversation at the other end of the flier in the early afternoon of the following day, while Tara and I sat together at the prow, where I could keep one eye on the ship's controls and the other on the unfolding countryside as we neared out destination.

"Though I do not approve of his unorthodox method of joining our expedition," I remarked to my daughter, "I am actually glad that Ghek is here to act as playfellow to our scholar. It restores a sense of equilibrium to our journey to have the two of them so occupied with one another—though I am sorry you will now be further delayed in arriving home to Gathol."

Tara's lips crooked in a wry smile. "I am sure you have noticed my lack of concern about any deferment. In fact, I am no more fond of presiding over affairs of state than are you, Father, while Gathol, like any other modern principality, teems with bureaucrats and functionaries who will jump at the chance to steer the nation's course for a few days." She leaned back into the cushioned bench and stretched her arms out to the sides. "This has been a delightful interlude so far, and were it not for a certain impending familial event that I dearly hope not to miss, I would gladly extend my holiday until Gahan is returned from his expedition and seated once again upon his diamond throne."

"Familial event?" I repeated.

Tara nodded. "My daughter and her mate are soon to become parents," she told me. "Five years have passed so quickly—though naturally Llana does not see it that way." She chuckled at my expression. "Yes, John Carter, you are but a few weeks away from becoming a great-grandfather."

"Another generation," I mused. "And so it goes. Llana and Pan Dan Chee shall soon have their own child to guide down the twisting path of life."

"Indeed," said Tara. "For their sakes, let us hope their young one is more appreciative of parental guidance than those of the previous crop. We would not want Vara Martis to have to fly in and take charge." Her tone grew wistful. "It has caused me to think deep thoughts about the future, however. Gahan may well miss the child's arrival because he must be off tending to those foolish forays carried out by outlaws from Manator in the west. You used to speak often of your desire for a peaceful Barsoom. Tell me, O Warlord, do you truly think that a people such as we, born and bred into conflict, will ever achieve that halcyon state?"

It was a question I had contemplated myself from time to time.

"Individuals can surely change," I told her, "as evidenced by Ghek's conversion under your own influence from the undifferentiated member of a nation of cold, unfeeling calculators into a being with hopes and aspirations, who would now gladly lay down his own life for those he considers his friends.

"Whether an entire people may be persuaded to another perspective is a different matter," I added with a shrug. "Still, there are many among the formerly arrogant therns and the even more imperious First Born who have now pledged to devote themselves to serving the human community, when half a century ago they would have thought nothing of enslaving members of those races they had then considered inferior. The yellow folk of the north once slaughtered or imprisoned any representatives of the red race who ventured beyond the great ice barrier, yet now we of Helium count them as staunch friends and allies. Well . . . the great majority of them," I amended, thinking that there was a certain hunting party from Illall whom I would not trust to act in my best interests should my back be turned. "And you know that Tars Tarkas continues to labor at his grand plan of uniting the various hordes of green men that range the dead sea bottoms."

"Do you suppose this flexibility of nature extends to the intelligent inhabitants of other worlds?" my daughter inquired. "Did you not see endless strife among the peoples of Jasoom during the many years you dwelled there? As a more recent example, have you any reason to believe the so-called Skeleton Men you encountered on distant Sasoom might ever learn to live in harmony with their human fellows? From your descriptions of the Morgors, they seemed a race devoted solely to warfare." Tara was referring to an unexpected visit Dejah Thoris and I had paid several years back to the giant planet Earthmen call Jupiter. "I was in Gathol when first you and then my mother were abducted, and from what little I have heard of your adventures there, you were lucky to escape with your lives! How did you manage to get away from that dreadful place?"

"Have we never told you this tale?" I asked in surprise. "Here is yet another reason for establishing a network of reliable Gridley Wave stations around the globe. It is absurd that I and others have been edifying your cousin back on Earth with stories of our exploits on Barsoom and elsewhere for decades, while relating them to my own daughter must wait upon our infrequent visits."

Tara's expression at once grew pensive. "I was so very sorry to hear of the loss of your great friend," she said, placing her hand on my arm. "It seemed he would be there for you forever. I often forget that with but few exceptions the people of Jasoom have such fleeting lives."

"As do I." I covered her hand with my own and we sat in silence for a moment. "But let me tell you now about the strange end to our adventure among the Skeleton Men, a fascinating tale in itself. It will come as no surprise to you that—"

At that moment a soft musical chime sounded from the *Kantim*'s control panel, indicating that we were nearing our destination.

Ghek at once came skittering along the deck like a crab before the tide and hopped up on the forward railing to survey the scene. The others moved to join him as I took back control of the ship and slowed our approach. According to Ghek, the kaldanes of Bantoom possessed no flying craft, nor any long-range weapons that might bring us down or do damage to the ship; still, the success of our plan to make off with a pair of bodies that night depended upon employing a certain degree of stealth while the sun still shone.

A professed amateur artist among his other pursuits, Talo Thoran had brought forth from his belongings a set of variously colored pieces of chalk and a roll of heavy paper, and now he began to deploy them with the aim of recording for posterity his impressions of the valley of the kaldanes.

At Ghek's suggestion, I lowered the *Kantim* to skim a few feet above the tree-lined summit of the last of a series of gently rolling hills and eased us forward until we could see what lay in the valley below without ourselves being observed.

Tara had previously described for me in some detail this deceptively pleasant vale—the very place in which she had been taken captive by the kaldanes when her lost flier drifted here long years ago in the aftermath of the most powerful windstorm to ravage Barsoom in human memory. In my mind's eye I had prepared an image of a beautiful, cultivated area nestled among low, tree-covered hills and dotted with numerous dome-capped circular towers of gray stone. It being midafternoon, the fields should have been filled with farm workers, nearly naked red men and women with perfect bodies and peculiarly large heads, toiling away beneath the bright sun. Upon closer inspection, of course, the workers would be revealed to be kaldanes mounted upon the rykors they had employed for countless ages as surrogate bodies, steeds, and—most disturbing to our human sensibilities—food stock. I was well prepared for all these sights and so doubly surprised by what I saw.

Below us spread a scene of utter devastation.

12
IN SEARCH OF OLD BURROWS

THE VALLEY OF BANTOOM had been reduced from a serene vista of rolling hills to a flattened plane of huge, overlapping craters that extended as far up and down the ancient vale as the eye could see. I thought at once of the glimpses I had been given years ago by means of the marvelous Heliumetic telescopes of the Great War in Europe, where repeated detonations generated by both sides had turned idyllic meadows into a wasteland of sterile pits. There had been a second, even greater war on my former home planet since then, and although I had found little appetite for viewing its consequences, my imagination had supplied me with frightening visions of the havoc that the employment of ever more powerful weapons of destruction must have wrought there.

Talo Thoran broke the silence. "Could the controlling destination compass have malfunctioned? Have we arrived at the wrong location?"

"I do not think so," Tara said in a quiet voice when Ghek did not immediately respond. She pointed a trembling finger at a crumbled mass of gray stone in the center of one of the craters, to which remnants of vivid paint still clung. "Was not that once the Tower of Luud?"

"Indeed it was," said the kaldane in his usual monotone, the immobile features of his great head giving no indication of what emotions swirled within. "That edifice stood at the precise center of

111

Luud's prosperous fields, where at one time I strove as third foreman, and far beneath it lay my own sheltered burrow." He lifted one of his claws. "Just there down the slope may be seen the pulverized remains of the neighboring Tower of Moak."

"Could your own people have done this?" Talo Thoran inquired. "Do the various kaldane monarchs ever war among themselves? And are they in possession of armaments capable of wreaking such havoc?"

Tara turned me a searching look. Before the kaldane could reply, she said: "Father? You have seen this sort of thing before, have you not?"

I nodded. "I have. This is very like the circles of devastation I came upon during my recent travels up north—though on a far grander scale." I related to the scholar and the kaldane the tale of the mysterious crater I had first happened upon, and of the second one whose creation had almost spelled my doom. As I spoke, I could see plainly writ on my daughter's face the same doubts I myself had begun to harbor concerning my repeated experiences with these deadly phenomena. Coincidences do occur—in my adventures I have experienced numerous occurrences that would have seemed beyond the odds of chance—but there comes a time when one starts to wonder.

We still hovered just above the crown of the hill. Tara went to peer over the side of the ship. "Might there be survivors? Do you think we should be hurled to the ground if we ventured any closer?" she asked.

"I believe the answer to both questions is no, Princess," said Talo Thoran. "Look there." We turned at his gesture to see a small band of sinuous animals darting among the rubble.

I brought forth my spyglass and examined the area. "Ulsios," I confirmed, as I watched one of the odious beasts, a hairless, hound-sized Martian equivalent of the terrestrial rat, burrowing vigorously into the soft earth with its powerful teeth. "And quite well fed, by the looks of them. They must have dined like jeddaks once the crushing effect subsided."

"Your grim analysis has the ring of truth," Ghek confirmed once I had passed him the spyglass. "There would have been many hundreds of kaldanes and rykors, both dead and wounded, for the scavengers to consume, and while a living kaldane could easily have fended off even a pack of the creatures, a rykor would have been quite helpless to defend itself against a single one. This suggests, however, that the destruction extends much deeper into the earth than I would have thought possible. As I can attest from my own encounters with them in the pits of Manator, both the flesh and the blood of ulsios are quite pleasing to the kaldane palate, which is what led to their being hunted to extinction in this valley by my people thousands of years ago. These could only have emerged from deep subterranean tunnels broached by whatever power razed the towers and so thoroughly crushed the surrounding countryside."

"I am very sorry that you have traveled all this way for naught," Tara said gently. "Even though you are no longer a member of your swarm, this must come as a terrible shock."

"It is an interesting situation," he replied simply. "I am pondering the possibility that I may well be the last of my kind."

"Just a moment," I said. "Is this area before us the full extent of the kaldane lands?"

"Actually, no." Ghek scampered along the railing to gaze off at a wooded region to the south. "These fields were merely the latest settlements of my people, having been founded some twelve thousand years ago. Beyond that forest, the valley continues to the south for some ways, and there one may find far older burrows—assuming they have not also fallen victim to the force that obliterated this area."

"Well then, we shall seek them out, and do it before nightfall," I said.

With Ghek acting as my navigator, we rose from the hilltop and took off toward the southeast above a range of alternating grassy dells and copses of stunted trees. We saw no further signs of destruction along the way; half an hour later we coasted to a stop above the last dozen yards of sparse growth and I lowered the *Kantim* to hang just within the edge of the forest. Crowding the forward rail, we peered out through a thin lattice of branches at a panorama that was radically different from the devastated region we had just departed.

Here I was at last able to match Tara's description to a living example, albeit in an unforeseen location. The fields that filled this gently sloping valley were well manicured and abounded in a variety of fruit and vegetable crops, the precise rows separated by swaths of the scarlet sward common to the cultivated regions of the planet and bordered by gaily flowering shrubs. Irrigation was provided by half a dozen small streams that flowed here and there among the planted areas.

Grayish green stone towers marked with elaborate insignias dotted the countryside. Even more imposing than the ones my daughter had described in the fields to the north, they ranged from fifty to eighty feet in diameter and averaged a hundred feet in height. Each was surmounted by a faceted dome constructed of prismatic glass, so that the structures resembled a field of enormous Arizona barrel cactus topped with crystalline flowers in the afternoon sunlight. Around the base of each stood a tall, plastered wall built of the same gray-green stone as the towers.

The fields themselves were thronged with workers both male and female, some tilling the earth, others pruning the various trees and vines, while still others passed along the rows, plucking ripe produce that they dropped into cloth slings draped over one shoulder. The meager trappings that barely concealed the perfect bodies of the laborers were of plain unadorned leather; these stood out in marked contrast to the elaborate bands dripping with jewels and precious metals that were wound about each grotesquely large head.

The pastoral scene was at once familiar and uncanny. I had grown quite used to the sight of Ghek's extraordinary appearance over the years he had spent in Helium, eventually coming to view him as a friend. As the sole kaldane in a nation of human beings, however, he was a nonesuch, and I found the spectacle of scores of his ilk going to and fro in workaday fashion among their towers and tillage to have an entirely different effect.

"Behold the fields of Duab," the kaldane intoned from his perch on the railing, neither his voice nor his inexpressive features giving any hint as to his own reaction to the sight.

Ghek requested the loan of my spyglass, and for the next several minutes he seemed content to roost on the narrow railing, turning his great head slowly this way and that. In the meantime, Talo Thoran had once again taken up his drawing materials and was producing creditable sketches of the environs and the inhabitants in colored chalks. He sat on a small folding stool, looking incongruously like a wealthy tourist taking his ease on the veranda of his hostelry. Tara stood close by my side, her expression for the moment as unreadable as Ghek's, though I suspected she was feeling a mixture of conflicting emotions, having once been imprisoned and in fear for her life in the warrens beneath a tower very much like one of these.

Ghek returned my spyglass. "As it happens, not all of the kaldanes were eradicated in the attack on the northern fields. It is clear from the metal of several of these workers that there are survivors here from the hives of Moak and Nolach, though I have so far glimpsed none from those fields once ruled by Luud or Otzak. Perhaps those latter hives were the first to be destroyed, and so the others had sufficient warning to allow some to escape through the underground ways that connect all of Bantoom."

The afternoon wore on and long shadows began to extend from the towers. Soon it would be time to put our plan into action.

Outwardly composed, Ghek betrayed his impatience as the sun neared the horizon by roaming ceaselessly about the ship, at one moment capering like an agitated crustacean across the deck, only to disappear over the side to circumnavigate the keel and appear half a minute later on the opposite rail just behind Talo Thoran, who jumped with a small shriek when one of the kaldane's jointed legs accidentally brushed the back of his neck.

Soon the workers began to quit the fields, filing in orderly procession through gates in the high walls surrounding the various towers. According to Ghek, the majority of the rykors would be left in the courtyards overnight, as many of the kaldanes repaired to the narrow tunnels and small burrows in which they felt most comfortable. Only a few would continue to serve their masters in various ways deep inside the tower itself.

At last darkness spread across the land. At Ghek's assurance that we would now be safe from detection, I maneuvered the *Kantim* out of the woods and brought it skimming noiselessly over the deserted fields to the tower the kaldane had selected as the one most likely to contain the superior quality of rykor he sought.

With Tara at the helm to maintain our position about twenty feet above the courtyard, I lowered the *Kantim*'s rope ladder and climbed down. Ghek followed swiftly, perching just above my head as I brought out my torch, and we directed our gazes into the enclosure. The kaldane uttered a small croak of dismay. The courtyard was empty.

"What has happened?" I asked him in a low whisper. "Where are all the bodies?"

"I am not sure. Even the feeding troughs are missing."

"Perhaps the attack up north has made them more cautious, and they have brought all the rykors inside the towers?"

"Possibly, though we are a sensitive people. In my former fields it would have been considered most unseemly to allow the beasts to feed and sleep in the very tower where the kaldanes make their homes."

"During periods of national emergency, even the most hidebound societies are obliged to effect adjustments to age-old customs," I reminded him.

The kaldane hung motionless by one chela for a long moment, until I turned the torch upward upon his pale face. "Ghek?"

"I have it now," he said. "Though I have never visited these fields myself, my ancient ancestors originated here, and so I merely reached back and examined their memories. Some one hundred and fourteen thousand years ago a predacious swarm of nocturnal flying creatures infested this valley for several weeks, raiding the pens after dark and carrying off many valuable rykors. During that time, all rykors were housed overnight in a large, roofed enclosure formerly used to store silage, with access provided through tunnels from beneath the several towers belonging to Duab. After a short time these malagaths grew frustrated with the lack of available prey and departed the area. This same strategy was successfully employed when the creatures briefly returned twenty-five thousand years later. Then, thirty-two thousand years after that, the enclosure was again occupied when fire destroyed a neighboring tower and its survivors and their rykors were allowed to shelter temporarily in Duab's fields."

"And you think they may be using this structure for a similar purpose now, due to the influx of individuals from the north? Would the building still be standing after all this time?"

"Why, naturally," Ghek said. "Why would it not?"

I reminded myself that, even without the kaldanes' access to an almost endless species memory, the recorded histories of most civilized nations on Barsoom were commonly measured in hundreds of thousands of years, rather than the paltry few thousands or even hundreds of years more typically observed on Earth. On this planet, things were built to last. "All right, then," I said. "Where will we find this place?"

He pointed his free claw toward the south.

We climbed back into the ship and with Ghek's guidance I brought us to an area near the edge of the forest at the far southern end of the valley. By now it was quite dark and neither of the moons had yet appeared in the sky. I had extinguished the *Kantim*'s running lights, fearing they might be too apparent to any kaldanes out for an evening stroll; not possessing Ghek's miraculous night-sight, I instructed Tara and Talo Thoran to flash their torches occasionally from either side of the flier to illuminate the way. After about fifteen minutes of creeping along in this fashion, a long, flat building bulked out of the darkness ahead of us. I halted the ship and shined my own light down.

"Here is a new wrinkle to our problem," I told Ghek. "As you had described, the structure is enclosed not simply along the sides, but with a broad roof. There is thus no way for us to confirm the presence of any rykors from the air, let alone look them over so that you may make your selection from among the latest models."

"They are there," the kaldane said. "I can sense the presence of many rykors within that space."

"I see. I do not suppose you could mentally induce a couple to let themselves discreetly out the back door and climb up our ladder?"

"Unfortunately, the minute brain of a rykor, whether flesh or metal, may only be controlled to that extent from very close proximity—though were I endowed with the enhanced mental powers of a kaldane monarch the story might be different."

Floating in darkness in a hostile land and now drifting far from our original plan, I was of half a mind to crown someone myself at that point. Instead, I merely raised my shoulders in a shrug. "Have you a solution to this conundrum? Do your borrowed memories perchance tell of any openings in the enclosure through which we might enter—other than those that connect by means of subterranean tunnels with the towers of Duab?"

"Yes and no," Ghek said after a moment's silence. "Although there are two large doors, one located on each of the pen's narrower sides, they may be opened only from the inside and are naturally heavily fortified."

"Naturally."

"In addition, there are small apertures designed to provide ventilation set just below the roof at several points around the structure. These are of a size that would accommodate only kaldanes, however. You would never be able to pass through to the interior."

"Would I?" asked Tara, who along with Talo Thoran had been closely following our conversation.

Ghek turned to appraise her slender form with his saucer eyes. "Possibly, yes."

More than discomfited by the idea of my daughter exposing herself to even greater danger in these unfamiliar surroundings, I said: "Ghek, if you could affix yourself to one blue-ribbon rykor, you should be able to wrangle a second and then make your way to the exit with both, correct?"

"In theory, yes. Assuming I met with no opposition."

"Then once you have entered through one of those ventilation apertures I shall observe you from just outside the opening, pistol drawn, and alert you immediately if I spot any warders who may wish to interfere with your shopping expedition. You can make your choices with celerity and meet us at the right-hand door. With luck, we will be back aboard the ship with our parcels and on our way before anyone is the wiser."

Hearing no better ideas, I maneuvered the *Kantim* to the eastern end of the long structure. The downward-slanting rooftop extended several feet beyond the enclosure wall, making an aerial transfer to one of the small openings impractical. With Tara once again at the controls, Ghek and I clambered back down the ladder to alight on the ground at the base of the wall. The locked door was directly before us, while one of the apertures was located just beneath the roof at a height of some thirty-five feet above the door.

We made for a fine pair of second-story men: I waited on lookout below while Ghek exercised his remarkable spiderlike ability to climb directly up the outer surface of the wall. Once he had disappeared within, I jumped up to the opening myself. The aperture was round as a porthole above a small curving stone sill and, as Ghek had predicted, a few inches too narrow to admit both my shoulders. By propping myself up on my elbows on the sill, I was able to hunch forward, pistol in one hand and torch in the other. Reflecting that I would not wish to remain in this contorted position for very long, I craned my neck as far as I could into the building, casting my eyes this way and that as I played the torch at its lowest luminance upon the gathered masses below.

The interior of the place was permeated by an intense barnyard odor. Feeding troughs lined the walls and there was a constant tide of movement before them as rykors groped their way out of the herd, knelt to shovel food into the cavities atop their open necks, and then, sated, rose to squeeze back among their fellows, while others stumbled forth to replace them at the receptacles. Because of the great number of bodies packed into the space, many of the rykors had remained on their feet, rather than fumbling aimlessly about on hands and knees, as would be their more typical behavior without kaldanes astride their shoulders to guide them. The center of the room evoked the macabre aftermath of an intemperate use of the guillotine, for here scores of the headless bodies lay sprawled one upon the other in a disordered pile, limbs relaxed, apparently sleeping.

Ghek appeared in my roving circle of wan torchlight. He moved slowly among the tightly packed creatures, picking his way from shoulder to naked shoulder as he performed his examinations. I saw that he was making deliberate headway toward a section of the en-closure where resided several creatures that were obviously of more heroic proportions than their fellows—the royal rykors of which he had spoken. Just then I noted a flurry of unexpectedly rapid movement at the far end of the building. I brought up my torch to see that a trio of other kaldanes mounted upon rykors had entered the room. They turned away instinctively from the pale white light, their lidless eyes gleaming.

"Ghek!" I called in a hoarse whisper, hefting my radium pistol awkwardly in the cramped space. "Beware—you are not alone!"

He was turning to peer in the direction of my beam when I heard a rush of sudden noise behind me, like that of many small objects hurtling through the air. I cried out as white-hot pain lanced in a dozen spots along my upper back, then something unseen yanked me roughly back from the aperture and bore me up into the night.

13

Spirited Away

I SHOT UPWARD through the darkness at dizzying speed, the fiery pain spreading quickly from my shoulders to my neck and upper torso as my whole body spasmed uncontrollably.

I had dropped my torch in the confusion and could see nothing of my captor as I thrashed about, though something very large was blotting out a cylindrical patch of stars directly above me. What felt like damp cables of enormous tensile strength were coiled tightly about the upper half of my body, pinning both arms close to my sides.

For a time I could get no clear impression of the thing from which I hung, beyond the strong and most disagreeable odor that filled my nostrils even though we hurtled through the night at breakneck speed. As my eyes adjusted to the darkness I became aware of a ghostly, greenish-yellow glimmering emanating from the thing. Combined with the rank odor, it conjured up the incongruous image of spoiled meat.

At first I struggled against my bonds to no avail, my fiercest exertions doing no more than amplifying the burning pain that suffused my body beneath the unyielding coils. I resolved to halt my efforts and conserve my strength against the possibility that whatever held me would at some point relax its grip.

We had been traveling for perhaps thirty minutes when there came a sudden tremendous jarring impact. Something had dealt a violent blow to the creature or vessel that was carrying me! We lurched to the side and dropped several yards, then began to rise again unsteadily. I was still trying to gather my wits from the first collision when we were rocked by another one, considerably more powerful than the first. All of this had occurred in relative silence, the only noises the rush of air and the sound of two large bodies coming together. Following the second assault, the bonds that held me squeezed even tighter for a long moment, until I feared I would be cut in two—and then abruptly withdrew altogether. Released in midair at an unknown altitude, I plummeted down through darkness.

I had just felt the first rasping touch of treetop foliage against the skin of my legs when I was caught again, iron cables wrapping around my torso in a grasp that was every bit as tight as before, and we soared upward with a nauseating swiftness. I cried out as a new wave of fiery pain lanced through my body.

I had somehow managed to retain my pistol in a tight grip in my right hand through all of this, though I had been unable to raise it due to the straitjacket of cables. The renewed onslaught of pain was excruciating, accompanied this time by waves of increasing light-headedness. Sensing that I was on the verge of blacking out, I managed to maneuver the pistol back into its holster.

We were still flying when I came to. I had the sense that considerable time had passed, which would mean that Thuria had already completed her first circuit through the heavens while I was insensible, and that I had missed my chance to examine under her cold light the thing that now held me. The foul odor was no longer evident. Craning my neck, I realized that the weird glimmering was also gone, and further that the shape of the thing had altered unmistakably from its initial outline. Could it be possible that whatever had plucked me from the side of the rykor storehouse was not what carried me now? It dawned on me that I must have been knocked loose from my original abductor by the forceful attack and then stolen in midair by a new captor.

Ever the latecomer, Cluros at last began to edge above the horizon in his tentative fashion a few minutes later, and I saw by his wan glow what appeared to be the outlines of a flying insect of titanic proportions.

I have always considered the Red Planet to be relatively free of insect life—at least as we define such creatures on Earth. Here there are no ants mustering by the millions, no clouds of miniscule gnats, no vampiric mosquitoes to swat at on a summer's evening. Perhaps as an act of overcompensation, Barsoom is host to multiple species of extremely large invertebrates that possess in magnified form many of the least desirable characteristics of their diminutive terrestrial cousins. Though they have now been hunted almost to extinction, the venomous, hornet-like and bull-sized beasts known as siths had at one time thronged the forests of Kaol, while in the Valley Hohr can be found a race of massive and murderous twelve-legged spiders.

What carried me now at a blistering pace through the night resembled nothing more than a gargantuan variant on the humble dragonfly—what we used to call a "devil's darning needle" back in Virginia—but one with an astounding wingspan of perhaps thirty-five feet. As the minutes passed and Cluros eased further into view, I was able to discern some additional features of this beast that set it apart from the little creatures one could find darting on glittering wings above the pond on a hot afternoon. My captor's head was dominated by four huge hemispheres of clustered ocelli, to the fore of which were located mouth parts more similar to those of an earthly moth or butterfly, in that they consisted of coiled proboscis-like organs in place of dentition. But where the moth might possess a single delicate proboscis, this nightmarish variation boasted an even dozen powerful graspers, these resembling the tentacles of a cephalopod more than any appurtenances one might expect to find on a winged insect. It was these prehensile extensions, some of which must have measured ten feet in length, in which I was currently tightly bound. I could only deduce from the searing pain still radiating along my back, and the body-wide tremors that were just now starting to abate, that the tips of these members secreted some sort of caustic fluid designed to shock the monster's prey into submission. Directly behind the bulbous head, three pairs of black-furred legs lay folded up against a chitinous thorax, which was itself some twenty feet in length.

Was my current captor then the predacious malagath of which Ghek had spoken—and had its noisome predecessor been a smaller, less powerful member of the same species? Any nascent rancor I might have felt about the kaldane's thoughtlessness in keeping to himself the news of their recent return to the vicinity vanished as I recalled that what memories he possessed of the southernmost portion of Bantoom would have left off some twelve thousand years in the past, when his own ancestors had departed those ancient burrows to colonize the northern valleys.

My concern, both for myself and for my erstwhile companions, grew ever deeper as my captor and I soared on, the huge wings above me an iridescent blur in the dim Cluros-light. By now we were many miles from the valley where I had been spirited away from Tara, Ghek, and Talo Thoran. So far I had seen no indication of pursuit by the *Kantim*—nor did I really expect any, owing to the abrupt nature of the first thing's attack and subsequent departure into the night.

The creature showed no signs of slowing, its two pairs of wings carrying us with a darting speed that seemed effortless. Time ticked away, as Thuria rose to rejoin her distant mate in the heavens, making a complete circuit overhead and disappearing below the horizon while he plodded stolidly far above. At last I decided I must find a way to extricate myself from the thing before we ventured so far afield that I would be hopelessly separated from the others. But how?

As it flew, the creature I had decided to identify as a malagath occasionally made small adjustments to the grip of its proboscides, certain of the tentacular members loosening slightly while others tightened even more painfully about my torso. Easing my pistol from its holster, I began to take advantage of these periodic occurrences, focusing all my considerable strength in an effort to extract my right arm each time there was the merest bit of slack among the powerful cables holding it against my side. Finally the hand that held my radium pistol was free.

We had been flying over open territory for a short while, below us one of the vast ranges of arid and desolate wilderness that cover much of the globe. With my captor deserting the higher reaches of the air to skim low above a range of moss-clad hillocks, I realized that there might be no better opportunity for me to persuade it to release its unwilling passenger. Taking what careful aim I could in the diffuse moonlight, I fired several bullets into the periphery of its thorax.

Unfortunately, the creature was constructed of much sterner stuff than I had anticipated. Responding with a small jolt at the impact of each slug, it did not seem otherwise impaired by my assault, and I realized in retrospect that this had been far from the wisest course of action. The projectile fired from a Martian pistol is explosive, and features an opaque outer coating that is broken by its impact upon the target, thus revealing the transparent inner cylinder in which reside a few particles of the Barsoomian element I have chosen to call radium, for I believe that to be its nearest earthly analogue. Quiescent in darkness, this powder detonates with violent force the moment it is exposed to natural sunlight. In this case, I had hoped the bullets would tear straight through the creature's flesh, imparting sufficient discomfort to cause it to either settle to the earth to inspect its wounds or at the least reflexively retract the imprisoning probos-cides and allow me to drop from its clutches while we were relatively close to the ground. Though neither of these events had come to pass, I could see at least two of the small missiles had lodged on the surface of what must have been an almost impregnable layer of chitin girding the belly of the beast. Now, if we did not reach our unknown destination before dawn, there was a great likelihood that the first rays of the rising sun would ignite the powder, and that I, riding a scant few feet from its underside, would be blown, along with my means of transport, straight to kingdom come.

After another several miles of level terrain, the ground beneath us began to rise sharply and the malagath adjusted its altitude accordingly. It was obvious to me that we had reached the edge of what had been one of Barsoom's ancient seabeds, though I knew not which great body of water had once flowed there, so turned about was I by our hectic flight. Presently we attained the top of a vast stretch of low tableland, whereupon I sensed that the malagath was nearing its destination, for its velocity abruptly increased. The outlines of an immense city appeared on the horizon and it was toward this the creature sped.

I am sure that to many who have read the accounts of my

adventures over the years, it must seem as if Barsoom is fairly overrun with long-abandoned cities. I assure you that this is not the case. As the vast expanses of water that once covered much of the surface of the planet began to dissipate, the great seagoing nations of antiquity crept vainly after the receding shorelines for millennia, in some cases extending their boundaries down into the former seabeds. When the life-giving water finally evaporated in all but a few isolated regions of the planet, once-thriving avenues of trade vanished with it, while the cities themselves fell prey to the roving hordes of the green race now free to spread across the world.

Before me in the predawn dimness rose the towers and domes of what I presumed to be one such sacked and despoiled maritime metropolis, most likely now no more than an empty shell. My captor began to slow as we flew over the great half-opened gate and entered the outer precincts, dipping low into a large courtyard close within the stout stone walls that encircled the nameless city. I could see a hint of rosy light far to the east and mentally crossed my fingers in the hope that we had indeed reached the end of our journey and that I might very soon discover the means to distance myself from my companion and its deadly cargo.

In the center of the plaza, surrounded by a once-beautiful mosaic of marble flooring now cracked and overgrown with the ubiquitous ocher moss, sat a low conical construction topped by a circular opening about ten feet in diameter.

We circled this structure, then shot up into the air directly above it. Flipping suddenly head-for-tail in a maneuver that left my stomach searching for its proper place in my body, the malagath folded its flickering wings tightly against its sides and dove straight down into the aperture, immediately spreading them wide again in the larger space within. We spiraled gently downward.

The shadowed interior below was shaped like an enormous laboratory beaker. Inward-sloping walls rose some eighty or ninety feet above the broad circular bottom, narrowed into a tube, and then continued up for another fifteen feet to the single opening into the plaza. The sides were smooth as glass from top to bottom, convincing me that it had not been a natural formation. I pondered its previous use before the demise of the city, deciding it had probably been employed as a well in bygone days. Indeed, a layer of murky water currently covered the bottom to an unknown depth. A small hummock of refuse rose from the center of the submerged floor, and it was there that my abductor decided to deposit me, hovering a few yards above the mass as it abruptly withdrew its proboscides. I fell with a clatter, then scrambled to my knees to find that the rubble upon which I knelt consisted mainly of bones—both human and animal—along with other less identifiable remains, which no doubt accounted for the odor of putrefaction that suffused the space.

As I teetered to my feet upon the grisly isle, I spotted several dark shapes lazing just under the surface of the water. Becoming aware of my presence, one after the other of them lifted its head above the surface, until five sets of glittering, multifaceted eyes peered in my direction. Perhaps eight feet in length, the creatures resembled the adult malagath in general construction, though they appeared to be entirely wingless, and their heads were much larger in proportion to their bodies.

Gathering side by side in a loose formation, they began to glide slowly toward me. I stepped backward down the far side of the mound of bones, finding to my relief that the clouded water rose no farther than my lower thighs. The floor beneath was extremely slippery, being coated with algal growths and littered with more of the detritus left behind, so I presumed, from previous meals.

The adult malagath had continued to hover above us while these wordless introductions occurred. Having satisfied herself that her young were well on their way to taking their morning meal, she rose upward on vibrating wings, perhaps to go in search of tomorrow's blue plate special.

By now the brief Martian dawn was in full swing and it was becoming quite light outside. Keeping one eye on my new companions, I backed quickly up against the sloping wall opposite them and peered upward to follow their mother's progress. She flitted up to the bottom of the tube, folded her wings, and crawled up to the outer rim, where she sat poised for a moment before flicking them open again. Then she soared up into the bright morning sunlight.

Three distinct explosions sounded. A five-foot section of iridescent wing fluttered down into the cone to land a few feet from me on the water's surface, and then all was silent.

I felt a brief stab of perverse sympathy for the creature's brood, who would never know why their mother did not return after providing them with what I am sure she had intended to be a filling breakfast.

My thoughts flew to the missing member of my own family. I wondered again what had occurred in Bantoom following my abrupt departure. Did Tara have any idea where I was? Were she familiar enough with the workings of her brother's improvement on the controlling destination compass—which, in its current sophisticated form, could be used to fix upon any moving object and then track it unerringly wheresoever it went—there was a slight chance that she had managed to train it on my departing form. It occurred to me that the mechanism might have been befuddled by my exchange of captors. Would it lead her on a wild-goose chase by tracing my initial kidnapper's route, or follow the second malagath to the dead city? I decided that there was a slim possibility she might eventually make her way here, in which case I hoped I would still be alive to greet her.

The sharp noise of the explosions had startled the young ones into momentary immobility. Now they resumed their steady movement toward me through the turbid water. I could see in the golden shafts of sunlight slanting down from above that in lieu of the adult's proboscides the children bore wicked-looking, scythe-like mandibles which clacked menacingly as they approached. One, perhaps more peckish than the rest and irritated by my disinclination to hop into its maw, suddenly stretched its jaws wide and aimed a jet of orange liquid at me. I managed to sidestep the stream, though the few droplets that landed on my ankle were enough to convince me it was the same caustic substance that their mother had excreted through the tips of her graspers.

Snatching the five-foot fragment of wing up from the surface of the pool, I held it as a glittering shield before my body as a second child and then a third aped the actions of their brother and orange fluid again shot across the water. As I had hoped, the material was impervious to the effects of the acid, and so I kept it angled between myself and the prospective diners as they pursued me doggedly around the floor of the well.

Fortunately for me, the little monsters preferred to move in a pack; if they had each come at me from a different direction, I would have been sunk—quite literally—in a very short time. As it was, long minutes dragged by as we kept up a circular dance about the central pile of refuse. I am sure our gyrations would have presented quite a comical show to an observer, with me pausing in my backward splashing and floundering to essay occasional desperate leaps toward the top of the funnel-like opening almost a hundred feet above. Even at my most agile, that distance would have been a challenge; with the floor beneath me slick with slime and no handholds on the glassy walls above, it was all but impossible. At the fifth or sixth try I twisted inadvertently in midair and fell back clumsily to land heavily right on the back of one of my pursuers. As I splashed away in the filthy water, he screamed at me with a wholly unexpected shrillness that threatened to pierce my eardrums—and then they all began to screech, venting their frustration at the inappropriate behavior exhibited by the tempting meal their doting mother had delivered them. I longed to clap my hands over my ears, but that would have meant abandoning my protection against their corrosive emissions. Even to draw my sword would be deleterious to maintaining my perilous footing and put me at the mercy of the jets of acid coming at me from various angles.

I began to wonder how long it would be before my stamina—not to mention my hearing—was exhausted and I met my doom at the clacking mandibles of these five. Even if I did dispatch my tormentors, I did not find the prospect of being trapped down here for the foreseeable future along with five decomposing corpses to be a pleasant one.

Then a shadow fell upon me from above. I craned my neck to see the outline of a woman's head and upper body in the gloomy distance beyond the opening, her long black hair falling past slender shoulders.

I was overjoyed. "Tara!" I cried above the clamor of my angry pursuers. "I am here!"

I had noticed the presence of a large coil of rope lying to one side of the well when we made our initial pass over the plaza. I was about to call it to my daughter's attention when a line came snaking down, halting just a few feet short of the surface of the water. Flinging my shield at my tormentors, I executed a shaky leap from the slippery pool and grasped the rope about ten feet up from the bottom.

Aware that something was not going according to plan, the malagath imps at once crowded together beneath my feet and began aiming their streams of acid upward. I made haste to scramble up the rope.

I reckoned that Tara must have tied the line around the base of the well or some other convenient immovable object, for I felt no slackness in the rope as I toiled upward. At last I reached the top of the cone and grasped her proffered hand. Voicing my fervent relief at her presence, I swung my legs up over the rim and dropped to the ground. I spun around, a broad smile upon my lips, and for the first time saw my savior without the sun's bright glare behind her. It was not my daughter.

14
THE WANDERER

THE WOMAN WHO STOOD before me did bear a superficial resemblance to a red Martian, in that her hair was black and her eyes were very nearly so. Yet her skin—and I could see a great deal of it, for she was completely without clothing—was cream colored with a hint of olive, and lighter even than mine, as if she had spent but little time beneath the sun. Her face was lively and intelligent, though at the moment she was regarding me with something akin to puzzlement.

Bitterly disappointed that I had not in fact been reunited with my daughter, I nonetheless offered my sincere thanks to my unknown rescuer for her timely assistance and inquired as to her identity.

She had begun drawing the rope up from the well, methodically coiling it as it passed through her fingers. It was shorter by several feet than when she had tossed it in, the bottom section having been eaten away by the corrosive jets of the youngsters' parting shots. She responded to my words with a shake of her head.

"I'm sorry, but I can't understand you," she told me as she worked. "Will you say that again more slowly?"

So preoccupied was I by the substitution of this complete stranger for my lost daughter that it took me several long moments to register that she had delivered her request in clear English!

"I was thanking you for helping me," I answered slowly in the same tongue. "And then I asked you your name."

"My name is . . . Loto," she said, her brow wrinkling in concentration, as if there might be more to it than that which she could not presently remember.

Barsoomian names, much like those employed by certain of the Indian tribes native to the Americas, often have distinct meanings bestowed in connection with some salient characteristic—actual or hoped for—of the person who receives them. You may think this is not dissimilar to the appellations borne by those of us in the English-speaking nations, yet nowadays these are more often handed down within families or simply chosen for their pleasing sounds, rather than given for any perceived application to the named individual. Thus you might address your acquaintances as Flora or Cooper or Prudence, without automatically comparing her beauty to a flower, assuming he earns his living making barrels, or reflecting on her history of wise decisions. At any rate, as near as I could figure, Loto signified "Wanderer" or "Drifter" in the Barsoomian common tongue—a language this young woman so far seemed unable to produce or comprehend. I decided to stick with English.

"Greetings to you, Loto. My name is John Carter," I told her in turn. This statement elicited another furrowed brow.

"Carter . . ." she repeated, her gaze becoming distant. "I knew someone by that name. No, not Carter—Carson! Carson *kum Amtor, Tanjong kum Korva*," she recited quickly, then turned back to me. "Do you know what that means?"

I shook my head. "I haven't a clue."

She looked disappointed. "Nor have I." She gazed around at the sunlit courtyard with its carpet of yellow moss as if noticing it for the first time. "But I think that Amtor is a place. A place much different from this one." She shaded her eyes with her hand and squinted skyward. "There the heavens are not so empty and there is no one very bright light, no, no . . ." She stopped again, at a loss.

"No sun?" I offered. "If there is no sun, then it must be very dark and cold there."

"Oh no, it is not dark at all, except at night. By day the clouds glow brightly with a pleasing warmth. I don't understand how that one bright light—that sun—can blaze there above us without causing great storms to ravage the land."

"Then I agree with you that this cannot be Amtor," I said. "For here on Barsoom the sun shines all through the day, yet storms are exceedingly rare."

Loto had finished coiling up the rope. She set it down carefully at the base of the well and looked around as if unsure what to do next.

I suggested that we seek some shade from the mounting morning heat in one of the nearby buildings, where I thought we might also endeavor to find her some form of apparel. We do not wear much upon our bodies here on Barsoom, but most persons deem a certain minimum of covering necessary for comfort and protection from injury. As we moved across the moss-covered marble of the plaza, I could not help but notice that my companion walked with a slight unsteadiness, in much the same way as a lifelong landlubber might traverse the deck on his first ocean voyage. With a growing suspicion as to the likely cause, I inquired how long she had been here in this nameless dead city. I was surprised when she said that just this morning she had found herself standing in sight of the outer gates. She assumed it was morning, at any rate, assuring me that there had been no period of darkness since her arrival. Loto told me that she could remember nothing from before she had opened her eyes in what she felt sure was a new place to her, and that she had no idea by what agency she had come here.

"Until I heard the sounds of explosions, which drew me into the plaza to investigate, and then a few minutes later the shrieks emanating from the creatures in the well, I had spent a good deal of my time wandering about the nearby courtyards simply practicing how to walk," she confided. "I am strangely light on my feet in this place, to the point of extreme awkwardness. I can't tell you how many times I landed on my face—and other areas—before I finally got the knack of walking upright again! However, once I learned to proceed from here to there without falling flat on my dignity in between, I quickly discovered how to do other, far more entertaining things," she added, her expression turning suddenly mischievous. "Watch!"

With that, Loto sprang up from the moss with a joyful cry, her prodigious leap carrying her fifteen yards across the plaza to land somewhat shakily on her feet at the base of a section of partially collapsed colonnade. Then, beckoning me to follow with a playful grin, she pointed to the top of the marble portico and launched herself straight up into the air.

As it turned out, mine were not the only ears her exultant cry had reached. An instant after she left the ground a towering manlike figure emerged suddenly from behind the structure, and, rearing up to its full height, reached out to wrap long green fingers about her ankle and snatch her from the air.

My blood ran cold as the green man stalked fully into the open, immediately followed by no less than seven more of the giant brutes.

Though I was dismayed by their unwelcome appearance, the presence of green warriors in the dead city did not surprise me. By ancient tradition, the green hordes are a nomadic people who pride themselves on building nothing, ever preferring to utilize the deserted relics of civilizations long past over demeaning themselves with what they consider to be lowly manual labor. Along with the savage great white apes, they infest many of Barsoom's otherwise deserted cities.

Loto was struggling vainly within her giant captor's grasp. Her expression, compounded of one part dread to two parts wonderment, convinced me that she had never before laid eyes on a green Martian.

Looking at these eight representatives of the green race as if through my companion's eyes, it was not difficult for me to divine the source of her wonder. Completely hairless, with skin colored a shade of dark olive, they are six-limbed creatures, each possessing two arms and two legs, while an intermediate pair of appendages that may be employed in either fashion sprouts from the torso at the midpoint between shoulder and hip. Their eyes protrude from opposite sides of a spherical head and are capable of moving independently of one another, not unlike those of the African chameleon. Ears like small cups, mounted high upon the skull on short antennae, and a pair of snowy white tusks curving up from the lower jaw to terminate just below the blood-red irises of their eyes, round out the utterly unearthly picture. All these strange details aside, the single most arresting feature of these formidable creatures may be their height, which in adult males such as these can range anywhere from thirteen to fifteen feet.

"Behold—I have snared me a little skeetan!" the green brute crowed to his comrades. He had chosen an unflattering epithet for my newfound companion: a skeetan is a small Martian animal that typically makes its nests in the walls of deserted cities. An amalgam of reptile and marsupial, it might have been assembled from equal parts horned toad and opossum. With a wide-lipped, grinning countenance and the thieving talents of a trade rat, it employs the front and hindmost pair of its eight spindly legs to propel it in prodigious vertical hops, while the two innermost are tipped with sharp grasping claws used to snatch the items it fancies. These are then stored in the pouch about its ample middle—often to the discomfiture of the helpless young who must also occupy the place as a nursery until they mature.

"Now we shall have something to play with later at the fireside when the night grows cold," Loto's captor continued. At this the others erupted in raucous laughter, as if in appreciation of a clever jest.

Clutched tightly to the man's breast, Loto strove even more vigorously against his iron grip, the menace in his voice clear to her even if she could not understand his words. At that moment one of the other warriors glanced across the plaza and his eyes fell upon me. "Look you—yonder crouches its mate!" he exclaimed. "We must seize him as well, so that we may wager as to which will bleat the loudest beneath our tender ministrations." Peals of laughter rang through the plaza.

To me, he called: "There's a good hopper! Come here, and be quick about it, if you do not want us to wring your beloved's neck on the spot."

I had seen by their metal that they were members of the Torquasian tribe. Still unsure of my own whereabouts, I wondered if they belonged to that group that had recently taken leave of the main horde to range over the area of dead seabed not far from Exum, which had been one of the original destinations of our disrupted voyage. Either way, I was certain they were not among those tribes that Tars Tarkas had so far succeeded in bringing under his tenuous banner of peace and cooperation, and so there would be little chance I could appeal to their better natures in his name. For thousands of years, warriors such as these had been taught from childhood to regard the prolonged torture of any red Martian captive unlucky enough to fall into their clutches as the most sublime form of entertainment. Though it was obvious that neither Loto nor I were of the red race, I highly doubted these fellows would permit the subtle distinctions of human skin pigmentation to cause them any qualms when the prospect of several hours of amusement was at stake.

Mulling the few options left open to me by this unpleasant turn of events, I proceeded to walk slowly toward the group, my head bent down as if I were thoroughly cowed.

When I was about halfway there I called out to Loto, telling her in English that when she was free she should immediately jump atop the portico. The structure reared more than thirty feet above the plaza and I was confident that the green men, tall as they were, would not be able to reach her there. At her quick nod of understanding, I took a few more plodding steps, pretended to stumble, and then—hoots of wild hilarity at my ineptitude ringing through the courtyard—vaulted toward the gathering in an arc carefully calculated to carry me right into their midst, my longsword already drawn.

This was a far cry from the behavior they had expected out of their timid hopper. Confusion reigned as the eight warriors tripped over one another, fumbling with their own weapons. The first swipe of my blade sent the head of the man holding Loto rolling onto the moss, while the second relieved his nearest companion of both the upper and intermediary limbs along his right side, together with the swords he had brandished in each. Roars of pain and outrage reverberated through the plaza as I darted back several feet, ducking my head just in time to avoid a shot from a radium pistol; the bullet passed an inch above my scalp to lodge deep in the belly of a third man.

Even as her captor slumped lifeless to earth, Loto had pushed free of his headless corpse. Now she hopped nimbly up onto the colonnade as the remaining warriors pounded toward me like juggernauts.

I squatted low and then soared over their heads, twisting in midair to score a vicious cut along the flank of the one who had fired his pistol, thus driving him to his knees with an agonized wail while I landed, feinted left, and then thrust the point of my blade through the heart of the man on my right. Were I the sort of fighter who enjoys conversing with his opponents while they spar, I might have offered a comment at that moment to the effect that even the smallest of skeetans may possess sharp claws—but I am not by nature a garrulous combatant and so I kept the observation to myself. The green warriors, on the other hand, were raising quite a racket, filling the plaza with great oaths and shouted imprecations as they swiped and lunged at their elusive foe.

With only three of my giant adversaries still remaining upright and all of them armed with swords, I curbed my leaps and engaged them directly with my feet upon the ground, my own blade weaving such a swift net of steel back and forth before them that it was as if each faced his own opponent. The tip of my longsword quickly found gaps here and there in their defenses, pursuing the openings almost before my brain could issue to my arm the appropriate commands. Soon I found myself with the old fighting smile playing upon my lips that always appears in the midst of spirited battle. Though I do not particularly relish killing, I greatly enjoy the act of fighting—perhaps because each contest feels unlike the last to me, and so I am never bored.

Loto remained crouched atop the portico while I fought, though she leaned forward to follow the exercise with avid interest. I was glad of this, as her presence within harm's way would have added an additional degree of distraction to the melee that might have endangered us both. As it was, I suspected she hung back not out of fear, but because she was currently naked and unarmed, while I had a deadly weapon and clearly knew how to employ it to best advantage. A minute or two later, as the last of the green men collapsed twitching onto the moss, I stepped back to salute her with my blade and then bade her join me on the ground. "We should not linger too long in this vicinity," I informed her, "since I have no idea as to the size of their company, and a great many more may soon come looking for their absent comrades."

Loto dropped lightly to earth a few yards away.

"You are very good with that," she observed with a gesture to my longsword, as I bent to clean it on a patch of moss. "The *kloozan* had no chance."

I did not know who or what a *kloozan* might be, but I got the gist of her compliment. "Thank you," I said. "I have had some practice."

Indeed, though I had arrived on Barsoom with uncounted years of experience in wielding my weapon of choice already under my belt, once here I quickly discovered that fighting a green Martian was quite unlike any other exercise in swordplay. For one thing, one's opponent is usually twice one's own height and more. As if the possibility of severe neck cramp were not aggravation enough, there is the additional complication of facing an adversary who may come at you swinging two, three, or even four sharp blades simultaneously. Fortunately, the very earliest tests of fighting proficiency to which I had been subjected upon arriving on my adopted planet had involved the members of various green hordes, and since then I have been afforded plenty more opportunities to hone my skills.

Rather than coming straight to my side, Loto wended her way among the fallen warriors, bending here and there for a closer inspection—though not for the reason I had anticipated, for she seemed far more interested in their accoutrements than in their unique physiology. At length she selected a short cape of black fur from one, a wide band of yellow silk from another, the same in purple from a third, and a section of belted leather from yet another. Requesting the loan of my dagger, she used it to quickly fashion herself a knee-length skirt out of the cape. From the silks she contrived a loose mantle and a scarf, draping the former over her shoulders and confining her long black hair in the latter, finally tying the tails of bright cloth beneath her narrow chin. Seeing my bemusement at her unorthodox tailoring, she flourished the tip of the dagger to where the "one very bright light" sat in the sky and said simply: "Sunburn."

I could see from the way her gaze darted back and forth between the outsized sandals worn by the green men and her own bare feet that she was contemplating the construction of some form of footwear, but the moss that covered the ground around us was soft and springy, and with time at a premium she decided to forgo the luxury.

"Much better," she said, tucking the dagger into her new-made belt. She stepped lightly over one of the green corpses, as if it were a dead tree limb that had fallen inconveniently into her path, and came to stand next to me. "Where shall we go now?"

"Where do you wish to go?" I asked. "I must be off at once to attempt to reunite with my daughter and our friends, but you are welcome to accompany me—if you have no other destination in mind."

"I have very little in mind," she replied with a small grimace. "There are too many important things missing from my memory."

"Well then, you shall come with me until they turn up again. And even beyond, if you wish, for you saved me from an unpleasant fate this morning and my country will welcome you with gratitude once we make our way back there."

"Thank you for the offer," she said. "Though I have a feeling I might not be here long enough to take advantage of it."

"Oh? And what makes you think that?" I asked.

She gave a little shrug. "It's more a premonition than a thought. It is pleasantly exciting here, but something tells me that I am seldom allowed to remain in one place for very long."

Before we departed the plaza, I made my own tour of the deceased warriors, adding a dagger to replace the one appropriated by Loto, some cartridges for my pistol, and a pair of waterskins to our stores.

"Where there are green men there are bound to be thoats, for they are a far-ranging race and rely heavily upon their mounts," I told her. I proposed that we make a quick inspection of the neighborhood in hopes of locating their pen. If we could separate one of the animals from the herd unobserved and then quit the city without being apprehended, we would be in much better shape.

As we prepared to leave the scene of battle and begin our search, something occurred to me. I explained my idea to Loto. It took us several trips, but we hauled the eight corpses across the plaza to the side of the now-silent well. I heaved them one by one over the rim, their arrival below occasioning a great commotion of splashing and shrill cries. With luck, by the time anyone came searching for the missing men there would be but little left of them to hint at their fate, while the five imps in the well might at least enjoy a final hearty meal before they either grew wings of their own or were overtaken by starvation.

15
OF THOATS AND THURIA

WE LEFT THE PLAZA and penetrated deeper into the city, my own previous experience dwelling among members of a green horde in the dead city of Korad guiding my selection of which buildings would be most likely to house the warriors' mounts.

Not wishing to gain the attention of any current inhabitants, we skulked quietly through the deserted halls, Loto marveling at the occasional large mural we encountered whose bright pigments had miraculously withstood the passage of thousands of years. Here were depicted scenes of a light-skinned, fair-haired people clad in flowing robes, delighting in the luxuriant, flower-dotted meadows and bountiful rivers now almost entirely absent from the sere and dying orb that is present-day Barsoom. I explained in response to my companion's whispered queries that these were the Orovars, one of the triad of peace-loving ancient peoples whose intermingling in later years had produced the current red race of which I now considered myself a member, in spirit if not in blood.

It was not until shortly after my second advent upon the planet that my adventures in the Valley Dor revealed to the wider world, for the first time in millennia, the existence of remnants of the original three races. Moreover, only during the past few decades did the historians of several nations begin working in collaboration to piece together the story of Barsoom's dim past. As the planet's innate vitality had continued to falter, the broad oceans retreating and the air growing thin and dry, humanity had scattered. Small enclaves of Orovars had remained in hiding in a handful of their ancient cities scattered over the globe, while an offshoot of religious zealots calling themselves believers—or "therns" in the common tongue—had fled the depredations of the green hordes to settle in the lush beauty of the Valley Dor, that supposed paradise at the south pole. Evolving after millennia of inbreeding to their current completely hairless state, these pale-skinned villains had established the cruel religion centered around the goddess Issus that had gone on to claim so many innocent lives, both red and green. Also dwelling in a few hidden reserves, as well as within the precincts of the blessed valley itself, were the fierce First Born, ebony-skinned descendants of the original peaceable Parovars who secretly preyed in turn upon the predatory Holy Therns. The Kalovars, a golden-skinned people with hair of dark gold or reddish bronze, had also been reputed to exist in antiquity—though when the great Ice Barrier at the northern pole had finally been breached, the race that had been revealed, perhaps their partial descendants, had been found to have coal-black hair and skin the color of ripe lemons.*

Luck was with our search. As we entered the fourth edifice to be explored, I could already hear the ill-tempered squeals that denoted the presence of a goodly quantity of the animals we sought. I crept forward through the halls to the inner courtyard, a great, roofless, rectangular atrium whose floor was sunk a few feet below the level of the rest of the building. Here a temporary paddock had been devised by pressing some large slabs of gold-threaded marble into service as a makeshift gate atop the ramp at one end of the walled space. Once I had ascertained that no one was present save ourselves and the thoats, I signaled for Loto to join me.

Our presence had not gone unnoticed; easily irritated, the thoats now began to circle in a restless herd around the paddock, emitting snorts and sharp squeals.

Standing quietly so as not to excite them further, I surveyed the herd, which consisted of some sixty or seventy animals—proof that the eight warriors I had dispatched were but a small sampling of those who currently occupied the city.

---

* See Chapter Eleven of *A Princess of Mars* by Edgar Rice Burroughs, in which Dejah Thoris tells John Carter of a "reddish yellow" race that flourished in Barsoom's distant past.

After a few minutes of observation, I focused my attention on one animal huddled in the corner nearest the gate that was noticeably smaller than the rest, standing a mere eight feet at the shoulder. The red race breeds a more diminutive and tractable species of saddle thoat than the irascible titans favored by the giant green men, and I speculated that this fellow had previously belonged to a red traveler unfortunate enough to have crossed paths with the Torquasians. Obviously wishing as little contact as possible with his fiercer companions, the poor soul pressed tightly against the wall as the others kept up their ceaseless circling. I pointed him out to Loto, who had been scrutinizing the rambunctious mob with obvious disapproval.

"You mean to attempt to climb atop one of those ill-favored behemoths?" she asked with skepticism. "Even the small one looks like it could swallow us in two bites!"

I could not fault my companion's first impression of our prospective mount. As a man who has spent a considerable portion of his life on both this world and another in the saddle, I have personally always found the thoat to be a lovely beast—in all aspects, that is, save appearance and temperament. Some might argue that they possess a certain sleek comeliness with their hairless hides of dark slate set off by a white undercarriage and heavily padded yellow feet—and I will readily admit that a swift steed racing beneath one across the dead sea bottom, leaving all pursuit far behind while the moons hurtle above through the gorgeous nighttime sky of Mars, can indeed be a thing of beauty. In the stark light of day, however, that same fleet-footed savior is too often transformed into a dyspeptic hulk with a snout like a crocodile's and fully eight muscular legs, each one poised to kick the unwary rider into the middle of next week the instant he dismounts.

It was shortly after my advent on Barsoom that I had encountered my first thoats—massive creatures with hair-trigger tempers, like the majority of these. With fond memories of the many noble horses I had trained and come to regard with great affection on Earth, I had been appalled by the state of near warfare that seemed to exist between the green men and their steeds, occasioned in large part by the brutal treatment to which the thoats were subjected on a daily basis. Applying the techniques of kindness and reward that I had successfully used in training my horses back on Earth, I was swiftly able to demonstrate to my Tharkian hosts that obedience and docility could be won from their mounts as easily as could unrelenting savagery and rebellion.

Now faced with an exacting timetable, I did my best to introduce the beast I had selected to an accelerated course in human kindness. I had noticed a small sack of nutmeats and bits of dried fruit among the saddles and riding cloths just outside the paddock—undoubtedly the property of one of the riders, as the thoats themselves subsist almost entirely on the ubiquitous ocher moss that, highly absorbent of moisture, provides them with both food and drink. Taking a few morsels in my hand, I sidled along the wall, all the while sending telepathic advertisements of my benign intentions to the mind of my chosen mount.

Waiting until none of the beast's burly fellows was nearby, I dropped a bit of food directly in front of him, and was gratified to see him lean over to sniff the tidbit and then gobble it up, whereafter he regarded me with a somewhat puzzled expression. I repeated this act several times over the next few minutes, always taking care to bestow my gifts when they would not be snatched away by one of the larger beasts. It was not long before he became complicit in my plan, and would turn me an expectant eye whenever the ceaseless motion of the others took them to the far end of the paddock. Continuing to soothe him with both words and thoughts, I dared to reach in and pat his great neck now and then as I doled out my bits of food, encouraging those moments when he behaved civilly and withholding the reward when he seemed about to lash out.

It took less than half an hour until I felt I could trust him well enough to ease open one side of the makeshift gate and urge him from the pen, after which I swung it quickly shut again. A few minutes later I was successful in applying a riding cloth and saddle to his back. Then, while continuing to rub his neck and tempting him with a final handful of treats, I hopped up behind his broad shoulders. Scattering the morsels on the ground at his feet as a distraction, I reached down to pull up Loto, who easily fit behind me on the capacious saddle, which had been designed to accommodate the more generous proportions of a green warrior.

Thoats are guided telepathically, so there was no time lost in fitting him with either bridle or reins. We made our way quickly back the way we had come and headed straight for the city gates. Just before we departed the paddock I had moved one of the marble slabs aside to leave the gate partially open, in hopes that the remainder of the herd would soon discover the gap and make their own escape, thus reducing the chance of any immediate pursuit were we spotted. Even if the remaining beasts lingered behind, the springy moss carpeting the land outside the city gates would not register the tracks of even a beast encumbered with two riders, and so long as we made our way swiftly out of view, I had little fear we would be successfully tracked by any Torquasians who might eventually note the theft of the smallest of their mounts.

Still, we galloped across the arid sea bottom for several hours just to be safe, not pausing until late afternoon, when I proposed we make camp atop a mossy knoll screened from view on two sides by tall, copper-leafed bushes of wild pimalia.

Loto confessed at this time that among the many items missing from her memory were the date and time of her last meal. I had exhausted the contents of the small sack of nutmeats and fruit over the course of my training of our mount; nor had I seen aught that might pass for game in the vicinity. Fortunately, I espied a grove of the milk-producing mantalia trees that dot the dead sea bottoms growing handily only a few yards from the hillock I had selected as our campground. After emptying the remaining water from one of the flasks I had appropriated from the Torquasians, I used my shortsword to tap the likeliest trunk and in short order had collected almost a gallon of the rich liquid.

Loto looked askance at my suggestion that we should dine on tree sap, but after I extolled the plant milk's highly nutritive attributes and she took a dainty sip to confirm my claim that its taste was not at all objectionable, she accepted my offer of half the bounty with thanks. With the thoat—whom Loto had variously referred to during our trek as "Bucephalus," "Marengo," and "Gray Beauty"—tethered to a mantalia tree where he could crop the moss that would provide him with his own dinner and drink, we sat atop the knoll and passed the flask back and forth as the sun dropped into the west.

Loto found the night sky even more fascinating than she had its predecessor.

"Just look at all the beautiful little suns!" she exclaimed. "Wait— *stars*. They are called stars, are they not?"

She beamed in triumph when I assured her that they were. A moment later her eyes grew round with wonder again. "And what is *that*?" she whispered in awed tones, pointing past my shoulder. I turned to see that Thuria, the mad queen of the heavens, was rising into the sky above the line of low hills at my back.

"That is Thuria, one of the two moons that circle this planet," I told her. "Her mate Cluros will appear later to keep her company, though he is never swift enough to match her pace as she races across the skies."

"Thuria—one of *two* moons!" she echoed with delight. Though I sincerely hoped her memory would soon be restored to her— if only so we could get to the bottom of who she was and how she had arrived on Barsoom speaking English like one born to it— I must admit I enjoyed introducing Loto to the natural wonders of this world for the very first time, much as one might do for a child fresh from the egg. "I do not think we had any of those on Amtor," she mused. "Although I seem to recall a similar thing, much larger, in yet another darkened sky."

"Perhaps you are thinking of the Earth's moon," I suggested. "Do you recall anything of Earth? This language we are speaking, as well as your fine jumping abilities, tell me that you have probably spent some time there."

"Earth . . ." She knitted her brows in concentration. "I remember a place called Brooklyn. Is Earth on Brooklyn?"

"The other way around, I believe," I said with a smile. "But this is encouraging, Loto! You are starting to recall more things."

"Loto," she repeated, frowning. "Why did you call me that? My name is Betty."

"Betty from Brooklyn," I mused. "Now we are indeed getting somewhere."

"Yes," she said solemnly. "It is always good to get somewhere." Her attention wandered back to the sky behind my head. "Have you ever been there?"

"To Thuria?" I asked with some amusement. "It is an odd question—yet as it happens, I have. Or at least, I think so."

"You think so? You cannot be sure whether you have been to the moon? Now whose memory is faulty?"

I laughed. "*Touché!* But it is a complicated matter." I gave her a brief sketch of the weird journey to the nearer moon that I had made in a spaceship years ago, and of how when we arrived at the diminutive rock—for our astronomers insist that it is barely fifteen miles from end to end—we found a planet that was quite as large as Barsoom and populated by humans and other creatures of perfectly normal dimension. I explained that since that trip I had often pondered the veracity of the eccentric scientist who had designed the spacecraft and later glibly explained away the phenomenon by insisting that some sort of bizarre inverse relationship existed between Barsoom and its two satellites, such that persons approaching one of the tiny bodies from the surface of the planet below would magically shrink in size during their journey—vessel and all—so that they would maintain upon arrival the same physical proportions to the moon they had enjoyed on their planet of origin. He called it a "compensatory adjustment of masses," an impressive-sounding phrase which seemed credible enough at the time, but over the years had begun to give off the rank odor of hokum.

"But how can you doubt it?" Loto—now Betty—asked me. "You went there yourself, or so you say."

"I definitely went somewhere," I said. "Yet in the ensuing years skeptical savants in my own country have propounded several alternate explanations for the experience—shared hallucination, for one, though I do believe that we made the trip and that the blue-haired folk and the one-eyed cat-men we encountered there were as real as you or I." I shrugged. "My personal preference is a theory that posits the existence of an invisible gateway of some sort surrounding

Thuria—and perhaps Cluros, as well—through which one may pass to other worlds entirely."

"That would be my preference also," Betty said. "I wonder if a traveler to Thuria must always end up on that planet of the blue-eyed cats, or if you might be allowed to choose your own world?" She lifted her arm and rotated her hand lazily in the air. "As a child, when I walked through the revolving door of a department store with Mother, I used to hope each time I went round that I would come out on a different sidewalk in some faraway land."

It was growing late and so I did not press her for the name of the department store, though it was evident that more and more of her memories were coming back to her. We spoke for a few more minutes and then I suggested that we try to get some sleep, so that we might rise before dawn and be on our way.

"Good night, John Carter," she said as she leaned back against the pillow she had devised from her purple scarf and some handfuls of moss. "Thank you for your kindness today."

"Good night, Loto—or, I should say, Betty."

"Betty will do fine," she told me, stifling a yawn with her fist. "'Miss Callwell' would sound far too formal coming from someone who has gone to the trouble of slaying a pack of gigantic *Brokols* on one's behalf, don't you agree?"*

I slept well, waking once in the middle of the night to hear a voice softly murmuring "Thuria . . ." When I glanced over, I could see that Miss Callwell was also awake, lying amid her plundered Torquasian silks and furs with her head on her folded arms, and staring up with rapt attention at the racing moon, which was beginning its second rapid circuit through the heavens. I turned over with a smile and went back to sleep.

When I awoke the next morning, she was gone.

---

* For more on the unusual life of Betty Callwell, see the novel *Escape on Venus* by Edgar Rice Burroughs.

16
AN ILL WIND

THE DAGGER I HAD GIVEN Loto lay atop her motley garments, which still bore the undisturbed impression of her recumbent form. I scanned the empty horizon, then looked to where the thoat stood close by, munching placidly on the day's first course of moss. His uncomplicated mind, aglow with contentment at no longer finding himself being jostled by much larger beasts in a crowded paddock, had nothing to report of any excitement in the night.

Bucephalus and I trotted around the area, scouring the surroundings to the extent a person traveling on foot might reasonably be expected to attain in a few hours, but we came upon no clues in the barren countryside to the whereabouts of our missing companion.

Reflecting upon the mystery surrounding her initial appearance and her presentiment that she might not be here for very long, I decided that until I received evidence to the contrary, I must admit the strong possibility that Miss Callwell was no longer even on Barsoom. Wherever she had gone, I already missed the wide-eyed wanderer; her eccentric conversation and naive appreciation of what seemed a wholly new world to her had made the prospect of setting off in search of the others more agreeable—and I had a strong feeling that she and my daughter might have become fast friends.

As for myself, the fact that I was on Barsoom was about the extent of my knowledge concerning my own current location. My intuition, which was all I had to go on at this point, told me that the far-ranging flights of my mysterious initial captor and the wily devil's darning needle that had usurped its catch two nights previous had brought me a good distance south and probably east of Bantoom. It had

149

occurred to me that the dead city where Betty and I had begun our brief association might well be ancient Xanator on the west coast of the Gulf of Torquas, where Tan Hadron of Hastor told me he had once sojourned; but never having been there myself, I had no way to confirm my guess. Nor was I likely to have it confirmed by Tan Hadron: that gallant warrior, one of the most splendid officers in Helium's navy, had disappeared over a decade ago while assisting me in the rescue of my granddaughter Llana from a northern dictator named Hin Abtol. Ruminating gloomily over the recurrence of loss in my life, I resolved to recover my daughter and our companions as soon as humanly possible. To that end, I set out toward the northwest, hoping to encounter before too long some identifying landmarks that would let me know if I was headed in anything approximating the right direction.

For hours we tramped through the largely unvarying landscape of the dead sea bottom, the carpet of yellowish moss broken only by the occasional glint of low quartz outcroppings and here and there a stand of bent-limbed trees. The sun was approaching the zenith when I beheld a gleaming object approaching through the cloudless sky from the west. It was a flier, which as I watched broke suddenly from its straightforward course and began bobbing and darting around the sky like a child's kite caught in an updraft. Bringing forth my spyglass, I identified it with mingled astonishment and delight as the *Kantim*!

From my position on the ground, I could not ascertain how many were aboard the ship; nor could I descry any obvious damage to its exterior that might account for such eccentric behavior. My first thought was that they had adopted a deliberately erratic course in an attempt to elude pursuit, but I could detect no other craft in the vicinity.

I was not sure if they had spotted me yet. Betty's former trappings lay in a bundle before me on the saddle; quickly I tied the strips of purple and yellow silk to my longsword and brandished them above my head like a gaudy pennant. A moment later the *Kantim* dipped suddenly, then swerved in a wide arc and headed in my direction, still jerking and lurching in the same peculiar fashion as it flew.

The craft swooped over us at a height of about fifty feet, continued on past, and then turned abruptly to repeat the motion. On its third such identical pass a familiar face appeared over the starboard railing. It was Talo Thoran, his features distorted by anxiety.

"Good afternoon, John Carter," he cried. "I do not know how to make it stop!"

"What of my daughter?" I called back to him, feeling a prickling of alarm. "Is she not able to pilot the ship?"

Before he could respond, the *Kantim* shot out of range again, circling back half a minute later.

"The princess insisted on remaining in Bantoom to aid the kaldane!" he shouted. "She sent—" The rest of the utterance was lost as the ship once more swung away.

I realized that my chief priority at that moment was to assist Talo Thoran in gaining control of the flier—or, more preferably, to wrest control of it from him altogether—lest we spend the next hour exchanging information in parcels of a dozen words each.

I therefore dismounted and, waiting for the *Kantim* to dip low above us on its next pass, leaped straight up for the side. I vaulted over the railing and hastened to the bow, where I found Talo Thoran muttering furiously to himself while he jabbed at the controls with his fingers. Nudging him to one side, I brought us about and stilled the engine. We coasted to a stop and descended to alight on the moss a few feet from the wide-eyed thoat.

"Now," I said to the quaking scholar. "Explain."

Talo Thoran recounted the events that had taken place following my abduction by my first captor. Those still aboard the flier had been shocked to see a faintly glowing form sweep in out of the night and snatch me from my perch at the ventilation port of the rykor pen. Tara had kept her head and instantly activated the tracking component of the destination compass, which she fixed on my retreating figure. Lowering the ship several feet, she brought it in to hover close to the wall and used her own half-Earthling muscles to leap up to the small window. She shined her torch inside, and reported that she believed Ghek was in need of assistance, then had Talo Thoran quickly retrieve some items from the cargo locker, which he bound with a strap of leather and tossed to her. Directing the scholar to wait no more than half an hour for her to return before taking the *Kantim* in search of me, she slipped in through the window, and he had not seen her again.

"I explained to the princess that I had no skill in piloting a flier, but she assured me that the automatic destination compass would do all of the work for me, and then instructed me as to which button I should press to activate it," Talo Thoran went on. "Please believe me, Warlord, I did not wish to leave your daughter there, even though she commanded me to obey her wishes. She said you would understand that she could not abandon her friend to an uncertain fate, while she had full confidence that you would most certainly overcome whatever malefic foe had made off with you. I believe that the Princess Tara is the most amazing person I have ever known," he concluded in a rush, his eyes shining with a look that I readily recognized.

I could see that the fellow was in a wretched state, torn between his concern for Tara's safety and his dread that I would excoriate him for leaving her, even at her own command. I reassured him that he had done the right thing by departing in search of me when she did not reappear from out of the pen. I did not add that, although I abhorred the thought that my daughter might now be alone in a nation of hostile creatures, I could not honestly say I believed the presence of Talo Thoran at her side would have significantly improved her lot.

Much relieved, he went on to tell me that his own flight from Bantoom had been largely uneventful—albeit somewhat leisurely, as he had somehow gotten the throttle stuck at its lowest speed shortly after departing. The only problem had arisen minutes ago, when he sighted a lone thoat and rider near the course the destination compass had been following. In order to investigate, he attempted to disengage the device, which had left him at the controls with no knowledge of how to operate them.

It was a simple matter for me to set the mechanism to retrace its path and carry us back to Bantoom. All that remained was to deal with my mount.

I removed the saddle from Bucephalus and bade him farewell,

taking some time to impress upon him as I stroked his broad neck that he was now free to roam as he liked, and advising him to avoid any unfamiliar beasts or men he might encounter.

The little thoat stood blinking up at us as we rose into the air. A few moments later Talo Thoran informed me that the animal was following us, and I looked back to see him galloping over the moss beneath the flier. Regretfully, I increased the engine to full speed, whereupon he quickly fell behind and was soon lost in the distance.

I kept the throttle wide open. Conservation of fuel was no consideration, as all modern Heliumetic fliers employ a motor that derives its limitless energy from the very magnetic field of the planet. We made excellent time as we raced beneath the hot sun, and I thought there was a chance we would arrive at our destination before nightfall.

After about two hours the ground began to slope upward out of the barren seabed and a high plateau fringed with patches of trees showed up ahead. I judged we were not far from that place where the second malagath had snatched me from its malodorous rival.

My attention was drawn to a bank of low clouds just becoming visible on the horizon. As I have previously noted, clouds of any significant magnitude rarely appear in the thin and arid atmosphere of Barsoom, and almost never in such an imposing array as now loomed before us. The sky behind them was a dull iron gray, while the clouds themselves stretched in a dark wall from east to west for as far as the eye could see. Although this forbidding display lay directly in our path, I was not overly concerned. Having previously piloted airships through clouds without incident on more than one occasion, I was confident that passing through even a few hundred yards of the insubstantial mist would not interfere with the functioning of the destination compass that currently bore us unerringly toward the valley of Bantoom and an overdue reunion with Tara.

As we drew nearer to the clouds, a sudden wind came up. Seemingly arising out of nowhere, it whipped the bottom of the bank into black tatters while the top surface expanded ominously upward like an oceanic tidal wave. As is customary when in flight, Talo Thoran and I had both secured our harnesses to the deck, but now

I attached the additional stouter lashings designed for adverse conditions, and signaled to my companion to do the same.

We had acted none too quickly, for a moment later the wind slammed into us with incredible force, seizing the *Kantim* and whirling it end over end as if it were a toy. I fought to right us, working furiously at the controls in an attempt to rise above the wall of roiling cloud now but a few hundred feet in front of us, but the wild currents seemed to be converging on us from several directions at once and a moment later we were plunged sidewise into a cold and damp world of streaming gray vapor. I redoubled my efforts to force the craft up above the rushing currents, wrestling with the controls until my shoulders ached and I felt like some winged creature desperate to win free of the imprisoning winds and into the bright sunlight I knew still shone but a short distance above us. Thwarted in that attempt, I reversed tactics, adjusted the buoyancy levels, and sought to dive downward toward the earth. Yet again the sheer power of the gale resisted my efforts, holding us almost stationary at the center of its howling violence. I took my eyes from the controls long enough to spare a glance over my shoulder at Talo Thoran, finding him grim-faced, his countenance somewhat greenish beneath its usual copper as he clung for dear life to the lashings that held him fast to the deck.

Though all my attempts to bring the ship back on course had been for naught, the dials of the control panel soon informed me we were no longer trapped in utter stasis, as the winds had begun to force us sharply westward.

My attention divided between making sure we maintained ourselves upright and simultaneously fighting to return us to our previous course, I was thus too preoccupied with the controls to pay any heed to the terrain above which we flew. With the force of the gale only increasing and my attempts to counter it merely serving to subject the flier's motor to possibly damaging strain, I decided to cease my battle for the time being and switched off the engine entirely, after which our halting progress to the west accelerated dramatically. It was then that I began to catch glimpses of a strange object becoming visible through the clouds below and ahead of us: a large, low structure toward which our prow seemed to be directly pointing.

The thing was constructed in the form of a stone octagon covering some three square miles of ground. This was not in itself that out of the ordinary: on Mars as on Earth, human habitations come in many shapes. As I peered down through the gaps in the clouds, however, it was soon evident to me that this was something other than a dwelling place. The structure was entirely roofless, and within the towering outer walls, each perhaps fifty feet in height and another twenty in thickness, the pattern was reduplicated, with at least a dozen sets of shorter walls nested within, but no sign of dwellings or inhabitants. Each of the diminishing octagons was offset from the one outside it by several degrees, and though I soon discerned that each succeeding internal wall actually rose an identical height from the ground, the terrain beneath them was graduated into a downward-sloping depression far too precise to have occurred naturally, giving the whole peculiar structure the look of a child's puzzle.

As the ship was propelled ever nearer to the imposing edifice it also began to lose altitude, the winds now bent on forcing us down into the heart of the weird funnel-like structure. I resumed my battle for control of the flier with the growing apprehension that we were not at the mercy of mindless elements, but were in fact being herded toward this place—as frankly impossible as that seemed.

Talo Thoran had recovered his equilibrium to the extent that he had also turned to peer over the side of the flier. "John Carter!" he called to me over the shriek of the wind. "Are you going to land us inside that strange enclosure?"

"Not by choice," I shouted back. "I have been trying for some time to return us to our proper path, but the storm seems to have a different notion."

In the end I brought us down just within the first and second walls of the structure, the shepherding winds reducing their force as we descended, as if to reward us for giving in to their obvious desires.

The gale was still roaring above us, which I took to be a sign that we were not to attempt to move from this spot. With Talo Thoran's assistance, I did my utmost to secure the *Kantim* within the first wall, but the best we could accomplish, even after lashing the craft to an array of stakes driven into the ground, still left it swaying and heaving violently from side to side. I had hoped we might take refuge in the flier's small cabin to wait out the storm, but since this would involve being continuously buffeted from one wall to the other—and perhaps even hurled back into the air so long as the tempest raged—I decided we should make our way deeper into the interior of the structure, on the theory that the further we descended into the earth, the more protected we should be from the brutal winds.

Not knowing how far we might have to venture before we found a place of safety, we gathered some meager supplies, which we wrapped in our sleeping silks and furs.

We set off in a clockwise direction, hoping to quickly encounter an opening in the second wall that would grant us ingress to the next inward circle. We trudged halfway round the structure before we discovered a small doorway. We repeated the process between the second and third walls, only to find our progress blocked by an interior wall set perpendicular to the others, which necessitated our turning around and heading back the other way, until we finally located another small opening on the far side of the edifice. Indeed, I soon realized that the structure had been deliberately conceived as a giant maze that funneled any visitor gradually into the ground, with one or two small openings placed at seemingly random intervals around the circumference of each of the dozen or more eight-sided walls, and interior barriers set here and there that forced one to turn and retrace one's steps. In possession of neither breadcrumbs nor a spool of thread, I had a moment's trepidation about continuing in this manner and eventually finding ourselves unable to locate the way out. The afternoon was drawing to a close, and I had hoped that the storm might quiet enough to allow us to return to the flier and take flight again before nightfall, as the varied dangers that stalk the less civilized regions of Barsoom by day are only multiplied after dark. Though I did not mention it to Talo Thoran, I had no wish to be caught in this weird structure at night by a troupe of great white apes or stumble into some other nest of monsters accustomed to chasing down their prey until the victim fell exhausted among the many twists and turns.

In the end I was reassured by the height of the walls, for twenty feet was as nothing to my leaping skills. If worse came to worst, I knew that in the event of pursuit I would be able to carry both myself and my companion up and over any such barrier we encountered. The force of the winds penetrated less and less the deeper we went, though the sound of their howling indicated that the storm had in no way abated.

We spent the better part of an hour traversing the descending pathways without coming upon any signs of recent habitation, though we did begin to note traces of a slimy substance on walls and pavement that glittered in the wan daylight. The farther down we went, the more prevalent these became. Curious, I touched a fingertip to one of the shining trails and brought it to my face. My stomach lurched at the smell, which was unpleasant in the extreme, but also familiar, for I was sure I had experienced its like before—first in the crater surrounding the downed flier far to the north, later in the pits beneath my own palace, and most recently emanating from the flying creature that had snatched me from my perch in Bantoom. I paused to rub my hands as free of the stuff as I could on the silky leaves of a stunted clump of gloresta I found growing defiantly at the base of one wall.

I was surprised to feel almost no fatigue after a protracted stretch of almost continuous walking, nor had Talo Thoran evinced a desire to stop and rest. In fact, my step felt lighter the deeper I penetrated, now urged on by the conviction that a construction this elaborate must conceal something of great importance at its hub.

Eventually we reached the center, a roofless circular chamber thirty feet in diameter, constructed of highly polished marble and absolutely bare of any furnishings. The wind had finally died down above us, and after a cursory inspection of the empty space I turned with some regret and signaled to my companion that we should start to make our way back up the sloping levels to the ship if we hoped to be airborne again by sunset. My steps were heavy as we set out, and after a minute or two I found myself trudging up the slightly tilted floor of the outer corridor as if I were climbing a steep slope. At my back, I heard Talo Thoran groan and looked back to see him slouch against the wall and then slide to the floor with an expression of utter weariness. There was obviously something untoward occurring.

Recalling the force that had knocked the *Tarkim* out of the sky, and worried that the debilitating pressure might suddenly increase, I hurried back to Talo Thoran's side and with some effort lifted him up into my arms. "We must get out of here," I told him. Gathering my strength, I moved to the base of the nearest wall and launched myself into the air. To my amazement I was unable to clear more than a few feet from the ground before I slammed shoulder-first into the stone wall.

I realized that it was as if I were back on Earth—more than that, as if I were a native Martian transported to the Earth and having to cope with the heavier gravity there. Talo Thoran was gasping for breath in my arms. I trudged doggedly back to the central circle and set him down on the floor, where he said at once that it was as if a great weight had been removed from his chest. I found that my strength and agility had returned as well—but only so long as I stayed within the bounds of the empty chamber. It was obvious that we were not intended to leave the central circle.

Evening approached and we resigned ourselves to spending the duration of the gale here. We took refuge against a wall on the opposite side of the single small doorway, the better to watch for any intruders in the night. I tested the opening from time to time, always with the same result: so long as we remained within the chamber, there was no oppressive force. Venture but an inch beyond, however, and an invisible hand pressed us downward.

We sat with our backs propped up against the polished wall in disconsolate silence. Talo Thoran was examining the contents of his pocket pouch in the rapidly waning light when he gave vent to an anguished gasp. "Oh no!" he cried. "Forgive me, John Carter. My memory has been upended by the events of the past few days. The princess charged me with conveying this to you!"

With that he handed me a small slip of folded paper. I opened it to find a single line written in my daughter's own dear hand: *I still live!*

Feeling my spirits rise, I reassured Talo Thoran that in spite of himself he had delivered me the message at just the right moment. Clasping the treasured words to my breast, I bade him good night and lay back in the increasing shadows with a smile upon my lips. I had not quite made it past the threshold of sleep when the floor opened up beneath us.

17
BROUGHT LOW

PERHAPS YOU ARE FAMILIAR with that disquieting sensation of falling into emptiness that occasionally intrudes upon the mind just as sleep takes hold, and causes even the most enervated body to spasm in mad anxiety. Placing a hand onto the smooth marble to steady myself, I realized there was something more than misguided reflex at work, as my body evinced a strong desire to persist in its downward motion. I flailed about in the darkness, groping at my pocket pouch until I remembered I had lost my radium torch at the rykor storehouse. I called out to Talo Thoran, who responded in groggy confusion: "Now what is happening?"

"Your torch, man. Give us some light!"

After a few moments, wavering light flared. My companion held the torch in one hand while bracing himself against the marble with his legs and elbows, a look of beleaguered incomprehension on his face.

Indeed, the sight that met our eyes was difficult to fathom. The smooth flooring upon which we had laid ourselves down to sleep was now divided into distinct wedges, much as one would slice a pie. As we watched in growing consternation, the tip of each section sank slowly toward the center of the room to the accompaniment of a low and labored grinding noise. A small aperture had appeared there and was slowly widening as the wedges dipped ever lower.

My thoughts whirled while I groped about for some purchase on the smooth surface: there was something strikingly familiar about this wholly unexpected development. In a sudden rush I remembered Carthoris telling me of a trap constructed much like this one in the

160

palace of the ruler of the ancient Orovar stronghold of Lothar, where he and his future mate Thuvia had once been detained against their will. At a command from the evil jed who held them prisoner, the floor beneath the captives had transformed itself in similar fashion, sending them sliding to the doom that waited beneath the chamber. I tried to recall how Carthoris and Thuvia had escaped the inexorable plunge into the darkness below, and then realized the sobering truth: they had not! It was only Thuvia's extraordinary ability to exert control over the ravenous giant banth that waited for them on the floor directly beneath that had prevented the putative god of the Lotharians from succeeding in making a meal of them. Continuing to claw futilely at the ever-tilting sides of polished marble with one hand, I sought the hilt of my longsword with the other. My daughter-in-law was not with us to exert her uncanny influence, and with no clue as to whether a bloodthirsty banth-god or some different terror awaited us below, I knew I must rely upon myself for a solution to our problem.

Slowly yet surely we were sliding toward the yawning aperture. I cast about in frustration for something, anything, to hold onto, but the walls were as smooth as the floor, and equally bare. Quickly I unbuckled a three-foot length of my harness. Wrapping one end twice about my hand, I flung the other toward Talo Thoran. "Grab hold!" I shouted to him, intending that we should not be separated when we inevitably fell into the oubliette.

The torch in his right hand sending beams of light flashing crazily about the room as he scrabbled in vain for purchase, the scholar managed to snare the leather band with his left and gripped it tightly.

I was positioned lower than Talo Thoran, and thus destined to meet whatever fate awaited us below a few seconds in advance of my companion. Just as my heels reached the edge of the yawning hole, the tilting of the wedges abruptly slowed and then halted altogether with a great grinding noise, leaving a roughly circular opening some five feet in diameter. Had the ancient mechanism failed at the last moment? Without pausing to think, I flung out my arms and legs and sprang forward, finding myself a second later miraculously suspended in the opening, as the palms of my hands and the soles of my sandals strained in desperation against the slanted wedges of cold marble. Only for a heartbeat did I hang there, facedown above the darkness, before I felt the full weight of Talo Thoran crash down upon my back and the two of us plunged through the opening.

The scholar's reverberating wail terminated abruptly when we landed in a tangled heap a short distance below, to be replaced by low-voiced apologies as he attempted to push himself up off my back in the absolute darkness. He had lost hold of his torch in the fall and began to scrabble about the floor in search of it. I was about to caution him not to release the strap of leather that kept us connected, when there came another grumble of long-unused machinery beneath us and the polished floor upon which we now rested also began to tilt down in sections. As I slid down once more into darkness, one hand still gripped about a length of leather whose other end now flapped loosely, I heard a final cry of distress from my companion on the other side of the room, which diminished gradually into the unknown distance as we slid our separate ways.

I was not falling free this time. Instead, I found myself traveling rapidly downward at a steep angle, feetfirst through a large tube coated with some slick substance that made it impossible to create enough friction to slow my descent, no matter how I strained against the walls with my arms and legs, and I imagined that Talo Thoran had been routed into another like it. I cursed myself for a fool, for I had allowed us to be easily and thoroughly snared in this elaborate trap, and both myself and my companion would doubtless now pay the price. The conduit zigged and zagged, the angle of its descent sometimes almost flattening out, sometimes approaching the vertical. Downward into the earth I hurtled, with no idea how long the passage stretched, nor what awaited me at its terminus.

Time ticks by in an odd manner in such a situation. It felt as though I had been falling forever, and I had lapsed into a mental state near to a trance when, entering one of those infrequent sections where the tube ran at an angle that was nearly horizontal, suddenly my feet encountered a fleeting resistance and, my speed only minimally impeded, I slid quickly through a collection of hard, clattering objects that had been partially blocking the tube. My hand had closed upon the largest of them as I sped by and, examining it by touch in the blackness as I plunged on, I came to the horrified realization that it was a human skull. Unbidden, my mind supplied me with the ghastly image of a person somehow managing to crawl up the slick passage from an unknown distance below, only to falter from lack of food and water and eventually succumb. I released the object with a shudder.

I do not know how long I plummeted down before I suddenly came shooting out of the conduit through a hinged round doorway that clapped instantly shut behind me, and arced through the air to land on the stone floor of a dimly lit space. I rose quickly to my feet and surveyed the area as best I could in the faint, sourceless light, finding it to be a round chamber about the size of the one we had lain down in far above, with a single open doorway. Hearing a muffled noise from nearby, I stepped through into the darkness beyond, hoping the young scholar had been deposited in similar fashion nearby. "Talo Thoran," I called in a low voice as I moved cautiously forward. "Is it you?"

I was in another room, dimmer than the first, rather than a corridor as I had anticipated. As my sight adjusted to the darkness, I became aware of an array of large shapes before me. Suddenly a dozen pairs of eyes opened to blaze crimson. As I took a step back, the door behind me closed softly, whereat the things rose up silently to their full height, and I saw their massive shoulders and unnaturally extended arms as they towered all around me. Fangs set in weird, hairy faces gleamed in the faint illumination. A moment later they were upon me. I fought with ferocity, laying out not a few of them, but they were too many. At last I felt something sharp prick my neck, the gray light faded, and I was borne to the ground.

18
IN A PERFECT WORLD

I OPENED MY EYES in the strangest of places. My first thought was that I must still be asleep, even though I seldom dream, and never in such vivid detail as this. Dejah Thoris likes to say my waking life is sufficiently stimulating that I reserve my periods of slumber strictly for rest, rather than as a playground for fanciful adventures.

As I came more fully to myself, the sights and sounds and various other sensations that assailed my body convinced me that this was indeed reality—albeit a form of reality I had never before imagined.

Many-colored lights came and went in a bewildering alternation that dazzled my vision, and an irregular throbbing hum filled the air.

I was lying supine on the cold, damp floor of a gargantuan tunnel—and when I choose those words to describe the place, I mean that the top of the vast cylinder arching above me was easily half a mile from where I lay at the bottom.

Shivering against the chill, I quickly found my attention focused on a more intrusive sensation: that of pain. Due to the unconventional illumination, I had to bring my left hand mere inches from my face before I could make out the source of the discomfort: my left palm now bore a strange mark in the shape of a black circle filled with intricate tracery, which burned as if it had been applied with a red-hot branding iron, though my fingertips could detect no blistering of the sensitive flesh.

I was completely naked, having been relieved while unconscious of not only my garments but my various weapons as well. Even more disturbing, I was as weak as a kitten. Had I been knocked unconscious? Drugged? How exactly had I gotten here? My thoughts came sluggishly. I recalled the hairy faces and bared fangs of the long-armed creatures that had sprung upon me out of the darkness, but nothing more. With a groan, I rose up onto my elbows, my head spinning wildly with each small movement, and looked behind and before me, to see the tunnel stretching off to the limit of my vision in both directions. Great lighted strips running lengthwise and distributed with regularity around the inner circumference of the tunnel glowed with a weird and ever-shifting phosphorescence, rendering it difficult to ascertain distances and impossible to clearly make out even close objects.

I had been witness to a less confounding version of such an effect in the past: in the gigantic cavern at Barsoom's south pole wherein lay the underground Sea of Omean, and in other places hidden from the sun where either radium ore or luminous plant growth had provided an eerie illumination, but never before had I seen it employed in such a deliberately organized—not to mention disorienting—fashion. It was obvious that whatever substance was responsible for the constantly rippling interplay of colors had been arranged in these orderly rows by some guiding intelligence—though perhaps a mad one. As it was, everything within the tunnel was bathed in a multitude of ever-changing hues, the various colors pulsing at different intervals, so that some grew brighter while others faded away. For a fraction of a moment my body was violet, the next it was the color of rust, then azure, vermilion, deep green, yellow-gold, and so forth.

I had come to my senses not far from the center of one of the broad tracks of smooth material that alternated with the strips of light. The closest of the latter began about fifty yards to my left, and they continued around the great cylinder in hundred-yard increments. As my vision began to clear, I saw that narrow pathways ran crosswise within the nearer lighted strips, most likely to make it possible to travel from one area of flooring to the next without treading on the source of the mysterious illumination.

With my mind already swimming in confusion, I could at first comprehend very little of my surroundings, and even after my eyes had grown accustomed to the phenomenon I still found it difficult to discern details in the chaos of throbbing colors. Raising my head to further inspect the tunnel's interior, I received another disconcerting shock: a person was standing on the wall several hundred yards above me, feet secured in some unseen fashion so that her body jutted out nearly perpendicular to the surface upon which she stood. Then, as I watched in amazement, the figure strode gracefully down the curving surface in my direction, using the pathways to pass through the illuminated strips that intervened.

"Kaor!" she called when we were within speaking distance, her voice echoing eerily up and down the tunnel amid the constant muffled hum. "I am pleased to see you awake."

I returned the greeting in a husky voice and struggled to a sitting position, though I was still too devitalized to rise to my feet.

"Here." She knelt by my side with a sympathetic smile and unstoppered a small flask. "This will help." Placing a hand behind my neck, she brought the bottle to my lips. Though I had some misgivings, I was too thirsty to be overly cautious and drank heartily. It was water, after all, though with a slight bite to it that hinted at some subtle addition, perhaps of spirits.

Almost immediately I felt renewed strength coursing through my body, as well as a sense of profound well-being. In half a minute I was able to clamber unaided to my feet.

In contrast to our fantastic surroundings, the woman appeared to be a quite ordinary specimen of humanity, with the beauty and timeless youthfulness of the typical Barsoomian adult, though her face was touched with a subtle weariness that bespoke the experience of many years. I say "appeared," because the unceasing play of lights made it impossible to properly appraise her features—nor did I know for certain that she was of the red race. Beneath the shifting polychrome veneer she could have been a representative of any of the several varieties of humans native to Mars—even a white-skinned thern, since the members of both sexes of that race commonly wear wigs to disguise their baldness. Unlike myself, she was clad from shoulder to knee in a thin tunic of lightweight material that seemed to have been constructed with a total disregard for style or proper fit, though she managed to wear it with a certain dignity. Like myself, she was also completely unarmed, a most unusual state for an adult anywhere upon Barsoom who was neither a slave nor a prisoner, which only served to confirm my growing suspicions as to the nature of this place.

"Welcome to the Perfect World," she said to me, her full lips curving in a smile in which I thought to detect a hint of sardonic humor. "Are you able to walk? If so, I shall conduct you to warmer climes." I was almost as disconcerted by her matter-of-fact manner as I was by my odd surroundings. My joints were still aching from ill use and the cold, but I told her I could manage, and we set off down the tunnel beneath the shifting lights.

Though my strength had returned with the draught from the flask, my mind seemed oddly sluggish. Perhaps oddest of all, I was not feeling particularly concerned to find myself in this untoward situation. I looked about with a mild curiosity as we walked, trying to piece together what information I could about the place as if it were an engaging puzzle to be solved, rather than a vital key to my own survival. While the floor beneath my bare soles felt like solid rock so smooth and polished as to suggest a volcanic origin, the lighted strips were of some irregular material that protruded from the surface like cobblestones. Meandering with my host to the edge of the nearest strip that I might examine it at close range, I beheld what seemed to be fist-sized nuggets of ore streaked with bands of glowing radium. The stones were swathed in a growth of luminous fungus upon which squirmed a host of tiny, sparkling creatures that I decided must be analogous to the glowworms I had glimpsed once in a tropical cave back on Earth. The three sources of illumination pulsed at different intervals, the combination producing an effect on the eyes and brain that was almost mesmeric. The visual onslaught was easier to bear from a distance, and after an initial close inspection I hastened back toward the center of the path. I noticed for the first time that the flooring itself bore intricate designs inlaid with metallic threads that might have been silver and gold, and I marveled at the workmanship that had produced artistry on so grand a scale. The woman had said nothing further as we strolled along, perhaps to allow me time to get my bearings. Finally I voiced the obvious question: "What is this place?"

"Your new home," she said, once again smiling broadly. "Welcome! From what I have been able to glean, your arrival has been long-awaited."

I pondered that unexpected statement as we continued on. Soon I began to notice that we were not alone in the tunnel, as I had first thought. Figures moved here and there on other strips of smooth rock—not only on the tunnel floor, but scattered around the entire inner surface of the great cylinder! Craning my neck, I saw that several individuals were making their way like ants on the ceiling directly above us.

I gestured to them in wonderment. "How are they doing that?" I asked.

She glanced upward. "The Masters have learned to bend the force of gravity to their will through a clever adaptation of the Eighth Ray. It is but the latest marvelous achievement in their ongoing preparations for the time to come."

Again, the unconcerned manner in which she spoke made her utterances seem all the more bizarre. Questions were accumulating in my mind, foremost among them how soon I might find my way out of the place and resume my search for my daughter, though the fog that persisted in my brain assured me that this was not an urgent mission. As I was for the moment naked and unarmed, I decided to hold my peace until I had gathered more information or until my fortunes had improved—especially in regard to armament.

As we walked on in silence, my attention was drawn to a series of large archways set into one side of the tunnel. I slowed to stare as I saw that each provided a glimpse into a chamber containing living beasts from different parts of the world, some familiar, all grotesque and strange. A pride of banths with ruffs of bristling quills surmounting their heads in place of manes prowled in one room, snapping their long jaws at us as we went by. None made any move to attack us, though the opening to their enclosure was blocked by no visible barrier. A single mammoth zitidar, the largest I had ever seen, glowered from another doorway, while a pair of huge, scaled reptiles of a type I had never before encountered circled each other warily in the next. Moving on, I was startled to see one of the so-called plant men, a species now almost extinct on Barsoom since the mass slaughter of their kind that had occurred following the overthrow of the Valley Dor. These fearsome monsters reproduce by growing their offspring on cords attached to their armpits; I could see two tiny replicas of the parent creature dangling at its sides when it paused in its grazing of the long-stemmed grass that floored its enclosure to regard us with its single great eye as we passed. The very next chamber was occupied by a dozen eight-legged things that looked to be more tree than animal, their rough, barklike integument dappled with small patches of flexing, leafy protuberances.

As we were passing between a pair of these fascinating zoological exhibits, I chanced to look over at the opposite side of the tunnel, where I glimpsed a row of much smaller circular designs. Before I could inquire as to their nature, my host led us across one of the nearby perpendicular pathways and then ushered me through another archway and out of the tunnel.

Here we found ourselves not among beasts, but in the company of other human beings, in a cavernous chamber whose walls and vaulted ceiling were, to my great disappointment, furnished with the same constantly altering illumination as the tunnel. No one was walking on the walls or ceiling here, however; scattered about the floor were several hundred men and women engaged in a variety of domestic tasks. After a few disinterested glances at our entrance they returned to their undertakings, and thenceforth ignored us.

It was noticeably warmer in here. Gazing around the chamber, I saw that my unadorned state was far from unique. Perhaps a quarter of the inhabitants, both male and female, were garbed like my companion in shapeless smocks or tunics extending halfway down their thighs; the rest were as bereft of covering as myself. Noting my appraisal, my host steered me to a section of the room where scores of shallow, T-shaped depressions of graduated sizes had been hollowed into the floor. A man approached laden with a large bale of some soft, silky substance. Setting it on a nearby table, he tore off several wads that he divided between a dozen of the molds, dropping down to his hands and knees as he smoothed the wispy material into a thin coating in each. Farther down the line, another worker was stooping to remove pairs of finished pieces from molds that had previously been lined. Setting one piece on a ledge of polished stone and then draping the second loosely on top of it, she kneaded the outer edges together with practiced motions of her fingertips until they adhered. After this, the completed garment was lifted, shaken out, and tossed on a pile corresponding to its approximate size.

As I was later to learn, the material involved was a form of almost indestructible silk produced by huge spiderlike creatures specially bred for the task. Legless and immobile, they spent their long lives in crowded enclosures, where they did nothing but eat and generate endless threads of the stuff. When compacted into one of the molds and left to cure for a day or two, these strands condensed permanently into a durable fabric.

My immediate surroundings were free of sharp protrusions, and warm enough to warrant no additional protection beyond one's own skin. I therefore felt no urgent need to clothe myself in one of the smocks, which possessed all the nobility of a potato sack. Even in my brain-numbed state, however, I recognized that such a covering could prove invaluable for the concealment of any potential weapon that might come to hand. Thus, when my host invited me to help myself to one of the just-completed garments, I did so, choosing from out of a stack of tunics one that had been augmented with a single, cockeyed pocket affixed to the left hip. I found the silken material not unpleasant against my skin, though the ragged seams formed by the mating of the two halves presented a decidedly rough and uncouth appearance, with numerous small gaps showing here and there. When I asked my host why they were not trimmed and sewn together to guarantee a better fit, she replied that needles and paring knives were as scarce and unnecessary in this place as would be daggers and swords. "All for the protection of the Numbers and the Hands, of course," she added with a languorous smile.

Though I was curious, I did not inquire as to what sharp implements or dissolving agents had been used to incise the molds for the tunics in the hard substance of the floor. At this point, it seemed more prudent to gather as much information as I could without inciting my new hosts to any unwanted speculation by a show of interest in items that might conceivably be used against them as weapons.

The pace of work at the surrounding stations was leisurely. As we moved through the room, I saw examples of containers and cooking utensils being molded from different materials, as well as various other implements whose purpose was unknown to me. If it was not a hive of enthusiastic activity, the chamber was at least filled with individuals working away steadily at a variety of strivings, though they did so blank-faced and mostly in silence. I asked my host how the tasks were assigned.

"Discerning judges of humanity such as myself evaluate the incoming stock and decide how each new Hand may best serve the Great Enterprise," she said in the same nonchalant fashion. "But do not fear—you will not be spending the rest of your days manufacturing smocks or spoons! In but a short while you will be taken before the Masters." Again I could ascertain from neither her countenance nor the tone of her voice whether she spoke with self-mockery or the earnestness of the fanatical convert.

"And how have you discerned that?" I inquired.

"Why, from your mark, of course," she responded, reaching for my left wrist and turning my hand over to expose the still tender palm. The caustic substance that had branded me stood out with a dull blackness even in the weird illumination, creating a lusterless design that reflected no light. "You have been designated for a scrutiny beyond that afforded most new arrivals."

"If that is the case, then I wish my hosts had chosen to hang a placard about my neck, rather than resorting to such a painful method of identification," I said.

"You are fortunate to have arrived when you did," she assured me. "In times long past such marks were applied using a much more powerful compound, which ate permanently into the flesh and, in contrast to the current transitory discomfort, never ceased to excite the bearer's nerves to agony. Indeed, before that it was customary to remove one or more fingers or even the entire hand as a means of special identification. You may still see those who have been so distinguished from time to time. Eventually, of course, the Masters realized the negative effect this had on the individual's capacity for efficient production and the practice was modified."

"How very considerate of them," I said. This remark earned me a quick sidelong glance from my host, but whether she accepted my sentiment on face value or suspected me of sarcasm, I could not tell. "When will I meet these Masters?" I asked in a milder tone. "And why do you suppose they have singled me out for their special attention?"

"Someone has no doubt already been dispatched to bring you to them. As for your second question—you would know the answer to that better than I. All I can imagine is that you are one who lived a life of significant import in the outer world, for rare nowadays is the arrival who arouses their interest to such a degree." She gave me an expectant look, but as I still had no idea of the extent to which I could trust her, I volunteered nothing, and after a moment we continued on our bizarre walking tour.

The chambers seemed to be arrayed like beads on a circular wire. Exiting through an archway on the opposite side from our entrance, we found ourselves in a nearly identical room, this one filled with tables and benches and the strong aroma of something that I decided after a moment did not smell much like food. Still quite thirsty, I paused to down a few more gulps of water out of a ladle from a communal basin. I was enormously hungry, but also feeling some doubts as to the nature of the offerings, which sat on large platters along the center of each table. At my host's repeated urging, I finally agreed to consume part of a small loaf of something that crumbled damply in my hand, for there were indeed no knives with which to subdivide it. I could not identify the substance, although its flavor was neither pleasing nor particularly disagreeable.

Another wave of calm washed over me moments later. Now I felt sure that the food and water had been tampered with, though the conviction did not disturb me in the least.

As we sat side by side on the bench, it occurred to me to attempt a probe of my host's thoughts. I found to my surprise that she had only the most superficial of mental shields. Her mind was as tranquil as my own, though I could gain very little information, other than that she was looking forward to the completion of this portion of her duties, so that she could return to some form of game or competition she had been observing.

I was on the verge of plying her with a random selection from my burgeoning storehouse of questions, when her face lit up at the appearance of someone in the doorway at the other end of the refectory. Urging me to my feet with obvious signs of relief, she handed me off to the newcomer with a bow and a broad smile of farewell.

My new guide was a tall, well-favored individual in a lopsided smock whose smile of welcome was more reserved. He placed his right hand on my left shoulder in the customary manner and I returned the greeting, just as if we were two acquaintances meeting on the Avenue of Ancestors in Greater Helium. Wondering if his mind was as casually protected as that of my original host, I sent out a questing thought as we departed the refectory, only to be met with the sort of impenetrable iron wall that typified an individual with perfect mental control.

He must have read my disappointment on my face and guessed what I had been about, for I saw that he was watching me from the corner of his eye with a slight smile. A moment later, his expression altered to one of puzzlement and he regarded me more speculatively. I wondered if he had decided to return the mental inspection and encountered the blankness that was my own inborn guard against mind-reading.

The next chamber was a good deal larger and furnished with workstations like the first. Most were located against the walls and too far away for me to figure out their purpose, other than that some sort of earthen disks were being manufactured at the nearest of them. My guide set out for the far doorway at a brisk pace, but after a few steps I laid my hand on his arm and drew him to a halt.

"Before you take me anywhere else," I asked him, "will you truthfully answer one question?"

The man regarded me silently for a moment. Then he nodded. "Of course."

"Have I been drugged? Is there something in the water or food I have been given since my arrival that is currently affecting my thinking?"

"Most assuredly. A powerful sedative is present in both the food and the water."

I stared at him. I had not expected such an easy admission.

"Adapting to one's new life here can be a challenge, especially at the outset," he went on. "Many new arrivals find the calming influence of the additives to have a benevolent effect. Of course," he acknowledged with a small quirk of his lips, "this also makes easier work for those of us who are tasked with welcoming the newcomers and getting them situated. Do you not wish to experience this artificial calm?"

"I do not."

He led me to a nearby stone bench. "Wait here, please." He disappeared back through the doorway to the refectory, emerging a minute later with an earthen goblet and a flask. He handed me the first. "Drink this and you will be free of the soothing agents in but a moment or two." He hefted the flask. "This is unadulterated water, should you desire something further to slake your thirst."

Stowing the flask in my newly acquired pocket, I downed the contents of the goblet, which were somewhat sweet, as if fruit juice had been used to mask a more acrid flavor. Seconds later I was looking around with a new keenness, as clarity flooded back into my brain.

I thanked him. "Now that I am in my right mind, I have a second question."

"I am not at all surprised," he said, eyebrows raised politely. "Ask away."

"Very well. Where are we and why have I been brought here?"

"These are actually two questions," he told me judiciously, "but I shall answer both. We are in a region of nine great interconnecting cavities lying some miles beneath the planet's surface. You have been brought here as a guest of the Oolscar—which is to say in plainer speech, as a valued captive of the Masters who rule this place."

Oolscar translates freely as "Ever-Below." While that title revealed little by itself, the term Masters had a decidedly ominous ring to it—and there was no ambivalence at all to the word captive.

I was on the verge of inquiring after the whereabouts of Talo Thoran, but thought better of it. There was always the possibility his own conduit had conveyed him to a different destination, and he had somehow eluded capture. If so, the last thing I wanted to do was initiate a search for him. Instead, I said: "The woman who greeted me in the great tunnel told me that I would be meeting these Masters before long. Is that where you are taking me now?"

"It is," said my guide. "Though along the way I aim to acquaint you with certain aspects of your new home." As had been true of his predecessor, this man's placid manner was at odds with the disquieting import of his words. "Shall we walk?"

I rose to my feet, considerably more on my guard than I had been scant minutes earlier, but determined to resist the growing urge to knock the fellow down and seek immediate egress from this insane place—at least until I had learned more about the forces that might bar my way. I was not yet sure whether my genial new guide was a prisoner of these Oolscar like myself, or if he did his Masters' bidding willingly.

We had gone only a little way when shouts of a heated dispute rang out from a knot of people clustered up ahead, not far from the center of the chamber.

My guide knitted his brows and lifted a hand. "Wait here," he instructed, then took off at a trot to the scene of the disturbance.

Deciding there was more to be gained by observing the interaction at close hand than by cooling my heels in the corner like a well-trained calot, I followed behind him at a slower pace. Several individuals faced one another in belligerent confrontation: three men on one side, a woman and two men—one of the latter almost seven feet tall and muscled like a bull—on the other. A growing crowd of workers had quit their stations to gather around them, maintaining a respectful distance of several yards as if to allow the six a sizable arena for the expected coming battle. Pausing just outside the circle, my guide raised his voice in commanding tones, though the throbbing hum that filled the place made it impossible for me to make out his words. Later I would learn that the sound was caused by the great fans that periodically drew air down from the surface here and elsewhere and sent it by means of the tunnel throughout the Perfect World. Whatever he said carried some weight, for the ring of onlookers parted at once for him to advance. Stopping not far from the would-be combatants, he addressed them in firm tones. His argument must have been persuasive: after a brief hesitation, all but the very large man and one of his opponents slunk silently away into the crowd. At another word from my guide, the smaller of the two remaining brutes winced, looked about anxiously, and then made to depart the circle as well. The big man stepped in his way, his broad face distorted by rage, and hauled him back with a massive hand on his shoulder. My guide edged closer and uttered a few more sentences in urgent tones, but the furious giant shook his head stubbornly.

The smaller man had taken advantage of the distraction to slip free of his grasp. With a roar of anger, the large man took a single step in pursuit, then suddenly stumbled as if from an unseen blow and collapsed to his knees with a hoarse cry. The crowd drew back even farther. The man struggled mightily to rise, sheer panic replacing the pugnacity on his face. Then he gave a shrill scream as his entire body seemed to fall in upon itself. There came a sickening crunch of bones, and blood spurted forth from several places. In another moment there was nothing left of him that resembled a human being—merely a perfectly circular, semiliquid outline on the stone floor. The crowd dissolved, the onlookers hastening back to their stations without a backward glance.

19

AMONG VERMIN

MY GUIDE STOOD for a moment with shoulders bowed. He turned around to find me standing just behind him. "I asked you to await me yonder," he said.

"Yes," I replied. "I heard you."

"Hm." He eyed me thoughtfully. "Well, perhaps it is best that you witnessed such a thing so early on. I hope you will not forget what happens when one refuses to heed the wishes of the Masters."

"It was an impressive lesson," I told him. "Tell me, did that terrible retribution come at your direct command? Are you yourself one of these Masters?"

He was momentarily startled out of his composure. Then his expression hardened beneath the shifting lights. *"I am not,"* he said with such heartfelt vehemence that I had no doubt he was telling the truth. After a moment he added more calmly: "I am merely one who understands the laws of cause and effect, and as best I can I attempt to pass along these insights to those who are fated to dwell here. The Masters abhor waste, and so they allow me some small measure of influence." He gestured to the horrid mess on the floor. "In this case, the man had reached his breaking point and traveled to a place where reason could no longer follow him. Now he is no longer a man, but a memory." As if released from some invisible barrier, the circular puddle of glutinous liquid suddenly began to stream outward toward our feet. He signaled to a nearby worker, who reluctantly fetched a bucket and a brush and fell to cleaning it up.

My guide proposed that we resume our tour. Newly aware of what my fate might be should I demur, I nonetheless presumed to

177

halt him again with a suggestion. "Before we continue, let us properly introduce ourselves. I am—"

But he raised his hand in a peremptory gesture before I could reveal my identity.

"In the interest of harmonious cooperation, we discard our former names, our races, our countries of origin, and a good many of our beliefs when we are brought below," he said, a new coldness entering his voice. "They have no meaning here and thus it is our custom to leave them in the outer world where they belong."

"I see. Then how do you identify each other when the need arises? I should imagine shouting 'You there!' and pointing a finger would become tiresome after a while, especially beneath these maddening lights."

"Indeed it would. Fortunately, you will soon be admitted to the hallowed ranks of the Numbered. I stand before you as Tor-ov Ov-tor, all the identification I require in this quite appropriately illuminated madhouse." He performed a mocking bow, his good humor quickly restored. "Pray do not be envious. Soon the Masters will take you for a thorough examination, after which they will deign to bestow a similarly descriptive appellation upon yourself."

In the Barsoomian common tongue, "Tor-ov Ov-tor" indicates the numerals "Four-seven Seven-four." I was reminded at once of the number-based categorization systems employed by the old Toonolian surgeon and onetime rascal Ras Thavas, originally to classify the unfortunate subjects of his fantastic medical experiments in the tower of horrors where he once traded in bodies and brains, until my countryman Ulysses Paxton put an end to the practice and persuaded him to apply his genius to more altruistic endeavors. Years later, Ras Thavas revived the system as a means of identification for the synthetic men he had begun producing en masse on the doomed island of Morbus, where each was supplied a numerical label according to the order of his emergence from the chemical vats that gave them life. Curious, I inquired whether my host's designation denoted that he was the 4,774th captive to have been taken by these mysterious Masters, a prospect I found chilling.

He shook his head with a mirthless chuckle. "If only that were the case, the suffering of this world would have been much decreased. Multiply that paltry figure by one million and you might approach a more accurate estimate. No, the Oolscar, both blind and deaf as we define such states, yet possessed of other means of perception far beyond our ken, assign to us each a numerical value which corresponds to our unique position on some abstruse vibratory scale mere humans cannot perceive. For myself, I am pleased to occupy the 4,774th niche on the spectrum of brain-wave oscillations perceptible only to their peculiar sensory apparatus. Naturally, the numbers by which they identify their chattels are as meaningless to us as they would consider the various pet names we have bestowed upon them over the years."

I lapsed back into silence as we walked on, chewing over these new morsels of information—most telling among them the fact that whoever the Masters were, they were not human beings.

The next room in which we found ourselves was considerably larger than the previous, and more natural cavern than chamber, with rough-hewn walls and vaulted ceilings pocked with small indentations and festooned with the same weird combination of radium ore and fungus crawling with glowing insects. The interior was subdivided by immense stalagmites rearing up from the floor, each decorated with intricate carvings so that they resembled sculpted pillars. Fascinated, I went over to examine one, leaving my host waiting patiently on the smooth pathway that wound through the rougher rock of the floor. I was hoping to find some recognizable designs among the ornamentation that would provide a clue as to the society that had sculpted them, but the reliefs, though beautiful and hauntingly familiar, were meaningless to me.

The constantly changing illumination made it difficult to track movement in the environment, and so I did not see the two who had followed us from the previous chamber, making their way stealthily from pillar to pillar, until it was almost too late. I turned just in time to see them race up and set upon my unsuspecting guide from behind, the man bludgeoning the back of Tor-ov Ov-tor's head with his doubled fists so that he fell forward onto the rough floor, while the woman darted in to crouch over him, a sharpened fragment of rock raised menacingly above her head. Scarcely pausing to think, I leaped the yards between us and disarmed her with a swipe of my hand, sending the makeshift dagger flying to shatter against the nearest stalagmite. I pivoted on my heel in time to meet the bellowing charge of the enraged man with a quick uppercut to the chin and had the satisfaction of seeing him go down like a felled ox. Grasping him by the neck of his tunic, I hauled him up with one hand and deposited him on his feet, where he stood swaying groggily at the side of his accomplice.

I quickly assisted Tor-ov Ov-tor to rise and we faced the attackers together. I recognized them as two of the recent disputants from the previous chamber, both allies of the dead giant.

The object of their assault was rubbing the back of his head. He regarded the pair for a long moment before speaking.

"Now then," he said at last. "You have chosen to take your exercise long before the appointed break period. Will you return to your stations and retain what is left of your lives, or shall I summon the Long-arms?"

The man had been looking sullenly back and forth between the two of us. Finally he threw up his hands and stalked back toward the previous chamber. The woman stood half-crouched, breast heaving with emotion. "From the moment he arrived, you never liked Thoatek!" she cried, jabbing a trembling finger at my guide. "This is why you allowed him to be taken from me."

"Truth be told, I do not like a single one of you," Tor-ov Ov-tor returned dryly. "Yet I did my best to persuade Dan-tel Dan-mak to set aside his grudge. You could read his disposition as well as I: he was poised on the brink and determined to hurl himself over it one way or the other."

At this, the woman clapped her hands to her cheeks and collapsed into wailing, gasping sobs. To my surprise, Tor-ov Ov-tor stepped forward and put his arm about her shoulders. "Go back to the tiling room, Il-tan Tee," he said softly. "Carry on with your work." He watched her stumble off with a weary look, and then turned back to me.

"You stood fifty feet away, inspecting that stele," he observed.

"Yet half a second later, here you were fending off their attack and hoisting Ay-Barmak into the air as easily as if he were a hair from a sorak's tail." He narrowed his eyes at me. "You are a most unusual person."

"That is because I am from another world," I said.

He responded with a crooked smile. "I am sure everyone feels that way upon their arrival below. And yet . . ."

"Or perhaps the light in here deceives the eye," I told him with a shrug.

He grunted. "Be that as it may, I am grateful for your swift action on my behalf. At the very least, you saved me from considerable discomfort."

"Why did your Masters not intervene and crush those two into pulp before they could assault you?" I inquired, as we began to walk again.

Tor-ov Ov-tor indicated the ever-changing lights on the ceiling of the cavern, which I now noticed showed dark gaps in a few spots here and there above the path. "From time to time, certain isolated areas are free from the Masters' vigilance, due to fluctuations in the nature of the luminous mixture. Inevitably, a few of the Hands and Numbers become familiar with these locations and learn where they may temporarily act unobserved."

My original guide had also used that odd nomenclature to describe the captives. At my query, Tor-ov Ov-tor explained that those who engaged in generalized manual labor in the caverns were referred to collectively as Hands, while the more specialized workers, those who received numerical labels from the Oolscar, were known as Numbers and granted the honor of sporting those ill-fitting tunics. Apparently the mark on my left palm, which I now realized had almost ceased to throb with pain, had accorded me the privilege of clothing myself even before I had been gifted with my very own string of numerals.

There were no workstations in this chamber. Following the path around another of the stalagmite pillars, we came upon a place where the floor of the cavern was pitted with large craterlike formations. As the pathway wound past the first of them, I was surprised to see a large number of men and women reclining within, a few propped up against the sloping walls while others sprawled on the rough rock floor. To a person they looked exhausted, drained, with half-closed eyes. Some of them were a good deal worse off than the others, their expressionless faces gaunt as skulls and their skin swollen and heavily scarred in places, almost as if they had been partially flayed. I noted an odd residue on the unclad bodies of several of them which sparkled in the shifting light as if they had been powdered with diamond dust.

The next depression held an even more disturbing display. It was crawling with vermin of many different sorts, from repulsive, dog-sized ulsios with their naked, bony jaws, to hopping skeetans sporting wide, humorous grins, and creeping insects of all varieties, including a large number of the sixteen-legged sacred worms known as sarovans for which I had an abiding dislike. Some of these last were giants of their species, stretching over four feet in length.

For all their ubiquity in the cellars of the red race, I had experienced over the years neither the occasion nor the desire to closely examine one of these revered pests, for they abhor bright light, the beam of a radium torch inevitably sending them skittering at top speed into the nearest dark crevice. The great size of these specimens only served to accentuate their loathsome appearance. Each worm had seventeen distinct segments, with pairs of legs occurring on every other section, and stiff bristles protruding in between. Both repelled and fascinated, I paused to survey the beasts, realizing for the first time that their bodies were divided laterally into two parts: a soft, almost translucent underbelly surmounted by a dorsal shell of pliable chitin that glimmered with oily iridescence under the fluctuating illumination. The gelatinous underside was webbed with wrinkles and dotted with irregularly shaped nodules of flaccid tissue, the shell festooned with warty excrescences. Both ends of the serpentine bodies were blunt and featureless, making it impossible to distinguish the head from its opposite unless the things were engaged in forward motion or, I imagined, feeding.

I was able to observe the second circumstance firsthand when we passed on to the third crater, where an even more unappealing sight awaited me, for this depression proved to be more of a grotesque dining hall for vermin than a mere social club like the last. Here snarling ulsios darted cautiously past large holes sunken into the rock. In about half the cavities sat rounded protrusions which I recognized with a start as the heads—or tails—of more and even larger sarovans. If I had thought the worms in the previous pit were giants, those who inhabited these tunnels must be classified as leviathans of the species; their blunt domes, which bore no discernible sensory organs, were easily twice the diameter of those of the previous crew.

As I stared on in disgust, an ulsio happened to venture near one of the holes, the resident worm appearing to take no notice of the ratlike interloper until the ragged creature was just above its den. Then it acted with terrifying swiftness, the head darting out beneath its prey and splitting open to reveal dozens of evenly spaced grasping mandibles curving inward over a complicated set of razor-sharp incisors. The mandibles yawned wide, then closed with an audible crunch about the ulsio's midsection. The captured beast struggled wildly, raising a terrible din as it was slowly but inexorably devoured by the hidden mouthparts burrowing into its belly. As I watched, the victim seemed to grow smaller and smaller in convulsive jerks, its blood fountaining outward, like a liquid-filled bladder being forcibly drawn through a narrow ring. I looked away. Ulsios are hideous beasts, with no redeeming qualities of which I am aware, yet it has ever been my tendency to throw my lot in with the underdog, and for once I found myself in sympathy with the lesser of two monsters. I pondered the consequences should one of the worms desire a change of fare and find its way into the crater we had first encountered with its complement of near-helpless men and women. Tor-ov Ov-tor, standing at my side, had observed my reaction.

"It is only during this brief stage while they lurk inside their holes that they consume flesh," he told me. "Their mandibles alter considerably as they continue to grow, and are employed for other purposes."

These monumental variations on the humble cellar worm appeared to be held in no less high regard here below the surface than their diminutive relatives were throughout the rest of Barsoom, and as we made our way across the cavern floor I glimpsed other craters wherein even larger versions of the grotesque creatures mingled freely with more of the reclining human captives. Indeed, I even saw one crawl right across the naked torso of a prostrate woman, who—though trembling violently, her eyes clamped shut and her face betraying her uttermost horror at the contact—did nothing whatsoever to escape the behemoth. My stomach turned to see the trail of glistening slime left behind on her flesh.

When I expressed my surprise at the beasts' gigantic proportions, Tor-ov Ov-tor informed me that the largest examples in this cavern were actually considered juvenile members of the particular species.

"If those are youthful specimens, I should not care to see their progenitors," I commented with heartfelt distaste.

"And yet you shall, ere long," he promised me.

20

THE NINE CIRCLES

S WE WENDED OUR WAY through what I had begun to think
of as the Chamber of Vermin, I began to notice my guide
casting distracted looks at the luminous ceiling, his brow creased
in thought. When I asked him what the matter was, he told me that
he had expected we would be summoned for my examination and
subsequent Numbering by now. Since we had not been called, he
decided we might as well extend our tour to the other cavernous
spaces that made up this underground realm.

I was relieved to depart the gruesome cavern. In addition to the
abundance of repulsive sights, the entire space reeked of a mixture
of unpleasant odors. We made our way quickly through two more
chambers, the first of these once again home to numerous workstations. In this case, great disks or lenses in a variety of peculiar shapes
were being fashioned out of what looked like volcanic glass. I was
unable to discern how the material was worked as we moved briskly
by, but the process seemed to involve the vigorous application of
chemical-soaked rags rather than heat. I supposed this made sense,
as the Masters would surely deem fire too potentially destructive a
force to be entrusted to the hands of their slaves. The last chamber
was another natural cavern containing sculpted stalagmites and
several large depressions in the rocky floor. I was relieved to see that
not a single one of the latter was currently occupied. Walking through
a low archway on the far side, we emerged back in the great tunnel
where I had originally regained consciousness—or so I believed,
until I saw none of the fantastic zoological exhibits I had glimpsed
upon my arrival. When I questioned Tor-ov Ov-tor, he directed my

185

attention three-quarters of the way around the cylinder above us, where I could just make out the series of archways. Even though I felt the floor of the tunnel as firmly beneath my bare soles as I had before, it seemed that we were now the ones walking on the ceiling!

I realized the hum that had formerly pervaded the tunnel and beyond had ceased, and the tunnel itself was no longer so cold. Tor-ov Ov-tor told me that the conduits housing mammoth fans alternated in drawing fresh air an unknown distance down from the surface and into the tunnel, whence it was distributed throughout the underground realm. He led me along a walkway and up to a section of the sloping wall upon which were incised a long row of circles similar to those I had noticed earlier. Each of these was marked with a different symbol, none of which meant anything to me.

"The caverns are separated from one another by several miles," he remarked. "And so, while it is possible to traverse the distance between them on foot, we shall employ a less time-consuming method." Motioning me to stand to one side, my guide touched his hand to a ceramic plate set into the wall. With a loud hiss, a metal tube about a yard in diameter extruded to a distance of just over a dozen feet into the tunnel, and a moveable lid slid back to reveal a hollow interior. Tor-ov Ov-tor stepped inside, lay down upon the floor with his legs stretched out toward the wall and his head resting near the center of the tube, and then instructed me to do the same in reverse, my own feet pointing into the tunnel, so that our heads practically touched one another. He tapped a panel at his side and the lid snapped shut, the capsule retreating with another hiss into the wall to leave us in utter darkness—a welcome relief after the constant assault of shifting lights, though I was somewhat appre-hensive about being shut up in the confining container. There was a second's pause and then the sense of great motion all around us.

After perhaps half a minute the conveyance halted, with no sense at all of having gradually slowed from a high velocity, and slid into place in its new berth with a dull click. The lid retracted and we climbed out. My guide was watching me closely—perhaps to gauge from my reaction whether I had been awed by this display of advanced technology. Separated by approximately seventy-five miles, the centers of Greater and Lesser Helium are connected by a not dissimilar pneumatic network, which whisks travelers from one metropolis to the other in mere seconds. And so, while I had certainly not anticipated the experience, any surprise I felt was merely at finding such a modern transportation system—still a rarity among the less advanced nations of the surface—in use down here, an unknown distance beneath Barsoom's crust.

We had emerged into a tunnel no less colossal than the one in which I had first found myself. The ever-changing illumination was in effect here as well, though I noted with some relief that the throbbing hum of the other place was also absent here.

Tor-ov Ov-tor informed me that the Perfect World, as the Masters named it, consisted of nine caverns, each of them laid out in circular fashion, and connected to one another to form a gigantic ring. We had begun in the Ninth Circle, which I later learned was the last constructed and a sort of catchall for the other regions, containing small manufactory areas, storehouses, and sleeping quarters for many of the workers, along with the place where new arrivals deemed worthy of becoming Numbers were judged by the Oolscar. In the end our tour encompassed only four of the Circles—five, including our starting point—using the transport cars to work our way in reverse order around the great ring.

The Eighth Circle presented itself as a collection of enormous indoor gardens branching off from the central tunnel. Tor-ov Ov-tor described it as a place of botanical experimentation and production, in which food crops and the raw materials for the various chemical additives were being cultivated beneath artificial skies. Each of the ceilings outside the tunnel was covered in luminous fungus that radiated a single rich hue, a slightly less off-putting alternative to the ever-changing lights found elsewhere. The archways leading from the central tunnel brought us out onto catwalks from which we could look out over seemingly endless fields of growing things, tended by naked Hands bathed in aquamarine, violet, or maroon illumination. After a few minutes, we returned to the pneumatic car and were sent hurtling on our way.

Our next stop was composed entirely of manufactories, including a collection of colossal caverns in which massive machine parts were being produced. The shifting lights were again in use here, and for the first time I glimpsed hundreds of captive green men and women— unmistakable with their towering stature and six-limbed physiques, no matter the vagaries of illumination. According to Tor-ov Ov-tor, they predominated among the Hands and Numbers in this Circle, due to the advantages afforded them by their superior height and extra set of grasping limbs.

The biological laboratories that composed the Sixth Circle were next on our agenda. As Tor-ov Ov-tor had previously told me, the Oolscar were a practical race, and very keen on producing to order, whether by means of scientific crossbreeding or surgical manipulation, those men and creatures they thought could best assist them. Apparently they allowed the Numbers who worked in this Circle to do some experimentation on their own, for along with great flying insects reminiscent of my glimpses of the sparkling malagath-like creature that had first abducted me in Bantoom, I espied many odd animal variants that seemed to have little useful application, including bizarrely modified creatures such as the spine-maned banths I had seen in the zoological displays back in the Ninth Circle. There were also a disturbing number of equally distorted humans—most of these, I was told, altered by some arcane means while still in the egg during those occasional periods when the Oolscar bred their captives like prized livestock. Among these I was surprised to see legions of the hulking, long-armed, hairy-faced beasts that had subdued me after my descent.

The laboratories and pens we observed teemed with a veritable catalog of other unspeakable monstrosities achieved by both inter-breeding and scientific wizardry, their only goal seeming to be the production of grotesque parodies of both animal life and humanity. I was both moved and sickened by the sight and only too glad to move on from the place.

When we exited the transportation tube in the next great tunnel, Tor-ov Ov-tor informed me that the Fifth Circle would be our final stop, the remaining four regions currently designated off-limits to those captives not directly employed in them. This Circle was the most unexpected of them all, for it was laid out as a series of large amphitheaters in which humans and beasts engaged in battle, while tiers of raucous Hands and Numbers cheered them on. Of the human combatants, only the Hands, deemed easily replaceable, were permitted to fight; of the animals, only captives from the outer world of which the Masters had grown tired, or those products of the laboratories judged unsuited for useful service made their way into the arenas, along with a selection of bizarre individuals that no longer seemed to belong to either category.

I was somewhat surprised to learn the Masters allowed their slaves to entertain themselves in this fashion during their rest periods, though upon reflection I imagined the principle of bread and circuses must be deemed as useful here as in other tightly controlled societies—especially when the bread was liberally dosed with drugs that kept the masses calm and biddable.

Having not yet received his summons from the Oolscar, Tor-ov Ov-tor was in no hurry to leave this realm. He led me to a prime vantage point in one of the arenas which had apparently been reserved for him, though those around us did not seem overly pleased by his presence. There my guide surprised me by wagering enthusiastically on the outcomes of several different matches by means of small, geometrically shaped, ceramic tokens he drew from his single pocket. These, he told me, could be redeemed in the dining halls in exchange for various amenities of food or drink not otherwise available to the human prisoners. The tokens themselves were manufactured in the Ninth Circle and distributed in equal quantity to the Numbers and Hands once every year—a chronological unit which was observed here underground just as it was on the surface, the term "cycles" being substituted for days. When I asked how the passage of time was marked down here where the sun could not be seen, my guide promised me that once I grew accustomed to life beneath the infernal lights of the Circles I would quickly learn to track the recurring progression of colors that elapsed during a day and soon find myself able to judge the time as well as did he. I said nothing, privately vowing that I would not spend enough time in this place to grow accustomed to anything about it.

Apparently the Masters did not deign to observe their slaves at play; the Circle of the amphitheaters was another area, like the fields of the Eighth Circle, where only a single richly colored illumination shone steadily down from the ceiling above each arena. While we observed the contests, all of which were fought without weaponry—or, in my opinion, any appreciable skill on the part of the human combatants—I plied my guide with questions about the various regions. I was most surprised to learn that the tour we had made had encompassed but a small sampling of the different areas to be found in a particular Circle, each of which was composed of many interconnected concentric rings clustered about its central tunnel. With a sinking feeling, I began to comprehend for the first time just how vast this underground realm truly was—and how replete with enslaved captives of various sorts, Tor-ov Ov-tor estimating the present total human population to be well in excess of one and a half million souls.

I looked around at my fellow captives as the matches played out. Though my guide had assured me it was the custom to leave one's race and place of origin at the door when entering the Perfect World, I saw sprinkled among the tiers of onlookers several whose hairless scalps proclaimed them to be therns, pale-skinned promulgators and beneficiaries of the false religion of Issus that had for thousands of years preyed on the other peoples of Barsoom. Though skin color was masked by the various forms of colored illumination, this feature marked them unmistakably, and I asked my companion how they fared among the other captives, since news of their dastardly deeds on the surface had presumably seeped into the Perfect World with the arrival of more recent prisoners. He told me that in fact many of the Hands and Numbers of both sexes chose to employ a depilatory powder which, when applied with water, removed all hair from the head and body for several months, preventing infestations of several strains of tiny vermin endemic to some Circles. Thus, even the one characteristic I had thought a foolproof method of racial or national identification was rendered immaterial.

Wagering was rife among the Hands and Numbers that crowded the stands, with designated agents moving constantly up and down the tiers of spectators to record bets and distribute winnings. Tor-ov Ov-tor confined his own wagers to those matches held between teams of opposing humans or among different strains of nonhuman creatures, assuring me that when humans were sent into the arena against the Long-arms or any similar artificially engendered species, the outcome was always the same—the humans quickly perished. When I asked him why any would then volunteer themselves for such matches, he replied with a sigh that death in the arena was but one of several ways available here for ending one's life when it no longer seemed worth living.

Most of the contests were fairly quick affairs. Tor-ov Ov-tor had wagered successfully on five matches and lost tokens on another two when he suddenly winced, his hand flying to his temple as if he had been stung by an insect. He informed me with a pained smile that the Masters inflicted these small jabs of discomfort as a means of communicating their basic wants to their Numbers.

We had been summoned to my examination.

21
JUDGMENT

WHEN WE NEXT CLIMBED from our car, we were back in the
Ninth Circle in the tunnel of my first awakening. A trio of
newly arrived valued guests of the Oolscar awaited us on the
pathway, along with a pair of the grotesque Long-arms. Tor-ov Ov-tor
went to address the two women and one man in soothing tones;
their unfocused gazes and muted responses suggested to me that
they had partaken of a goodly amount of the calming food and drink
I had been given upon my own arrival. I noticed they had not yet
been awarded their tunics, and I was the only one among the four
of us who had been gifted with a mark upon my palm.

Knowing now that they had been derived by scientific means
from human stock, I could not resist casting sidelong glances at
our brutish guards as they escorted us into the chamber Tor-ov
Ov-tor and I had last visited in this Circle. Their wedge-shaped
torsos were capped by massive shoulders from which arms knotted
with muscle depended to the floor, causing them to brachiate as
they walked, their shaggy heads and shoulders thrust forward in a
manner that called to mind the great apes of Earth. Their faces were
uniformly prognathous and more reminiscent of a bat than a man,
fanged and terrible with eyes that glowed in the shifting light. I
was by now convinced I had encountered their like long before I
ever came here. More than once I had glimpsed red eyes burning
atop hulking shapes in the darkness of the various dungeons in
which I had been forced to spend time over the years. Tor-ov Ov-tor
had told me when we visited the Sixth Circle of biological experimentation that a certain number of the Long-arms, both male and

192

female, that had been sent forth over the centuries on retrieval missions had failed to make their way back to the Perfect World when the Masters' hold on them had faded; it was believed these had multiplied and gone on to haunt the interconnected pits in many a city on the surface, where they preyed upon prisoner and jailer alike for their sustenance.

I saw with distaste that the nearest of the heretofore vacant depressions in the cavernous chamber was now crawling with a menagerie of verminous creatures, including three enormous sarovans, the largest I had yet seen. These wallowed near the pit's edge, nearly covered by a constantly moving tide of slinking ulsios, hopping skeetans, skittish ollcos from the far north, and countless other crawling and skittering creatures. When we halted at this crater rather than continuing on to one of the other chambers, I wondered incredulously if the vermin had been deposited there so that they might be evaluated along with the rest of us—or, conversely, if those among us who failed to live up to expectations during the examination of our brain oscillations would simply be toppled over the rim and fed to them as entertainment for the watching Masters. As if in confirmation of my second supposition, the Long-arms herded us up to the very edge of the pit, where the great centipedes lay in a roiling, grotesque array beneath their cloaks of lesser pestiferous creatures, their obscenely bloated bodies undulating and the small nodules on their bellies trembling at our approach. I covered my mouth and nose with my hand; the unpleasant miasma of odors was now present in this chamber as well.

For all their exposure to the calming drugs, my fellow newcomers had begun to fidget and glance about in nervous anticipation, and even the imperturbable Tor-ov Ov-tor looked tense.

I felt a growing unease myself. What if the Oolscar peered within my soul and found me wanting in whatever attributes were required to attain the benefits of a Number? Would they decide simply to dispose of me, as they seemed ready to do with so many of their subpar experiments and superfluous Hands? Just behind our little row of examinees, the Long-arms towered like a pair of hideous statues to either side of Tor-ov Ov-tor, who waited with his head bowed as if in prayer. Still, I told myself, there were only two of the beast-men in attendance. My muscles taut and at the ready, I scanned the surroundings as we awaited the arrival of the Masters, determined to sell my life dearly if this was in fact to be an execution party.

After about five minutes of unmoving silence, the guards abruptly stirred. Reaching their elongated limbs forward, they seized my three companions by the shoulders and led them back toward the tunnel of the transport cars.

Had the others passed the test and earned their numerals? I studied the rippling lights in the ceiling above us, wondering if the evaluation was being conducted by whatever surveillance mechanisms the Oolscar had concealed in the illumination, and if the Long-arms would soon return to take me away as well—or to pitch me into the noisome crater.

Tor-ov Ov-tor had remained motionless while the guards conducted the trio from the chamber. Now he raised his head in obvious perplexity. Squinting through the lights, I fancied that even the worms were looking agitated as the wave of vermin began to move in a writhing tide to the other side of the pit, perhaps irritated by the tiny creatures that hopped and scampered across their backs as they attempted to crawl away. Tor-ov Ov-tor stepped forward to my side and watched the retreating monsters with a look of deep confusion.

"I do not understand what just occurred," I said.

"Nor do I," he said slowly. "It is almost as if the Masters could not see you."

"And this surprises you?" I asked. I turned to scan the ceiling again. Were the Oolscar still there, judging me from afar in one of their secret Circles, through the radiation generated by the weird lights? "You said that all of them were blind."

"Yes, blind as we understand such things. But as I also explained to you, the Oolscar rely upon their own unique senses to perceive the world. Though they cannot read our actual thoughts, they identify and track humans by the activity within our brains—and even the most potent mental shield is as nothing to their probing minds. And yet—" He paused as if a new thought had occurred to him. "Forgive me if I intrude upon your privacy . . ." Taking a step back, he raked me with his gaze, as if searching for some overlooked clue. His eyes widened. "You have a very strange mind!"

I grinned. "So I have been told. Perhaps now you will believe that I am not from this world."

He made no response, peering down at the rocky floor again as if lost in thought. When he raised his eyes I saw disbelief in them, mixed with a dawning hope.

"But this has never happened before!" He turned about in a slow circle as if he had forgotten where we were, and then pointed in the direction of the other chambers. "Come—I must consider the ramifications of such a momentous event."

We made our way back through the room where the great lenses were being shaped and polished, Tor-ov Ov-tor looking about apprehensively as we crossed the chamber. Though no one appeared to be paying us any mind, I could see from the clenched muscles in his jaw that it was costing him a great effort to maintain a moderate pace, when it was obvious that he wanted to be racing along the path.

We passed through the next chamber in similar fashion. When we were almost to the doorway of the tiling room, I saw that one of the poor souls I had previously observed lying spent on the bottom of the first crater had somehow managed to drag himself up and over the rim. As we neared, he rose to his feet, shambled across the rocky floor, and fell to his knees directly before us.

My guide had been looking back over his shoulder. I nudged his side.

Tor-ov Ov-tor started at the sight of the kneeling man as if at a viper coiled in our path. Coming to an abrupt halt, he seemed on the verge of heading us back the way we had come; then he glanced to one side and flinched again as if at a blow. I followed his gaze to see that one of the huge sarovans from the crater where our supposed judgment had been enacted was now creeping across the rocky floor of this chamber, and seemed to be making its way toward the man blinking stuporously up at us. Not sure whether this specimen was advanced enough in development to have set aside its carnivorous proclivities, I stepped forward at once and interposed myself between the two, prepared to fend off the loathsome creature with my bare hands if it came to that. Tor-ov Ov-tor grasped my arm.

"No! Stay back!" he said urgently. "Go quickly now and stand behind that pillar. Do not let yourself be seen and I pray you not to interfere, no matter what you may witness." Seeing my reaction to being ordered about in such peremptory fashion writ plainly upon my face, he addressed me in a quieter tone, his voice shaking with conviction: "Trust me, I will explain it all to you when I can—but you must not interfere or more lives than your own will be in danger."

It has never been my nature to hang back when an obvious threat arises, but the passion in the man's voice was such that I heeded his entreaty and moved swiftly to stand behind the ornate pillar several yards away, confident that the cover offered by the shifting lights would allow me to peer around its edge without being apprehended by the man swaying drunkenly on the cavern floor.

What I next beheld filled me with horror and disgust, and sorely tested my resolve to honor Tor-ov Ov-tor's wishes.

While I took up my station behind the pillar, the great worm, its long body moving sinuously and with an almost serpentine grace, had crept slowly up behind the kneeling man. My hands tightened into fists at my sides as it suddenly reared up behind his quaking head, mandibles spreading and wide mouth agape.

Things happened swiftly after that. The wrinkled tissue of its underbelly fanning out to form something like the hood of a king cobra, the monster dropped down to envelop the back of the poor fellow's head, shoulders, and upper torso in a translucent cloak, the pathetic object of its attentions flinching at each new point of contact. The creature further extended itself over the man's skull until the upper rim of its flexible maw rested against his forehead just below the hairline, the topmost pair of mandibles curving about his brow like outlandish curls. The man jerked as if at the bite of an animal when their points sank into the flesh at his temples, though no blood came trickling forth to indicate that they had punctured his skin. With a gurgling cry, he thrust shakily to his feet, the worm draping itself over his back as he rose and its soft, gelatinous tissue oozing forward in undulating pulses around his bare torso, until it seemed he wore a slick, shiny cloak that stretched over the rear portion of his body from the crown of his head to his heels before trailing off several feet behind in a grotesque train. Then, with another sickening pulse, the front surfaces of his body were covered as well, as the creeping substance flowed in from both sides to join seamlessly across his chest and groin, and then enrobed both arms and legs in filmy sheaths, the worm's own spindly limbs curving around to tightly grip the quivering flesh beneath. Riveted, I squinted through the play of colored lights to see that the flaps of worm-skin had thinned on the victim's face, so that small openings now appeared over his eyes. A third aperture yawned as his mouth suddenly gaped open beneath the cloudy face mask and he took in a shuddering breath.

Tor-ov Ov-tor had been standing by in a posture of incongruous dignity during this revolting procedure. Now he stepped forward and, after an obsequious bow, addressed the pitiful captive. I was too far away to hear his words, yet when the man turned to look at him, I saw with amazement that the earlier terror had vanished completely from his face, to be replaced behind the thin, gelatinous mask by a supercilious sneer.

The two conversed for about five minutes, their exchange punctuated by a series of sharp gestures on the part of the transformed man, and much nodding and placatory posturing from Tor-ov Ov-tor. When the former made an abrupt sign of dismissal in the midst of a statement from my guide, Tor-ov Ov-tor at once performed a second low bow and took several steps back from the hideously burdened creature. Some instinct warning me, I ducked back behind the shattered pillar just as the worm-man turned his head in a slow, suspicious arc to scan the chamber. When I peered out a moment later, he had sunk back to the filthy floor, where he now crouched on all fours in a pose of bestial abasement. His glistening second skin was racked by shuddering waves, and then the worm slowly detached itself from his body and oozed back onto the floor, heaving and twitching as it separated from its host and gradually resumed its normal dimensions. Bristles waving, the creature crawled sinuously away in the direction of one of the farther craters. Once free, the man uttered a series of hoarse grunts and toppled over onto his side. His chest was heaving and I saw that the skin above his spine now sparkled with those same bright pinpoints I had noticed before among the men and women in the craters. With painful slowness, he half crawled, half dragged himself back over the rim and down into the nearest depression to once again sprawl upon its floor.

I was staring at the abhorrent spectacle with such rapt attention that I did not realize Tor-ov Ov-tor had slipped away at the end of the audience to take a circuitous route past several stalagmites and come up next to me. I started when he spoke, turning to find him standing close by my shoulder behind the pillar.

"I thank you," he said earnestly. "Things would have gone badly for us all had you made your presence known."

"Badly?" I echoed with incredulity. "How much worse could they have gone—especially for that poor lunatic?"

"Horribly worse," he assured me.

The ghoulish exhibition had worn on my already taxed nerves and I was losing my tolerance for his cryptic comments. At this point, my mind was rife with weird suppositions. Was this some brand of parasitic feeding rite imposed upon the captives in the craters by the watching Oolscar? Or, conversely, did the denizens of this hellish place assume increased stature among their fellow inmates through the repulsive act of draping themselves in holy vermin the way a jeddak might don a royal cloak?

"What exactly was the purpose of that extraordinary spectacle?" I demanded. "Is that wretched man your superior? Why did he permit the monster to crawl upon him in that hideous fashion? And why then did he appear to admonish you?"

"That Number is Hel-tee Bar, to his own profound misfortune one of the Masters' current favored instruments. The Oolscar are trying to ferret out the whereabouts of their latest prize—that is to say, yourself. Apparently they hold you responsible for an impressive list of crimes committed against their vital interests, though I was given no details. Suffice it to say that a grimmer fate than mere cataloging awaited you had they been aware of your presence just now." He took in a deep breath and looked me in the eye. "My many years spent languishing in this place have furnished me ample time to hone my skills at judging my fellow man, and I seldom err in my estimation of an individual's integrity. Thus, prompted by your earlier actions on my behalf and my general impression of your character, I took a great gamble just now and claimed that you had mysteriously slipped away earlier while I was dealing with the disturbance in the tiling room, and that I not seen you since. I believe I have convinced it, at least for the time being, though it is a suspicious old thoat."

I was further confounded by this explanation, as well as by the notion that I had ever before encountered an Oolscar, much less knowingly caused one harm. "Was this Hel-tee Bar individual referring to myself? But he had just seen us together with his own two eyes! He watched me scurry off behind this pillar."

"Only Hel-tee Bar saw us together," Tor-ov Ov-tor said with weary patience. "Thanks to your prudence just now in remaining out of sight, no Master has yet to see you with anyone's eyes."

I scowled. "I am sick to death of riddles, man," I told him. "If you expect my further cooperation in your deceptions, I think you had better let me in on exactly what is happening here."

"Yes, I believe that time has arrived," said Tor-ov Ov-tor. Wincing suddenly, he touched his palm to his right temple. He squinted up at the ceiling, seeming to glean something meaningful from the ever-changing play of colors. "I am called now to sort out those recently Numbered, but I will answer all of your questions in but a short while."

We retraced our steps quickly, Tor-ov Ov-tor continuing to display more nervous excitement than I had previously seen from him. He halted a few feet before the opening to the tiling chamber. "We must part company beyond this archway. I shall use another exit along the side wall just inside the door that will conduct me to the next outermost ring, while you continue on to the place where you first ate and drank. There will be small bins of round cakes against the wall that are free of additives, should you wish more food, and you have your flask if the sight of the water tempts you."

"Where shall I find you?" I asked. "And for that matter, how will I know when the time is nigh? I have yet to discern a clock face among those throbbing lights."

"I will seek you out. Now go, and try to lose yourself among the Hands and Numbers in the refectory. Speak as little as possible and look no one in the eye. Conceal the mark on your palm, and do not remain too long in one area."

But we were not yet free of the vermin that seemed to infest the place. As we stepped toward the archway, one of the larger sarovans, a bloated beast about ten feet in length, glided suddenly out from behind a stalagmite. I could not tell if it was the same creature that Hel-tee Bar had allowed to enfold him, or one of its kin. Tor-ov Ov-tor froze in his tracks as it slithered directly into our path and settled its coils there as if preparing to enjoy a long nap.

The comment concerning food had reminded me that I had not eaten anything substantial since my abduction an unknown number of hours ago. In addition to being famished and not a little baffled, I was about fed up with this universal worm worship, and in no mood to kowtow to one of the baser representatives of the animal kingdom when its inconvenient bulk was delaying me from finding a place to sit down for a bit, before whatever villains ruled this hellish place finally saw fit to make their presence known to me.

I had drawn back my foot, intending to encourage the creature out of our way with a swift kick to that area of its gelatinous underbelly I had identified as its fundament, when my guide stepped quickly in front of me. "What are you doing?" he cried, a look of horror distorting his handsome features.

"Forgive me," I said dryly. "I have never quite adjusted myself to the notion that an overgrown centipede should enjoy such exalted status, no matter what holy tree it dropped from at the dawn of time. I will not deny that these great creepers are more physically imposing than their diminutive counterparts, yet to me they remain not deities, but loathsome vermin, regardless of whether they are the precious pets of your mysterious Masters. And now you may add blasphemy to my lengthy list of supposed crimes."

"Blaspheme all you like," Tor-ov Ov-tor told me. Taking me

firmly by the elbow, he led me in a wide circuit about the lounging serpentine creature and quickly through the archway. "Just do not do it in a manner that will likely get you killed before I have concluded your introduction to this abominable place, or I will regret the time I have squandered acting as your guide."

"Killed!" I repeated incredulously. "By whom, and for what reason? You told me earlier that those wicked mandibles are no longer used to inflict harm when the worms grow to such gargantuan proportions, and I am certainly not about to invite one of the things to drape itself across my back. Does that glittering slime they spew contain a venom—or do you, your gods, and your masters love the crawling pests so profoundly that abusing one would cause the lot of you to turn against me?"

The man regarded me with disbelief.

"You have not yet guessed?" He gestured behind us at the lolling monster. "Those crawling pests, as you deem them, are the Oolscar, and they are both our Gods and our Masters."

22
GODS AND MASTERS

WITH THAT OUTRAGEOUS statement ringing in my ears, I watched in stunned silence as my guide ducked swiftly through the nearby doorway and I was left to my own devices.

I forced myself to move casually through the tiling room, wondering if the two workers who had assaulted my guide were still here, and whether they might recognize me under the distortion of the changing lights and attempt to chastise me for my earlier behavior, thus calling down upon us all further retribution from the Masters. Eager to put as much distance between myself and what I had now been told were the devils in charge of this infernal prison, I continued on to the refectory, where I selected one of the small, hard cakes Tor-ov Ov-tor had certified as untouched by tampering, and sat myself down at the most sparsely occupied table to gnaw at it, trying my best to look like someone who had been down here rubbing shoulders with my fellow inmates for many years. When others came to sit nearby, I waited a minute or two and then made my unhurried way to the other end of the chamber, where I repeated the process in a new venue. On my third such move I became aware that a tunic-clad man sitting at a table by the wall was watching me covertly from the corner of his eye. He changed his own seat twice before finally coming over to me.

Leaning with his hand on the table's edge a few feet from where I sat, and reaching down as if to brush something from the sole of his bare foot, he said in a low voice: "You are as jumpy as a skeetan! But never fear: Tor-ov Ov-tor has sent me to collect you. When I leave here, you must wait a few moments and then follow me, but do not make a show of it."

I nodded my understanding. After a moment he stretched out his arms with a prodigious yawn and strolled toward one of the smaller archways. I counted out half a minute, then rose and crossed the room toward the food bins, where I seemingly thought better of a second helping and turned with a shrug toward the same portal.

He was waiting for me outside the archway. We ambled along as if unaware of each other's presence until he passed through yet another doorway into a narrow corridor. Here he looked about quickly, then signaled for me to catch up. He conducted me several yards along the corridor to a stretch of rough wall, where he halted. Once more checking to make sure no one had followed, he motioned me to stand directly in front of him, so close that I could feel his nervous exhalations upon my neck. He hesitated for just a moment, then seemed to make up his mind and reached past me to touch the wall in several places in rapid succession. A four-foot-wide section of the featureless rock before us turned noiselessly on a central pivot, whereat the man grasped me by the shoulders and thrust me through the narrow opening before it swung back into place. With the door once more shut, we stood in total darkness.

He took my arm and guided me along for another several paces. I could hear the soft sound of his hand brushing along the wall while he counted beneath his breath, before he drew me to stand in front of him again and tapped the wall.

This time we found ourselves in a long, narrow, curving room that paralleled the passage we had just traversed. The interior was illuminated in a deep emerald green that emanated from the fungus-clad ceiling, untroubled by winking glowworms and similar to the rich, unvarying hues I had encountered earlier in some of the other Circles.

"Kaor. I am called Bor-ay-bor," said the man. "Tor-ov Ov-tor has told me little about you beyond the peculiar incident that occurred at your Numbering. Apparently, he now deems you to be a person of potential value to our cause." He eyed me with a measuring gaze. "For decades he has carefully observed the new arrivals, selecting to bring into his confidence only those in whom he felt the utmost faith. Yet never has he admitted one so quickly to our ranks."

"I am hopeful his judgment of me is sound and I can indeed contribute to your cause, Bor-ay-bor—once someone enlightens me as to its exact nature," I replied. "As for introductions, I am afraid I cannot tell you what number I occupy in the Masters' brain-catalog, for the fickle worms have not seen fit to award me one—but my name is John Carter."

I thought the man's eyes would start from his head. "John Carter!" he cried, bending close to peer into my face through the emerald light. "But I am San Tothis of Gathol! I commanded the *Vanator*, the Gatholian cruiser which at the behest of our noble jed Gahan set off from Helium in search of your daughter upon the fateful night of her disappearance, lo these many years ago. Tell me, Prince, was she ever found?"

Touched that this was the first question he had for me, I assured him that she had been, by Gahan himself, and that she had thereafter resided in Gathol as his beloved mate for many years.

"But what of you, San Tothis?" I asked. "The *Vanator* was assumed destroyed with all hands more than three decades ago, though its wreckage was never recovered. How came you here?

"Our ship was borne to the earth by the wild winds and its crew set upon by monsters and taken prisoner. Some have since perished in this accursed place, yet many still live," he said. "They will be as thankful as am I to learn that neither the princess nor our great jed fell victim to that foul experiment of the Oolscar!"

"Experiment?" I echoed in puzzlement.

"Surely you recall the mighty gale into which the Princess Tara went flying. That fierce tempest, whose like had never before swept the surface of Barsoom, was no natural occurrence, but a creation of the destructive atmospheric engines of the Oolscar, built with the assistance of those they snatched from above to serve them as their clever hands and scientific minds."

I had questions about those engines, having recently been on the business end of them myself. Before we went any further, I asked San Tothis if there was a chance we were under the watchful eyes of the Masters in this room. He assured me that, like the fields in the Eighth Circle and the arenas in the Fifth, this chamber was secure against the Masters' direct surveillance, due to the fact that the illumination from the ceiling was provided only by a single strain of monochromatic fungus, rather than the queer mixture of light sources common to other areas. He did not know whether this space and others like it had been deliberately designed to provide a refuge from observation, nor who had crafted the secret ways that provided these havens between the rings of this Circle.

"If what Tor-ov Ov-tor told me is true, even were the Oolscar somehow able to peer into this chamber, they would perceive naught but myself," he added in a wondering tone. "Can it be true that you are invisible to the worms?"

I spread my hands. "I have only just arrived here in this mad place," I told him. "I have no more to go on than what Tor-ov Ov-tor and now you yourself have told me. For the time being, my main concern is figuring out a way to shorten my stay here—and that of the rest of the inmates, as well—though I will probably need the help of others to accomplish this."

I watched San Tothis' hand fly to his hip as though a scabbard still hung there. "Old habits die hard, John Carter," he said with a sheepish grin, "but if I still possessed a sword, you may rest assured both it and my undying loyalty would now lie at your feet. There are many of us here who would be yours to command in any effort against the Masters!"

At that moment our conversation was interrupted as the nearby wall turned silently again on its pivot and Tor-ov Ov-tor and another man stepped quickly through.

Tor-ov Ov-tor was carrying a small parcel. Pausing to identify his new companion as Helten En, he headed for a storage closet at the far end of the chamber to prepare us some food and drink. When he had gone out of earshot, San Tothis remarked in a low voice that although Tor-ov Ov-tor was adamant our previous names and allegiances not be used in the Perfect World, not all of his followers adhered strictly to that rule—especially those who had known one another in their previous lives. "This is John Carter, Prince of Helium and Warlord of all Barsoom," he told Helten En. I saw the other man's brows shoot up in surprise and he turned me a quick, calculating look, but before he could confide his own true name Tor-ov Ov-tor had returned with a platter of cold usa and some earthenware goblets of water, and the four of us tucked into the first meal of honest victuals I had been offered since my awakening in the great tunnel. The emerald-tinted room contained no furnishings, so we hunkered down to sit cross-legged on the rock floor as we ate. We were barefoot and wearing only our ragged smocks, yet the four of us might as well have been clad in jeweled leather and seated on cushioned chairs to enjoy a feast in the palace of a jeddak, for how much I savored the meal and the friendly company. Rarely had humble usa tasted so fine!

There were no utensils to accompany our repast. A few minutes later I licked my fingers clean as I lifted my eyes to the other three.

"Now," I said. "Might someone be so good as to enlighten me on a few points? I am especially interested to learn how sixteen-legged worms went from infesting the dank pits beneath our houses to assuming rulership of an underground kingdom—not to mention by what means we may swiftly divest them of their royal offices and find our ways out of this place."

San Tothis and Helten En exchanged guarded glances at my flippancy, while Tor-ov Ov-tor gave a little frown. He told me first that he had asked Helten En to accompany him to our clandestine meeting because of his work as supervisor in one of the horticultural rings located in the Eighth Circle, this granting him access to various chemical additives and thus the wherewithal to remove the identifying mark from my palm. The quiet man took a small vial from his pocket and indicated that I should stretch out my left hand to him.

"It is an unpleasant procedure," Tor-ov Ov-tor warned me. "Perhaps attending to our tale will help distance your mind from the discomfort."

He had not exaggerated. I gave a small jump when Helten En applied the first droplet of solution to my skin, and then set my jaw while he dabbed meticulously with a slender stylus for the following several minutes.

Tor-ov Ov-tor tented his fingers in his lap like a judicious scholar and began. The incredible story he went on to relate, with occasional interjections from San Tothis, did indeed help to divert my attention from the ordeal, and a few hours later my hand was back to its normal state, albeit a bit swollen for a while and tender to the touch.

What they told me had been pieced together over many years by the human captives in the underground realm, with information garnered both from the worms themselves and from those who had served them the longest.

According to their own beliefs, the Oolscar had indeed been among the original beings to find themselves dangling in pods from the Tree of Life some twenty-odd millions of years ago. After finding their way down to the surface of Barsoom—and then swiftly into the crevices that led beneath it—they had lived as near-brainless animals for an unknown period of time before being taken in hand by a race of godlike beings who awakened them to sentience, imbued them with great longevity, and started them on the path to their own strange subterranean civilization. For a long time they lived contentedly in nearly airless pockets below the ground, having little intercourse with the surface world due to their aversion to natural sunlight and the deleterious effects that prolonged exposure to oxygen now had on their altered forms, which gradually lost the ability to see and hear, but gained other strange senses as they aged. Their beloved gods, who continued to visit them periodically in their underground retreats to teach and enlighten, promised to deliver them to a paradise of their own one day: a dark and airless world where they would be free to roam as they liked beneath the stars. Alas for the worms, this day never arrived. Instead, there came a terrible time when the gods departed but did not return, though the decades and then the long centuries rolled by.

Callously abandoned, as they saw it, the worms at last decided to assume the role of gods themselves, believing this to be no less than their destiny. If they were not to be granted their dark paradise aboveground, they must create it themselves down below, they decided—and to accomplish this they would need members of other species to serve them in substitution for the various sensory organs and manipulating appendages they lacked.

For many thousands of years they took what they needed from above, working with the hands and eyes of others to reshape their underground kingdom and extend its reach until it encompassed the supposed Perfect World they inhabited today.

It occurred to me as I listened that I might have been more skeptical of some aspects of this tale—particularly the assertion that the worms did not require the consumption of oxygen to sustain their lives—had I not already been familiar with the kaldanes of Bantoom, who also claimed to exist happily without the need to breathe. I did, however, have other questions.

"So they have always abducted men and beasts from the surface?" I inquired. "How has this never come to light?"

"Because, with but a few exceptions, they have been most careful to keep it in the dark," Tor-ov Ov-tor replied. "In ages far beyond the reckoning of any surviving civilization, they ruled openly. However, since the worms have always been few in number, and because as they aged the air itself choked them, while the rays of the sun filtering through the atmosphere burned and disoriented them, they eventually renounced active participation in the affairs of the surface and kept themselves scrupulously hidden from those above. Thus were the Oolscar born—those who are ever below, yet never seen."

He went on to tell me that the worms had never relinquished the idea of gaining a world of their own, where they might come forth to sprawl on barren rock for all eternity. With their immense life spans, they viewed time differently from other creatures and were capable of great patience, most of their number content to remake their underground strongholds as congenial biding places while they waited for the outer world to die, as all worlds must.

Two altered factors tested their patience.

Having witnessed the gradual dissipation of most of the world's surface water, the Masters were confident that the breathable air would follow suit in another million years or so. The discovery by the red race of a method of sustaining the atmosphere of their dying planet on the very eve of its extinction came as a great surprise to the worms, for they had paid little attention to the advancements of the surface civilizations from which they drew their chattel. While most of the Masters considered this to be a minor inconvenience, capable of extending the dying planet's life by only a few more hundreds of thousands of years, an impetuous minority had hatched a plan to render the lone Atmosphere Plant inoperable. This was not accomplished overnight. Slowly they collected the necessary supplies from the surface, dispatching their agents to bring below scientists that might be forced to aid them in interfering with the functioning of the single vital plant and ridding the planet once and for all of the air that sustained life for those who dwelled on the surface, while also rendering it increasingly inimical to the Oolscar. Then, on a single fateful day, their operatives assassinated both the Keeper of the Atmosphere Plant and his sole replacement, the two men whose responsibility it was to maintain the system of great pumps that now alone ensured a sufficient quantity of air for the billions of humans and beasts that covered the surface. At the same time, others traversed secret tunnels up from beneath the mighty structure itself to fatally disable those pumps. The deadly plan almost succeeded, being thwarted at the very last instant only by the timely intervention of a man who had mysteriously come into possession of the telepathic key to the impenetrable gates of the Atmosphere Plant, and was thus able to grant entry in the final minutes before extinction to engineers who then staggered inside and restarted the equipment.

(At this point, San Tothis shot me a meaningful glance from his place slightly behind the others. He, at least, knew full well that the personage alluded to by Tor-ov Ov-tor—he who by the grace of Fortune had been able to intervene in time to save the world from suffocation on that grim day—now sat before them on the rough stone floor!)

The failed attempt on the Atmosphere Plant was not in itself sufficient to persuade the majority of the Oolscar to step up their timetable.

From the beginning, fashioning their Nine Circles below the surface had required a constant flow of slaves from above. Thanks to the unwitting collaboration of the Holy Therns, for a very long time the worms were able to obtain a nearly unlimited supply of fresh Hands by the simple means of siphoning off a small percentage of those tens of thousands who yearly made the final voluntary pilgrimage down the subterranean tributaries of the River Iss to their own imagined paradise in the Valley Dor. These were men and women already counted among the dead by those they had left behind, while the therns who harvested them for slavery and worse in the Blessed Valley had no way of knowing that a portion of their own steady supply of human fodder was being pilfered en route by the Oolscar from the very banks of the River of Death. This system, which for millennia had worked well for all concerned excepting the victims, was all but halted once the shocking betrayal of the therns and the perfidy of the false goddess Issus was revealed to the world.

(Here I earned another significant look from San Tothis, for by some cosmic coincidence I had also been the author of that world-changing revelation.)

After that, Tor-ov Ov-tor continued, all but the most fanatical followers turned away from the age-old traditions, and what had for eons been a flood of willing travelers down the underground water-ways diminished to a mere trickle of stubborn zealots.

A small faction of the worms, no longer content to wait out the long years of Barsoom's lingering death, had already attempted to hasten the inevitable, and it was at this point that others among the Oolscar began to successfully agitate for more decisive action. The Great Enterprise had begun.

The impetus behind the several attempts that had finally resulted in my abduction was now becoming clear to me, though Tor-ov Ov-tor himself—with his determination to cut himself off from the outer world—seemed unaware that he had just enumerated two of the major crimes that had no doubt figured prominently in the Masters' dissatisfaction with my continued existence.

I had mostly held my tongue during this lengthy declamation; now I decided to pose some inquiries that had arisen along the way.

"You said the Oolscar were few in number. How many constitute a 'few' in this circumstance? I know I have rarely set foot in a pit or cellar without encountering at least one of the undersized variety."

Tor-ov Ov-tor gave a curt nod. "In order to answer that, we must first refine our definition of 'Oolscar,' for the profound alterations wrought by their purported gods upon the brains and bodies of the original worms did not extend to their countless descendants."

He went on to explain that each of the Masters was capable of generating and fertilizing numerous eggs, every one of which hatched to produce hundreds of minute larvae that, I was startled to learn, were in fact the tiny glowing insects I had seen writhing in the light-generating mixture spread in great swaths in the tunnels and across the ceilings of most other areas in the Circles. Eventually these were collected from the fungus upon which they fed and became identical to the small sarovans so common across Barsoom. If nourished with secretions from an adult Oolscar, they would ultimately grow into much larger monsters, such as those I had seen disporting themselves in the craters in the Chamber of Vermin. Those that never received the growth secretions went on to attain a maximum of two feet in length, at which time they were capable of producing their own eggs and beginning a new cycle of the common cellar worms. None of these offspring—including the midsized creatures in the craters—ever achieved sentience, nor did any live longer than a few decades.

"It is only those original Oolscar that have survived the millennia who bear those attributes," he concluded. "We estimate that they total perhaps one hundred worms. You saw three of them earlier during the judgment, though they could not see you."

"A hundred!" I exclaimed. I shook my head. "So much misery wrought upon humanity by such a small pack of villains."

"They are few in number, yet their influence in the history of our world has been vast," San Tothis put in. "Have you ever wondered why only the oldest of human structures employ stairways rather than runways and ramps? In ancient days, the Masters would occasionally venture up to choose among their livestock themselves. Naturally it was easier for them to make their way through our dwellings on inclined surfaces, so the use of stairs was gradually discontinued."

"The true Oolscar are able to extend their perceptions to a certain extent through their own nonsentient offspring," Tor-ov Ov-tor said. "This is how they observe us through the minute brains and sensing organs of the larvae in the ceiling lights. The effect is more transitory when they assume control of humans and other creatures—though, once possessed, the subject's mind gradually becomes increasingly easier for them to manipulate. Thus it is with many of the Long-arms, who have little intelligence of their own, but are repeatedly possessed from the time they hatch until they may be readily influenced by the Masters, even at a distance."

"What of those poor wretches I saw prostrate in the craters?" I asked. "When the Oolscar wrapped itself around one of them, it was as if the man became a worm himself."

"Rather the Master became the man," he answered. "When they engage in that sort of intimate contact, they seize full control of the host's perceptions and actions for a time—though thankfully they cannot access his thoughts or memories. This is why the Oolscar had no awareness that Hel-tee Bar had already laid eyes on you when it climbed upon him. Nor would Hel-tee Bar now recollect any of what transpired while the Master questioned me."

"It is a substance they produce that acts for a brief time like an extension of their own consciousness," San Tothis said. "The Oolscar are like living chemical manufactories. Perhaps you noticed the sparkling slime left on the possessed, most noticeably along the spine? We do not know just how it works, but it allows the worms to maintain a modest level of contact and control even when they have quit the body. Beware of anyone or anything you see bearing that glittering residue, and know that such a creature is at least partially under the direction of the Masters for so long as the glow endures—though it is only during full possession that they may see with the host's eyes and hear with its ears. Luckily, the effects do not last more than a few days at the most."

"What happens to them afterward?" I asked. "The women and men in those craters looked to be in extremis, and a few could easily have passed for dead."

"Those are the favorites," Tor-ov Ov-tor responded. "The Oolscar have their particular pets among the captives; we believe it has something to do with the brain index. But repeated possessions quickly take their toll on the host. Unfortunately for those chosen ones—or perhaps it is a blessing—both their flesh and their minds soon break down under the strain, and they are never long for this world."

Tucking his stylus and now-empty vial back into his pocket, Helten En contributed to the conversation for the first time. "We call them corpse-men," he said.

There was a long moment of silence. Then Tor-ov Ov-tor rose to his feet. "We three must return to our duties lest we be missed," he said. "There will be time for more discussion when we are able to return."

Tor-ov Ov-tor requested that I spend as much time as possible in the Green Room, even sleeping there, rather than arousing suspicion by venturing out to one of the barracks in the surrounding rings where Hands and Numbers bedded down. He had obtained an extra pair of smocks from one of the textile workers, and these he offered to be used in substitution for sleeping silks and furs on the rough floor. "I do not know to what level of comfort you were accustomed in your former life," he said, "but you seem like a man who can make do with less than opulent accommodations."

As was the case with all of the cells that served as barracks, and many of the other chambers, a small but vigorous stream of water ran across the far end of the narrow room, and this was sufficient for my ablutions and other needs. I was frankly more than happy to make the Green Room my temporary bedchamber, if only to get away from the rippling colors outside, which I was told were never extinguished in this Circle—even in the sleeping quarters.

I was tired enough that I slept well, in spite of all that had transpired in a relatively short time. Early the next morning—for I continued to think in terms of the outer world, even though I no longer had any means of confirming my perceptions of the passage of time—Tor-ov Ov-tor reappeared and guided me out of the Green Room and back through the secret ways, acquainting me as we went with the locations and sequences of finger taps required to trigger the hidden doorways.

He told me that in addition to his other duties he had just been charged by the Masters with a new responsibility: tracking me down.

"Ironically, this provides us with an excellent means of sharing information outside the protected areas, for as I prowl dutifully through the various rings on my hunt for the missing mischief-maker, you may walk by my side undetected."

"Will not the Oolscar think something is amiss, if they catch you speaking into the thin air as you are doing now?"

He shook his head. "They are not so attuned to human behavior as that. We believe that their unamplified perception of us consists of little more than an intricately configured bright orb denoting brain activity, mounted upon a faint supporting haze that represents the body. So long as I do not whoop and gesticulate my moving lips will pass unnoticed."

As we made our way through the chamber of the lens shapers, I noticed a short length of gauzy silk on the ground next to one of the overflowing baskets from which the various workers chose cloths to polish the glass. I stooped and plucked it up, stuffing it into my pocket alongside the flask of water Tor-ov Ov-tor had given me.

I had found my onetime guide's new position as pursuer of the invisible man quite interesting. When I asked whether every communication with the Oolscar required an audience with one of those poor souls who had been possessed by a worm, he shook his head. "They have less complicated ways of communicating basic ideas to those of us who have been given our Numbers. The twinges of pain they transmit accompany the implantation of simple images in our brains, and commands in the form of emotional shading. Some of us are permitted to make our wants known to them in like fashion. The two who expressed their displeasure with me after the incident in the tiling room were persuaded to return to work in large part because they feared I would use my rapport with the Masters to summon a Long-arm to escort them if they did not go willingly."

From the lens-making room we entered the odious Chamber of Vermin, where I again saw in attendance three of the largest worms I now recognized as Oolscar. It required all my self-control to trust in my reputed invisibility as we strolled casually among them.

I could detect very little variation in their unlovely forms, nor did I have any idea whether this was the same triumvirate that had been present during my unsuccessful judgment. "You told me earlier that the prisoners knew the Masters as individuals and had even conferred names upon them," I said. "You are truly able to tell one worm from the other?"

"Oh, to be sure!" He nodded to a great segmented monstrosity making its way at an almost imperceptible pace at the base of the far wall. "There is old Slowcoach, for example, who can take an hour to traverse the distance his fellows cover in a few minutes. You do not want to have him on top of you." He let his gaze roam. "All of the Masters are noisome, as you have no doubt noticed—yet wallowing in that pit of ordure near the wall of the central crater is Flower Scent, a creature of particularly rank odor. And over there? We call that proud beast whose posterior you earlier wished to bruise with your heel Dotard. We believe him to be the oldest of these immortal fiends, and his behavior indicates he is becoming a bit of a mooncalf. You will eventually learn to identify them as do we, by some conspicuous characteristic of carcass or temperament."

"Not I!" I vowed. "Believe me, I do not plan to remain in this hell long enough to assemble a catalog of variegated worms."

Tor-ov Ov-tor favored me with a pitying look. "I can almost remember a time when I harbored such hopeless convictions myself. It was not long after my arrival that I decided to take up the work of hampering and disrupting the advancements which eventually became the Great Enterprise. As you will learn, it is a striving that serves to distract one from such impossible yearnings, and it will never cease."

"Until," I said cautiously, "the Great Enterprise itself is thwarted for good."

"Impossible, at least for the time being," he replied at once, "and far too dangerous to attempt. Were the Oolscar to become aware of our ongoing sabotage, then all the work of the past century would have been for naught and the world could end on the instant."

"From the sound of things, it may end shortly at any rate."

He shook his head. "Alarmist rumors, nothing more. As you

heard earlier, the Masters have tried more than once, and each time they have failed. We do not yet have the means to bring down their destructive engines, and so it is best we wait until we do, should it take a decade or a century." He gave me an understanding smile. "You are new to the Perfect World. Take time to acclimate yourself before rushing headlong into some possibly wrongheaded action."

I had no intention of postponing my departure from this realm for a year, let alone a century, but said nothing, not yet prepared to air my own nascent plans for bringing a decisive end to the reign of the Oolscar and setting free their long-suffering captives.

"We should return to the Green Room and take our morning meal," Tor-ov Ov-tor said after a short silence. "Some usa remains from what Helten En brought us yesterday, along with a few roots and berries from the fields. But first, in the interest of increasing your understanding of your new home . . ."

He led me through one of the side portals into a chamber in a ring I had not yet visited. "This is a storeroom, one of many. There are thousands of these chambers distributed among the Circles."

I peered past him into the vast, low-ceilinged cavern. The rough floor was covered from wall to wall with irregular rows of earthen disks, each about the diameter of a manhole cap, which I recognized as products of the tiling room. As far as I could make out in the shifting lights, the space was otherwise empty.

"I see nothing save these unremarkable tiles," I told Tor-ov Ov-tor. "What makes them valuable enough to store?"

"Oh, those are not the items being stored. In fact, this room contains examples of the Masters' most plentiful commodity and their most precious—by which, of course, I mean ourselves," he answered with a sardonic twist of his lips. "The floor in each storeroom is filled with hollows similar to those employed as dens by the carnivorous youthful worms—narrow tubular pockets that extend about eight feet down into the rock. When a Master wishes to set one of us aside so that he may be easily accessed for future use, it simply lowers the deserving fellow into one of the hollows. The Oolscar exits the body, the receptacle is filled to the top with a cold slime, and then swiftly sealed with one of these round tiles."

He followed my gaze as I turned to stare in repugnance at the long rows of disks stretching from wall to wall. "Brain activity continues unabated so long as we are alive, so the Masters may easily locate a specific Number when they once again have need of him. It is all very efficient."

As usual, the cool-headed manner in which Tor-ov Ov-tor imparted these details made the whole affair seem all the more abhorrent to me. "How does the occupant not drown to death when the receptacle fills with liquid?" I asked him.

He shrugged. "It is another miraculous potion excreted by a gland within the Masters themselves, as appalling as that sounds. Somehow a reaction is engendered in the human body by which one is able to obtain a sufficiency of oxygen, as well as a supply of nutrients that nourish the body without waste, so there is in theory no limit to how long one might survive in the receptacle. As I said, it is an eminently efficient process, perfected over many years until nowadays unintended deaths are infrequent. After you have been entombed in this fashion for a certain number of times—a score for some, a hundred score for those favored others—the ordeal becomes a commonplace and you learn not to thrash around so much as the odious substance invades your mouth and nostrils. Perhaps a quarter of the inhabitants of the Perfect World are presently preserved in such fashion."

This was not my first encounter with an insane attempt to stockpile human beings against some future use, but at least the frozen men of Panar were allowed the boon of remaining unconscious while in durance vile. I have never been partial to confined spaces; staring at the hundreds of disks dotting the chamber floor, I could not help but imagine myself as one of the wretched souls preserved in cold, choking slime and utter darkness within a narrow space—and then abandoned there for weeks! Years? Decades? I wondered how many days it would take before I began clawing at the sides until I wore my fingers to the bone, or finally resorted to bashing my brains out against the rocky wall of the hollow.

As if divining the nature of my ruminations, Tor-ov Ov-tor added: "The Oolscars' secretion affects the nerves and muscles in some inhibitory way, draining the occupant of vigor and rendering him incapable of all but the tiniest movements." He gave a bleak smile. "After all, the Masters would be ill served were they to dredge up a valued Number after a few months or years, only to find that he had damaged himself beyond all future usefulness in the interim."

I suppressed a shudder. "Can one sleep down there?"

He considered. "I would not call it that. There is, of course, no way to measure how long you lie in the receptacle, nor are you interred with any sure knowledge that you will eventually be retrieved. Might not the Master who placed you there with all good intentions decide later to replace you with a likelier Number to run its errands— or simply forget about you altogether? I am sure that both have happened many times. But would you languish there completely conscious of your state for a thousand years, unable to move, unable to die? It is my personal belief that after some period most captives enter into a sort of prolonged catatonia that may be compared to sleep. Or perhaps it is just that we go insane down there. Insofar as madness may be deemed a dream, then I suppose we would at least be able to flee into our dreams."

I was watching his impassive face as he spoke.

"You do not strike me as a madman, Tor-ov Ov-tor," I told him. "You have endured this yourself?"

"Oh yes, several times since my arrival." His tone had remained calm throughout the telling, but now I saw him swallow convulsively. "I do not know with any certainty how long I have been a guest of this venerable establishment," he added, "but I reckon that I have been down here for more than a century, and a not inconsiderable portion of that time has been spent beneath the floor of one of these rooms. I should add that interment in a storage hole is not reserved only for the favorites. The Masters also resort to the hollows when they wish to punish a recalcitrant slave deemed too useful to kill. And by far the largest number of occupants are what Helten En referred to earlier as the corpse-men, those whom the Oolscar routinely bring forth to send in alternation with the Long-arms upon their various missions to the surface. The preservation process prolongs their lives, though once they are decanted a rapid deterioration ensues."

He turned a speculative gaze to the dank walls and lowering ceiling of the cavern. "As to my own mental condition, I have no idea when I may be returned to storage myself—perhaps in this very chamber. For now, it would seem a terrible pity to waste one precious moment up here in this relative paradise by indulging in the shrieking and raving to which my mind occasionally urges me.

"Do not be fooled by my placid demeanor, however," he added, wagging his finger like a jovial professor. "Peering out at you from behind these calm eyes is a ragged soul who would as lief claw through the rock walls with his bare hands as spend another hour in this hell—let alone endure a single second in that far worse hell beneath our feet." His shoulders raised and then fell again. "And now—to breakfast."

With a wan smile, he turned and ambled across the floor. I felt a slow chill traverse my spine as I moved to follow.

23
IN THE ARENA

I HAD BEGUN FORMULATING my own plans concerning my place in the Perfect World, ones that I feared might not necessarily mesh with those of Tor-ov Ov-tor, the putative head of the resistance. The next time San Tothis and I were alone in the Green Room, I took him up on his vow of fealty to my person and his offer of abetment of my future crimes against the Masters. If headway was to be made in finding a means to escape this underground prison, I would need allies of my own.

One thing I had been unable to understand was why the captives had not long since found some way out of the Perfect World. There were apparently multiple entrances; could it be that there was no single unguarded passage back to the surface among the Nine Circles?

San Tothis assured me that there were many. The following cycle he brought me to the nearest, an aperture located on the far side of a largely deserted cavern in one of the outermost rings of our Circle. We smelled the stench of decaying flesh well before we reached the opening, beyond which a narrow tunnel could be glimpsed stretching upward into darkness. Three human corpses in various stages of decomposition lay atop one another just inside the threshold, while portions of skeletons were strewn liberally about them. "Occasionally a captive will rush the portal in an act of self-destruction," San Tothis said, going on to explain that all such openings had originally been guarded by the Long-arms, and that this more efficient solution represented the earliest use to which the broadcast gravity devices had been put. In such places the downward pressure fluctuated in strength beyond the opening, often allowing prisoners

220

to proceed a foot or two into the passage before increasing a second later to crush or trap them. In most cases the attempted escapees were killed instantly; if not, they lay in suffocating agony until they expired. The carrion was left there as a lesson, or a warning—or perhaps, San Tothis mused, because the Masters simply did not care. He asked if I had noted the zoological exhibitions in the entrance tunnel, in which a more powerful continuous effect served as an invisible barrier to escape from the various enclosures. "And what is the point of those displays?" I asked. "Do the Oolscar derive some weird pleasure from showing off their collection of unusual beasts?"

"No point whatsoever as far as the Masters are concerned," San Tothis told me. "The longer you are down here, the more you will come to realize that the Perfect World was constructed not by the worms alone, but by corrupted men working in concert with them. Just as some highly placed Numbers enjoy indulging their darker natures in the production of such freakish creatures in the laboratories of the Sixth Circle, others derive pleasure from observing them in their cages. It is the same as with the arenas in the Fifth Circle. Men originated the deadly contests for their own enjoyment, and the Oolscar do not interfere so long as the work gets done."

"At any rate, it would take us far too long to send the population of the Nine Circles back to the surface by means of such small passageways," I remarked as we made our way back through the rings.

"I and others like me have combed these caverns for countless years, searching for a true means of escape," San Tothis said in leaden tones. "Believe me, there is no way out."

"Well, then, we shall just have to create one," I replied, gesturing at the great central tunnel visible through a nearby archway. "I imagine the conduits that bring air down into the tunnels must be of a sizable nature."

He chuckled. "Yes, perhaps we might blow up one of those. It should only take a few thousand tons of explosives."

I shared his amusement, yet the kernel of an idea remained lodged in my brain.

When we were back in the Green Room, I asked him what he could tell me about the remaining four regions of the Perfect World, which Tor-ov Ov-tor had said were strictly forbidden to the captives. He explained that the Fourth Circle, the region directly beyond the arenas, was devoted to the study and implementation of atmospheric manipulation by means of the Ninth Solar Ray, and filled with mighty engines capable of generating and directing wind currents on the surface, such as had been done during the powerful tempest that had toppled the scarlet tower of Greater Helium after spiriting away both my daughter's frail flier and San Tothis' own *Vanator* years ago—not to mention the gale that had but recently brought the *Kantim* to ground above my own place of capture. Only those few Numbers like Tor-ov Ov-tor with expertise in such matters were granted ingress, and even then only to certain areas, the actual operation of the engines being left to a chosen handful.

The Third Circle followed a similar template: it was there that the Eighth Ray was employed to impose areas of increased gravity both above and below the earth, and there were none among Tor-ov Ov-tor's current roster of accomplices who had ever been inside. San Tothis listened with interest to my description of the various uses to which I had seen amplified gravitic fields applied on the surface. Familiar with their deadly effectiveness as a tool of punishment among the Circles, he took the downing of the fliers up north and the devastating attack on Bantoom as an ominous signal that the Masters were close to perfecting their long-range control of the phenomenon.

The Second Circle also remained completely unexplored by the conspirators, for the simple fact that it was said to consist of a series of dark and airless caverns utterly inhospitable to human life. A deadly environment even to their air-breathing offspring, this was where the Oolscar themselves dwelled whenever they were not required to travel elsewhere, their more perfect haven within the Perfect World.

This left the First Circle, believed to be the oldest of the nine underground realms. Located all the way around the great loop of linked regions and thus on the other side of our own caverns in the Ninth Circle, it was said to have been rendered uninhabitable millennia ago due to massive cave-ins as a disastrous result of one of the Oolscars' earliest forays into meddling with the force of gravity.

San Tothis lowered his voice, even though we were quite alone: "Tor-ov Ov-tor likely intended to reveal this to you himself in due time, but I have no qualms about telling you that we think the First Circle is far from the complete ruin the worms would have us believe. Unfortunately, though we have searched long and hard, we have uncovered no way of getting inside to confirm this."

I took some time to ponder all of this before announcing that I wished to do some exploring of my own. "I would like to take a trip to the Fifth Circle," I told him. "I can essay the journey alone, unless there is someone among our confederates who could bring me there without attracting undue attention."

As it happened, San Tothis, who worked as a foreman in the Seventh Circle manufactories, was free for the next half-cycle and elected to accompany me himself. I was glad of this, as I was not yet completely familiar with the operation of the transport system, nor was I certain where I could wander unchallenged. Although my supposed invisibility where the worms were concerned afforded a measure of protection from their murderous wrath, my lack of an official identity opened me up to scrutiny by my fellow captives, not all of whom I was prepared to trust.

I could tell my escort found it curious that I should choose to begin my tutelage in the ways of the Perfect World with a visit to its recreational center. Head-to-head, we rode the tube-car to the Fifth Circle, where I saw for the first time that the small, two-man capsules were not the only means of traveling between the regions. Farther down the central tunnel great carriers slid out of the wall to disgorge the hundreds of Hands and Numbers that flocked here every cycle to enjoy a brief hiatus from work.

I studied the scheduled bouts for this cycle, which were posted in simplistic pictogram fashion on large placards behind each amphitheater. Then we made a quick survey of the nearest arenas before I settled on one in which a motley group of Hands was scheduled to engage in combat against a team of the Long-arms. San Tothis informed me that this was by far the commonest match-up, these two categories being deemed by the Oolscar the most easily replaced—and thus the most disposable—representatives of both humans and monsters.

My companion was visibly taken aback when I announced that I planned to participate in one of these imminent matches myself. "These bouts amount to little more than light exercise for the Long-arms," he told me dubiously, "and almost always end in massacres."

With some reluctance, San Tothis showed me to a corridor just behind the stands that provided access to the waiting combatants. There he reminded me that Numbers, being more intrinsically valuable to the Masters owing to their specialized skills, were forbidden to compete in any of the contests. Looking around in the purple light to make sure we were not being observed, I quickly shucked my tunic, handed it to him, and told him to secure himself a seat in the spectators' section. I then made my way to the holding pen and slipped in among the dozen of my fellow human beings who for one reason or another had decided to test their fighting prowess—and most likely end their lives—during this short break in their work cycle.

With a nod to the superior strength and ferocity of the eight-foot-tall beast-men, contests such as these were typically arranged to allow two Hands for every Long-arm, and so there was some grumbling from the man tasked with readying the human contestants when he saw that we now numbered thirteen. His counterpart at the neighboring pen of Long-arms dismissed his concerns with a sneering laugh, claiming that the inclusion of a single additional Hand would do no more than add an extra bloody corpse to the rubble soon to be left behind by his half-dozen ogres.

Out on the field, another decidedly uneven contest was currently underway, pitting four of the eccentrically modified banths I had observed on display in the tunnel of my arrival against twice that many stalwart green men. I watched as the fierce leonine predators tore through their adversaries with their claws and tremendous jaws, only one banth falling to the combined efforts of two of the unarmed warriors, who managed to pin it down long enough to slash its flanks open with their gleaming tusks before being dispatched themselves. At this point, the lone surviving green man attempted to straddle the back of the largest of the banths with the hope of wrapping his upper four limbs about its neck to throttle it. Instead, the roaring creature gave its great head a backward toss, the man was pierced by dozens of the rapier-like quills with which the experimenters had endowed these monsters in place of their usual tawny manes, and the battle was over.

San Tothis had told me that the finish of a match was signaled by the gradually changing color of the ceiling illumination, providing a brief interlude before the next contest in which the survivors were allowed to exit the arena while workers rushed out to drag away the remains of those that had not fared as well. I sized up our beastly opponents as I waited for the field to be cleared, then let my gaze wander to the nine men and three women who shared the holding pen with me, marveling at how relatively puny and unprotected they seemed without the weaponry and garments common to the world above. Though it has occasionally been my lot to battle for my life completely unclothed, I have never done so by choice. The vulnerability of certain regions of the body when in the presence of honed edges and sharp points can cause even the doughtiest warrior to act with added caution, to the inevitable detriment of his fighting ability. At least in this arena we would be confronted by no weapons other than those borne naturally by our opponents—which was not to imply that the fangs and claws of the beastly Long-arms were to be discounted as harmless. To my mind, the single benefit of being one of a dozen naked Hands engaged in spirited combat beneath the weirdly colored illumination of the amphitheater was that the on-lookers would find it challenging, if not impossible, to keep track of us as individuals. I had picked out at least three other fighters whose size and build approached my own in the holding pen, and I resolved to make a point of doing my fighting in their general vicinity whenever possible.

"I am beginning to recall how pleasant it is to spend one's break time eating bliss-cake in the refectory," one of the men standing next to me muttered. "Still, I have made my choice and this cycle is as good as any to meet my doom."

"Courage," I told him, divining from the quaver in his voice that he had not quite convinced himself of the wisdom of his decision. "Perhaps it is the beast-men whose lives will be cut short this time around."

He gave a snort of sour amusement. "You have evidently not attended many of these matches. The Long-arms never lose and only a madman would expect otherwise."

"And yet here you are by my side," I reminded him.

He sighed. "I have labored in these dreadful caverns for sixty long years, ever since I was snatched from my boat while floating serenely down the Iss on my way to paradise in the Valley Dor." He gave his head a decisive shake. "No, I am sick of this Perfect World. I would rather be torn to bits on the instant than face another moment of hauling clay so some arrogant Number can turn it into tiles or goblets."

"Then let us at least give them a fight they will remember," I suggested.

"Maybe you are right," mused my morose friend, raising his chin just a bit. "Even if we are no longer capable of looking back upon this battle once it reaches its inevitable conclusion, perhaps some among the spectators will carry it forward in their own memories for a cycle or two, and our ancestors will not frown upon us with quite as much contempt."

"Spoken like a true warrior!" I said and clapped him on the shoulder.

At that moment the light from the ceiling of the cavern completed its shift from orange-yellow to scarlet. Before stripping down, I had removed from my pocket the short length of diaphanous silk I had pilfered from the lens-makers' room. Now I wound it swiftly about my face and knotted it at the back of my head. Though it was quite sheer and presented no obstacle to my vision, it rendered my features nearly unrecognizable under the colored light. The gates of our pen swung open and we thirteen warriors jogged or plodded onto the field of battle as was our wont.

The Long-arms were evidently accustomed to winning their matches with only token opposition from their foes, for they sauntered casually after us into the arena, making a great show of preening before the crowd and raising their mighty arms above their heads to pound them down again on the packed ground, all the while deliberately turning their backs upon their much smaller opponents.

After half a minute of their posturing, I decided it was past time for the show to commence. After waiting for one of the larger specimens to display his bulging muscles to the spectators and his backside to me, I leaped across the ten feet which separated us and came to rest upon his massive shoulders, wrapping my legs tightly about his neck like the Old Man of the Sea astride Sinbad. Quickly getting over his initial surprise, the great brute proceeded to treat me as more of an amusing nuisance than a genuine threat, reaching up to pin my ankles against his chest in a powerful grip as he capered about on his short legs. One of his fellows soon trotted over to join in the fun. As he leaned in to pluck me from his comrade's shoulders, I reached out and grasped his shaggy head firmly in both my hands, then gave a terrific pull and dashed it against the skull of my host, sending the one whom I rode spinning about in dazed agony, and his helpful friend to the ground, quite dead.

There was a moment of stunned silence, and then a roar of appreciation rose in the stands. My fellow Hands seemed no less inspired than the spectators. I watched with approval as two of the women rushed a lone Long-arm from either side, harrying the beast-man with frenzied cries and jabs of their fists while dancing just outside his considerable reach. As he turned his attention to one side to swipe at the nearest, I ran at full steam up to his unprotected chest, where I grabbed a knot of coarse fur in one hand and proceeded to rain rapid blows upon his face with the other until the blood gushed into his eyes and he toppled backward, half-blinded and roaring with pain and fury. I left his two assailants taking turns pummeling his head with their heels and raced to the aid of another member of our little battalion. It was my resigned friend from the holding pen, who was doing his desperate best to outrun the grinning Long-arm that had decided to make short work of him. I hooted and bellowed to draw the beast-man's attention to myself, then, banking on the inability of the dull-witted creature to follow the import of my words, shouted an order to the other man. After a moment's hesitation he dropped onto his knees and elbows behind the Long-arm, whereupon I made a prodigious leap headfirst into the latter's stomach that sent him tripping and flailing backward over my teammate. In an instant I was astraddle his chest and in another his head lolled back against the packed earth at the end of a broken neck.

Three of the beast-men were now out of the fight. I amended the tally to four as I saw several of the other Hands, emboldened by this unexpected success, swarm about the still disoriented Long-arm upon whose shoulders I had first leaped and manage to drag him to the ground, where they gouged his eyes and kicked at his ears until he crept away panting and groaning like a child beset by a hive of angry hornets.

Our side had suffered significant losses as well. The two remaining Long-arms had each accounted for the death of two of the Hands. Now they advanced menacingly toward the group of five that had just taken down their dazed comrade. They were as swift as the humans on their short legs and massive arms; in a moment they were in the midst of the little group and the bodies of two more men and a woman went flying like rag dolls through the air. Taking advantage of the melee, I circled behind them and then launched myself, arms outstretched, at the calves of the nearest. A moment later the beast-man was rising from the ground to limp on one foot and an arm, his right foot hanging at an unnatural angle from his ankle. I attached myself to his free arm and held on for dear life, my feet braced against his ribs as he swung me wildly about. At last there came an unpleasant popping sound and the powerfully muscled arm bulged from its socket to hang nervelessly from his shoulder. I administered a mighty backward kick to his side, heard ribs crack beneath my heel, and leaped over to the remaining brute, who was doing his best to wield the body of one hapless Hand as a cudgel against the four who harried him like hounds about a bear. Perching high on his back with my knees wedged into his armpits, I clasped my hands together and leaned forward. When he threw back his head to rake me with his fangs, I drove my fists with all my might into his nose, shattering it and sending fragments of bone into his brain.

I sprang lightly from his toppling body and took a moment to catch my breath while I surveyed the scene.

Only one of the Long-arms remained ambulatory. He cowered at the edge of the field, probably more incapacitated by shock at this wholly unforeseen turn of events than by the blows we had inflicted. Of our original complement of thirteen, six Hands were dead and two bore injuries that would need tending—if such was even provided here—leaving five of us in relatively good shape. From the near-hysterical reaction of those Hands and Numbers in the stands, I felt sure that even this costly victory was more than had been achieved by human fighters in many cycles.

The light began to alter from scarlet to royal blue. I untied the concealing strip of silk from my head and squeezed it into a small ball in my palm as we departed the field.

We were mobbed by enthusiastic onlookers. I spotted San Tothis at the edge of the crowd and shouldered my way through the con-gratulatory throng to his side. He handed me my tunic and we wound our way past the masses streaming from the stands and into a deserted back corridor, where to my surprise I found Tor-ov Ov-tor waiting, his arms folded across his breast and his expression unreadable.

"That was an extremely risky decision," he told me.

I shrugged. "I did not see it that way." I nodded to the handful of tokens he was stowing in his pocket. "Apparently you arrived in time to lay some decent bets."

"Yes. Bor-ay-bor persuaded me to a wager at the commencement of this contest that seemed ridiculous on the face of it, yet paid off handsomely in the end." He looked around as other celebrants began to spill into the corridor. "Are you finished here?"

"Not quite," I said. "Would you care to win a few more tokens?"

I next presented myself three fields over at the holding pen for a match-up between eight humans and four of the Long-arms. As I had expected, word of the previous match had not yet made its way to this amphitheater, and no one paid much heed as I sized up the six men and two women and then approached the one I deemed to be exhibiting the most second thoughts and offered to take his place. He yielded his spot to me without much soul-searching and soon I was out on the field again, where the results were even more

salubrious than in my first bout: not only did I leave the arena with
nothing more than an added bruise or two, but I was able to take a
pair of the beast-men out by myself fairly quickly. I then rallied my
teammates, one of whom showed himself to be quite talented in
hand-to-hand combat, against the remaining pair, with me serving
as decoy and stalking horse while they launched surprise attacks.
We lost a man and one of the women before we brought the last of
the Long-arms crashing to the ground with a resounding thud. I did
not linger, though my surviving teammates were eager to include
me in their celebrations. As before, I removed my face covering,
donned the tunic San Tothis tossed me and made myself scarce
behind the stands, where Tor-ov Ov-tor joined us, his pocket bulging
with another handful of tokens.

I had one more match to fight. Pointing out a secluded area to
one side of the neighboring stands to my companions, and advising
Tor-ov Ov-tor to place no bets this time, I once more doffed my
garments and took off briskly down the corridor toward the next
arena over. This match, as I had noted earlier on the posted schedule,
was between two teams that mixed humans and members of the
green race in their ranks. Both sides sported two males and two
females of each species, for a grand total of sixteen fighters on the
field. To distinguish between the teams, combatants were issued a
pair of wide silk ribbons, the members of one team tying them about
their left wrists and ankles, while their opponents applied them on
the right. This placement was necessitated owing to the richly tinted
light from the ceiling, which made it impossible to tell one colored
cloth from another.

I had no difficulty obtaining a spot in this match; most Hands
found the prospect of unarmed battle against a team featuring
fifteen-foot green warriors somewhat daunting: even if the giants
did not engage one directly, there was always the possibility of being
inadvertently trod upon.

The light turned from lavender to vermillion, I wrapped my strip
of silk about my head, and the match began.

My strategy for this engagement differed radically from the last.
From the start I hopped and sprang about the field like a madman,

doing my best to divest my fellow players of their ribbons without regard to which team they represented, and focusing my especial attention on the green warriors. "Which horde?" I shouted as I leaped from one to the next. "From whence do you hail?" Startled, most replied without thinking, and to the five out of eight who identified themselves as Tharks, Thurds, or Warhoons as I snatched the identifying ribbons from their limbs, I cried: "Tell all your tribesmen that Dotar Sojat has come to lead them out of this buried prison and back to their rightful places above!" My hope was that the green fighters would recognize the name I had earned in combat while a prisoner among the Tharks during my early days on Barsoom, and that my unexpected presence among them might serve to renew their courage.

With most of the fighters now unsure as to which was enemy and which was friend, I tossed the ribbons high into the air and vaulted over the holding pen, leaving shouts of outrage and confusion in my wake.

San Tothis and Tor-ov Ov-tor met me in the designated spot, the former grinning broadly and the latter looking puzzled. "What went wrong out there?" Tor-ov Ov-tor asked me as we hurried away in the direction of the tube-cars.

"Nothing at all," I told him. "My objectives in this match were not the same as in the first two."

"I see," he said, though I was fairly certain he did not. "And now we must return to the Green Room before you are recognized and we are followed."

When we entered the hidden space half a dozen men and women were already there, eyeing me curiously under the green light. Among them, I was startled to recognize the woman who had met me upon my arrival in the tunnel and served as my initial host. She was introduced to me by her Number as Ilmak Teeyil, though I later learned that her name in the outer world had been Sharu. While San Tothis regaled the others with the tale of our adventures in the Fifth Circle, she drew me aside to apologize for her listless behavior during our previous interaction. "I strive to play my part in the grand scheme, yet occasionally I give in to apathy and partake too freely of the bliss-water myself," she said by way of explanation. She was grateful when I reassured her that she had done nothing deserving of reproach, and went on to tell me that I reminded her of someone she had briefly known during her time back on the surface, when she had dwelled in a place that was in its own way as oppressive as the Perfect World. "Our city was ruled by a cruel monster who preyed upon both his own people and those infrequent visitors whose bad fortune led them into our secluded vale. A man came there once who was unlike the others, and I was able to help him and his companion escape the awful fate decreed for them by our mad jed—though I never learned whether it was to freedom or an even more frightful destiny that they departed. His determination and noble spirit during his short stay inspired me to make my own bid for liberty not long after. Alas, my freedom was short-lived, for my jubilant flight on the River Syl carried me here." She gave a sad little laugh. "It is not the life I would have chosen, but I try to do what meager good I can."

The others crowded around me at this point, incited to incredulity by San Tothis' colorful reenactments of my forays into the arena.

"If we expect them to follow us, we must remind people that they are more than Hands or Numbers," I said, when asked by several what had been the motivations behind my actions. "We must give them hope that things can change."

Standing at the edge of the little group, Tor-ov Ov-tor was skeptical. "And you believe such hope is to be imparted by fighting Long-arms in the arena?"

"By showing the captives that it is possible even here to fight and on occasion triumph, yes."

He raised an eyebrow at the nods and murmured words of affirmation that followed my simple statement.

"Even though you are invisible to the Oolscar, we should come up with a means of identifying you among ourselves," he said. "As has been noted, it becomes tiresome after a while to point and say 'you there.'"

"I have given some thought to this of late," I said with a smile.

"Since you eschew the use of our former names and the worms are unlikely to gift me with a proper Number, I have taken on the only numerical label fit for an invisible man. You may call me Vetj."

This evoked a ripple of amusement among the small gathering, and even Tor-ov Ov-tor allowed himself a modest smile. "Vetj" is the Barsoomian term for "Zero."

24
THE WAR ROOM

AND SO I WAS VETJ to the little band of conspirators; John Carter, Prince of Helium, to those captives with whom I shared a previous connection in the outer world; and soon, I hoped, Dotar Sojat to those green men and women with long memories who toiled in the Seventh Circle.

By the start of the next cycle, San Tothis reported that the five Circles frequented by human prisoners were abuzz with news of the performance of the unknown Hand who had almost single-handedly defeated two hundred of the monstrous Long-arms. As I had hoped, his solitary fame did not endure for long: shortly after the first match, at least two of my fellow combatants—one of them a woman—had graciously accepted credit from the crowd for most of my own maneuvers, which suited my plans perfectly. By the end of the cycle, several prisoners who had apparently been watching the second match from the safety of the stands had themselves come forth claiming to be the mysterious warrior.

The next cycle I returned to the arenas, inserting myself discreetly into several more bouts and continuing to compete with a thin layer of silk wrapped around my face. I knew all combatants would soon be subjected to increased scrutiny from the spectators; to my satisfaction, by the end of the day others had begun to obscure their features, with members of the audience tossing balls of silk out to the contestants as they entered the field.

Since the arenas in the Fifth Circle were not under the Masters' direct surveillance, we had apparently not yet attracted the notice of the worms, though I suspected that would soon follow.

Subsequent to Tor-ov Ov-tor's decision years ago to recruit San Tothis to work with him in indefinitely postponing realization of the Great Enterprise, the two had cultivated the habit of walking through the chambers of the First Circle at certain times when they were not required to be elsewhere. This gave them the opportunity to exchange information with each other and with other members of the group without attracting undue attention. So far neither had been asked to account for those occasions when they absented themselves in the Green Room, and they spent as little time there as possible in an effort to keep things that way. With my new status of nonexistence confirmed, I began to join them on their walks as often as possible, asking questions and adding to my growing store of knowledge of the Perfect World.

Tor-ov Ov-tor remained the titular head of the resistance, although San Tothis had now begun to add new members to the cause at a much faster pace than before, using the reaction of certain Numbers and Hands to the news from the arenas as one way of gauging their trustworthiness. Exactly what that cause was seemed to vary according to the man or woman who spoke about it. Tor-ov Ov-tor's original goals had been twofold: to covertly sabotage the Masters' efforts to obliterate all life on the surface, as embodied in the Great Enterprise, and to preserve as many lives among the captives as possible. San Tothis had long aspired to more direct action. He welcomed my presence as a catalyst for a more pointed type of rebellion—one designed, as he told me, to function as a spear rather than a shield. He had not allowed these new developments to make him reckless in seeking out accomplices, however, cautioning me that there were an unknown number of traitors and collaborators among the captives. "Consigned to this miserable half-existence, many have been only too happy to seek favored status with their enslavers—even if it means the inevitable extinction of life upon the surface world."

I gave a bark of laughter, then quickly sobered as I saw his expression. "But that is madness," I said flatly. "And suicide. Why would anyone willingly assist them in this regard? Every one of us is dependent for survival upon a breathable atmosphere, and once there is no more air for the Oolscar to funnel down from the surface that will be the end for all. Surely they must understand that when Barsoom dies, they will perish as well!"

"The Masters feed them lies," San Tothis said bitterly, "denying that the abolishment of all life above is their goal. It is true that there are some whose involvement necessitates an understanding of the actual plot. The worms deal with those by promising that an exalted few will be preserved in some unspecified fashion and—just as in the case of the Oolscar themselves—finally installed in the paradise they feel was long ago denied them. Remember: though many of those who are now designated Numbers were torn from their lives on account of their reputed knowledge or skills, the vast majority of the population of Hands is made up of those unfortunates who embarked upon the last pilgrimage down the Iss, some because they had reached the conclusion of a full life, but many more because they felt obliged to terminate their own existence for a host of darker reasons: shame, guilt, fear, despair. Expecting a surcease of pain and an afterlife of peace and plenty, they were instead snatched from the bosom of the River of Death and brought here."

"And what of Tor-ov Ov-tor himself?" I inquired. "He told me that he has been here for more than a hundred years. Since he is assigned to the atmospheric research area, I assume he was one of those taken for his specialized knowledge?"

"Yes." San Tothis studied the ground. "His is a difficult story. He was seized along with many other experts in the midst of a scientific expedition, back when the Oolscar first went looking for learned individuals to assist them in ridding the planet of its atmosphere. When he and his colleagues unanimously refused to do the Masters' bidding, the Oolscar brought forth the members of their crew and began to slaughter them horribly, one by one. Tor-ov Ov-tor could not bear this and sought to halt the atrocities by claiming that he would aid the monsters in their enterprise."

"Claiming? He never intended to further their cause?"

"In no wise did he intend to help them. In fact, for scores of years he has been doing everything in his power to secretly subvert their efforts. The Oolscar are not scientists themselves, forever having to rely upon the minds and hands of others to fulfill their plans. Tor-ov Ov-tor reasoned that if he feigned compliance and gained their trust, he would be granted access to the machinery they had already had constructed, and might be able to slow and frustrate their progress beneath their very noses. The Masters accepted his offer, installing him in the Fourth Circle at once. It was not until later that he learned to his vast horror and regret that the rest of those he had been captured with, scientists and crew alike, had soon after been summarily executed as superfluous. By ingratiating himself with the Oolscar, he has been able to save a great many more lives over the past hundred years, though at the cost of being branded a traitor and collaborator by many of the prisoners." San Tothis sighed. "To this day he blames himself for all of it, and has little regard for the great good he has accomplished during his stay, no matter how often his friends have tried to convince him otherwise."

I was glad to have heard the story, tragic though it was, as I had found myself from time to time uncertain of Tor-ov Ov-tor's motivations—and thus of the extent to which he might be relied upon to support my own plans to fan the coals of resistance into the hot flames of rebellion.

Tor-ov Ov-tor himself responded with a doubtful grimace when I told him later of my expectation that more and more of the captives—Hands as well as Numbers—would soon rally to our side. "The spurned lover," he said, "the exposed cheat, the liar, the debtor, the thief—this is a pretty gang of miscreants and suicides you would choose to mold into your rebel army."

I looked him in the eye. "You might be surprised how many men and women, no matter how fallen in their own regard, would leap at the chance to redeem themselves from the supposed errors of their early lives."

We gained a much-needed lift in morale when one of the latest additions to our growing band of conspirators brought with her word of a small repository she had stumbled upon in an outer ring of our Circle, where some of the garments stripped from the more recent captives had been deposited. No one was certain why they had not been destroyed, as was believed to be the usual practice, but over the next few cycles the Numbers among us began to smuggle them piece by piece into the Green Room beneath our own shapeless tunics. From then on, it became our custom to garb ourselves like men and women of the outer world while inside our little sanctuary— even if we had to leave the harnesses and silks behind with many a regretful look whenever we ventured elsewhere in the Perfect World. Pocket pouches were included with some of the trappings, and these yielded a plethora of useful items. The only things missing were the swords and daggers to fill the empty scabbards!

An equally unexpected, and far more significant, discovery oc-curred not long after. My work in the arenas was coming along well, though I took care to mete out my own appearances while allowing others to do their share of fighting in my stead. More new recruits reported in to the Green Room each cycle—substantially more than could comfortably occupy the little chamber at one time, which made coordination on a large scale difficult. San Tothis reported that he had heard the name of Dotar Sojat whispered with admiration among the members of the green race with whom he labored in the Seventh Circle, and he expected that we might soon see a sizable number of recruits from that quarter as well. Still I chafed under the slow pace of the plan and the need to spend most of my days in idleness in such cramped quarters when I wasn't off bedeviling the Long-arms or wooing the green men in the amphitheaters. Among the items recovered from the few pocket pouches found with the discarded harnesses were several radium torches. With too much time on my hands in the often untenanted chamber, I sometimes left off my restless pacing to prowl the unlit warren of hidden cor-ridors while thinking on the best and most expedient ways to bring my developing plans to fruition.

One time my absentminded explorations brought me down a hitherto ignored passageway that I had previously taken for a dead end, the undisturbed dust beneath my borrowed sandals telling me that others had come to the same conclusion and chosen more frequented routes for their exercise. I had started to get a sense of the overarching pattern of these hidden ways that threaded between the rings, however, and something about the abrupt termination of this particular passage struck me as not quite right.

On a whim, I tried the usual tapping code in several locations near the far end, each time to no avail, until finally I sensed the slightest bit of movement in the stone beneath my fingertips. Bracing my feet against the floor, I placed my shoulder to the wall and tapped again while pushing forward with all my strength. The wall gave, reluctantly at first, but then suddenly swung wide with a puff of stale air to reveal Stygian darkness beyond. After first wedging my sandals between the wall and the door, lest it pivot shut and entomb me far out of earshot of my comrades, I stepped cautiously through. I uncapped my torch, finding in one direction the heaped debris from a partially collapsed stretch of ceiling that had been blocking the door from turning. The other direction showed a long, curving corridor that paralleled the one I had just quit. I made my way carefully, seeing more evidence of destruction to the walls and ceiling that made me distrustful of the structure's general integrity. This passage eventually connected with a much broader one, which in turn brought me to a second hidden doorway that responded instantly to my touch.

Stepping through, I found myself in a large circular chamber, where my torch revealed the outlines of eight horizontal ovals, each about twelve feet in width and three in height, etched at equal distances into the smooth stone wall. Could they be entrances to the tube-car system? If true, it was obvious from the webs of dust that lay heavily across them that they had not been accessed in a very long time.

I crossed the floor and pressed the nearest activation plate, gratified when a low grinding noise began at once and a capsule resembling one of the mass carriers I had seen in the tunnel outside the arenas pushed itself slowly out into the chamber and shuddered to a stop. The lid moved back in fits and starts to expose an interior that was large enough to accommodate a dozen men arranged side by side and head-to-head.

I stood cogitating over this new development. At this juncture, the sensible move would be to retrace my steps and hunker down in the Green Room until I could notify either San Tothis or Tor-ov Ov-tor of my discovery. Would it not be foolhardy to trust myself to a transport system that had obviously lain dormant for many years? Might not the mechanism fail en route to its destination, stranding me in the but slightly larger equivalent of one of the Oolscar's storage hollows for the rest of my days? And what of that destination? The only markings I could discern on the wall next to the capsules were in a foreign script. Suppose I sat up at the end of the journey only to find myself gasping for breath in the heart of the Masters' own dark and airless lair?

But my luck had carried me this far. *In for a pi, in for a tanpi*, I said to myself, using the Barsoomian counterpart of an old saying from Earth.* I stepped into the capsule, stretched out on my back, and touched the side plate. The lid creaked shut and there was a sense of great motion outside the car.

The space in which I sat up a minute later was not airless, but it was as dark as a moonless night. I uncapped my torch and moved it in a slow arc. I was in another station of the tube-car system, this one much larger than the previous. Exiting the capsule and stepping to a nearby doorway, I found myself at one end of a vast, vaulted chamber that stretched out before me into shadow.

I found evidence of long disuse here as well, though I saw no signs of damage. The floor, of ebon marble shot with a tracery of gold and silver, was furnished with large round tables, chairs, desks, and a scattering of chest-high cylindrical platforms, all of a variety of materials, including wood, marble, and metal, and all in a condition of excellent preservation beneath their thick coating of dust. The great central room gave onto other chambers that were almost equally spacious and high-ceilinged, each of which might comfortably accommodate several hundred individuals. Everywhere was elegant crafting and artistic design. Indeed, the place looked like nothing

---

* A *pi* is the smallest of the coins of the Barsoomian monetary system, made of copper and roughly similar to the American cent. A *tanpi* is composed of gold and the equivalent of the dollar.

that the worms and their human Hands and Numbers had patched together in the Circles I had already visited, the grand scale and richness of detail reminding me more of some of the long-dead Orovar cities I had visited.

Filled with excitement, I rode the capsule back to the chamber from which I had embarked, noting with relief that the mechanism seemed to run more, rather than less, smoothly during the return trip. Backtracking through the hidden ways, I reentered the Green Room scant moments before the arrival of San Tothis and a pair of other conspirators. I waited for them to discard their ragged smocks and buckle themselves into the harness that transformed them into civilized men again, and then told them I had something of interest to show them. They followed me wide-eyed through the newer passageways and into the tube-car room. I confess I relished the expressions of profound shock on their faces when the lid of the transport slid open and we climbed out into the great chamber.

We quickly spread out, exploring the place with our torches, the most welcome discovery occurring when Tanus, a likable fellow who had served under San Tothis aboard the *Vanator*, happened to depress an ornamental knob on one of the small upright podiums. Light instantly appeared in the room, beginning pale and rosy in the far spaces where the walls met the vaulted ceiling and flowing upward like dawn until the whole room was bathed in the purest, warmest illumination I had seen in days—and they in decades: an unwavering facsimile of early morning sunlight produced neither from radium-infused ore nor luminous fungus, nor—most importantly—scintillating worm larvae! I thought these doughty warriors would weep as they raised their faces to the warm glow from above and I am not ashamed to say I felt a lump rise in my own throat.

"My friends," I said to them as we surveyed the enormous space, "I think we have found our new headquarters."

Tor-ov Ov-tor was quietly impressed when I brought him there some time later. I noticed him glancing at my skin—not quite its normal hue in the rosy glow from the ceiling, yet still several shades lighter than the typical red Martian's—but he made no comment. After seeing the scope of the place, which seemed to stretch on in an endless array of interconnected chambers, he agreed with my assessment that it more resembled part of an ancient city than it did the other portions of the Perfect World. "Perhaps this place was already in existence when the worms stumbled upon it, and it became the template for their further construction," he said. "For now we have a larger place in which to gather, but we must continue our explorations. There is every chance that we have found our way through the back door into the supposedly destroyed First Circle, and who knows what useful treasures it may contain?"

Hope was tempered with foreboding, for Tor-ov Ov-tor had brought with him sobering news. The engines fueled by the Ninth Ray that were designed to engender vast windstorms upon the surface of Barsoom were being checked and double-checked. Though the Oolscar had made no official declaration of their intentions to those Numbers of his rank assigned to the Fourth Circle, it was apparent that something significant was in the works, and the increased scrutiny had made it almost impossible for Tor-ov Ov-tor to continue to perpetrate his small acts of sabotage.

We spent the next several cycles acquainting the growing band of conspirators with the route to the First Circle, as we believed it to be, and gradually clearing away the dust of ages in our newly christened War Room.

Then, after an unusually extended stay in the Fourth Circle, a haggard Tor-ov Ov-tor reappeared and announced grimly that a new phase in the Masters' Great Enterprise was definitely underway. "We have at most twenty cycles before the storms are unleashed to scour the planet," he said, "while shortly thereafter the full effect of the gravity engines will be concentrated on the Atmosphere Plant and elsewhere. Apparently auxiliary plants have been under construction for some time on the surface, and are now nearing completion. This is undoubtedly behind the sudden acceleration in the Great Enterprise, for they are determined to demolish the original plant before any others can be activated."

He took me aside to impart additional information. "There is much discussion among the Masters concerning the missing captive. Several other high-ranking Numbers and I were privy to a debate carried on by half a dozen worms while in possession of various corpse-men and women so that we humans could follow the conversation—something that is rarely allowed. They have started receiving reports of strange goings-on in the arenas, though this does not greatly concern them as yet. Interestingly, a number of the Masters flatly refuse to acknowledge the existence of this invisible trickster in the Perfect World, while others believe that his presence here may actually work to their benefit, since escape is patently impossible and maintaining their foe here beneath the surface will guarantee his inability to once more thwart their designs above.

"Some among the worms claim that he is simply a man, who can and will be killed like other men, while others verge on a superstitious awe of his abilities. They recounted some of his supposed crimes." Here he fixed me with a calculating stare. "Tell me, Vetj—are you truly the individual who frustrated the Masters' first attempt at destroying the Atmosphere Plant?"

"I am."

"And were you then also responsible for the downfall of the erstwhile goddess Issus and her false religion?"

When I acknowledged my hand in that matter as well, he took a step back as if to get a better view of me. "How can this be true?" he whispered.

I shrugged. "You said so yourself some time ago, my friend. I am an unusual person."

Tanus of Gathol, whose Number I had never committed to memory, strove along with his former commander in the Seventh Circle, where he designed microscopic bits of instrumentation—often secretly incorporating minor flaws that prolonged and complicated their manufacture—to be used in the gravity engines. As it turned out, he was also a talented engineer and draftsman, and it was he who commandeered one of the War Room's massive ersite tables to devise an elaborate map of the Nine Circles. Using information amassed over the centuries, he presented the underground region as a grid of connected realms, with various objects standing in for proposed target sites and small colored markers for the different conspirators assigned to them—until the whole resembled nothing so much as an insanely complex game of jetan being played out on half a dozen boards at once.

Mounting the dais at the front of the room before the largest gathering of conspirators we had yet assembled, I looked at the Perfect World spread out in miniature before me, and assessed the efforts already underway: here were the fields of the Eighth Circle, where Helten En and his trusted assistants were beginning to slowly decrease the potency of the chemical additives that calmed and cheered. Soon bliss-cakes and bliss-water would be merely food and drink, and the Numbers and Hands who habitually consumed them would find a growing dissatisfaction with their lot in life. I continued to participate in contests in the arenas of the Fifth Circle, though many others had stepped up to demonstrate to the spectators that human fighters were capable of holding their own against a variety of adversaries formerly deemed invincible. Exploration was continuing here in the First Circle, as well; a rumor had been circulating that the vault where the Oolscar kept the daggers and other weapons that they doled out to their corpse-men and Long-arms when it became necessary to arm them was located somewhere on the far side of the supposedly devastated Circle, and we raced to find an internal entrance to it.

Looking out over the assemblage beneath the clear illumination of the War Room, I could understand Tor-ov Ov-tor's desire to leave past national and racial identities behind, as there were several here who would have been at each other's throats were we still on the surface. My audience consisted of some two hundred red men and women of various nations, along with a smattering of dark-skinned First Born, a pair of pale-skinned, fair-haired brothers who identified themselves as Orovars from the ancient Citadel of Horz, and six green men of Thark and a green woman of Warhoon who towered over all at the back of the gathering. The time had come, however, for all to unite as freedom-seeking enemies of the Masters and throw off the yoke of enslavement and the chains of captivity.

I began by describing those efforts now in progress and then detailed my plans for the near future. Above all, I exhorted them to continue to make contact with others they were sure they could trust, forging a chain of conspirators to spread the word that great change was coming and that we must be ready to take advantage of it.

"But how can this be accomplished without word reaching the Oolscar through their human agents?" asked one of the Orovars. Both he and his brother had been down here for some hundreds of years since they had been snatched from the pits beneath their ruined city, as evidenced by the missing fingers on their left hands.

"It is true that we must proceed with great caution and discernment," I responded. "And yet I know it can be done. Decades ago, before the downfall of Issus and her evil religion, the beloved princess of Barsoom's mightiest nation fell into the clutches of evil men in the Valley Dor. Those who wished to secure her release plotted for close to a year in utmost secrecy, for the country itself was at that time under the rule of an unfriendly neighboring nation, and one loose tongue would have betrayed their plans and scuttled the entire endeavor. Yet over a million trustworthy followers of the princess were enrolled in the cause with nary a word reaching the foreign pretenders who held their nation in sway, each man limiting his recruitment only to those about whose absolute loyalty he had not a shred of doubt."

"Yet they had a year!" cried another. "We have a few weeks, at the most."

"All the more reason to begin at once," I told him. "And to be doubly circumspect in your choice of confidants."

As the crowd dispersed to make their way back to their various Circles, I reflected on the complicated combination of strategies we had set in motion, and the fact that all of these endeavors were more by way of carefully coordinated groundwork for the main acts of rebellion that must soon follow.

Yet it was not long before some new and wholly unforeseen pieces were introduced into the game.

25
AN UNEXPECTED CALLER

SHARU ALERTED US after she found him unannounced on the floor in the tunnel of the Ninth Circle, and we quickly removed him and brought him here through the hidden ways for your inspection, Prince," San Tothis told me, with a jerk of his thumb at the naked man watching us warily as he leaned in the shadows against the doorjamb in the main entrance to the War Room. "He is either a simpleton or a very good liar, for he professes not to understand our speech."

"He also staggers like one who has drunk too much, though we smelled no spirits on his breath," put in Tanus.

In accordance with our recently established customs, I asked Tanus to furnish the newcomer with a harness and some silks, and then, after watching him awkwardly buckle himself into the leather like one who has never done so before, I instructed them to seek out Tor-ov Ov-tor and see if there was aught new to report on his efforts at sabotage in the Air Control Center.

"In the meantime, I will attempt to get some answers from this one and decide whether he should be allowed to leave the chamber after what he has already witnessed."

"At once, John Carter!"

The individual in question, who had taken a seat at the great table once he finished dressing himself, had been watching me with his head tilted to one side in an attitude of close appraisal. As the others left to take up their duties he pushed carefully to his feet and shuffled over. "At last a pair of words I understand!" he said in perfect

American English. "If you are truly John Carter, then I suppose I have found my way to the planet Mars."

"Indeed you have," I replied after a single moment's hesitation. Now that he was standing before me I was struck by the relative paleness of his tanned skin and noted that with that thatch of dark hair he was obviously no thern or Orovar. I was beginning to wonder if Barsoom had become a stop on some interplanetary railway line from Earth. "And if you are but newly arrived here, it seems from your forthright announcement that you have made the journey with wits intact."

"Reasonably," he said with a grin. He was a handsome fellow; the smile he flashed would have done credit to a matinee idol back on Earth. "Although I confess I'm a bit perplexed that it's the coherence of my speech you find worthy of note, rather than my mere presence here on another world."

"We wayfarers from Earth are a less exclusive society than I had once assumed," I acknowledged. "Though our previous guest barely seemed to grasp the significance of her whereabouts before she once again resumed her travels."

His eyes widened. "She's been here then, and recently?" This time his smile reflected a combination of surprise and relief. "This is welcome news! I hadn't expected to arrive so close on Victory's heels!"

His remark puzzled me. "Are you and the young lady engaged in some form of relay race?" I inquired. "If so, this strikes me as one situation where a miss is as good as a mile. Or fifty million miles, to be exact. Especially as the young miss seemed ignorant of any pursuit when we spoke. In fact, she had but recently recalled her own name."

He looked thoughtful.

"Odd," he said. "I expected she might not have been aware that I had entered the vortex at her back, but I'm pretty certain she's since been apprised of my own peregrinations. But you say that she was experiencing memory loss? That's troubling! I've had no such lapses."

"Nor have I during my own travels," I told him. "But Betty was only just emerging from a state of deep confusion when she disappeared again."

"Excuse me—what did you call her?" he asked, his dark brows contracted in a frown.

"Betty, though I suppose she was christened Elizabeth. Don't tell me it is Loto, after all," I added with a skeptical smile. "That hardly seems a likely name for a Brooklyn girl, though perhaps customs have changed in the years since I last visited New York."

"Brooklyn! Victory told you that she was from New York City?"

"Victory?" I echoed. We eyed one another in mutual confusion.

"I think," I said, "that we had best take a few paces back and begin again. For starters, you might tell me your own name and how you came to recognize mine."

"Of course—my apologies! I'm Jason Gridley of California. You and I share an acquaintance in Tarzana—or at least we did until a short time ago." A melancholy shadow flitted across his features. "And I've spent many an hour communicating with your friend Paxton and the Martian technicians he's been training to operate the equipment."

"Gridley," I repeated. "Of course—the Gridley Wave is your brainchild! You're the fellow behind our communications revolution." I extended my hand and we performed a good old-fashioned American handshake.

"None other," he said with a smile. "I have read some mighty interesting accounts of your exploits, John Carter, and it's good to finally meet you—though I never dreamed it would be under these fraught circumstances. Circumstances that I am still trying to unravel."

I wondered if he would retain his good humor once I had explained our present situation, trapped here beneath the surface of Barsoom in a madhouse ruled by giant, sapient centipedes and their corrupt human servants. At his request I first recounted my experiences with the woman I had known variously as Loto, Betty, and Miss Callwell. Gridley listened with rapt attention, interjecting a question here and there. At last he shook his head.

"It's all very fascinating," he told me, "though frankly more perplexing than enlightening, and, I must confess, disappointing in terms of my present objective. What do you suppose happened to her?"

"She seemed unable to account for the impetus behind her own comings and goings," I said. "The last time I saw her, she was fascinated by one of our moons. Whether her travels took her there, I have no idea, but it seems no more improbable than any other theory. But what about yourself? What strange twist of fate brings you here to Barsoom?"

Gridley gave a gusty sigh. "I can't offer too much more in the way of accounting for my own travels. I embarked on this odyssey in an attempt to recover my godchild and fellow scientist, Victory Harben, whom I last glimpsed as she was being swept into a glowing vortex of purplish light in the land of Pellucidar, that fantastic realm situated at the Earth's core of which you have doubtless heard in your many conversations with our mutual friend. I leaped into the maelstrom just behind her, intent on bringing her back, but our paths diverged at once and I have caromed helplessly from place to place ever since. My latest stop was the planet Venus, if you can believe it, where I learned that Victory had also briefly appeared. Unfortunately, our paths never crossed on that cloud-shrouded world, despite the fact that I sojourned there for some time before being swept away again." He surveyed the War Room with a dejected expression. "Now I find myself here on Mars in dire straits, and apparently no closer to my original goal."

"Venus!" I marveled. "I have often wondered what it would be like to visit Cosoom, as we name it here. Our scientists have long claimed that it is home to highly intelligent life."

Gridley gave a wan smile. "Its own inhabitants call it Amtor, and I can attest from recent personal experience that it is a lively place."

"Amtor . . ." I was puzzled again. "Loto—Betty—spoke of such a place! It seems that you two have also come close to crossing paths, yet she is clearly not the Victory you seek." I shook my head. "You are right. It is all very baffling."

When I asked Gridley how long he had been on Barsoom and by what means he had made his way down here into the Perfect World, he informed me that he had been traveling on Venus with a small group led by his friend Carson Napier—yet another transplant from Mother Earth, whose own journey through the void had apparently been conducted in a rocket ship originally intended to carry him here to Barsoom! One night Gridley had felt himself drawn down a tunnel at the back of a cave in which they had sought shelter. He found his way to a chamber where blue light flickered, and beheld a strange creature, quite dead and quite unlike anything he had seen on Venus or any other world in his travels thus far. From the description Gridley offered I soon realized that he was speaking of a Barsoomian green man—on Cosoom! Approaching the corpse, he suddenly felt the electric tingling he had come to recognize as the precursor to transportation to another world. The next thing he knew, he was in a new and unknown place, lying in near darkness on a rocky surface from where he could hear the nearby rush of moving water.

"I was fortunate to find myself on dry land, as my first appearance on Amtor had me several fathoms down in an alien ocean without a diving suit—though luckily I vanished again before I had time to drown! When I returned there much later, it was to a location not far from my first materialization. Several months of adventures on other worlds had gone by for me—yet according to my friend Carson only a few hours had elapsed in his own reality since he had glimpsed me struggling in the water during my first appearance. Since then, I've come to the realization that Victory and I are untethered in time as well as space."* He shook his head. "At any rate . . . lacking garments and weaponry—my usual state after one of these jaunts— my first priority was to strike out in search of both, and then to find some means of identifying where in the universe I had come to ground this time.

"I was lying on a narrow pathway that was bordered on one side by a wall of rough black rock which curved up and over me to form a roof about fifty feet above my head, the only illumination emanating

---

* For more on Jason Gridley's and Victory Harben's unanticipated tours through the vagaries of space-time, see the ERB Universe novel *Carson of Venus: The Edge of All Worlds* by Matt Betts and its bonus novelette, "Pellucidar: Dark of the Sun" by Christopher Paul Carey, as well as "Victory Harben: Clash on Caspak" by Mike Wolfer, the bonus novelette in *Tarzan: Battle for Pellucidar* by Win Scott Eckert.

from a few large nuggets of some sort of glowing ore that protruded here and there from the wall. On the other side of the path was a partial barrier of jagged rocks, from beyond which came the sound of moving water. Feeling a bit wobbly—another common aftereffect of these journeys through the ether—I reached out and cautiously pulled myself to my feet and peered out between two of the upthrust rocks. The path ran alongside a sizable waterway, its opposite shore lost in the shadows across the water. I was debating whether to set out to the left or right along the pathway, when my attention was drawn to a glimmering of pale light from upstream. A moment later I was spellbound by a vision that seemed to come straight from an old-time fairytale."

26

ON THE RIVER OF MYSTERY

A PPROACHING SILENTLY on the black waters," Jason Gridley
continued, "I beheld a fleet of nine stately barges of ivory-
colored wood, each of them flat-bottomed, long and graceful,
and tapered in the front like a fancy slipper out of the Arabian Nights
to an inward-curving point from which were hung golden lanterns
that shed brilliant white light."

Gridley was shielded from the view of those aboard the flotilla
by the partial wall of jagged rocks. Thinking it unwise to leave his
place of concealment until he had determined the character of the
newcomers, he crouched low and surveyed the fleet as it drew near
his vantage point. In each of the first four boats, rows of raised
benches held individuals cloaked and hooded in azure blue, whom
he took to be warriors by the broadsword hanging in its white
scabbard from each man's hip. Half a dozen similarly clad oarsmen
sat along either side from prow to stern. Their ivory oars rose and
dipped, cutting the water at precise angles so that the barges whispered
along in near silence, only adding to the aura of unreality.

Four identical vessels led the procession and four more brought
up the rear. The craft at the center of the group was larger than its
escorts, a good forty feet from stem to stern, with a gleaming hull
carved with fanciful designs and decorated in bright accents of gold
and azure. Gridley found it a captivating sight, its splendor reflected
in the dark waters beneath the high and craggy ceiling of black rock.

Seated amidship on an ivory dais was a most fantastic apparition,
beside which the fairyland vessels themselves paled into insignificance:
a life-size statue of a golden goddess, minutely detailed, its skin

tinted a warm, ruddy gold and its copper-red hair sculpted in a complicated design and caught in a tiara of gold filigree wound with azure ribbons. The exquisite figure's only garment was a gauzy scarf of the same pure blue wrapped loosely around the perfectly executed form. Ten attendants bearing staves of gold in addition to the swords at their sides stood at attention about the raised platform, their own forms disguised in hooded cloaks of alternating white and blue, while twice as many oarsmen sat on the benches that ran along either side from prow to stern.

Wonderstruck, and momentarily forgetting his caution, Gridley rose up out of his place of concealment as the barge drew near. Then, as he stood silently staring, the most unexpected thing of all occurred: the golden statue turned its head and met his gaze!

If possible, her face was even more beautiful when animated than he had judged it in repose. Azure eyes widened in startlement above her slightly parted ruby lips. A thrill passed up his spine as he stepped out from behind the fang of rock, returning her astonished scrutiny across the black water. Only for an instant did they lock eyes, and then they were wrenched apart by a chorus of hoarse shouts from the quartet of smaller vessels preceding the central barge down the waterway. But it was not Gridley's sudden appearance that had occasioned the exclamations of alarm. He turned to face a sight that was as unspeakable as it was incredible.

A score of slender ropes had dropped silently from the shadowed ceiling several yards in front of the foremost craft. The cords dangled like great spider threads in the gloom, while along their lengths hung the makings of a gruesome feast for some monster as yet unseen, for rotting human corpses festooned the ropes like sausages in a butcher's window. Gridley felt his gorge rise as he squinted at the glazed eyes and the sparkling sheen of decay that overlaid the torn and empurpled flesh. Was this a ghoulish warning from some unseen foe, upon whose territory the ivory boats had unwittingly trespassed?

Gridley was not the only one so affected, for the weird spectacle had caused great consternation among the cloaked warriors who manned the barges. The oarsmen on the lead ship strained against the powerful current to reverse their headlong motion, and the vessel began to slow, its stern nearly bumping into the forepart of the one just behind it. But it was too late, and the graceful prow of the first barge slid beneath that awful tableau of ghastly, swaying bodies.

It was then that Gridley felt a shiver traverse his spine for the second time since his arrival on the banks of the black river, as that which had heretofore seemed inanimate sprang unexpectedly to life.

Yet these were not exquisite golden statues invested suddenly with vitality, but monstrous travesties of humanity, and he watched in horrified disbelief as the lowest dozen of the dangling abominations released their holds upon the spider ropes and dropped onto the ivory deck. Only then did he note the slim blades that hung at the side of each rotted flank, needlelike daggers that flashed in the lantern light as the living corpses brandished them above their gruesome heads.

As if a spell had been broken, the warriors on the escort boats threw back the hoods and cloaks that had obscured their features, and Gridley saw for the first time that their skin was as ruddily golden and their hair as coppery red as that of the woman, as they rose from their benches as one man to defend their vessel from the horrific boarding party.

The battle was quickly joined. No longer mindful of his own concealment, Gridley hurried along the path to follow their progress, his heart surging in frank admiration of the courage and prowess with which they fought.

By contrast, there seemed not an ounce of martial skill among the corpselike attackers, who stabbed and thrust haphazardly with their daggers at aught who moved about them; yet what they lacked in finesse they more than made up for in numbers. Dozens of the decaying bodies slid down the spider threads, and Gridley realized for the first time that the ropes were not affixed to the rocky surface of the shadowed ceiling itself, as he had first presumed, but had been lowered out of concealed apertures, down through which an increasing army of the monstrous creatures continued to crawl. Soon the leading barge rocked back and forth beneath their weight, its pristine deck aswarm with shambling invaders, as the next ship in line hastened forward to succor its fellow.

Gridley looked to the dim tunnel ahead, alarmed to see more

spider ropes unfurling, each one bearing its hideous complement of dangling creatures, while still more of the living corpses appeared above to crawl insect fashion down ropes already shed of their burdens. The current swept the ivory ships along and a second barge was boarded and then a third, their own valiant crews at once engaged in desperate battle.

Shortly after the commencement of the attack, Gridley had become aware of an incongruous noise: a high-pitched clashing, as of a multitude of tiny bells being vigorously shaken. As the defenders threw off their cloaks and stood at the ready in the barges nearest to him, he saw that their broadswords were constructed after a most peculiar design: all of a single piece of silver metal from hilt to point, with a narrow slit down the center of each sword that was strung with dozens of small golden bells. The warriors handled the weapons with incredible skill, balancing the blades in their hands so that they remained utterly silent until their masters wished them to speak, at which point they rang out in a shivering chorus he thought must be designed to unnerve their foes. If such was the case, they appeared to be ineffectual against this breed of insensate opponent.

The invaders themselves, about a third of whom were female, fought in an unnatural silence that was as unnerving as the clashing bells. They had little regard for the deadly accuracy of the golden warriors' weapons, pressing forward to wield their own slender blades with no seeming awareness of any pain or injury they themselves incurred. Even a wicked sword thrust through the breast did little to slow them, while those whose arms were hacked away fought on with tooth and clawed toenail, as reinforcements dropped from overhead to pry the daggers from severed hands and brandish them anew. Indeed, nothing short of decapitation could fell them, and even then the headless bodies persisted in creeping about among the feet of the combatants, legs convulsing, arms flailing, and skeletal fingers groping, until they either dropped or were kicked overboard into the black waters, where each sank immediately, leaving a peculiar glistening stain on the surface that soon vanished.

Though the living corpses fought without stratagem or subterfuge, it soon became apparent that by sheer numbers alone they could not fail to eventually overmaster the golden warriors, and Gridley's heart contracted with horror as he became aware of an additional fact that would surely hasten that inevitable conclusion: the slim daggers wielded by the living corpses were poisoned!

Moments after even the smallest nick from one of these blades, a golden defender would begin to sway and falter, and then crash unmoving to the ivory deck. Mere slaughter was not the sole aim of the shambling creatures, however, as Gridley realized when the next wave of attackers came crawling down the spider ropes, these not armed with daggers but clutching tightly bound coils of cordage to their emaciated flanks.

As Gridley looked on in horrified fascination, the newcomers stalked among the fallen golden warriors, each one choosing an unconscious victim whom he then bound tightly and, showing surprising strength, hauled up from the deck and across his shoulders before shinnying back up the rope, to vanish into the aperture in the roof like a man-sized spider with its paralyzed prey.

Gridley looked about with a sudden sick feeling to see the largest ship with its precious cargo drawing ever nearer to those curtains of dangling ropes and their monstrous burdens.

All of this, Gridley assured me, though long in the telling, had occurred within the space of only a minute or two.

The golden goddess had risen to her feet at the onset of the attack, the expression of anguish upon her perfect features at once convincing him that she was more distressed by the decimation of her brave escort than by any worries concerning her own fate.

It was when he saw a dozen narrow passages open above the central barge itself and spider threads beginning to lower toward that ivory deck that Gridley reacted in a completely irrational fashion.

"I've always been partial to red hair," he confided with a rueful grin, "and perhaps that slight resemblance to Jana, the Red Flower of Zoram—my own dear wife, whom I have not seen since I embarked on this incredible odyssey—provided some of the impetus for what I did next."

Futile—and possibly fatal—though he knew the gesture to be, Gridley could not suppress the instinct that sent him bursting from his place of observation and leaping outward toward the expanse of black water in one smooth motion. What happened next was no less a shock to himself than he imagined it to be to those aboard the flotilla of ivory vessels.

Far from sending him plunging into the icy depths of the underground river, Gridley's impetuous leap carried him in a great arc that brought the top of his head within mere inches of the rocky ceiling far above—so close that he gazed for a frozen instant into the dead, glistening eyes of one of the animated corpses emerging upside down from his hole—before depositing him squarely on the deck of the central barge, scarcely a yard from she whose imminent peril had prompted his unreasoned actions. He teetered there for a few heartbeats, gathering his wits amid the mounting chaos of battle, then lunged forward and swept the golden woman into his arms.

Unarmed as he was, there was but one thing he could do to ensure her safety. Crouching low, he vaulted upward again, narrowly avoiding the rush of agitated golden warriors and the edges of their ringing blades as he soared out above the black water toward the opposite shore, hoping against hope that a pathway ran there as well—and that fortune might somehow permit him to duplicate the prodigious leap that had delivered him to the barge. Again, to his wonderment, Gridley landed lightly with his burden upon the narrow path that paralleled the river on that side.

Thrusting her way free of his grasp, the golden woman spun around to stare in obvious horror at the melee occurring among the vessels. As more of the monsters dropped onto the ivory decks only to scurry back up into the shadows moments later, their bound victims in tow, it became evident to Gridley that there would be few, if any, survivors among the golden people. Then, even while he strove to restrain the woman from leaping back over the jagged rocks that bordered the path in a fruitless attempt to return to her brave defenders, he saw an even more disheartening sight.

Gridley flinched as a score of those dead faces glistening with decay swung simultaneously in their direction, almost as if controlled by a single intelligence. Having overwhelmed their golden adversaries by sheer force of numbers, the attackers of the central vessel now turned their full attention toward the two of them. At once some fastened themselves like giant insects to the upturned end at the vessel's prow, while others clasped their limbs and then reached upward to still others who hung from the spider ropes above, thus effectively anchoring the vessel to the ceiling and halting its progress down the river, while the remaining ships upon which the fighting still raged swept helplessly past them on either side.

The creatures were as silent as before, yet somehow commands passed among them. More ropes uncoiled from the rock ceiling to be released at a sharp tug from below, whereupon they fell into the skeletal hands. These lines terminated in nooses and soon the creatures began to hurl them with surprising precision toward the bank where Gridley and the golden goddess stood. It did not take long before one of the throws snagged a tapered rock and held. Gridley lunged forward at once and tried to pry it off, but several of the monsters on the boat pulled it taut and he could not budge the thing. First one and then another of the creatures crept out from the deck and, clinging by hands and feet, began to make their way inexorably toward them. At the same time, other ropes were flung outward to settle over the upthrust rocks both up and down the bank.

"I would have been inclined to stay and fight had I been alone," Gridley said, his face tense with the memory. "Yet I knew that a single prick from one of those tainted blades could spell my end, leaving my golden companion to fend for herself against a horde of corpses. I was trying to decide whether we should run upriver or down, when I heard a man's voice cry out nearby in a foreign tongue I did not recognize. I turned to see a half-naked man with copper-red skin and an urgent expression beckoning to us from an opening in the side of the rock wall a few yards down the path that I was sure had not been there before.

"'Who are you?' I exclaimed. 'Are you a friend?'

"The fellow's expression had changed from urgency to astonishment when he gazed on my face. For a brief second he paused in confusion. Then he said, in strangely accented English: 'Yes— a friend! Hurry!'

"The creatures were almost upon us. 'Go with him!' I told the golden woman, knowing she would most likely understand my gestures if not my words. 'I'll try to buy you some time.' And to the man I called: 'Keep her safe!'

"The man hesitated again, then took the shortsword from his belt and, bending low, slid it to me across the pathway, before taking the woman's hand and drawing her into the dark crevice." Seeing the doorway close flush with the rock behind them, Gridley had turned back to face the living corpses as they poured onto the path and swarmed over him. Conscious of an unfamiliar power surging through his muscles, he wielded the sword with herculean strength. Soon the pathway was littered with dissevered bodies, yet still they came, hurling themselves at him from all sides. One of them at last worked its way behind him while he was fending off another three, and Gridley felt the point of a slim dagger pierce his side. At once numbness began to radiate through his body from the site of the wound. He swung the sword in a final powerful arc that sent two of his assailants reeling back over the rocks and into the black water, then crumpled to the ground. Sound faded from his ears and his eyes lost focus, his vision reduced to a jumble of light and shadow.

Gridley felt as if from a great distance clammy hands bundling him into a net of coarse fibers. There came a jerking motion as his body was passed from one creature to another along the rope between the shore and the vessel. Then one of the creatures slung him roughly over its back and he was carried up the spider thread into darkness

27

THE INVISIBLE MEN

RIDLEY LEANED BACK against the wall, eyes veiled in recollection.

"If ever there had been a time when I wished to be transported suddenly elsewhere, that was it," he concluded ruefully. "Naturally, whatever force has been sending me ricocheting from world to world chose that moment to allow me to linger in one place."

He nodded to the far entrance. "When I came to my senses I was in a gigantic tunnel, where I was found by some of your agents, who I am sure deduced from my jabbering in an unknown tongue that I was not from around here. They hustled me through a succession of secret passageways to some sort of transport capsule that eventually brought us here, where they gave me to understand that I was to wait my turn until the head panjandrum requested my presence.

"Naturally, once I had time to think without distraction, I deduced that I had found my way to a world whose gravity was substantially less than that of the Earth, which explained my increased strength and amazing agility—not to mention my continuing tendency to trip over my own two feet. It hadn't occurred to me that this might be Mars, however, until I heard one of the men call you by name just now. You know the rest."

I was not sure what to make of much of his tale. I knew all too well the experience of being snatched from one world and transported willy-nilly to another, while his description of the golden goddess stirred vague memories in me. It was obvious that the creatures he had fought were corpse-men dispatched by the Oolscar to intercept the fleet of ivory barges. But who was the man who had appeared on the pathway next to the black river and responded to his query in English? My mind went instantly to the possibility of still more excursionists from Earth—yet Gridley's description had been of a red Martian.

Another possible explanation occurred to me. "Do you recall what the red man you met by the river first called out to you?" I asked.

Gridley wrinkled his brows in recollection. "It was something on the order of 'ma-morthin,'" he replied after a moment.

"Aha. *Madmorthan* is the Barsoomian word for 'Warlord,'" I told him. "That is actually one of my titles here, and the fact that the fellow was then able to converse with you in English leads me to believe that he was none other than Talo Thoran, a Barsoomian scholar and linguist who was with me shortly before I was taken by the Oolscar, but whom I have not laid eyes on since. It is good to know that he may have managed to escape their grasp!"

"Well, then, I hope that it was he," he said. "But what, pray tell, is an Oolscar when it's at home?"

I spent the next long while detailing to Gridley my adventures belowground and bringing him up to date on all that I had learned of our current captors.

He shook his head in amazement at the conclusion of my peroration. "It would be a pleasant change of pace to find myself in a dull and peaceful corner of the universe at the end of one of my unintended journeys," he said. "Though I am beginning to suspect that no such place exists. At any rate, I am here now, and more than glad to offer whatever assistance you may deem useful until I'm once more borne away on the winds of fate and subatomic entanglement."

I was not familiar with the last concept, which he proceeded to explain to me in great detail—after which I found myself only a little more confused than when he had started.

San Tothis and the others soon returned to the War Room with Tor-ov Ov-tor in tow, and I introduced them all to our new arrival. Tor-ov Ov-tor stared at me when I said that Gridley was a fellow traveler from Jasoom. "Jasoom?" he said. "What are you talking about?"

"I am sure that I have mentioned my otherworldly origins to you on at least two previous occasions," I told him. "But perhaps you were preoccupied at the time." In the face of his obvious skepticism, I persuaded Gridley to take turns with me leaping twenty or thirty feet to the nearest wall and back, at which point Tor-ov Ov-tor sank into one of the elegant ersite chairs and mopped his brow. "You said that I was an unusual person," I reminded him with a smile. "Maybe now that there are two of us, you will not find me so remarkable."

I provided Gridley with some food and drink and then took him at his word and put him to use in our plan. Gaining confirmation from the others that his skull was as impenetrable as my own when it came to mind-reading, I concluded that he must also be invisible to the Masters, and thus as immune as myself from the summary justice in the form of extreme gravity that they were wont to mete out to those who crossed them. Gridley had acquainted me with some of his more dramatic exploits in the Stone Age land at the Earth's core and professed himself both able and willing to try his luck at continuing to invert the status quo in the arenas. Soon the two of us were working mischief together at opposite ends of the Fifth Circle, and word quickly spread that the mysterious leaping phantom had now gained the ability to battle in two amphitheaters at once.

Though Gridley's success in picking up the Barsoomian common tongue was spotty at best, he had noticed early on that most of the conspirators referred to me by something other than my given name. When I explained the significance of the system of Numbers established by the Oolscar and told him of the particular meaning of the epithet he was hearing as "vetch," he inquired at once after the Barsoomian translation of "Zero minus one," and thereafter proudly introduced himself to newcomers as "Vetj vem-Ay."

Useful in the arenas, Gridley soon proved indispensable in other matters when it came to a series of colossal chambers filled with damaged and apparently inoperable machinery to which we had just gained access on the outskirts of the War Room. A Hand with a good memory who had once delivered provisions to one of the refectories located in the Third Circle had tentatively identified the rows of mammoth engines as closely resembling apparatus he had glimpsed in the Gravity Control Center. I brought Gridley along to see if he could make heads or tails of the assemblage.

"I can't pretend to fully understand the purpose of most of these," he told me after wandering for an hour among the great engines, "but I'm pretty sure that with the right tools and supplies I can at least partially repair the major damage. Give me a few uninterrupted days with them and they just might be doing again whatever it was they were originally designed to accomplish."

This gave me an idea. "If you can repair these, do you think you might also cause enough damage to ones that are intact to render them nonfunctioning? If our suspicions are proven correct, there may be some similar devices in the Third Circle that could present a major threat to the world above."

"By all means," he said with a smile. "It goes against my nature to vandalize machinery, but I'd happily do it for a good cause."

Gridley came to me at the end of an intense couple of cycles for both of us, his brow creased with concern. We were alone in the small room not far from the main chamber that I had set aside for those in need of rest who did not wish to return to their customary barracks.

"We may have a problem, John. The more I travel in this singular fashion, the more attuned I've become to the unique sensations that seem to surge through my body like the tingle of a mild electric current just prior to my being swept away," he told me. "Lately I've been feeling them again. I'm not nearly done with my restoration project here, and we still haven't gotten me into the Third Circle, so I'd like to hold on for at least a few more days.

"In light of that, it's occurred to me that an unpredictable providence may have delivered me to the one person in the solar system who could possibly aid me in gaining some control over when and where I go—while incidentally assisting me in taking advantage of your hospitality here on Barsoom for a longer period," he said. "I know that you were originally flung through space when you least expected it, but that since then you have somehow learned to come and go solely at your own behest. Have you any pearls of wisdom regarding the fine art of transmigration through the ether that you might care to share with me?"

"You mentioned that you were familiar with some of the published accounts of my life here on Barsoom," I said. "Do you by any chance recall the strange story of Kar Komak, the bowman of Lothar who was instrumental in aiding my son Carthoris in his rescue of Thuvia of Ptarth?

Gridley acknowledged that he remembered it well. "He was originally one of that army of phantom archers conjured up by the potent minds of the surviving Orovars of Lothar to protect them from the marauding green men who perpetually laid siege to their walled city. At the end of one day-long battle, Kar Komak found himself miraculously still in existence, though all his fellows had returned to the nothingness from whence they sprang. I found the notion a wonderful fantasy!"

"Exactly so, though of course it was no fantasy. Kar Komak is a unique visitor from out of Barsoom's ancient past, having lived his first life some half million years ago as commander of the mightiest fleet of sailing ships to ply the five oceans of that far-gone world. Later he ceased to be the mere figment of a Lotharian's overdeveloped brain, and through some vagary of fate was granted a second existence here in latter-day Barsoom. Over the years, he and Carthoris have become fast friends, and when he is not roaming the world he spends much of his time as our guest in Helium, where I have had occasion to converse with him often.

"I was most interested when Kar Komak told me that for a time following his rebirth he would feel an occasional ethereal pull, as if his spirit were being summoned back to the Beyond from whence it came. He told me that at first it took a conscious effort of will, especially when he was feeling fatigued or overwrought, to keep himself from fading back into the void, but that after a short while it was as if an unseen switch had been thrown inside his brain and the call to nothingness ceased, never to return. From that moment on he has felt as real as you or I. Indeed, he has gone on from being the phantasmal creation of the advanced mental abilities of the Lotharians to exploring the power within his own mind.

"We were deep in discussion on such matters in Helium one day, when Kar Komak provided me with a tangible illustration of this power. In front of my eyes, he gestured to the empty tabletop between us and suddenly a goblet of wine appeared, which he offered me. I took a sip and tasted the fine vintage that, so he claimed, he had summoned from out of his memory of half a million years in the past. Kar Komak confided to me that the only drawback—or perhaps benefit—to this conjured libation was that it would neither assuage my thirst nor provide me with the slightest inebriation, no matter how much of it I consumed."

Smiling at the look on Gridley's face, I added, "In retrospect, it made for an unsettling conversation, though a useful one, for Kar Komak offered to perform a demonstration more pertinent to my own interests when next we met. Accordingly, I entered his apartments one evening not long after to find him seated cross-legged on the carpet, his face creased in concentration, after the manner of a yogi of the Far East. I took a seat facing him and waited quietly. A few minutes passed. Thinking to hear a small noise in the antechamber, I looked away for but an instant and when I turned back he was gone. Startled, I leaped to my feet just in time to see the door at the far end of the chamber slide open and there was my host, grinning broadly as he strolled in from the adjoining room."

"It wasn't a trick?" Gridley asked.

"Kar Komak assured me that the phenomenon was real, though it had taken much practice to perfect and still required intense concentration to accomplish. I had noted at once that he had made the transition from one location to another not only clad in his harness, silks and sandals, but—perhaps more importantly on a world where personal weapons are considered a necessary component of the attire of any adult citizen—still fully armed. He explained that it was a matter of forming a precise mental image of himself, trappings and all, in his present environment, and then picturing that same image duplicated at some other location well known to him.

"Heretofore my own experience with this uncanny mode of travel had been limited, as you know, first to being whisked back and forth across the void by some unknown agent, and then later at my own instigation. Even after I had learned to accomplish the transition through my own desire, I had found myself drawn exclusively to a single spot on Earth: the specially constructed tomb in Virginia in which my unaccountably preserved corpse resides to this day.

"At once Kar Komak's deceptively simple explanation set me thinking that perhaps I could learn to use the power of my own not inconsiderable will in similar fashion in order to dictate the terms of any future transportation: not from room to antechamber, but across the trackless interplanetary wastes, even down to choosing my preferred destination and the objects that accompanied me. The pursuit of this goal proceeded in stages, my first triumph being to materialize inside that crypt in the Richmond cemetery without the grim necessity of merging with my own discarded body, a practice I had found increasingly repugnant. Once I had gotten past the seeming paradox of standing in tangible form next to my own recumbent corpse, it was but a short while before I was able to project myself to ever more distant locales. Because I still appeared on Earth stripped of my clothing and other accoutrements, these brief visits were always made to isolated areas familiar to me, and usually in the dead of night. Once I stood for a cold November minute near my former cottage high above the Hudson River; once I roamed for almost half an hour beneath the silver moonlight after paying my respects at the burial site of a fallen friend outside a certain cave in the Arizona desert."

I paused in contemplation of those early expeditions.

"Yet at some point you did succeed in bringing other items along," Gridley prompted. "I remember hearing that you cut quite a figure, striding into the Admiral's sedate Tarzana living room decked out as the Warlord of Mars!"

I responded with a grunt of wry amusement. "Admiral, is it? Did Ed reenlist in the service of his country and neglect to tell me about it?"

He laughed. "Not quite. I liked to tease him about a certain grand-looking yachting cap he was accustomed to wear at the beach. He had told me early on not to call him Mr. Burroughs, and I don't think he minded the nickname."

We shared a few quiet moments in fond recollection, and then Gridley reminded me that I had been telling him of my progress in mastering the art of translocation while fully clothed.

"It was far from a case of instantaneous mastery, I assure you," I told him. "Long before that evening when I paid my call on our mutual friend clad in my familiar Barsoomian habiliments, I had conducted several trial excursions, not all of them concluding as I might have wished!"

I proceeded to tell him the details of a memorable early jaunt I had made to the Chicago World's Fair of 1893 that had culminated with the components of my fine worsted suit, carefully constructed to the fashions of the day by Martian haberdashers, unexpectedly making the return trip to Barsoom some minutes before their wearer, thus subjecting me to several awkward moments on the Midway.

As entertaining as Gridley found the tale of my gradual mastery of such travel, he did not fail to grasp the lesson at its heart: that in order to voluntarily cross the trackless void—whether it be from chamber to chamber or planet to planet—I, at least, required a sure knowledge of my starting point, information that was currently impossible to obtain, and of where I wished to end up, not to mention a calm and meditative environment in which to marshal my will. Absent any certain understanding of where beneath the surface of Mars we had been imprisoned, I had resigned myself early on to the fact that if I were to escape the Perfect World, it would have to be through the tried-and-true method of slipping out unnoticed through a carelessly guarded exit. Since then I had learned of the worms' intention to cleanse the planet of all life save their own, and any thoughts of my own imminent departure had taken a back seat to making sure that objective was never realized.

Gridley returned to his work on the damaged machines, reporting back to me later that after engaging in some meditative exercises he believed he may have started on the path to being able to delay his next leap to a time more of his choosing. "As I told you, I'm beginning to be able to sense when I'm about to be drawn away, and I plan to concentrate with all my might upon an image of myself in the here-and-now and see if that helps anchor me to my current location."

28
REUNIONS

FOR MYSELF I WAS FINDING IT difficult to fix my mind wholly on the future when the unresolved issues of the past persisted in laying claim to my heart. As our plans to frustrate the Great Enterprise continued to unfold, I could not help but find my thoughts wandering often to those with whom I had set out upon the journey that had brought me to this place. Naturally paramount in my concern were the fate and current whereabouts of my daughter. Had Tara been able to assist Ghek in eluding the wrath of the kaldanes that had long ago condemned him to death—or had she herself once more fallen captive in that strangest of lands? I also continued to wonder about the fact that Talo Thoran had not yet turned up, and began to fear that he was not, after all, the man who had appeared at the side of the River Iss just in time to spirit away Gridley's golden goddess. Though he was a clever fellow, I judged the scholar's survival instincts to be of a somewhat lower order than my daughter's, and it grieved me to think that perhaps he had met his end trapped in a dark conduit somewhere between the surface of Barsoom and the Perfect World.

Then one day, when Gridley and I had just returned to the First Circle from an invigorating few hours in the arenas, a puzzled conspirator brought us news of a sequence of faint rhythmic noises that had begun to be heard at certain locations in a newly explored stretch of corridor some distance from the War Room. We hastened to the passage. At first we heard nothing, but then a series of muffled rapping sounds began to issue from somewhere behind one of the panels. Gridley stared wide-eyed at the wall. "That's Morse Code!" he exclaimed.

269

Placing his ear against the polished stone, he brought forth from his pocket pouch a stylus and a scrap of paper upon which he began to scribble as the rest of us waited in tense silence. The sequence repeated itself three times and then ceased.

Shaking his head in bemusement, Gridley handed me his transcription:

ENSCONCED IN PASSAGE WITHOUT OBVIOUS MEANS OF EGRESS IMMEDIATE SUCCOR IMMENSELY APPRECIATED

"Loose translation," Gridley said over my shoulder, "'Get me out of here!'"

I told him I had little doubt that we had found our missing linguist.

We had only that day come across a series of charts of the surrounding complex of chambers and passages engraved on metal tablets inside one of the desks in the War Room. The inscriptions on them were unreadable, yet what we had so far inspected presented an accurate picture of the vicinity and we had hopes that in time we could use them to explore the rest of the First Circle. I dispatched a man to bring us the plans for this section of the complex, over which we pored until we were sure we had pinpointed the nearest hidden doorways. Gridley then rapped out a brief reply, instructing the trapped man to make his way toward the white light when it appeared. We propped doors open in three separate corridors, with someone stationed in each to observe. After a few anxious minutes, a cry drew us to the next passage over. There was the hurried scuff of feet on the floor and Talo Thoran poked his head out. He was gaunt-faced, covered in dust and cobwebs, and talking so rapidly as to be almost incoherent, especially when he recognized Jason Gridley and began a jumbled alternation between Barsoomian and English.

After we had calmed him down sufficiently for an intelligible exchange of information, he conducted us at a near run back through a maze of inner corridors to an area that, unlike those we had heretofore examined, appeared to consist solely of residential quarters. Here he slowed his pace, leading us almost on tiptoe into a great circular chamber whose walls were of polished palthon, a rare stone of a rich blood-red color adorned with traceries of purest white, and decorated in elaborate frescoes depicting carefree scenes of men and women with jet-black hair and skin the color of polished ebony. In the center of the room, a concave disk of metal hung from the high marble ceiling on thick gold chains, and there upon a thin layer of azure-blue silk a beautiful maiden lay sleeping. Her skin gleamed like ruddy gold, while her hair was the red of burnished copper in the light of our several radium torches, and I found myself staring at her with an odd sensation of recognition.

After some searching we discovered an ornamental boss near the doorway that turned to flood the chamber with the same rosy white light found in other sections of what we were now beginning to see as an ancient city in its own right, rather than the crude cavernous environs of the rest of the Nine Circles. I sent for food and water and we settled on marble benches just outside the room while the linguist told us that the two of them had spent the time since he had drawn her into the passageway by the river prowling through a maze of connected corridors. "We wandered for several days, eventually attaining these deserted chambers, but without knowing your method of opening the doors we could not find a way out, nor did we ever encounter another living being. We had been occupying ourselves by teaching our languages to one another," he said in reverent tones between the bites of food he was ravenously devouring. He swallowed. "Do you understand what I am saying? She speaks another language—on Barsoom!—and it is one that I had never heard before, though it does bear some passing resemblance to the ancient tongue of the First Born!" He composed himself with effort and went on: "We were resting to conserve our strength after several days without food or water when she said something to the effect that she must go in search of her people. She closed her eyes and I have not been able to rouse her since."

The golden woman's heartbeat was strong and her breathing slow but steady. One of the conspirators was a green woman who had some medical knowledge. She examined her, but could offer no explanation for her unconscious state.

Talo Thoran installed himself just outside her room, where he remained for several cycles warily eyeing any prospective visitors in the manner of a calot guarding his mistress' chamber—except for short intervals during which he was persuaded to take nourishment or paced up and down the nearby corridors to stretch his muscles. I accompanied him on several of these walks, at which times I enlightened him as to the current situation and tried to glean what further information I could about the newcomer. He said that she had seemed stunned to the point of bewilderment by what had befallen her on the river, and that they had exchanged little actual information as they taught each other simple words and phrases while searching for a way out of the endless corridors.

"Were you at least able to discern her name?" I asked him. "It would be useful to have a way to refer to her other than 'the golden woman.'"

"I did," he said, then paused in obvious reluctance. "She told me early on that her name was . . . Issus."

I stared at him, imagining the effect that notorious appellation would have on many both above and beneath the surface of Barsoom. "I see," I said at last. "Well, perhaps 'the golden woman' will suffice for now."

The section of the First Circle we had entered when we discovered Talo Thoran had brought us to a much older part of what we hypothesized had once been an extensive underground city inhabited by the dark-skinned Parovars. The investigations he had conducted with the golden woman had been largely confined to one area; what our exploration team encountered when they moved forth in the opposite direction seemed to prove our point. I was summoned to a broad portico that overlooked a magnificent cavern larger than any other I had glimpsed in the Nine Circles. Spreading out before us were great edifices of palthon and alabaster beneath a far ceiling that glowed with the same rosy-white light we had found in the War Room and elsewhere.

I would have liked nothing better than to spend the days that followed exploring the place. Unfortunately, the pressing need to save our imperiled planet meant that we must focus our attention only on those aspects of this new discovery that would further our goal of defeating the Great Enterprise. Luckily, one of the first buildings we entered when we reached the floor of this new cavern was yet another transportation nexus containing a multitude of tube-car entrances. We set about immediately to discover where they would bring us and soon had found alternate routes to the interiors of each of the other Circles, all apparently concealed from view at their far ends following the disaster that had caused the Masters to declare the First Circle forbidden territory.

With the culmination of the Great Enterprise drawing near, our master plan involved gaining access over the next several cycles to the engines of potential mass destruction located in the Third and Fourth Circles. After determining that we could use the new system to surreptitiously enter those Circles the Oolscar had declared off-limits to unauthorized individuals, I asked Gridley to accompany me to the Third Circle where the gravity engines were located.

Unlike the case in the Fourth Circle, where his own elevated status could be relied upon to see us past the outer walls of the Air Control Center, Tor-ov Ov-tor had assured me that there was no way we could expect to penetrate the locked gates of its counterpart in the Gravity Circle without explicit authorization from the Masters. Hoping to learn something useful from closer study, Gridley and I donned the ragged tunics of Numbers near the end of one work cycle and took a two-man tube-car to the Third Circle, where we emerged behind a false wall and then fell in with a crowd of male workers heading to the barracks that surrounded the central tunnel.

It was my first time in one of these compartments. Each small cell was designed to accommodate no more than two persons, and was furnished with the requisite small stream of flowing water and a high ceiling that was pitted in these particular caverns by numerous hollows and openings set against the inevitable shifting background of fungus, ore, and worm larvae. As advised by San Tothis, we slipped into the first unoccupied cell we came to. Knowing that we two were effectively invisible to the Oolscar even with their offspring squirming above our heads, we busied ourselves by attempting to appear to our fellow men as if we belonged there—this effort mostly consisting of lying in view of the doorway in a state of feigned exhaustion, with one of us always leaning against the wall facing the opening, legs crossed tailor-fashion and eyes half-closed, so that we might be on the alert for any unwanted scrutiny by agents of the Masters. Soon the traffic of Hands and Numbers seeking a place to rest dwindled.

We had decided to wait for the end of the sleep cycle, so that we could emerge with the others and make our inspection of the center. After standing the first watch, I was roused from what seemed a very brief period of slumber by a sharp elbow to the ribs and a hiss of alarm from my cellmate.

"We have company," Gridley informed me in a hoarse whisper. "Either that or I've nodded off and tumbled smack into the middle of a nightmare."

Rising cautiously up on my elbows, I glanced at the empty doorway, then swung my head to left and right, but saw nothing. Gridley tilted his chin toward the ceiling and I raised my eyes.

A singularly peculiar countenance peered down from one of the roughly circular cavities in the luminous rock some twenty feet above where we lay. The lower rim of the opening was gripped by the tips of six spiderlike legs, while a pair of powerful chelae waved slowly to either side of a grotesque face that was dominated by bulging, lidless eyes and a puckered round hole of a mouth, the combination producing an effect that I had to admit would be nightmarish indeed for the uninitiated.

"Ghek!" I called out in delighted amazement.

"Greetings, John Carter. I am pleased to have finally located you," said our visitor. "Your companion seems quite discomfited by my presence, though I have been attempting to reassure him as to my benign intentions."

Gridley cleared his throat.

"What is a 'gekk,' if I may ask, and how does it know your name?" he inquired in low-voiced wonder, staring back and forth between the two of us.

"Ghek is a kaldane, originally from the valley of Bantoom, first captor and then staunch friend of my daughter Tara, when she found herself by misadventure in the country of his people," I explained to him in English. To Ghek I said: "Jason Gridley is a recent arrival from Jasoom and comprehends but a few words in the common tongue."

"Intriguing," Ghek observed in his toneless voice. "Yourself, Vad Varo, and now this one. Our world would seem to be aswarm with Jasoomians."

"You have no idea," I replied. "But tell me, Ghek—how did you come here and what of my daughter?"

"It is a long story, John Carter. In essence, the princess aided me in avoiding a situation that would surely have resulted in my death, and in the process allowed me to gain a valued new position among my fellow kaldanes. Now a group of us have come here to exact retribution from the Oolscar for their murderous attack on our burrows.

"Since the talkative one had departed with your flier by the time I achieved a new understanding with my people, your daughter accompanied me down through the narrow ways as far as she could and then struck out on her own just before we reached the caverns. We had arranged to meet in a certain location a short time ago, but she did not appear. I have since ranged far and wide throughout the tunnels connecting the various regions, but have as yet not located the princess. She does not seem to be in this grouping of cells, nor do any other human females," he added. "It is my theory that the Oolscar prudently separate their captives by sex to prevent unauthorized breeding."

I relayed the gist of our exchange to Gridley.

"I would be hard pressed to find these filthy warrens conducive to romance," he said with a grimace of distaste. "But tell me: how has your friend managed to elude his own captivity? Is that space above our heads easily navigable? Perhaps we can gain entry to otherwise inaccessible areas by emulating his methods."

Already guessing at the answers, I put the questions to Ghek, who crawled down over the rim of the opening before responding. As Gridley looked on open-mouthed, the nimble kaldane proceeded to perambulate upside down about the ceiling fungus while he spoke.

"I was never in danger of captivity to begin with," he explained. "The Oolscar foolishly look upon those of my race as barely sentient vermin and appear to have no more than a passing awareness of our existence—except when they are in search of some place to test their deadly weaponry. The truth is that our minds are so different from their own that they could not possess us if they tried. For all of that, I must admit that their offspring are quite tasty at this stage." He paused to pluck several of the wriggling larvae from the fungus before him and popped them into his round mouth before continuing. "The strata between the layers of these cells are honey-combed with pleasantly narrow tunnels that open only into the upper crust of the various chambers. Perhaps due to the height of these openings above the floor, as well as their constricted diameter, the Oolscar are not overly concerned that their human captives will utilize them for escape."

I was naturally both heartened and disturbed to learn of Tara's presence here belowground, and clung to the hope that she would curb her innate impetuosity and proceed cautiously until I could discern her whereabouts. In the meantime, Ghek's comments had given me an idea.

"Ghek, there is a large complex located in this Circle that should be filled with sizable amounts of sophisticated machinery. Do you think you would be able to gain entrance to it, and if so, assist Jason Gridley and myself to discreetly enter?"

Ghek told me that he was aware of the location of the Gravity Center and offered to investigate it at once.

"Your friend has no body," Gridley remarked with what I thought was a considerable degree of composure, once Ghek had departed the cell by the same means he had used to enter.

"You are a very observant man," I replied with a grin. "He does occasionally avail himself of the odd beast of burden, however, and it was a desire to pilfer himself a pair of brand-new models that prompted him to come along on the journey that eventually led us to this bleak place."

The kaldane soon returned with the news that he had easily entered the complex via one of the many natural ceiling openings and had moreover been able to surreptitiously locate an isolated doorway through which we could slip inside when we wished. Though it was securely locked from within, Ghek claimed that either he or one of the other kaldanes would have no difficulty in opening it for us whenever we desired.

Two of my former companions were now accounted for, with only the most important to me still among the missing.

Word had reached us of ever more Hands and a growing proportion of Numbers who were performing ably in the arenas, each using a band of silk to disguise his or her features. Two days later San Tothis asked me to accompany him to the Fifth Circle, there being a particular contest he wished me to observe.

With the growing success enjoyed by human combatants against their opponents, the ratio of humans to other species had been adjusted, and so the match he brought me to watch featured a team of three men and three women against two male and two female Long-arms. Following the new fashion, all of the human fighters had emerged from the holding pen sporting lengths of sheer silk wrapped about their heads and some had adorned themselves with other strips about their waists and thighs.

"Is there anything in particular that I should be watching out for?" I asked as the illumination changed from blue-green to maroon and the combatants entered the field.

"I heard rumors last cycle of a new fighter who was having great success in the arenas," he said, "someone far stronger and more agile than one would expect from such a slender frame. I think it will not take you long to discern the one I mean."

The contest began and one of the female Hands immediately distinguished herself from her teammates due to the unorthodox way in which she confronted the opposing force. As her comrades lunged and feinted before the Long-arms, she darted among them like an animated bolt of lightning, positioning herself directly in front of one towering antagonist after another. If you have ever seen the ancient paintings of the bull-leapers of Crete, then you will have some idea of what next transpired. Slim and graceful, she always lingered until mere seconds before the lumbering Long-arm could grasp her in its massive paw, at which time she would spring high into the air and play leapfrog over its head, stripping one of the additional lengths of silk from her body as she flew and pulling it taut over the Long-arm's face to force the creature's head sharply backward. Touching down lightly on the ground, she somersaulted on to the next, while her teammates moved in to shower the cloth-shrouded head of the one she had left behind with expertly aimed blows.

It was my daughter.

My eyes riveted to the potentially deadly scene, I started up from my seat, prepared to hurl myself into the arena at her side, but San Tothis entreated me to restraint. "Patience, Prince—it will soon be over. Look you how she maddens and confuses them with her antics, so that they may be easily taken by the others!"

He was right. With Tara in the lead, the group moved like a well-rehearsed troupe of deadly dancers, each sequence choreographed to confound the slow-witted Long-arms and leave them tripping over one another, as the other Hands singled them out in turn and swarmed over them like ants, gouging eyes and cracking necks. Soon only a single beast-woman remained on her feet. Confronted by the half-dozen Hands, she stumbled from the field on her powerful arms to the great delight of the spectators.

The light began to change from dark red to lavender and then I did desert my seat to leap out onto the field, landing directly in front of the slim, panting form. Tara looked me up and down as she unwound the silken length from her head.

"John Carter, at last!" she cried. "I was wondering how many of these energetic performances I would have to give before you got wind of me, Father!" We embraced and I hurried her from the amphitheater to where San Tothis stood waiting. We had taken to bringing extra tunics with us to the arena, and she slipped gracefully into the ragged smock while we shielded her from those who might seek her out to bestow their congratulations.

San Tothis had been eyeing Tara with an almost fearful intensity. I made formal introductions on our way back to the War Room.

Tears came to my daughter's eyes when she heard that he was one of those gallant warriors who had gone in search of her during the great storm that ravaged Barsoom so many years ago, only to end up a captive of the Oolscar. Taking his hands in hers, she expressed her gratitude so eloquently that the onetime commander of the *Vanator* found himself choking back sobs.

Once we were safe from prying eyes both human and Oolscar, we caught each other up on what had transpired since we had last been together in Bantoom.

I concluded my own account by telling her that the worms had eventually snared me by summoning up another fierce windstorm— though on a much smaller scale than that which she had once experienced. "Talo Thoran and I went our separate ways for a while," I told her. "However, he has also recently turned up here, with a most interesting companion, and Ghek has made his presence known, as well. But now tell me of your own adventures and how they happened to lead you to this unlikely place."

She began with the moment I had been spirited away from the rykor storehouse by the Oolscar-controlled malagath, leaving her and the scholar aboard the *Kantim* and Ghek somewhere inside the building. After setting the controlling destination compass, she had leaped from the flier to the window of the storeroom and peered within to find Ghek being pursued by three guards, the four agitated kaldanes producing shrill whistling noises that set her nerves on edge.

After waiting long enough to have Talo Thoran bring her certain items from the flier's cargo locker, she had squeezed in through the window and dropped onto a narrow ledge directly below that ran all the way around the interior of the building, no doubt for the convenience of kaldanes who wished to inspect the contents from above. There she crouched, playing her torch upon the drama below.

Never in her life had Tara observed a stranger tableau. Pursuers and pursued alike sprang from body to body among the listlessly moving herd, now pausing to animate a rykor when necessary to gain some ground, then abandoning it once the crush of shuffling bodies rendered such movement impractical, to skitter ahead on spider legs to the next advantageously situated host, Ghek distinguishing himself by the daring leaps he made from one pair of headless shoulders to another. Perhaps spoiled by more prolonged dependency upon their rykors, the pursuing kaldanes seemed less nimble, though they had the benefit of being able to act in concert to keep him hemmed in between them. Edging along the narrow ledge above them, Tara found it difficult to decide which species made for the more ghastly spectacle: the whistling, capering, great-headed spider-things or the tightly packed mass of headless humans, some crawling on their hands and knees, others on two feet as they shambled their way about the pen—until suddenly one of the kaldanes would halt long enough to squat on an unoccupied neck and thrust the small bundle of writhing tentacles at the rear of its head into the cavity just behind the rykor's mouth. Then the blindly groping body would jerk upright with purposeful movement, arms stretching out to shove its fellows brusquely aside as it stalked through the herd.

Differences of sex were immaterial in this grotesque enterprise. At one moment four women strove with desperate purpose through the mass of flesh; seconds later one of the pursuers was a man; then it was two males and a female chasing another female, two females and a male in earnest pursuit of a leaping, scampering, disembodied head, and so on and on. Though Tara was prepared to aid Ghek in his flight however she could, keeping track of which kaldane was which in a given moment was a dizzying prospect as she crept along the high ledge. Differentiation was made possible only by the ornamented leather straps worn by Ghek's three pursuers, as the bejeweled headdresses flashed in her torch beam and glittered under the pale moonlight now streaming in from the high-set portals.

"At last I saw my opening," she told me, "just after Ghek quit the latest body he had commandeered. He had been gradually backed into a far corner of the warehouse and it looked as if there was finally no possibility of eluding his pursuers. Placing my thumb and fore-finger between my lips, I produced a surprisingly shrill whistle of my own. At this the action halted and all four swung about to stare. 'Ghek!' I cried. 'Catch!' I hurled the metal ball I had obtained from the flier in a low arc and watched it fall out of sight between the shuffling bodies and the wall. Immediately dismissing my actions as inconsequential, the trio of guards pushed forward through the sea of rykors with obvious confidence."

Suddenly Tara saw a disturbance in the crowd milling before the wall, and Ghek rose above the headless bodies, his head now poised on a gleaming metal torso. He took a step toward his pursuers, then another, his four flexible arms hurling the rykors to either side as if they were weightless. The kaldane guards stood stricken, their great lidless eyes staring. They muttered to one another for a moment, then came to a swift decision and lowered themselves slowly to the floor upon the knees of their mounts as if before a god.

"You should have seen him, John Carter!" Tara told me. "Never have I beheld Ghek so forceful. He confided to me later that it was mostly bravado, learned during his years in Helium, but he addressed those kaldanes as if they were children who had gone astray and they cowered before him. Summoning me to his side, he bade them conduct us to their leaders, and so we set off through the tunnel to the main tower, where he strode like a god indeed among the other kaldanes and their mere flesh-and-blood rykors.

"Ghek had told me years ago that the kaldane mind is so constructed that the thoughts and attitudes of one are as an index of the entire race. I was therefore not surprised when the assembled monarchs shared the feelings of awe we had witnessed in the guards. From them we learned that the attack that had decimated the northern valley had originated from deep below the earth, perpetrated by beings whom they referred to as Oolscar. As you know, the kaldanes are creatures of unwavering custom and routine, bound to their own burrows, and it has never been their way to venture from their valleys to wage war. Yet never had they been subjected to such a ruthless assault. Ghek conferred with the monarchs for long hours before the decision was made to follow the ancient subterranean tunnels to the enemy stronghold, and in the end all agreed that retribution must be sought and any further occurrence of this atrocity prevented."

The tunnels beneath Bantoom are extensive, and the kaldanes had been acquainted with the Oolscar in antiquity, all such experience still retained in their prodigious memories. It was not long before they had found their way to the Perfect World. Once there, a small contingent quit their rykors and spread out through the narrower passages within the walls and ceilings through which only they could move in order to reconnoiter. Word soon came back to the main body that there was unrest among the many thousands of prisoners, most of it traced to the presence of a strange newcomer. Suspecting the identity of the troublemaker, Tara left the kaldanes at this time to slip into the Perfect World alone. There she joined the captives, discarding her silks and harness to disguise herself as a lowly Hand. "It was far easier than I expected to pass unnoticed," she told me. "I suppose these self-styled Masters have grown more accustomed to men and women attempting to break out of their prison rather than into it."

Certain that her sire was behind the recent unusual developments in the arenas of the Fifth Circle, she hit upon a plan to notify me of her presence.

"And now I am here and you may consider yourself all but rescued," she concluded with an arch smile. "So! What must we do to tie up the loose ends of this insurrection and hasten our return to the surface world?"

I greatly appreciated my daughter's optimism.

29
THE GOLDEN MEN OF MARS

THOUGH I SHARED WITH the rest an intense curiosity regarding her identity and origins, there had been little time to spare as yet for the mystery of the golden woman, she whom Jason Gridley had first spied on her ivory barge on the River Iss and who now lay unconscious in a room in the First Circle. A few days after her arrival, I was prowling the corridors in search of some solitude and found myself outside the blood-red chamber. A tired and disheveled Talo Thoran was drowsing in a chair by the door. He leaped to his feet when he saw me, obviously most eager to speak with me, but I instructed him to find himself something to eat and take some exercise first, telling him when he demurred that this was an order rather than a suggestion, and promising that I would stay with his charge until he returned.

Part of this was for my own benefit, as I knew few besides the scholar had yet made their way to this newly opened part of the First Circle, and I was greatly desirous of the opportunity to be alone with my thoughts as the culmination of our plans drew near.

After his reluctant departure, I found myself drawn to the side of the pendant bed, where I stood gazing down at the sleeper, fascinated once again by the strange familiarity of her features. Then, moved by some unnameable impulse, I leaned over and placed my palm gently upon her golden brow. At once I heard a vast rushing sound and the room swam about me.

"Almost had I despaired of meeting you again, my ghost-man!" a voice announced in a rich contralto. I wheeled about at a warm touch on my shoulder and there she was, wide awake and standing

283

before me. Eyes of a startling azure blue sparkled against the rose-tinged gold of her face, the whole framed in lustrous waves of copper-red. The chamber itself seemed to have vanished and we stood facing one another, sole inhabitants of an otherwise featureless realm suffused with drifting clouds of glowing particles.

"Ghost-man?" I echoed. "And again, you say?" I gazed about, my wits beguiled by the dreamlike quality of our surroundings.

"Indeed," she said, her voice tinged with amusement. "When once before I attempted to lay my hand upon you, it passed on through your flesh as if penetrating a lambent mist. Do you not recall our shared astoundment?"

"I do now," I said thoughtfully, for it was as if a mist inside my own mind was beginning to clear. "You are the woman from the ghostly city!"

"A matter of perspective only," she said. She tilted her head to the side, measuring me with those startling eyes. "Examined from one angle, a man wandered for a short time through a silent, half-real metropolis peopled by phantoms. Considered from another, a glowing specter appeared among us in our City of Ten Thousand Names and tantalized our curiosity for years as he grew ever more substantial."

Watching the movement of her lips, I realized that she was not speaking in the common tongue, yet I understood her perfectly, the sense arriving a few moments after I heard the strange words.

Then the import of those words struck me. "Years!" I said. "That was certainly not true from my perspective."

"There was much conjecture when first you entered our secluded realm," she continued. "Scarce could we believe that during the short span, as we then judged it, of our sequestration, another Barsoomian had gained the ability to move at will through the angles."

"I am not from Barsoom," I told her.

"Be that as it may, we recognize that you are indeed quite unique. Perhaps you have noticed it yourself, how a furious tempest of the improbable seems to swirl around you, intertwining you with unlikely events and fateful confluences. No, you may not be from Barsoom, but neither is it certain that you are from—"

At that moment there was a disturbance in the glowing haze about us, tiny points of light streaming by us like particles of snow caught in a wintry gust. She looked past me.

"Forgive me," she said. "I have located my scattered escort and summoned them hither. I can trace in your thoughts the way they must follow to arrive unimpeded."

I did not know what she meant by this, and was puzzled by her claim that she could see into my mind. If so, she would be the first upon Barsoom ever to do so. Yet where were we now, standing in this swirling haze—if not in the depths of my own mind?

"The longer you tarried with us, the closer we felt you moving through the angles," she went on. "It was marvelous to observe, as are all new things! But then, after but a few years in our midst, you abruptly sought to leave us, for what reason we knew not. It was on that final day, as we witnessed your titanic struggle that we realized for the first time that the walls of an impenetrable prison now stood about the simple veil of seclusion we ourselves had woven. Then, when finally you succeeded in piercing through that barricade, so vast were the forces you invoked that you bore us with you out of confinement as well." She pronounced the last with something like awe in her voice. "Had not you done that, ghost-man, we might have remained there, in ignorance of our own peril, for all eternity."

I recalled with sudden clarity that moment when I had summoned all my will and shattered the barrier that was preventing my escape from the ghostly city.

"When you freed us and brought us back into the world, we had no idea how much time had elapsed on Barsoom during our immurement. In search of a tranquil space in which to ponder certain weighty matters, it had been our intention to grant ourselves no more than ten years within the veil of seclusion, with but an instant passing in the outer world. Now, based upon the revelation that time had elapsed without as well as within, we set about preparing to fulfill our obligations as part of the ancient agreement. Paramount among these was the delivery to the Blessed Valley of the new Issus, goddess of peace and love, overdue to take the place of she whose reign of ten thousand years had nearly elapsed when we entered our sequestration.

"It was not until well after I had embarked with my escort upon the River of Life that the savants in our city more closely examined the stars, and thus came to realize to their profound dismay how long we had languished unsuspecting in the captivity visited upon us by those distant Others: that ten years within had surpassed nearly two million without . . ." Her voice dropped to a whisper, as if even she could not comprehend such a span. "After the bewildering truth was communicated to us we forged on, now all uncertain of what we would discover at the end of our voyage. But a short while later we were attacked by an army of those half-alive creatures, my escort was taken, and I was spirited away through the actions of two of your friends."

"So you truly are . . . Issus?"

She gave a graceful nod. "That at least was to be my destiny, had not the deceitful Others walled us away from the here and now."

"Two million years! How did such a thing come to pass?" I asked.

Reading the bafflement and disbelief in my own face, she extended her hands palms up to me. "This method of communing is too wasteful of time, nor can I sustain it for very much longer. If you would truly understand, there is a quicker, surer way."

After a moment's hesitation I rested my own palms on top of hers. From that moment on, our conversation continued in a fashion I can scarcely describe, save that it involved pure understanding rather than words, in an exchange of knowledge which I had never before experienced.

The world was young, a Barsoom so different from the dying planet I now called my home that I might not have recognized it. Five great oceans teemed with life, as did the continents they encircled. The fertile land was striated with soaring mountains and dotted with lakes and meadows, while broad rivers meandered among towering forests of multihued trees and rolling hills carpeted with scarlet grasses. In addition to the abundant flora and fauna, much of which was strange to me, I saw the three great races of humans that together held dominion over the world: the dark-skinned Parovars, the light-skinned Orovars, and the golden-skinned Kalovars.

Millennia beyond war and strife, they dwelled in peaceful cooperation, symbolically united in the person of a god or goddess who ruled in the Blessed Valley for successive terms of ten thousand years, while each race embraced the world in its own fashion.

The Orovars plied the seas and harvested the bounty of the ocean, their great metropolises spreading across the land as havens of culture and art.

The Parovars built cities that sat encased in crystalline bubbles beneath the waves or drifted like clouds through the air, devised new scientific instruments that allowed them to observe the nearby planets, and more thoroughly investigate their own.

For ages the golden Kalovars had looked both inward and outward, their mental explorations ranging from deep within themselves to out beyond the farthest star. Through their examination of the capabilities of the human brain, they learned to cast their thoughts across the trackless infinite, until distance held little meaning for them. Intoxicated with knowledge itself, in their thirst for understanding they had reached out and hurled their questions into the void.

Unexpectedly, they were answered.

"Father?"

"Warlord?"

"John?"

The voices came from nowhere, urging me against my will from the misty space.

I raised my arms as if to fend them off and was abruptly back in the palthon chamber, surrounded by Talo Thoran, Jason Gridley, and my daughter, their faces showing various degrees of apprehension and concern. I stood once more by the golden bed upon which reposed the golden woman, her eyes still closed, her face serene.

Talo Thoran informed me that he had met Tara on his quest for a meal. She had decided to accompany him back to the chamber, and on their way the two of them had encountered Gridley.

"Were you speaking with her?" Talo Thoran inquired. Rather than evincing the skepticism I expected from such a remark, the others regarded me with keen interest.

"I . . . thought I was," I began. Looking at the untroubled countenance against the folds of azure silk, still apparently as deep in slumber as when I had entered the chamber, I was not so certain.

Had my overtired brain manufactured a vivid hallucination to give me the answers I could not otherwise obtain?

"You were," he assured me. "She communicated with me in the same fashion not an hour ago. It is what I wished to tell you. I believe that she and her people possess the ability to access and utilize in unexpected ways the purported world-mind we once discussed, which connects all sentient life on our planet. Given your own brain's divergence from that of the typical Barsoomian, I find it extraordinary that she was also able to commune with you in this way."

"Well?" said Tara. "What did she have to say to you both? Or must Jason Gridley and I venture inside her dreaming head ourselves?"

The scholar and I related by turns what we had each been told, piecing together more of the fantastic tale of a world some two million years in the past.

It was the Parovars who discovered that their fertile planet was dying, and that eventually the broad seas would dissipate, the atmosphere give way to nothingness. The death of a planet is part of a natural progression, for nothing lives forever, yet this was accelerating beyond any previous predictions. Faced with the challenge of staving off—or at least surviving—the inevitable changes to their world, each of the three races approached the dilemma in its own fashion.

The Orovars pondered how the peoples of the world could remain united in the face of such massive changes, proposing the construction of great waterways to bring life-giving liquid from the polar ice caps to a globe left sere and desolate as the seas receded.

Ever the mechanists, the Parovars constructed machines to search beneath the earth for hidden reservoirs of life-giving water, while simultaneously pursuing technological solutions to the loss of atmosphere, hoping to find a way to use the newly discovered Ninth Ray to coax breathable air back into existence.

The Kalovars had been experimenting upon living things for centuries, bringing about the careful alteration and enhancement of various animal species. After much internal debate, they presented the others with a plan to convert the biology of humanity itself, in hopes that a changed human race might successfully adapt to the harsher conditions that would inevitably prevail. To this end, they proposed a fundamental transformation of the human species into a state of oviparity matching that of the vast majority of Barsoomian animals. No longer then would children be born in the time-honored fashion, helpless before the elements and vulnerable in their leisurely development.

We four fell silent following this unthinkable revelation.

"Do you think this is true, Father?" my daughter asked in a tremulous voice. "If so, these ancients saw themselves as gods indeed!"

Talo Thoran answered first: "I believe that it is, Princess. The Kalovars had already wrought many experimental changes upon the fauna of our planet. In fact . . ." His voice dwindled, his copper face grown pale.

"Go on, man," I urged him. "What more did you learn?"

The scholar took in a deep breath and began again. "It was the Kalovars who had long thought to see the potential for intelligence in many of the lower orders, they who raised up the green race and brought them from the seas, reshaping them so that they could live upon the land like the other thinking beings. It was they—" he faltered again, recovering in a moment to continue resolutely: "It was the Kalovars who, as one of their many experiments, unlocked the potential for intelligence and advanced development by adding a new stage to the life cycle of a selected group of the lowly sarovans."

"Sarovans?" Jason Gridley repeated. He had been following along as best he could, with Talo Thoran or myself pausing to add explanations in English here and there as need be. "Isn't that the original name of the—"

"*The worms!*" Tara interjected in a hushed voice. "But that would mean . . ."

"Yes," Talo Thoran confirmed almost unwillingly. "It was the Kalovars who set in motion those alterations that ultimately created the Oolscar."

We turned as one to regard the peaceful sleeping countenance of the beautiful woman.

"So the Masters' ancient tale of the gods who raised them up and then abandoned them is true," I said. "These golden folk are the gods of the Oolscar, whose unexplained desertion led to the worms' eternal war against the surface world."

"That abandonment was not by their choice," the scholar insisted. He then went on to narrate the full tale of the golden race's imprisonment, of which I had been vouchsafed only a small portion.

It was a profound surprise to the Kalovars when their call was answered.

This was their first meeting with those unfathomable beings from another plane of existence entirely, whom they came to know only as the Others.

These Others came among them professing open friendship and bearing many gifts of advanced knowledge, including the means by which a veil of energy could be spun to temporarily isolate in time and space any designated region, from a thimble to a continent. Faced now with the weighty decisions concerning the transformation of humanity itself, the Kalovars welcomed the opportunity to sequester themselves from the rest of Barsoom and contemplate this grave move. With conflict and strife only faint memories, they never suspected the possibility of a hidden motive behind the Others' gifts—while the distrustful Others found it inconceivable that the swiftly ascending Kalovars might gain a measure of understanding approaching their own without seeking to employ it against those who had taught them. And so, as the Kalovars gathered their race in their greatest city and then raised the veil about themselves, these Others acted at once to seal them behind an impenetrable wall, imprisoning them, as they thought, for all eternity.

As sobering as the revelations concerning the Kalovars' relationship to the Oolscar were, we had little time in which to consider them, for the day of the Masters' bid to annihilate all life upon the surface was fast approaching, and with it our final chance to stop them.

The golden woman's claim that she had communed with her lost escort was borne out over the next cycle, when a steady flow of unfamiliar newcomers began to appear outside the hidden entrance to the Green Room: several dozens of unclad men who would not, or could not, speak the common tongue, but loitered about stubbornly until those who watched the area ushered them quickly in and though the hidden ways. When they came into the rosy-white illumination of the First Circle, we saw that they too had golden skin. As if drawn by some unheard summons, they moved unerringly to the chamber in which the sleeping woman lay; nor, to Talo Thoran's poorly disguised exasperation, would they leave their mistress, presenting themselves as a mute barrier to any who would approach her.

30
AIR

PUSHING TINY MARKERS ACROSS a map is a very different exercise from implementing an actual strategy against one's enemy. In the real world, the markers have a tendency to find their way to places where they have not been pushed, and some of them turn out to have been incorrectly labeled from the beginning.

We had more than a few close calls before our plans reached final fruition.

"Warlord, did you send Parthak to the Air Control Center on some errand?" San Tothis asked me as we met to confer in the nearly deserted tiling room when we were but a few cycles away from the eve of revolution. "I saw him taking the hidden route there just now and wondered if something had gone amiss with the plans for tomorrow."

"Since secrecy is of the utmost importance at this stage, I sent no one there," I replied. "But who is Parthak, and where have I heard that name before?"

He blinked in surprise. "Why, that is Helten En's true name. I thought that you and he were old acquaintances, for he told me shortly after your arrival that he knew you long ago in Helium. He said something odd: that this was not the first time his path had crossed with yours in a prison."

When I returned to the War Room I asked Talo Thoran if he knew much about the man. "There is something familiar about him which I cannot pin down. He claims to have been acquainted with me in Helium many years ago."

"Helium?" said the linguist thoughtfully. "That is interesting, for the small idiosyncrasies of his speech betray him to be a Zodangan, and they have not always been on the best terms with we Heliumites."

"Zodangan!" Suddenly it clicked into place. Prior to the great plot to rescue Dejah Thoris from the First Born, I had been held prisoner in the pits beneath my own city for close to a year. Much of Helium's great aerial navy was scattered over Barsoom in search of their missing princess at that time, and the enemy forces of neighboring Zodanga had swooped in under the leadership of the foul jeddak Zat Arrras to seize control of the nation. Upon my hard-won return from the Valley Dor I had been branded a blasphemer by the new regime and sent to the dungeons, where it was thought I could not act as inspiration for the millions of loyal Heliumites who were all too ready to revolt against the foreign ruler. With no other way to notify my supporters of my whereabouts, I had finally resorted to tricking the young Zodangan noble who had been tasked with bringing me my meals into presenting himself at the palace of my son to receive a reward, as I told him, for the courteous treatment he had accorded me. Carthoris had delivered the reward, thus fulfilling my promise—and promptly clapped the fellow into irons in a cell in his own pits. Parthak had stood steadfast in his loyalty to his jeddak and refused all attempts to winnow out the secret of my location, which was finally obtained from him only by means of further subterfuge on the part of my wily son. Bearing the lad no ill will for his allegiance to his own nation, Carthoris had later returned to the pits to release him, only to find him gone, yet another victim of the inexplicable disappearances that had transpired in dungeons around the world for centuries.

"That must have been when he was taken by the Oolscar," I remarked to Talo Thoran. "If ever a man had reason to hold John Carter responsible for the cruel blows dealt to him by fate, it is he." I stepped to the doorway. "Tell San Tothis that I have gone to the Air Center, hopefully to avert our undoing at the hands of a traitor to the cause, if there is still time."

I rode the tube-car to the Fourth Circle, where I raced down the hidden tunnel, arriving in the anteroom in time to see an aged green woman standing by the communication grille on the far side of the chamber. Like its counterpart in the Third Circle, the Air Control Center was equipped with an alarm system, by means of which information could be conveyed to those inside in the event of some dire emergency. There was no hope of my reaching her in time, but just as she extended a bony finger to press the alarm bell that would summon an agent of the worms and most likely scuttle our plans, a man dashed out of a nearby alcove and accosted her with an angry cry. The giantess turned on him with lightning swiftness, piercing his chest with a vicious cut of her dagger. Unsheathing his shortsword as he fell back under her assault, he made a desperate lunge forward, and just as swiftly ran her through the heart. As the green woman fell dying to the floor I raced to the wounded man's side.

"Parthak!" I cried. "I thought—"

"You believed that I had come to betray our cause because of what befell me decades ago in the pits of Helium," he said, essaying a smile through pain-clenched teeth. "Since that day when I was abducted from my cell and brought here by the Long-arms, I have listened to many stirring tales of John Carter from countless new arrivals, and oft pondered how my blind loyalty to a corrupt ruler nearly robbed Barsoom of one of its greatest champions. Recently I overheard comments that led me to suspect this creature of plotting to expose us to the Oolscar. I had no solid proof to back up my mistrust until I just now found her reaching for the warning bell. I thank my ancestors that I had made up my mind to follow her this cycle and thus was near enough to dissuade her."

Examining his wound, I was relieved to find that the dagger had glanced from one of his ribs, leaving him with an injury that, though painful, should not prove fatal. "I thank them, as well," I told the man, drawing from the pocket of my tunic the strip of silk I had taken to carrying with me to disguise myself in the arenas and pressing it tightly to his side to staunch the blood. "For you have likely saved our mission with your actions."

I looked down at the lifeless body of the ancient green woman.

"I suppose we will never learn what prompted this one to such a foul deed. I do not even know her Number, much less her true name."

"I know her name," said Parthak, "though I have no clue as to the source of her enmity. My suspicion was sparked when I overheard her speaking with contempt of Dotar Sojat to one of her fellow workers in the refectory of the Seventh Circle. She is a Thark and her name was Sarkoja."

I stared down through the ruby light into the dead and distorted visage of one of my bitterest enemies, she who had shortly after my arrival on this world visited so much abuse upon myself and my beloved princess—and done even more harm long before that to those great friends of ours among the Tharks, Tars Tarkas and Sola. I wondered if I would ever have the chance to tell them that as wicked a villainess as we four had ever encountered had finally met her just deserts.

With more than three quarters of a million lost souls from above swelling the ranks of the Perfect World, it was little surprise that more than one forgotten shade from years gone by resurfaced like corphals—those baleful spirits of Barsoomian mythology—in the last days of the underground realm. Yet so did unexpected heroes emerge from the shadows of the past.

The time had arrived for Tor-ov Ov-tor and me to follow through on our plan to infiltrate the Air Control Center. His favored status gained us entry to the complex, as I walked humbly behind him as his newest assistant, after which he led us through a maze of largely deserted passages until we finally reached the first in a series of broad windows, this one overlooking a lower level upon which sat row upon row of gigantic machines.

"Those are the great engines," he whispered. "The chamber of the Air Controller should be just up here."

Moving cautiously to the next window, we looked down on a smaller room and in it a lone man sitting with his back to us, hunched over a semicircular desk inset with flickering glass panels and covered by a profusion of buttons and switches. "That is he," confirmed

Tor-ov Ov-tor. "From all that I have heard of him, I have no reason to believe he can be persuaded to our cause. Still, if we can but overpower him, I shall replace him at the controls and command of the atmospheric engines shall be ours."

A ramp at the end of the corridor brought us to the level of the control chamber, where we found an unguarded doorway. It seemed almost too easy.

We crept forward silently into the room and were a few feet from the man when he emitted a sudden cackle of laughter and swung around in his seat. At the same time, a hollow transparent cylinder some six feet in diameter rose swiftly from a circular slot in the floor beneath us, only to be met by a similar one dropping from the ceiling. They fitted together seamlessly, effectively trapping us in a gigantic test tube.

Inspecting us with a wicked smile, the old man toggled a switch on the desk and his voice sounded sharply within the tube: "What a pleasure it is to settle scores both old and new! I have long suspected Tor-ov Ov-tor of ongoing sabotage, while his accomplice must be the infamous Vetj, whispers of whose recent feats have reached even this cloistered citadel. But hold—" He leaned forward to gaze into my eyes, a look of shocked amazement on his cruel features. "Did I not once know you as Vandor, supposed panthan and duplicitous bodyguard?* Haha! What a small Perfect World it is, after all!"

"Vandor? How many names do you have, Vetj?" my companion asked me in a low voice.

"If we survive these next few days, I shall make you a list," I promised.

"And you know this creature?" Tor-ov Ov-tor continued. "For twenty years Dur Bordar has been one of the worms' leading experimentalists, though it has long been rumored that he has used his favored position to commit unspeakable acts upon his fellow human beings, especially those female Hands to which he has formed an unwholesome attraction."

"Of course he knows me, though most certainly not by that absurd number-name!" jeered the old man at the desk. "When

---

* A panthan is a Barsoomian soldier of fortune.

Vandor served me briefly in my great mansion on Silk Market Avenue, he addressed me respectfully as Fal Sivas—when he was not trying to make off with my inventions, that is."

Tor-ov Ov-tor shook his head. "You have led a most interesting life, Vetj," he murmured.

I could not dispute that. Nor could I think upon the astronomical coincidence that I had run across three figures from my past—Parthak, Sarkoja, and Fal Sivas—in such a short span and not recall the golden woman's assertion that a storm of improbability swirled around me. But that was a mystery to solve at a time less pressing. I raised my voice: "You were a wicked man in the world above, Fal Sivas, but I never took you for a stupid one. Why are you colluding with the worms in an enterprise that must surely result in your own destruction?"

The scientist gave a sour smile. "You always were insolent, but your barbs can cause me no pain down here. In fact, it is you I have to thank for giving me the means to survive the imminent alterations to the planet. Had your interference in my life not resulted in my unjust imprisonment in the pits beneath my city, I would never have ended up in the Nine Circles, and thus would surely have perished along with the rest of humanity in the days to come. As it is, my diligent labors on their behalf have inspired the Oolscar to deem me one of those worthy few who will be spared when the world gasps its final breath. Fortunately, the spacefaring ship that you once stole from me still resides in a secure warehouse in Zodanga. As you yourself know, that ship is fully capable of bringing me safely to either Thuria or Cluros—to one of which I shall flee with the Masters' blessings and a sizable harem of my choosing, immediately prior to the end of all life on Barsoom."

Just then a large man in a tunic entered the control room.

The old scientist beckoned the newcomer over. "Look who has come calling, Ur Jan!" he said with a sneering chuckle. "Do you not recognize the master swordsman who laid several of your fellows to rest when you led the Assassins' Guild in Zodanga? Another reason you owe me your undying gratitude for allowing you the honor of becoming my assistant following our capture, rather than dooming you to toil with the rest of the naked Hands, as you so obviously deserved. Now, here by my side, you shall witness his violent demise! But first, what news?"

After a single wondering glance at me, the hulking former assassin bent to whisper something into Fal Sivas' ear. At a peremptory gesture from the latter he then took up a post just behind his master, where he stared at us without expression.

"Ah, the time grows ever nearer," Fal Sivas crowed. "Since you two will never leave these holy precincts of science, would you like to see the control mechanism by which I shall soon send forth the great tempests to scour clean the surface of Barsoom?"

Not waiting for a reply, he jabbed at a button with his thumb, then twisted in his seat to gaze over his shoulder as the great metal wall behind him parted in the middle. In truth, this was exactly what we had come to see, though it had never been part of our plan to view it from within a thick wall of glass—nor had I for a moment anticipated the terrible sight that was revealed as the wall drew slowly open. At my side, Tor-ov Ov-tor choked back a cry, while I was racked by a shudder of sick revulsion.

Arrayed before us on tiers of marble shelves were no less than fifty glass jars, and inside each reposed what appeared to be a naked human brain. Wires led from beneath the disembodied organs through small openings in the base of each jar, while a tiny flow of bubbles streamed upward through the clear liquid that filled them.

Fal Sivas' eyes lingered on the appalling tableau with unconcealed admiration before he turned back to us. He smirked at our expressions. "Ah, Vandor, perhaps you recall my penchant for beautiful girls? Let me assure you that each one of these lovelies was once housed in a vessel of such pulchritude that I almost regretted reducing them to this state of perfect utility. Fortunately, I still cherish in my memory each and every charming curve and dimple."

A few years back I had gone in pursuit of a kidnapped Dejah Thoris by mentally commandeering a spacefaring ship Fal Sivas had designed to be operated exclusively by communicating one's wishes telepathically to a mechanical brain of his devising. Now I conquered my great repugnance and reached out with my mind in an attempt to similarly influence the rows of enslaved human brains, and thus gain dominance over the operation of the atmospheric engines. Fal Sivas was watching me carefully, his face split by a diabolical grin. "Haha! You are trying to wrest control from me, are you not? Fool to believe I would not take extra precautions with this ultimate creation!" He turned once more to stare in dreamy contemplation at the horrible display.

"Remember this, Vandor, for the few moments of life remaining to you: no matter how sophisticated, a mechanical calculating device can never match the power of the human brain. Over the long years since the Masters brought me below I have molded these jewels to accept only my instructions. Let the greatest thinkers of Barsoom try as they might—so long as my own mind holds the mechanism in thrall, no one else may hope to command it!" His eyes narrowed in satisfaction. "And now I shall have the pleasure of accomplishing a goal I set myself long ago. Invisible and innocuous in its quiescent state, air is often overlooked as a potential weapon—yet even a skilled warrior may die by having his brains dashed against an unyielding surface, just as surely as from the expert sword stroke of an opponent."

Eyes half closed in concentration, he raised his index finger.

Immediately lights began to blink along the shelves beneath the brains, while a noticeable breeze sprang up in the small chamber. Gathering force as Fal Sivas rotated his finger in the air, the breeze quickly progressed to a raging whirlwind, and soon we two were struggling to remain erect. The strength of the wind increased rapidly, until we were pulled from the floor and spun about like leaves, colliding with one another with bruising intensity. From the corner of my eye I saw Fal Sivas flourish his hand like a mad orchestra conductor and I knew that we were but an instant away from being hurled at gale force into the thick glass wall.

There was a blur of motion from behind the old inventor. Abruptly the wind vanished and Tor-ov Ov-tor and I tumbled to the floor.

My head still whirling dizzily, I sprang back to my feet, only to behold Fal Sivas slumped forward on his desk, blood leaking from his fractured skull. Looming above him, his hand clenched about a heavy metal bar, stood Ur Jan. The hulking man reached forward to depress a switch on the control board, whereupon the glass capsule about us parted, retracting silently back into the ceiling and the floor.

"It seemed the only solution," Ur Jan said mildly.

"I am happy that you thought so," I told my onetime adversary. "Tell me, could you yourself now assume control of the system?"

"I have no doubt of it," the big man said. "For so long as I have toiled beneath that ulsio in this pit of horrors, I have made it my mission to closely monitor his efforts, and secretly experimented when he was absent from the chamber by exerting my own mental control over the pitiable creatures, my ultimate goal to someday curtail his monstrous deeds. Were Fal Sivas still drawing breath, he would be shocked to witness what has been accomplished by one he had long since dismissed as a dim-witted clod." He cast a poignant glance at the bank of naked brains. "Warlord, I will assist you with whatever you require to achieve your objective—with the single stipulation that when we are finished I may put these poor souls out of their misery."

"Good man," I said and proceeded to outline our plan to him.

I departed a few minutes later, Tor-ov Ov-tor remaining behind to supervise Ur Jan in bringing the Air Control Center under our sole dominion. Due to Fal Sivas' insistence in maintaining complete authority and the worms' tendency to work their machinations at long-range, we were convinced that the evil inventor's death could be concealed from the Masters for long enough to achieve our goals.

31
GRAVITY

DURING HIS ATTEMPTED rehabilitation of the damaged machines in the First Circle, Jason Gridley had confirmed our suspicion that they were most likely earlier versions of the gravity engines located in the Third Circle, performing a brief demonstration in which he successfully projected a gravity field in order to flatten a clay goblet on a tabletop. Unfortunately, the mishap that had caused enough ruination to portions of the oldest Circle that the Oolscar had permanently sealed off the entire area had also fractured the mighty Eighth Ray reservoirs. Drained of all but a whiff of their contents, their function had been reduced nearly to zero—meaning that as matters stood a crushed goblet was likely to be the extent of our own offensive actions.

However, inspired by an incidental discovery Gridley had made while working on the machines, he and I had come up with another idea, one that we now moved swiftly to put into practice.

Accompanied by a small cadre of conspirators in case we encountered trouble, Gridley and I were approaching the nexus of the secret transport system in the newly discovered city that sat at the center of the First Circle, when I felt a heavy weight descending upon my shoulders like the onset of an overpowering fatigue. At my side, Gridley slumped against the wall with a look of surprised bewilderment, and cries and groans sounded behind us. I looked around to see the men of our escort dropping one by one to lie prostrate on the floor, their breath coming in labored gasps.

"This is the worms' doing!" I exclaimed.

Gridley gave a slow, effortful nod. "They've turned up the gravity,

301

probably blanketing the whole of the Nine Circles," he croaked, "though not yet to a lethal degree."

"I am wagering they have no real idea of what we are up to," I said, throwing back my shoulders and holding out a hand to him. "They dare not dispense with their slaves at this critical juncture and have chosen instead to pin everyone in place for a time while they attempt to figure things out. Fortunately, they have reckoned without the possibility of men from Earth among us! We must continue with our mission and trust that the effect will not extend to the inner areas of the Gravity Control Center."

The members of our escort would have to remain behind. Reassuring them that the paralyzing phenomenon would likely be of short duration, we trudged on along the passage until we finally stood before the tube-car we had previously determined would bring us to the Third Circle. "Will they still run?" Gridley wondered aloud.

With the several-mile distance that lay between each of the Circles along the great tunnel, I knew of no other route to reach our destination. "There is one way to find out." I pressed the activation plate. After a long moment, the car creaked out from the wall. Gridley and I heaved ourselves over the rim and lay down head-to-head on the floor. The lid crept shut above us and I touched the wall plate. There was another uncomfortably long pause and then the feeling of great motion.

I breathed a sigh of relief when the lid slid back in the hidden chamber on the outskirts of the Gravity Center and we clambered out. I was finding it easier to move around as I adjusted to the sensation of a gravitic pressure that was truthfully not much more oppressive than that I had once been subjected to on Earth. The next question was whether the kaldane whom Ghek had assigned to open the side door for us had managed to accomplish his task before the gravity was increased. We crept along the passageway.

"Look!" The door was ajar. Lying just inside in a small pool of liquid was a strange object like a partially deflated balloon.

Gridley stared as we stepped over it and eased inside. "Is it . . ?"

"Kaldanes have no skulls to protect their brains," I told him. "Even a small increase in gravitic force is therefore deadly. I only hope that Ghek and the rest of his people were safely out of range."

As we had hoped, the oppressive force of gravity decreased rapidly as we made our way cautiously along the interior corridor, and soon we were walking with our usual lightness.

It did not take us long to reach the chamber Ghek had identified as containing machinery similar to that found in our own Engine Room in the First Circle. Gridley gave a great smile of relief as we stood in the doorway and he confirmed the strong resemblance between these devices and those he had been tinkering with back in the First Circle. I stood watch at the entrance while he darted into the room and disappeared between two great metal domes. The minutes seemed to stretch into eternity as I awaited his return with mounting anxiety. Had he run into a trap like that which had snared Tor-ov Ov-tor and myself in the Air Control Center? I was on the verge of setting out to look for him when he finally reappeared and signaled to me across the room with a questioning look. I made a slow scan of the chamber and nodded that all was clear, whereupon he hastened to my side. He told me that he had seen no one inside save a few Hands performing what looked like ordinary maintenance on the machines. He was clad in a tunic and they had paid him no mind as he made his way confidently to the great mechanism he had judged to be the primary engine.

"Were you successful?" I asked.

"I was."

I smiled grimly. Things were about to become interesting, though the worms might not find them so. Now it was a matter of returning without detection to the First Circle and waiting for the Masters' next move.

32

HOLES IN THE UNIVERSE

OUR GREATEST ALLY during this period was, paradoxically, the imminent culmination of the Great Enterprise. With the worms' attention now focused almost exclusively on the surface, they became increasingly careless when it came to the strict maintenance of order and surveillance down below.

I had been searching for a way to quell the constantly altering illumination that pervaded the Perfect World, not simply to prevent the Oolscar from directly spying upon their chattel from far away, but also to restore to the captives an environment more closely resembling that which they had left behind on the surface of Barsoom. As our conspiracy expanded in size, a Number who worked in the biological laboratories of the Sixth Circle came forth with a means of paralyzing the glowing larvae that coated the ceilings of most of the caverns and thus provided the Oolscar with the ability to track and punish the Numbers below while remaining safe in their airless lair. According to him, the radium ore emitted an unwavering bluish light on its own, which was amplified by the yellowish luminescence produced by the fungus. It was the presence of the tiny larvae that incited the fungus and the ore to phosphoresce in the ever-changing sequence of colors that the Masters found soothing and the humans disconcerting. Without the tiny worms, the other two sources of luminosity shone with a steady light that could be electrically modified to continually produce one of several hues, as evidenced in the arenas and other regions. This researcher claimed to have derived a chemical substance that, when mixed with ordinary water, produced a solution harmless to humans that

304

could be released as a rising mist. Making its way to the ceiling of the shifting lights, this would over a period of a few hours cause the undeveloped worms to enter a state approaching catatonia and soon drop helplessly down onto the floor below. We tested the effect in a few isolated areas and discovered the illumination that remained was of an unwavering greenish hue. It was not the approximation of natural sunlight we had discovered in the First Circle, but it was a vast improvement over the disorienting status quo—with the happy side effect of potentially removing great swaths of territory from direct observation and potential peril. Scores of conspirators were given jars and flasks of the stuff and assigned areas in which to wander during their break periods, pretending to drink from the opened containers.

We had gradually reduced the amount of calming drugs in the food and water to mere traces and there was a noticeable disquiet growing among the captives. We hoped this would urge them to our side once the true rebellion began. In addition, conspirators from a variety of caverns had begun to smuggle food and other supplies into the First Circle to sustain the growing stream of Hands and Numbers whom our agents brought there to stay, in hopes that they would be at least temporarily safe from the unpredictable punishment of the Masters.

Gridley and I had a peculiar experience on our way back to the War Room. We had closed the door behind us when we departed the Gravity Center, hoping that if the expired kaldane were to be discovered it would be dismissed as just another example of the vermin the Oolscar considered beneath their notice. To our relief, the gravity wave that had temporarily paralyzed the human inhabitants of the Perfect World had been lifted while we were in the control center. Instead of heading directly back to headquarters, we first traveled in a two-man car to the Ninth Circle tunnel, as I wanted to gauge the progress of our steady evacuation of the environs. When we stepped out of the capsule, we found ourselves not far from where I had initially awakened, what already felt like a lifetime ago.

We had emptied the place of almost all of its inhabitants, both human and animal—or so I thought.

"Where do those lead?" Gridley asked, nodding to a series of empty archways on the other side of the now-deserted cylinder. I told him of the zoological exhibits that had originally been housed there.

"They were used to display some of the odder beasts either captured on the surface or created down here in the laboratories," I said. "Some of them have been freed to add to the general chaos and range the tunnels between the Circles, while the rest were removed by our allies among the biological workers and returned to the Sixth Circle until decisions can be made about their ultimate fate."

Gridley was looking back over his shoulder as we turned to go. "Apparently not all of them," he said.

I turned to see a flicker of motion from inside the nearest archway. Someone stood for a moment peering out at us, then ducked back out of sight.

"That's strange."

We walked to the edge of the archway. Just inside the opening was a creature of a sort I had never laid eyes on before. I was sure that I had seen an upright, humanlike being watching us from beyond the arch. Yet the thing that confronted us now was a four-legged beast about the size of a small horse, with a broad face that somehow combined elements both equine and human. Someone had covered it rather clumsily in a tunic like those worn by the Numbers, which had been torn at one seam and draped across its back like a saddle blanket.

Gridley and I moved with exaggerated slowness so as not to startle the thing, which watched us warily with great dark eyes, but did not back away. "What do you call that?" he asked softly.

"I . . . do not know," I replied. "I have never seen its like."

As we stood there, the creature slowly rose up on its hind legs—not as a horse might rear up for a moment or two, but as if it were almost as comfortable in that position as on all fours. As it remained poised there, returning our stares from its new height, I noted that it was female, and that the torn tunic had been loosely tied across her belly with a length of silk such as we had been wont to use in the arenas.

She shied away a little as I took a step closer, but did not retreat. I felt the familiar jangle of alarm along my nerves and a moment later my foot encountered pressure at the threshold. I snatched it back, realizing that a gravity barrier was still in effect in this cell.

The pocket of the tunic had been positioned in such fashion as to be within reach of the creature's left forelimb. As I watched in amazement she awkwardly inserted her three-toed paw and brought forth a few crumbs of food. She lifted the paw close to her mouth with an imploring gaze.

"Whatever she is, she's obviously famished," Gridley said. "And look—on her back. Isn't that . . ?"

She had been turning slightly whenever we did, always making sure to face us directly. Now I saw the tiny paw on her broad shoulder and behind it the small hump beneath the fabric of the tunic. There was a child clinging to her back.

I told him to wait there and ran to the deserted refectory, where I found a few leftover hard cakes and filled a flask of water. As I left the chamber I called ahead to Gridley to press his palm against the small disk beside the archway that would deactivate the barrier and grant us entry, but when I reached the cell he turned to me with a look of bewilderment.

"She's not here," he said. "She tried to say something to me, but I couldn't understand her speech. I was attempting to communicate through gestures that you had gone to get her something to eat, when suddenly I felt that familiar wave of electricity wash over me and I was sure I was about to be whisked away into the infinite. I shut my eyes and focused as hard as I could on being right here, at this moment. When I opened them the feeling had subsided, but she—they—had vanished."

"Still more unexpected visitors from somewhere else?" I mused, coming to stand beside him. Aside from the ragged tunic, which now lay on the floor, the chamber was empty. "Someone seems to be poking holes in the universe and all manner of strange beings are falling through."

As we made our way back to the War Room, I pondered the unusual appearance and sudden departure of the horse-woman, whose behavior had suggested that she was an intelligent being rather than another strange product of the animal laboratories. The puzzle of her origin was not solved that day; in fact, it would be many years before I saw her like again—and it was not on Barsoom.*

---

* See the bonus novelette *Victory Harben: Stormwinds of Va-nah* by Ann Tonsor Zeddies at the end of this book for more on this mystery.

33

ASCENSION

WITH BUT A FEW DAYS to go until the worms' planned attack on the surface world, the crew which had been extending the perimeter of explored areas in the First Circle at last uncovered the treasure trove we had sought, when a hidden doorway opened to reveal a large chamber, heaped like Ali Baba's cave with mounds of clothing and other belongings garnered from various abductions over the centuries, along with the greatest find of all: weaponry! Gridley marveled as I decked myself out with my usual pistol, dagger, and swords both short and long. "I'm amazed you don't clank with each step like an itinerant peddler of pots and pans," he observed, as he selected a pistol and dagger for himself. "And what is this odd contraption? It doesn't quite match what I've so far seen of Martian fashion or armament."

"Aha! Assuming it remains intact, that is something that may come in very handy once we blow the lid off things," I told him as I pulled the object from where it lay half-buried under a heap of wrist chronometers and pocket pouches.

The equilibrimotor is a wonderful product of modern Barsoomian technology that in general appearance brings to mind those life preservers commonly found on the passenger liners that ply the seas of Earth. Somewhat narrower in construction, the belt is filled with the Eighth Barsoomian Ray in a quantity carefully calibrated to offset the pull of gravity, allowing the user to float motionless in midair until the small radium motor attached to the back is activated and one rises or descends as desired. Directionality is determined by a pair of lightweight metal wings projecting from either side of the belt, whose position may be changed by the application of hand levers. It was indeed intact, as I was able to demonstrate to Gridley's delight a minute later. "Many is the time I have toured the upper reaches of Helium by use of one of these marvelous devices," I remarked as I donned the belt and drifted several feet off the floor.

"I could have made fine use of this at the Earth's core," Gridley said. "Though on second thought, attempting a tour of the upper reaches of Pellucidar in such fashion would no doubt have swiftly landed me in the maw of a hungry thipdar."

The fact remained that even should my mad plan to blast a tunnel directly up to the surface succeed, we had no idea how the many thousands down here would scale it—nor where on Barsoom we might find ourselves when we emerged. What was needed was some way of getting word of our whereabouts to those above.

As for those whereabouts, Tor-ov Ov-tor believed that precise coordinates—vital for the targeting of both atmospheric disturbances and gravitic enhancement—were kept in the hearts of both the Third and Fourth Circles, and he was doing his best to track them down from his new position in the Air Control Center. Assuming he was successful in ferreting out our precise location, we then needed to find a way to broadcast the information to friendly ears in the outside world.

Talo Thoran had shown us to the place in one of the more damaged areas of the First Circle where the corridor into which he had plunged had originally deposited him. He assured us that, unlike many of the other passageways from the outer world that twisted and angled, perhaps for miles, on their way down to the Perfect World, his had led downward at a nearly unvarying slope from the chamber wherein he and I had been snared. Though it would be almost impossible to ascend the slippery passageway on foot, it followed that a person with some sort of flying device could make his way with relative speed back up to the *Kantim*—assuming, of course, that the mechanical trapdoor remained open and that the ship was still moored nearby. Since one of the two Gridley Wave sets aboard the flier had been the master transceiver, someone with an intimate knowledge of such equipment could then use it to activate the whole of the dormant system and transmit a request for assistance.

"I think we all know who that someone should be," Gridley said. "With Talo Thoran's help getting past the language barrier, I've managed to train San Tothis and several others to operate the machinery we've modified in the Engine Room, meaning my presence is no longer required to carry out your plan." He looked around with a sigh. "It's a fascinating place you've got here, John. I could spend years just trying to understand the principles behind these various solar and planetary rays. And look here—" He ran his palm lightly along a metal wall panel that had survived the ancient disaster in this quarter of the First Circle and in fact seemed to have nary a scratch upon it, while the carved wood and other metals to which it had been affixed had long since been reduced to rubble. "A lost city beneath the crust of Mars is the last place I ever expected to find Harbenite!"

"We call it forandus," I told him. "It is wondrously strong and lightweight. Many of the finest battleships in Helium's navy incorporate it in their construction."

"I can well believe it, having myself flown from the Earth's surface down to its hollow core in an airship built entirely of the stuff."

Just then the long-awaited messenger arrived from the Air Control Center, bearing a card upon which Tor-ov Ov-tor had recorded the precise location of our cavern. I noted with interest that we were no more than ten miles beneath the surface of the planet, while the coordinates placed us much farther south than I had expected, though still well north of the formidable Otz Mountains that surround the Valley Dor at the southern pole.

"Well," I said, "we have our information. If you are still game, it may be time for you to accomplish your ascension."

There had been some discussion as to how best to compose our single dispatch. With no sense of how much longer Gridley might remain on Barsoom before his unfathomable entanglement sent him off again through the trackless wastes, in the end we decided that if he were successful in reaching the flier he would send out the signal activating the network, followed immediately by a brief repeating message in Morse Code requesting assistance and giving the location of that region on the surface that sat above the portion of tunnel just outside the First Circle where we proposed to create our opening. In addition to Vad Varo in Duhor, there were a handful of Barsoomian communication experts in Helium who were familiar enough with both code and the English language to decipher it.

Gridley adjusted the belt about his waist and experimentally lowered and raised the small wings attached to the sides. It had taken him but a few minutes of practice after we discovered the device until he was able to successfully maintain an upright position by adjusting the equilibrimotor's wings and felt comfortable steering himself up through the several miles of steep incline Talo Thoran had described.

"I may not come this way again, John Carter," Gridley said. "I must resume my search for my goddaughter and after that find some way home to my wife and son back in Pellucidar." He looked around with a wistful expression. "I should have liked to see more of Mars than the inside of these wretched caverns. That said, I have no doubt that you will succeed in your endeavors here. I do hope to find the means to visit you again someday after I've become subatomically disentangled—if science and whatever gods there be allow it."

I gave him my heartfelt thanks for his invaluable assistance and added that, insofar as I could speak for an entire planet, he would always be welcome on Barsoom. We shook hands for a final time, and he took up his position beneath the aperture and activated the radium motor. His feet left the ground, he floated upward into the dark cylinder, and we saw him no more.

34

CAPTURE!

WITH TOR-OV OV-TOR now surreptitiously in charge at the Air Control Center and the relatively small but potentially momentous addition Gridley had made to the gravity engines in the Third Circle at the ready, everything seemed to be in place for our rebellion. This was, of course, the ideal moment for something to go seriously wrong.

According to our best information, the attack on the surface world was mere hours away. I was conferring in the War Room with my daughter, who had appointed herself in charge of the ongoing effort to evacuate as many people as we could from the central rings of certain of the Circles in as subtle a fashion as possible—though at this point it seemed the Oolscar were largely oblivious to the actions of their soon-to-be doomed slaves, as long as they did not appear to directly interfere with the Great Enterprise. Ghek was also at the table in his capacity as liaison between our forces and the unknown number of kaldanes currently infesting the smaller passages of the Nine Circles.

Then a worried-looking Tanus burst into the chamber to report that San Tothis had requested my immediate presence to discuss an urgent matter that had arisen in the Engine Room. We hastened there to find him stretched out on his back beneath the housing of one of the mighty machines.

"Warlord!" he said, when he had crawled from beneath the cowl and regained his feet. "Although everything is functioning correctly on our end, we fear the small instrument that Vetj vem-Ay affixed to the central engine in the Third Circle has somehow become

313

dislodged, perhaps by an unwitting Hand during routine maintenance, thus severing our connection. Unless it is restored . . ."

Aided by Talo Thoran as interpreter, San Tothis had been working
closely with Gridley up to the latter's departure and understood best
how the device must be mounted in order to achieve our goal. I
could not let him make the journey alone. After requesting that
Ghek send one of his fellows to open the side door for us once again,
I checked the wrist chronometer I had appropriated from the treasure
chamber and turned back to San Tothis. "Come—time grows short.
We must return to the Third Circle at once!"

Ghek elected to do the job himself, and the three of us raced to
a small tube-car, the kaldane leaping from his perch upon my shoulder
to tuck himself snugly in between our two heads as we made the
quick trip to the Gravity Circle.

Once there we passed through the hidden door and crept out
from behind the false wall to find the area outside the building largely
deserted. Still, San Tothis and I donned our best expressions of
unconcern as we headed toward the far side of the complex, while
Ghek scurried up the nearest wall and disappeared into a hole in the
cavern's ceiling. We loitered in the shadows by the side of the building
for a tense minute or two until we finally heard a click and the door
eased open a crack. Once inside, we made our way swiftly back to
the chamber of the great engines, where we reenacted the visit I had
made with Gridley a few days earlier, as I stood watch while my
partner in crime crept across the open space and disappeared between
the two largest machines.

The adjustment went off without a hitch. Ghek was waiting for
us outside the complex and the three of us headed back to the false
wall and the camouflaged door that concealed the tube-car entrance.

The kaldane and the Gatholian had taken their places in the
capsule and I was moving to join them when a shadow loomed in
the doorway behind me. "Look out!" cried San Tothis. A massive
paw clamped like a vise on my shoulder and I turned to face half a
dozen hulking Long-arms. Wrenching free, I thrust myself between
them and the car.

"Hie yourselves to the Engine Room while I hold them off

and then send the car back for me!" I called to my companions. "Whether or not you see me again, follow the plan and act at the appointed time!"

San Tothis nodded his comprehension as the lid slid shut over his stricken face. I spun around as the capsule began to withdraw into the wall and hurled myself at the Long-arms.

I noted at once that these specimens conducted themselves with more shrewdness and cunning than the ones I was used to meeting in the arenas. As I ducked and dodged between them I noticed that about half showed the telltale gleam of recent possession along their spines, and that several of these carried stout cudgels, the first weapons I could recall seeing borne by any of their ilk. My strength and agility served me well for the first two minutes of the battle, after which their enhanced acumen and superior numbers began to get the better of me. I had successfully manipulated two of the brutes into colliding with one another so forcefully that the crunch of bones could be heard, and was crouching down in preparation of a mighty leap that would send me clear of the constricted space in which we fought and out into the open where I could maneuver more effectively, when something landed with a cracking sound upon the top of my head and blackness descended in my brain.

I awoke lying prone under dim maroon light in a large low-ceilinged chamber I recognized from the patterns on the flooring as part of the Gravity Control Center. The room was a wide oval, about one hundred feet in the long direction, with a bank of machinery filling the side nearer to me beneath a wall covered in lighted charts and maps before which several tunic-clad Numbers moved. The chamber's other side was lost to my sight in a jumble of shapes and shadows.

As I pushed cautiously up from the floor and into a sitting position I noticed a strongly unpleasant odor pervading the room like a miasma. At the same time I became aware of a constant faint sound, as of the rustling of dry leaves, emanating from the darker side of the chamber. I squinted into the shadows, my hackles rising as I began to make out a number of enormous serpentine shapes gliding restlessly to and fro. Another motion caught my eye: three

Long-arms shambled into the room, each bearing an ornately carved bench of ornamental wood. Depositing them in a semicircle about fifteen feet in front of me, they turned and took up positions to one side of the array.

After a long moment, a trio of naked manlike creatures emerged from the shadows, shuffling laboriously across the tiles until each had seated itself heavily upon a bench. They were followed by a like number of colossal, sinuous shapes that slithered out of the dimness to rear up, tiny limbs waving, directly behind the throne-like benches. I looked away, knowing what was to follow. With an appalling mixture of muttered groans and damp squelching sounds, the worms took possession of their hosts, their long bodies trailing off into darkness behind the trembling unfortunates. Three heads now shrouded in quivering flesh turned as one to face me.

"At last . . ." came a rasping voice from the central figure, an ancient female whose bones showed clearly through the drooping folds of her translucent skin. "How fitting that we confront our nemesis now at the moment of final victory!"

"Is it truly here, then?" asked the creature to her left, a hunched and cadaverous man whose eyes shone milky with cataracts in the lights from the control panel. "I perceive nothing."

"I see its loathsome form clearly with these eyes, brother," the third assured him. "Though like yourself, my higher senses detect naught but a yawning void." Like the woman who had spoken first, he was a bundle of skin and bones, with little resemblance left to a living human being. He pointed a tremulous hand in my direction. "What do you say for yourself, thing? Your reign of evil deeds has come to an end, and now, despite your unwarranted interference, we shall fulfill the promise made to us so long ago by our gods!"

I could not resist a low chuckle. "I have met one of your gods of late," I told him. "You would be surprised to hear her story."

"Blasphemer!" shrieked the woman in the middle. "Is it not enough that you have dedicated your life to thwarting our simple quest for happiness? Must you now profane the memory of our gods with your lies?"

I managed to tilt my arm so the light from behind me was cast upon my chronometer. By my calculations I had been unconscious for only a handful of minutes. I wondered if San Tothis had made it back to the Engine Room yet and begun preparing for our next move. Hoping the worms had not already discovered the alterations we had wrought to their machines, I determined to distract them from doing so for as long as possible, no matter the risk to my own survival.

"I fear you have me confused with someone else," I said lightly. The Long-arms stationed by the worms stirred as I rose carefully to my feet and allowed my eyes to rove over the hideously ravaged faces before me. "I could hardly have dedicated my life to inconveniencing you when until recently I was ignorant of your very existence—although I freely admit that had I known of you before I would have done everything in my power to halt your Great Enterprise and undo the monstrous deeds you have committed against mankind, whom you have stolen and enslaved for millennia."

The sightless man on the right made a series of gagging sounds which I belatedly recognized as laughter. "You dare castigate us for the few deluded souls we have plucked from their boats on the way to an unspeakable fate in the so-called Blessed Valley? You should be thanking us for providing them salvation."

"Imprisonment and murder do not constitute salvation," I scoffed.

"Rank hypocrisy." The corpse-man essayed a palsied shrug. "War and assassination have been practiced by Helium, and by every other so-called civilized nation on the surface, for countless generations! Your race has made an art of slaughtering its own people!"

I had been determined not to let the creatures get under my skin, yet I bristled at that accusation. "Mankind is far from perfect," I replied. "Yet it is my firm belief that eventually we shall achieve a world where peace and justice reign among the peoples of Barsoom. Even now, those who war beneath Helium's banners do so with honor, sword against sword, and not by cutting down our enemies with unseen weapons hurled by cowards from a hidden cave."

"Our war is of a different nature," said the hybrid of worm and man. "And unlike you, we do not quarrel among our own kind. But no matter. We know you came to the Third Circle in a final desperate bid to prevent the realization of the Great Enterprise. Fortunately we apprehended you before you were able to make your way into our stronghold and now it is too late."

It dawned on me then that the Masters believed they had snared their renowned enemy on his way into the Gravity Circle rather than out of it! With any luck, they would not realize that we had already accomplished our planned mischief until it was too late.

I glanced at my chronometer and decided that it was time to depart.

"That being the case, I am sure you understand that I would prefer to meet my doom among my own kind," I said to the ancient corpse-man. "Therefore, if you will excuse me . . ." I took a step toward the far doorway. Instantly the Long-arms guarding the thrones stepped forward. My hands tightened into fists as I prepared to battle my way either to freedom or to death. Then the corpse-woman on the central bench raised a shaking arm and the great brutes halted.

"It matters not," she said. "For decades we have waited to get a glimpse of this storied demon, only to find that he is just another prattling human animal. His sabotage attempt has failed and there is no more he can do to hinder our plan. Therefore, let us turn our attention to the matter at hand, while he scurries back into his hole like the vermin he is." She leered at me through the shadows, her ruined face alight with triumph and scorn. "Know this, monster: before you can draw one hundred breaths the engines will be activated. The Atmosphere Plant will be crushed into rubble and we will seize control of what air remains, unleashing great winds to cleanse the world of the disfiguring relics of mankind. In a matter of one or two days, no more air will find its way down the conduits from the surface. It is impossible to outrun suffocation, so flee where you will!"

I was already beginning to feel the all-too-familiar sense of uncanny foreboding and the jangling along my nerves that portended the presence of artificially manipulated gravity. I decided it was high time I took her advice.

Striding out the doorway I raced down the passage until I came to a connection to a larger corridor I hoped would deliver me to the main portal of the complex. A group of hulking Long-arm guards were clustered at the gateway, but as I approached they shuffled aside and the great doors opened slowly before me.

I shot out through the portal, bounding off in a series of tremendous leaps as soon as I was clear of the complex. I am not sure I have ever moved so swiftly in my life—and that is saying something. I had just made it to the hidden door outside the tube-car terminus when the terrible sounds of cracking pavement and collapsing walls began. In haste I tapped out the code, raced to the waiting capsule, and hurled myself inside. The ground was beginning to heave wildly beneath me. I heard more crashing and the blare of alarms. The lid slid shut above me with agonizing slowness, and then all was silent within the capsule.

During his examination of the ancient gravity engines in the First Circle, Jason Gridley had discovered a small instrument affixed to each of the great machines that he eventually deduced was designed to enable them to work in concert under the direction of a central guidance system. It had not taken him long to figure out how to modify the mechanism to focus on a single signal from our own Engine Room, while blocking out all others. Thanks to Gridley's attachment of the device to the main engine in the Third Circle—and to our eleventh-hour foray to reattach it after it had been dislodged—San Tothis had been able to successfully redirect the massive gravity waves meant to target the Atmosphere Plant on the surface back to their source in the Masters' Gravity Control Center within mere moments of my escape. We would soon learn that half the total number of Oolscar had been in attendance in the complex for the momentous event, and had thus been unceremoniously smashed into pulp when the entire building collapsed upon itself.

A careful watch had been kept on the worms during these last days, and now those that had been tending to other tasks elsewhere in the Nine Circles during the failed attack were surrounded in their wallows and their chambers as our fighters streamed out of the various hidden tube-car depots throughout the caverns. In desperation, the great hulks summoned to their defense all of the corpse-men and Long-arms within range of their mental calls for succor, and many a furious battle was fought, with hundreds of newly armed rebels competing for the opportunity to slay one of the hated Masters. I myself witnessed a scene of unparalleled savagery in the Chamber of Vermin of the Ninth Circle, as the trio of giant centipedes that regularly patronized that cavern were set upon and methodically sliced to shreds by the seething mob.

A few of the former Lords of the Perfect World had managed to escape; when those that remained alive, now less than a dozen by our calculations, retreated to the airless caverns in the Second Circle, we barricaded them in, blocking all entrances and disabling the tube-car system that led to and from their lair.

Putting the worms to rout by no means signaled an end to our campaign. With the Great Enterprise in tatters and their masters dead or captured, the many high-ranking human confederates of the Oolscar did not take kindly to having their own control over the underground realm challenged—nor did those pitiful creatures whose minds had been warped by repeated possession lay down their arms when their unhuman overlords perished.

Having harnessed the force of gravity itself to accomplish our goal of salvation for the unaware billions in the world above our heads, it was now our task to continue the battle below with flesh and steel to save ourselves.

35
REVOLUTION

I HAVE ALWAYS considered modesty to be both an admirable trait and a sensible one, for in the end the only person who is taken in by the man who indulges in boasting and vainglory is the braggart himself. False modesty, on the other hand, strikes me as merely another form of deceit, and often serves as little more than a waste of time for all concerned.

I have never vied for the title of greatest swordsman of two worlds. However, having engaged in countless contests on both Earth and Mars and been fairly defeated in none of them, I do not choose to expend either oxygen or precious time by denying the epithet. (I have also used my sword arm to good effect in whatever strange domain truly lay at the end of my voyage to the moon Thuria, as well as beneath the constant red glare of the volcanic eruptions that reflect from Jupiter's cloud banks—but have reached the conclusion that, accurate or not, adding two more worlds to my tally would surely begin to smack of excess.) Suffice it to say that with a longsword once again where it belonged in my right hand, I made my customary use of it here beneath the surface of Barsoom, and many were the belligerent beasts and corrupted men that fell beneath my blade in those final hours of rebellion.

I fought in esteemed company that day, surrounded by warriors both red and black, by pale therns from the south and yellow-skinned Okarians from the far north, as well as by many a towering green warrior out of the hordes that ranged the dead seabeds above our heads. In addition to these legions of united men, there was an unexpectedly large contingent of zealous kaldanes astride their rykors. These last, though they were by no means the most accomplished swordsmen among us, perhaps struck the enemy with the greatest consternation, as they leaped from their own fallen bodies to scamper spiderlike up the legs of their opponents and tear at head and shoulders with their sharp claws. Leading them was Ghek himself. Once an exile condemned to death by his own people, our friend was now an awe-inspiring sight. The mastery he had gained over his automated body since I had last seen him mounted upon its metal chassis was evident: a shortsword gripped tightly in each of the four flexible upper limbs, he strode like a juggernaut, cleaving through the mass of men and creatures before him as if they were made of water.

Fighting close by my side in the vanguard were San Tothis of Gathol and his crewmates from the *Vanator*, along with Ur Jan and Parthak of Zodanga, and surging behind us a veritable host of abductees from Helium and elsewhere about the globe, all eager to reclaim their lives after so many years in hell. Women joined in the battle equally with the men, and I learned later that my daughter, who had been schooled in swordplay by both myself and her warrior husband, had left the War Room to fight valiantly in our midst—though thankfully not within my sight, as I confess a father's concern might have proved too strong a distraction even for myself.

The fighting ranged throughout the Circles for more than a day, with unexpected foes rearing their heads whenever we thought we had successfully cleared out a cavern. Our side had also been at work unearthing new allies—quite literally—and so a great flood of decanted corpse-men was met with a tide of ardent rebels also recently released from the hollows, the former being no match for fighters in full control of their own actions. I was sorry to see the battered husks of the corpse-men fall, even though I understood they no longer retained the hearts and souls of men and women and had, in a sense, lost their lives to the depredations of the Oolscar long since.

The great tunnels of the Nine Circles ran with blood that day, and became progressively darker as bodies fell upon the glowing fungus and radium ore of the illumination strips that ran along the curved floor. At least no one battled on the walls or ceilings; with the engines of the Gravity Control Center now inoperable, both the floor of the tunnel and its roof had resumed their natural properties.

The former agents of the Masters had a few tricks yet remaining up their ragged sleeves. We had all but finished with the active fighting when word came that many of the enormous fields in the Eighth Circle had been set afire. Those Hands and Numbers who had not heeded the earlier calls to evacuate the food-producing caverns now raced through the choking billows of smoke to crowd into the tube-cars, joining latecomers from other caverns to be herded by our agents from Circle to Circle until soon the vacant buildings and empty spaces of the ancient city were teeming with refugees. We had brought some stores of food with us, but they would not last for more than a week or two, this development serving to highlight the importance of opening our path to the outer world as soon as possible—and then finding some way to transport many thousands of people up the ten-mile, near-vertical distance before they starved.

Accordingly, with our people now in control of the engines in the Air Center of the Fourth Circle, we acted in swift concert. The great conduit located above the now-empty Ninth Circle through which air had been propelled down to the Perfect World for centuries by a series of gigantic fans was blasted open by an artificially engendered whirlwind of staggering proportions, the tons of rock and machinery that would have rained down then sent hurtling upward through the channel. Far above us, for the first time, we saw the glint of daylight.

Still to be decided was the fate of those that remained of the former Gods and Masters of the Perfect World, who had for so long preyed upon the unwitting populace of Barsoom, and over the ages devoured the lives of millions of its lost souls. By our calculations, about a dozen of the creatures still survived within the locked and barricaded confines of the Second Circle, and opinions varied on the manner of their punishment, with the imposition of a slow and painful death finding slightly more favor among the rebels than a quick execution.

When I arrived with a delegation of rebels at the guarded barricade before the ornate doors to their airless and lightless sanctum sanctorum, I was surprised to find Talo Thoran there before us, and next to him, her head bowed as if in meditation, the slight figure of the golden woman who had introduced herself to me as the Goddess Issus. Standing in a silent group off to one side were the other Kalovar men that had once composed her escort.

"What is this about?" I asked the scholar. "Please do not tell me she has come to pray for the worms' souls, for I fear she will find them impossible to detect."

He shook his head. "No, John Carter, she has been communicating with the Oolscar on behalf of her people."

"What!"

The golden woman opened her eyes and I met again that startling azure gaze.

"Greetings, my ghost-man. As you now know, John Carter, we Kalovars are ultimately responsible for this sad state of affairs," she told me in her musical voice, "though it was through the intervention of those unimaginable Others that we ourselves were so long imprisoned and this tragedy allowed to unfold to such terrible proportions. The fact remains: as the Oolscar have harmed you, so did we harm them two million years ago." I noted that she was now speaking the common tongue of Barsoom, although with a slight accent, and surmised that she had acquired it through her mental communication with Talo Thoran and myself.

"Whatever your role in lifting them up from the status of beasts to thinking beings, you are by no means responsible for the worms' subsequent reprehensible actions," I told her. I indicated the group gathered at my back. "These representatives of the unwilling inhabitants of this hellish place have come to exact payment for the terrible wrongs wrought against the peoples of the surface world over so many thousands of years."

"I understand." She inclined her golden head. "However, my people have already determined what is to be our part in the matter, and carried it out."

I looked around. "Carried it out? Where? How?"

She nodded to the sealed doors. "Few barriers exist to those capable of moving through the angles, as you must surely know."

"Open the doors," I ordered. Silently the guards removed the barricade. Those behind me raised their weapons, while I stood at the ready, pistol in hand.

There was a rushing noise as the seal was broken. The great gates swung wide and air poured in along with light. The chamber was empty.

Incredulous, I turned back to the golden woman, whom I could not bring myself to call Issus. "You have destroyed them?"

"No. Unless unavoidable in the defense our own existence, we do not believe in taking life from those who have done harm, no matter how grievous their offenses."

"That alone places you in a small minority upon this planet," I observed. "What then have you done with them?"

For a moment she seemed at a loss. "There are words for which you have no counterparts in your tongue—nor are there yet suitable ones in ours. If I spoke to you of "fluilation" and "teteculence," would you grasp my meaning? However, it would not be incorrect to say that we have removed them from these caverns and delivered them elsewhere, to a place not so distant, yet far enough away that they will never again bring distress to you."

"Exactly where did you bring them?" I persisted, convinced that if the surviving worms were anywhere on or beneath Barsoom—even in the ghostly city of the Kalovars at the bottom of a chasm in the far north—then they must still be hunted down and dealt with once and for all, pity be damned, lest they attempt again one day to subjugate humanity.

"Not on Barsoom, but yet a little farther out." She gestured toward the unseen sky far above us. "To one of those remnants of The Broken World that once lay between this planet and Sasoom, a dark and airless rock that is as a paradise to them, though they may soon deem it as false a one as was created by a fallen humanity upon the shores of the once–Blessed Valley. Remember: after millions of years, their former ranks have now been decimated and their servants taken from them, and they will come to understand despair and loneliness ere long."

"You brought them to . . . an asteroid?" I considered the distance involved and thought absurdly of the graceful ivory barges Gridley had encountered upon the River Iss. "How? You have no ships that can travel through the void."

"Through the angles all destinations are equally near. Nonetheless, it was a considerable undertaking, as we have just begun to master our own fluilatory states."

Raising her hands palm outward, she bowed her head low before me.

"It will soon be time for us to depart, John Carter. However, if you wish to wreak vengeance upon the Kalovars for our actions, I am prepared to remain here to suffer your judgment without protest. Things must be set aright between us and the other peoples of Barsoom."

I stood awhile in thought, many conflicting emotions rising and falling in my breast. Then I told her that she was free to go, with the added caution that if she and her golden entourage planned to continue their interrupted voyage to the Valley Dor, they would find it a drastically changed land from the ancient paradise for which they had set out. "Nowadays the name of Issus is invoked more often as a curse than as a blessing," I told her. "Yet there may still be some there or elsewhere who are willing to welcome you as their goddess."

"No, John Carter. Barsoom has had enough of gods of any stripe to suit it for a very long time." She gave a pensive smile. "By your leave, we will soon return to our city. After peering out across infinity, it is our belief that those Others have long since turned their attention elsewhere and will not interfere with us again. Therefore we have reached the decision to raise the veils about our city and isolate ourselves once more, at least for a while, until we may decide if there is any place for our kind in this savage world at the end of time."

Talo Thoran had been standing slightly removed while we conversed, his eyes never leaving the golden face. Now he stepped forward and turned his earnest countenance to me. "Warlord, if you will grant me your permission, I should like to accompany them. I am making much progress with their language and she—that is, they— have agreed to allow me to join them in their hidden city. Do you think you might possibly find someone else to manage the communications station at Exum?"

I put my hand on his shoulder and drew him a few steps to the side. "You are sure of this?" I asked him in a low voice. "It sounds as though you could be gone for a very long time.".

"Oh, yes," Talo Thoran said. "There is so much more than just the language to be learned from them." Then, his eyes shining with a look that I knew all too well, he added: "Besides, John Carter: she is the most amazing person that I have ever known!"

Not long after, the golden goddess and her countrymen vanished from the caverns in the company of a lone scholar from Helium, returning to the City of Ten Thousand Names by their own unfathomable path.

36
OF DEATH AND LIFE

ROPPING DOWN OUT OF THE SKY in a seemingly endless stream came the massive battleships and cruisers. My heart swelled in my breast as I saw vessels bearing the insignia not only of the Empire of Helium, but of our great ally Ptarth, along with a swarm of smaller fliers sent by Xodar of the First Born. Touching down lightly in the newly opened expanse of the Ninth Circle, they discharged warriors from Kaol, Gathol, Duhor, and Okar, as well, all of whom we quickly put to work rounding up the dazed former Hands and Numbers so they might ferry to the surface those who wished to depart at once. This was by no means everyone: some there were who scurried in fear from the unfamiliar light of the open sky, and some who announced their wish to stay forever below in the remnants of the Perfect World, having long ago forgotten—or in some cases never experienced—what life was like above; but others were eager to resume their former lives and wept for joy to have the bright blue vault of the heavens over their heads again in place of the ceiling of shifting lights they had known for so many years.

One of the first to land was the *Xavarian*, proud flagship of the Heliumetic navy, and aboard it were its commander, my old friend Kantos Kan, and my son Carthoris, who bounded out to greet me with Woola in tow, the old calot nearly beside himself with mad delight at seeing me once again. As I embraced them both, and greeted many another stalwart friend and comrade, I was yet craning my neck over the throng of rebels and rescuers in search of one other.

Then I felt delicate fingers caress my shoulders from behind.

"When my indomitable Virginian did not return to me as promised, I came to him instead," said the beloved voice. I spun around and opened my arms to my princess.

It turned out that our coded message had reached all of the new communications stations—most importantly the one established in Duhor, where it had been quickly deciphered by Vad Varo, once a captain in the United States Infantry. The former Ulysses Paxton had then used the newly activated network to organize the rescue parties, which set out at once to converge on the coordinates contained in the message. Along their way, the contingent from Helium, led by my son, had come upon the *Kantim* and discovered the master Gridley Wave set, connected by its inventor in some improbable fashion to the endlessly powered engine of the flier, and still tirelessly sending out its signal of "SOS FROM JOHN CARTER LATITUDE 72.5S LONGITUDE 243.1W." Of Jason Gridley himself there was no sign, other than the discarded equilibrimotor and a folded sheet of drawing paper from Talo Thoran's art supplies bearing my initials, which they had found sticking out from beneath the tangle of equipment on the deck. Carthoris presented it to me with a wry smile. "Naturally, curiosity compelled me to attempt to make sense of it, but my aptitude for comprehending written English is even poorer than it is for the spoken variety."

I unfolded the paper and read the following:

John—

I hope that by the time you find this you will have managed to dig your way out of that fantastic underground prison and been reunited with your family. I found the flier just where our polyglot friend said it would be—though I must admit to a bit of a scare when I came to a place about halfway to the surface where ten or more identical passageways all diverged upward at different angles from the one through which I was rising. I hung there for several minutes, hoping to puzzle out which path to take before the flight-belt ran out of juice—or I ran out of time and space—before noticing by the light of my torch a strange symbol scratched onto the metal at the base of one of the passages. I recognized it immediately from my time spent with our mutual friend in Tarzana as one of the little doodads he and his children once used to mark their trails when they went on camping expeditions. I have no idea how it found its way to the bottom of that tunnel. Perhaps Talo Thoran somehow obtained from you the design of the crooked stick with the crossbars on one end and tiny circle at the other, and scrawled it there on his way down—or maybe I hallucinated the thing in my befuddlement and simply made a lucky guess! At any rate, that was the path I chose and it led me directly up to your ship, where I located the master transceiver and jury-rigged it to draw power from the flier's motor. I've set it to broadcast the coordinates you gave me until its parts wear out, and have crossed my fingers that your friends will find their way to the right spot.

Now I feel the all-too-familiar electric tingling returning to my nerves and this time I must not attempt to fight it. Kaor to you, John Carter, as the locals say—it has been an honor and a privilege!

> Yours sincerely,
> J. Gridley
> Formerly of California, Pellucidar,
> Amtor—and now Barsoom

When I showed the message to Talo Thoran he professed no knowledge of the "doodad," as Gridley had called it. I myself had recognized the description of the little marking with some surprise as something I had seen before, one summer afternoon many years ago, as I scratched idly with my walking stick in the sandy soil by the lake that lay to the east of the Carter manse. The children who regularly formed my rowdy escort on those supposedly solitary and contemplative walks had plucked twigs from the ground and joined me in my artistic endeavors. One of the little fellows, especially taken with the whimsical design he had sketched in the dirt, insisted on copying it several times until he was able to reproduce it with ease—and for some reason the simple shape had become lodged in my own memory, as well.

In the time that followed, those who had arrived from the outer world heard many versions of the tale of what had transpired down there in the Masters' Perfect World, both from relative newcomers like myself and from others who had languished below for centuries. As they left their fliers to explore the ancient city and the ruins of the Nine Circles beyond, I told them of the Oolscar and their ultimate fate at the hands and minds of the Kalovars, who had returned like wraiths to their city in the north and once more placed it beyond the reach of ordinary time and space.

It seemed that some additional good might come of this terrible time: listening to the colloquy of the gathered representatives of some of Barsoom's most powerful nations, I heard much determination to scour the pits and dungeons beneath their own cities, to ensure that the hidden ways used to spirit away prisoners and others over the centuries were closed off and the pits themselves emptied of their human castoffs.

Beyond this, there were still a few loose ends, as Tara had referred to them, to be tied up before we departed the ancient Parovar city and returned home at last.

As I entered the little chamber in the central building of the buried metropolis that had once been called the First Circle, my eyes fell on the end of a velvet-covered divan and the sandaled feet and shapely legs of the copper-skinned maiden who reclined upon it. She was attired in a harness inlaid with bits of platinum and gold and embellished with a sash of deep red silk, these garments serving to accentuate rather than conceal the statuesque form beneath them. She had a wide leather collar about her shoulders, and no head.

"Kaor, John Carter," said Ghek, crawling out from the shadows beneath the divan to spring up onto the cushions. Squatting over the collar, the kaldane extended a tight bundle of tentacles from his underside, folded his short spider legs beneath the great head, and tucked his powerful claws out of sight. Abruptly the woman arched her back and rose languorously to her feet. She was of almost heroic proportions, and with the addition of the kaldane's outsized bluish gray head upon her shoulders now stood nearly eye to eye with me.

"Kaor, Ghek. I was informed that you will be traveling the underground ways and returning to Bantoom, at least for now, and before you departed I wished to thank you personally for your assistance in the defeat of the Oolscar," I told him. *Her?* I had always known that—with the exception of their monarchs, who combined the reproductive capabilities of both sexes and were responsible for laying the eggs that produced all of the denizens of a given hive— kaldanes were themselves sexless. I was also aware that they made indiscriminate use of both male and female rykors. Witnessing that hitherto abstract knowledge firsthand, however, had a disconcerting effect, and I could see now that our original use of the male pronoun in regard to our friend had perhaps been ill-considered. Tara had once told me that among themselves the kaldanes referred to each other as "it," but in Helium we had ignored that custom as impolite. I made a mental note to consult Talo Thoran should our paths ever cross again. Perhaps the clever linguist would be able to come up with something more suitable after a few centuries of enlightenment among the golden folk in the City of Ten Thousand Names.

For the moment I focused my attention on Ghek's unlovely head, which for the first time was draped in the bejeweled leather trappings commonly worn by highly placed kaldanes in the hives of Bantoom. "You are looking rather magnificent these days," I observed. "Have you put away your metal rykor for good?"

"Not at all. As impressive as my fellow kaldanes find it, however, I believe that valued instrument is more suited to battle and affairs of state."

"Yes, I understand that you have recently become an honored leader among your people, due to your forceful role in the recent campaign. Are we to address you as 'jeddak' now, or is there another, more descriptive title employed exclusively by those of your race?"

The richly decorated head bobbed slowly from side to side, its saucer eyes avoiding my gaze. "Not precisely, John Carter . . ." the kaldane began hesitantly.

"Ghek! Father!" At that moment my daughter appeared in the doorway, her cheeks flushed with excitement. "I was told I would find you both here. Please allow me a moment to commit this historic meeting to my memory," she said, her eyes twinkling with merriment as she paused on the threshold. "Tell me, John Carter—how does it feel to bask in the august presence of the newly acclaimed Warlord of Bantoom?"

Ghek's expressionless face turned a somewhat deeper shade of blue.

The bodies of the slain rebels were transported to the surface, where great funeral pyres blazed across the dead sea bottom surrounding the new chasm; those identified as collaborators were brought to the Second Circle and entombed without ceremony in the now-empty chambers of their Masters, which were then pumped free of air and sealed once more.

Discussions were held with representatives of those who for one reason or another had elected to stay in the remnants of the Nine Circles, at least for the time being. Many of the surface nations, Helium included, were willing to negotiate trade agreements, whereby food and other perishable supplies would be exchanged for scientific equipment, as well as records of the botanical and biological experimentation that had been carried out below, at least until those fields not utterly destroyed by fire could be brought back into production. Certain of the surviving experimental animals were to be transported above for study, while others would be put into the care of those who remained below or released to roam the sea bottoms. Once these matters were taken care of, the various fleets began to depart, carrying with them former prisoners bound for their various homes.

One individual had not come forth to exchange greetings with those from above. I found Tor-ov Ov-tor alone in the War Room, standing at the central table and contemplating the elaborate map Tanus had laid out of the once–Perfect World. I came up to stand beside him.

"I have been looking for you," I said. "The last of those who plan to return to the surface at this time are departing in a few hours. I would like you to join me and my family in our flier."

Tor-ov Ov-tor considered my offer but a moment; then he gave his head a decisive shake.

"Thank you, my friend, but no. I no longer have a place in the world above. I shall remain down here to assist in the liberation of the uncounted thousands who still languish in these caverns. The remaining receptacles in all the storerooms must be opened and those of their occupants who yet retain some semblance of sanity given the opportunity to return to their various nations and to the loved ones from whom they were stolen so long ago. By staying here to ease their transition back into the living world, perhaps I may atone in some measure for the cowardly actions of my early life."

Placing my hand on his shoulder, I regarded him steadily.

"You are a good man, Tor-ov Ov-tor, and clearly no coward. It is not a sin to continue to live when circumstances beyond one's ability to alter have condemned others to death. Especially when by living one has effected the preservation of the lives of so many."

He stiffened. "Be that as it may," he said, "I have grown used to a life away from the sun. With luck, those who might once have cared for me have long since dried their tears and put my shade to rest."

I was feeling a touch exasperated with the noble fellow. Seeing him for the past several days free of the confusing interplay of colored lights had confirmed the suspicion that had been growing in my breast for a considerable time.

"I know that you are a betting man," I told him in a lighter tone. "And so I offer you a final wager. Will you agree to come back to the surface world with me, at least for a time, if I am able to divine your true name? Should I fail, I pledge to leave you to do penance in perpetuity here in your sunless world."

Tor-ov Ov-tor's eyes had brightened at the mention of a wager. Now he gave a snort of incredulity. "That is an easy bet to accept! No one here knows my name save myself, and my thoughts lie behind a wall of protection second only to your own."

"I do not need to read your mind to know your name, brother," I said with a smile.

Before he could respond, a commotion by the main entrance heralded the arrival of my children, who hastened across the floor to join us.

Tara kissed my cheek and then told me that final preparations were underway for our departure to the surface. At her side, Carthoris was studying Tor-ov Ov-tor's handsome visage with a puzzled frown.

"Well and good! We shall soon be on our way," I told Tara. "But first—introductions are in order."

I turned to the man by my side.

"My friend, this is my daughter, the matchless Tara, now Princess of Gathol, and my son, the redoubtable Carthoris, Prince of Helium. Tara, Carthoris, I am most pleased to present to you the man whose unwavering courage and ingenuity were indispensable in the defeat of the Oolscar and the salvation of all Barsoom. He is your mother's brother and his name is Kajan Dan."

On our flight back to Helium, I requested that the *Xavarian* stop again at the octagonal structure where the *Kantim* still rested, so that the flier might be brought aboard and delivered to the shipyards at Hastor, where Carthoris wished to inspect it for any damage incurred from our time in the punishing winds. When we touched down nearby, I was surprised to espy a lone thoat wandering along the outskirts of the edifice.

"A friend of yours, Father?" Carthoris inquired, as the beast trotted over eagerly and began to nuzzle my shoulder.

"Yes, indeed!" I replied. "This is Bucephalus, a most noble and loyal steed."

We brought the little thoat aboard the battleship as well. Once we reached Helium, I secured him a well-appointed paddock in the royal stables, against that day when Miss Callwell might again grace us with her presence and would surely welcome the sight of another familiar face.

There were many heartfelt scenes in the days that followed. Not least among them was that moment when I entered the main audience chamber of the palace of Tardos Mors in Greater Helium to join the other members of the family that had gathered there, and Vara Martis rose from the couch upon which she had been seated next to the beloved grandson she had believed to be dead for over a century, and, tears streaming down her cheeks, fell on her knees with gratitude before me. Reflecting that she had once again managed to catch me off guard, I assisted the empress to her feet, and, her pet sorak slinking suspiciously at our heels, escorted her into the grand hall.

Tardos Mors, Jeddak of the Empire of Helium, presided at the celebration along with his wife. Seated next to them were their son Mors Kajak, Jed of Lesser Helium, and his mate Thoria, who could scarce keep her brimming eyes from the son who had returned to them against all odds. My beloved Dejah Thoris was there, radiant in her joy, as were our children.

In addition to the reunited members of the House of Tardos Mors, there were treasured friends and staunch allies aplenty at that massive table: Tars Tarkas was there, and Sola his daughter, both towering above the rest of us in the huge chairs that had been constructed especially to accommodate them; my countryman from Earth, Vad Varo, with his mate Valla Dia, Princess of Duhor; Kantos Kan, jedwar of Helium's air navy; Talu of Marentina, who now ruled all of Okar in the distant north, and Xodar, jeddak of the newly forged nation composed of the First Born and the therns in the far south; Kulan Tith of Kaol; Thuvan Dihn of Ptarth, father to Thuvia, seated next to our mutual grandson Djon Dihn. San Tothis, Tanus, and other crew members of the lost cruiser *Vanator* sat proudly with their jed, Gahan of Gathol, husband of my daughter, along with his firstborn daughter Llana and her mate, the Orovar Pan-dan-chee, and their own new daughter Gala, whose name means "grace." In all it was a joyous time, though tears were also shed, both of thanksgiving and in recognition of the long years that had been lost while comrades and loved ones were parted due to the machinations of the Oolscar.

A few days later, I watched old Cluros wend his careful way high in the star-sprinkled heavens of late evening, while Thuria, his heedless and ever-youthful bride, danced across the sky below him.

Once more alone after the press of friends and family that had continued for several days, Dejah Thoris and I stood on our balcony overlooking the ancient domes and soaring towers of our beloved Helium. "Do you still have doubts that a man can live in two worlds?" my wife asked me, her eyes on the brilliant star blazing like a sapphire above us.

"Truth to tell, Earth has been more in my thoughts these past weeks than in many years," I answered with a smile. "Apparently I am far from the only one whose lifetime has spanned more than one world. It is good to know I have some company in that regard out here in the wider universe."

"So you will continue to maintain the old connections between your past life and this one?"

"I believe I shall," I said. "In fact, I performed a time-honored custom from back home just a few hours ago, when little Gala begged me to entertain her with a story as her parents were tucking her into her sleeping silks and furs. I think her venerable grandmother Tara put her up to it. I decided to tell her about a little boy I had once known on far Jasoom and of the unparalleled teller of wonderful tales that he himself had grown up to be." I gazed fondly at the pinpoint of blue light. "She wanted to know if he was still up there telling his stories now, and if one day she might go visit him."

"Large questions for such a small child!" Dejah Thoris rested her head against my shoulder. "And how did you answer her?"

"I told her that her path would be her own to choose, through all its twists and turns," I said with a smile. "As for the storyteller, that question has been much on my own mind—especially in light of recent events. And so, having lately come to understand it myself, I told her the simple truth."

Dejah Thoris turned her face up to me expectantly, her dark eyes shining. "And what would that be?" she asked.

"Why, that he still lives!" I said, and once more gathered my incomparable princess into my arms beneath the hurtling moons of Mars.

EDGAR RICE BURROUGHS UNIVERSE™

VICTORY HARBEN™
STORMWINDS OF VA-NAH™

AS RETOLD BY ANN TONSOR ZEDDIES

BASED ON GRIDLEY WAVE TRANSMISSIONS RECEIVED AT THE OFFICES OF
EDGAR RICE BURROUGHS, INC.,
TARZANA, CALIFORNIA

ERB
INC.

EDITOR'S NOTE
MORE TALES FROM THE VOID

IT IS NO LONGER A SECRET that here in Tarzana, California, at the offices of Edgar Rice Burroughs, Inc., we recently discovered a curious apparatus in a locked drawer in Mr. Burroughs' old desk. The device was a Gridley Wave transmitter-receiver, and with it we have been communicating with other worlds, just as the great author did in the first half of the twentieth century when he made contact with such legendary figures as David Innes and John Carter.

In the back pages of the book *Carson of Venus: The Edge of All Worlds*, one such transmission appeared, which I transcribed from my own communications with Jason Gridley himself, the discoverer of the Gridley Wave. "Pellucidar: Dark of the Sun" opens the Swords of Eternity super-arc, an epic cycle of tales that begins in early 1950 in the inner world of Pellucidar. There Jason Gridley and Victory Harben plumbed the ruins of the buried Mahar city of Mintra, seeking an ancient tablet in the archives of Pellucidar's former reptilian overlords in the attempt to "jump-start" the Gridley Wave, which had mysteriously ceased to be, both in function and as a principle of physics.

If you have read Win Scott Eckert's ERB Universe novel *Tarzan: Battle for Pellucidar*, you already know the story of how the eleven-year-old Victory encountered the Mahar queen Tu-al-sa at the dead city of Mintra. That is why Jason Gridley and his goddaughter returned there in 1950, for Victory remembered having seen records in the timeworn archives of the Mahars indicating that the intelligent reptilians knew of the Gridley Wave, and had knowledge concerning it far beyond Jason's and her understanding. But when Jason and Victory attempted to reactivate the Gridley Wave, their experiment generated a distressing result: the extinguishing of Pellucidar's once-eternal

341

noonday sun. Victory appealed to Tu-al-sa for help, but when the Mahar queen adjusted the settings on their portable Gridley Wave set, a beam of energy reflected off the face of the darkened sun and spawned a maelstrom-like vortex that swallowed Victory whole, appearing to hurl her out of our reality, perhaps to a dimension beyond our own.

Shortly after I transcribed that tale from Jason Gridley, I made contact with Victory Harben. In a strange development, I began receiving transmissions from Victory sent from an array of different points on the timeline of her life, such that I, from my viewpoint in the 2020s, might receive two transmissions on the same day from what were essentially *two different "Victorys"*—for example, one transmitting from 1955 and the other from 1951. Such, Victory tells me, is the oddity of the illusion we call time.

Consequently, it soon became apparent that I needed assistance, for I was becoming flooded with transmissions and could not hope to handle them all. Moreover, Victory began narrating to me an epic tale that requires my full concentration, which will be published as the novel *Victory Harben: Fires of Halos.* Thus, I have turned to others to transcribe the new tales received at Tarzana. In "Victory Harben: Clash on Caspak," author Mike Wolfer related the story of how Victory was transported to the Land That Time Forgot, met See-ta the Savage, and was confronted by a mysterious winged warrior named Lahvoh, who claimed to be traveling "the angles" in search of the wayward Victory at the behest of her "hungry gods." The present story has been recounted by author Ann Tonsor Zeddies, based on notes from Victory Harben sent via Gridley Wave. "Stormwinds of Va-nah" picks up directly following the events of "Clash on Caspak."

I would be remiss if I failed to mention that Jason's continuing search for his goddaughter led to his own fantastic adventures. Stay tuned for forthcoming tales of Jason Gridley of Earth!

Christopher Paul Carey
Director of Publishing
Edgar Rice Burroughs, Inc.

VICTORY HARBEN: STORMWINDS OF VA-NAH
A Tale of the Swords of Eternity Super-Arc

VICTORY HARBEN, RUSHED ALONG by unseen forces through a dark void beyond time and space, rejoiced briefly at the sudden reverberation, like a steel cord snapping, that heralded her arrival on a new world. In an instant, sound and color once again flooded her deprived senses, and her lungs gasped in sweet, oxygen-laden air. But she had only a moment to survey her new surroundings. For the first time in her wayward travels through the cosmos, she had materialized in midair, and was falling out of the sky.

Before she could orient herself enough to break her fall, she tumbled to earth with force enough to knock her newly reclaimed breath out of her. Her senses blurred with the impact. When her sight cleared, her field of vision was fully occupied by a fierce and apparently angry face, and next to it, a viciously barbed spearhead jabbing at her, only inches away.

She wondered if the fall had somehow affected her sight, for although the face appeared humanoid, with eyes, nose, and mouth in the expected places, it was oddly wide, and a deep purple in hue. It took a moment to register the fact that this being, whatever it was, was shouting at her—or was it chanting? The sounds had an odd, singsong quality, and they were completely incomprehensible. Perhaps her ears had suffered as well.

Incomprehensible or not, the fierce assault of verbiage demanded an answer, as was clearly indicated by another jab of the spearhead, now perilously close to piercing Victory's skin. She considered using one of the jiu-jitsu moves she had learned from her friend Tarzan to knock it aside, but she was unsure how far she could trust her own body, or what might lie behind the visage that blocked most of her view. She focused on drawing enough breath to speak.

"Please," she managed to articulate. "I mean you no harm. I can't understand your speech. Give me a moment. I'll do my best to answer you."

The frown deepened on the broad face, and the large dark eyes narrowed, as if in surprise. Again the voice demanded reply—but this time the tonal syllables almost made sense to Victory. It was like listening to a song she had once heard and almost remembered.

"Say again!" she pleaded. "I almost got it that time."

When the spear-wielder spoke again, the sense of the words seemed to arrive in Victory's mind a few seconds after the sound, trailing it like an echo.

"What are you?" Victory heard. "Are you Kalkar or U-ga? Speak! Tell me your business, before I make a flesh-meal of you."

Victory decided that it was unlikely that the purple-hued being would stab her before hearing her answer. Cautiously pushing the point of the spear away from her eyes, she rolled to her side. Feeling no pain in her back or legs, she sat up, raising an open hand in what usually was understood as a gesture of peace among humanoids.

"My name is Victory Harben," she said. "I don't know what a Kalkar or U-ga might be. I come from far away, and I come in peace."

"What city? What tribe?" the being asked.

"No city and no tribe of this place," Victory said. "My land is called Pellucidar. I've lived in many cities: most recently London and Los Angeles. Who are you? Will you tell me your name and your city?"

Again the creature frowned. It looked Victory over, taking in— Victory guessed—the fact that she had arrived without clothing or gear of any kind. Victory spread her hands in a "nothing-up-my-sleeve" gesture.

"You see I am unarmed," she said. "Can we not talk? Perhaps be friends?"

"I am Ren-ah-ree of the Va-gas. Va-gas have no friends among the flying people."

In spite of this statement, Ren-ah-ree of the Va-gas no longer seemed inclined to stab Victory, at least not imminently. Victory took advantage of the Va-gas' pause to examine Ren-ah-ree more closely. Ren-ah-ree had seemed at first to be taller than a human, but Victory realized that the Va-gas' body was shaped more like that of a quadruped than a bipedal human. As if to confirm this, the Va-gas dropped to all fours, one front paw or hand still clutching the spear. Victory noticed that the Va-gas had an organ that resembled the udder of a terrestrial mammal. She cautiously concluded that the alien was probably female. Pending an opportunity for discussion, Victory thought of Ren-ah-ree as "she."

"How is it that you speak to me in the language of Va-nah?" Ren-ah-ree said. "I see the purple wind around you. Have you come to take me captive?"

The reference to the "purple wind" stunned Victory. Did the stranger perceive an aura surrounding her, perhaps one generated by the unknown force that transported Victory through the continuum? That would confirm her own hypothesis that a quantum effect somehow enabled her to speak with the Va-gas, just as it had enabled Lahvoh, the Zerafim who had attacked Victory on Caspak, to speak with Victory in both English and the native tongue of her friend See-tah. Ideas whirled through her mind, struggling for expression.

Before Victory could speak any of her thoughts aloud, Ren-ah-ree again rose on her hind legs, raising the spear toward the horizon.

"More flying people come!" she cried. "Your friends, female of Pel-u-see-dah?"

Victory scrambled to her feet, determined not to be caught lying down if Ren-ah-ree chose to menace her again. She looked in the direction the Va-gas indicated.

"No friends of mine," she replied. "I've been here only for these few moments. I have no friends in this place—unless you will be my friend."

"They are Kalkars! Never have I seen Kalkars flying! This is bad news for us. And we are caught in the open. Run, if you are no Kalkar and if you value your life. Run, Vik-tah-ree of Pel-u-see-dah!"

The Va-gas dropped to all fours again and made off, bounding away at an amazing pace, toward a low hill about half a mile away, where a thick growth of vegetation promised cover.

Victory did not wait for a second invitation, but whirled and followed the Va-gas, as fast as she could. She winced as her feet struck the hard ground, expecting to feel the pain of impact on her bare feet, but was instead surprised to find herself as light as a feather. The gravity of this world must be significantly less than that of Earth. Despite her startlement, she hit the ground running and maintained her speed.

The dark shapes visible against the softly glowing clouds above grew larger with alarming swiftness. They wheeled in a flock, their wings beating like those of massive birds. They were closing fast, and it was soon evident that they were no birds, but humanoid forms with arms and legs, and hands that carried objects that looked very much like weapons. Knowing she could not make it to cover in time, Victory looked around for anything that might aid her defense against an attack, but saw nothing. The ground was hard, but no large stones were visible, nor could she see any vegetation that might yield a stick or branch.

The fliers had spotted her. She heard bellicose shouts of glee, and saw them waving the objects in her direction, in much the same way a human might point a gun. For the second time in mere minutes, Victory found herself targeted. She had never felt more defenseless. She stopped running and faced the fliers. Perhaps they, like Ren-ah-ree, could be persuaded to communicate. If not, agility and audacity had saved her skin more than once, and might again.

Boldly, she raised her open hand skyward.

"Stop!" she shouted. "I come as a friend."

If they, like the Va-gas, had the ability to understand her, they showed no sign of it. There were five of them, and all had aimed weapons at her. Had they coordinated their efforts, she would have had no chance, but instead, they seemed to be jockeying for position to claim the first shot. Just as the first to arrive aimed at her, a second knocked him off balance to try his own luck. That gave Victory time to dive and roll. A projectile of some kind hit the ground, scattering dust into her eyes, but missing her. The second flier shouted triumphantly and dove toward her. She rolled to a crouch and gathered herself for a leap. He did not seem to have very good control of his flying gear. Too close to the ground, he was forced to swerve upward again before firing.

At that moment, Victory sprang after him. She leaped higher than she had imagined she could. A fleeting wonder that the gravity was indeed different here passed through her mind as her reaching hand seized the attacker's ankle. Victory felt her own feet leave the ground for an instant, but before she could be tugged into the sky, the flier floundered and crashed to the ground with Victory on top of him.

He was sufficiently stunned by the impact that she wrested his weapon away from him. In seconds, her quick eye grasped its basic function. The design was much like a terrestrial gun, but the curved trigger guard protected a firing button rather than a lever. She had no idea what kind of damage it might do, and didn't wish to kill intelligent beings whose identities she didn't know. But neither did she wish to die or suffer damage herself. Targeting the nearest flier's wings, she depressed the button.

She felt a recoil, and something tore a hole in the wing. The same shot apparently grazed the flier's arm, for he shouted in pain, and a splash of red marked both the wound and the fact that this humanoid had blood like an earthling's. His wing crippled, he too crashed to the ground. Falling from a greater height than the first, he landed harder, and lay still.

Fearing she had killed him, Victory sprang to his side, but she had no time even to disarm him, much less check his condition. The remaining three, with bloodcurdling yells of threat and rage, swooped over her. She tried to take cover behind the fallen bodies, but it was scant defense against an aerial attack.

At that moment, a spear appeared as if by magic, transfixing the lead flier. A gout of blood sprayed into the air and pattered down like rain on the dust. Moments later, the flier hit the ground headfirst, with a sickening crunch of bone. The remaining fliers pulled up in midair, nearly stalling out in their haste, and executed a panicked ascent and retreat. They dwindled rapidly in the direction of a far-off mountain range.

Victory turned to see the Va-gas standing behind her, flanks heaving with exertion. Without ceremony, Ren-ah-ree set one forepaw on the body of the fallen flier and yanked her spear loose. She licked the fresh blood from the haft, wiped the point on the ground, and restowed the weapon in a holder on one side of the leather harness she wore around her torso.

"You killed him," Victory said, stunned by the unexpected violence of Ren-ah-ree's attack.

"I saved your life," the Va-gas replied coolly.

The flier Victory had winged stirred and groaned, showing signs of returning consciousness. Before Victory could act, Ren-ah-ree pulled a large knife from her harness. She drove it into the flier's chest. He went limp. The Va-gas moved to the attacker that Victory had pulled from the air, and gave him the coup de grace before Victory could voice her horror.

"Why did you do that?" she cried. "I wanted to speak with them!"

Victory moved from one fallen body to the next with frantic haste, fumbling with their garments to seek a pulse. She bloodied her hands in a vain effort to stanch their blood. All were dead, executed with swift efficiency.

"They are Kalkars," Ren-ah-ree said. "It is of no use to speak with them. They are good only for meat."

She shook herself and stamped her feet, jostling the bundle she carried on her back. Victory stared in shock as the bundle moved on its own, lifting a head and stirring limbs, then jumping down from Ren-ah-ree's back. Just like the Va-gas in miniature, it glowered up at Victory in a good imitation of Ren-ah-ree.

"You must run on your own legs, Da-va-ro," Ren-ah-ree said. "Hurry now and help load this fresh meat. Cast away these things they carried. We have no use for them."

The little one began to tug and drag the bodies, straining to lift them to Ren-ah-ree's back.

Sickened by the sight of a child dragging bloody corpses away with no more concern than a farmer handling plucked chickens, Victory turned away to focus on the unfamiliar gear the Va-gas had tossed to the ground. Salvaging a pouch one of the Kalkars had slung at his back, she placed their artifacts in it and shouldered it herself. Protection from this unfamiliar environment was her greatest need. Suppressing a shudder, she took the sandals from the feet of the smallest of the bodies, and with a hasty adjustment to the straps, she made them fit her own feet well enough to provide some protection and still permit her to move quickly. The question of further clothing would have to wait for a more convenient time.

"You might have thanked me for my help," Ren-ah-ree growled. "If you would thank me now, or if you would not throw away the life I saved for you, then get busy and help the young one. We must carry these away to shelter quickly, before we are seen by their kind or anyone else. If the other Kalkars find you here alone, you can only hope to die as quickly as these did."

Victory wished briefly that she could part ways with this blood-thirsty companion. But she had no reason to doubt Ren-ah-ree's assessment of their plight. Logic quelled disgust, and she turned resolutely to doing what must be done. The burden of the dead seemed heavy to carry.

"Can you bear so much weight?" she asked the Va-gas.

"I carry what I must," Ren-ah-ree replied stoically. "This is food for many days."

Victory found the first body, still strapped into its flying harness, curiously light. Between herself and the small Va-gas, they were able to heave it across Ren-ah-ree's back with some effort, but by no means the difficulty she had expected. The wings flopped at Ren-ah-ree's flanks, causing her to shy irritably like a spooked pony. The young one, Da-va-ro, started to unbuckle the flying harness from the next body on the ground. Victory saw that between the wings there was some kind of inflatable bag.

"Stop," she said. "You can cast away the wings that I damaged, but leave the others. It may be that this flying gear makes them lighter to carry. It could be an advantage to us. Let's not throw it away without examining it first."

The little Va-gas showed his teeth at her, and looked to Ren-ah-ree before obeying.

Ren-ah-ree growled and stamped her feet, testing the weight of her burden.

"Do as she says," the Va-gas ordered Da-va-ro. "Hurry and load them up. We'll deal with the gear later."

Soon all three bodies were piled across Ren-ah-ree's sturdy back, and roughly secured with the straps that lashed some additional bundles to her harness. The Va-gas set off at a steady pace toward the hills, but without any of the dramatic bounds and leaps she had displayed earlier. Da-va-ro trotted beside her. Victory noticed that, unlike the adult Va-gas, he was shod with what looked like stiff leather mittens on his forefeet. Victory herself ran alongside the Va-gas. She held to the harness straps with one hand, both to keep the burden balanced securely and to help herself keep up. It was a swift pace for her, even with sandals to protect her feet.

As they ran, a cool breeze began to blow. Victory welcomed it, for the climate was warmer and damper than she was used to. But Ren-ah-ree tossed her head in apparent unease.

The small Va-gas spoke for the first time.

"Mama, is it Zo-al's breath?" he piped up, in a hoarse but high voice. "What did we do wrong?"

"We did nothing wrong!" Ren-ah-ree responded fiercely. "Run faster! We must reach shelter!"

By the time they reached the first slopes of the hillside, they were fighting the wind's strength, and the little one was stumbling. A few raindrops spattered down as they entered the shade of vegetation and slowed to a walk. They passed over the first hill, and then down into a dell beyond. Here they found a thick bole, bigger around than the three of them together, with one bough sweeping low to earth, under the shoulder of another ascending slope. Ren-ah-ree swept her gaze around the area.

"Here," she said. "We must take shelter in this place until Zo-al is quiet once more."

Her voice was hard to hear above the shrieking of the wind. They hurried beneath the protection of the low-hanging foliage as the wind drove stinging droplets of rain against them.

Victory braced herself against the wind for a minute after the other two had taken shelter. She could see nothing beyond the curtain of rain, but she could hear thunderclaps in the air above. The storm was violent, but had come without the warning of clouds or any other weather signs with which she was familiar. Victory stood in the downpour long enough to wash away the blood that had splashed her from the fallen Kalkars. Their deaths had been disturbing enough without wearing the reminder.

In the gloomy shade beneath the branches, the two Va-gas huddled together next to the tree's sturdy bole. Outside, Victory could hear creaking and snapping as other vegetation was tumbled by the wind. Flashes like lightning intermittently illuminated the thicket with searing light. In spite of the heavy rain, Victory detected a scent of burning, and by the flared nostrils of the Va-gas, she guessed they could smell it too. Da-va-ro shivered and whimpered.

To sit still under the lash of the storm did not suit Victory. Restless, she searched for action that could be taken or knowledge to be gained.

"Let me undo your burden," she suggested. The Va-gas made no protest, so Victory loosed the straps and dragged the dead Kalkars off Ren-ah-ree's back into the farthest corner of their tiny shelter. There she busied herself with stripping off the rest of their gear. The flying devices, consisting of wings strapped to the arms, and an inflatable sac that rested on a harness between the shoulders, alarmed her by bouncing gently, as if they would float away like a helium balloon. Victory buckled their straps to a tree branch to secure them for later examination.

Her first concern was to equip herself. The Kalkars wore simple tunics. Among the three, one at least remained bloodless. It was easy enough to pull the garment over her own head, securing it with the previous owner's belt, which came with a wickedly large and sharp knife attached. Victory pushed the other tunics out into the rain, hoping they would be washed clean. Then she set to work with the knife to trim the sandals into a form that would fit her comfortably for the long term. It was unnerving to know that at any moment, the mysterious effect that had repeatedly seized her after traveling through the Mahar vortex might snatch her away and hurl her to yet another world. Yet at the same time, she had to plan for the possibility of an extended stay on this one.

She forced herself to take a good look at the Kalkar bodies as she stripped them. Unlike the Va-gas, they seemed completely human in form, which only added to Victory's distress at the brutality of their deaths. Their hair and nails were rough and ill-trimmed, but they had apparently shaved, having stubble but no beards. Their hands, feet, and other appendages all seemed those of male humans, and the now-dried blood had the same color and consistency as that of earthly humans. Among the three, there were variations in complexion and hair color. Bodies and faces bore scars both old and new, reinforcing her impression that Kalkars were a hostile and belligerent group. The Va-gas were no angels, either, as far as she could tell from Ren-ah-ree's warlike behavior.

I've come to another world of conflict, Victory thought ruefully. Is there any other kind? If so, I wish I could be hurled *there*.

Lifting her head from her work, she realized that the thunder and rain had died away to an occasional grumble and splash. Light again filtered through the long, frond-like leaves of their shelter. The Va-gas shook off the raindrops that still clung to them.

"I'm hungry," Da-va-ro said.

"Yes, it's past time to prepare this flesh." Ren-ah-ree bent over the bodies with her large knife in one forepaw. Victory had a chance to examine the Va-gas appendages. They appeared to be part paw, part grasping hand. There were only three digits, thick and powerful enough that the Va-gas could use them for locomotion, but also flexible enough to wield tools. Their manner of grasping appeared a bit awkward, and Victory was not sure if the digits were fully opposable, like the human fingers and thumb, but they served well enough.

"The kill was partly yours," Ren-ah-ree said. "Eat, if you are hungry."

Victory knew that the invitation was well intended, but she could not overcome her revulsion.

"Thank you, but I prefer other food. Are there fruits here that are edible?"

Ren-ah-ree snorted scornfully. "Yes, all the fruits you find here can be eaten. But you will find little strength in them. Without flesh, you will not be able to continue your journey."

"In my country, we do not eat the flesh of—of beings that speak, such as these."

Ren-ah-ree snorted again. "What, then, will you eat? The tor-ho? The rymph? We consume the Kalkars, and the U-ga when we can get them. Is it not better to eat our enemies than our own kind? If we did not eat them, they would eat us."

Victory wanted to pursue the issue, but the Va-gas shouldered her away.

"If you will not eat, then move aside. The young one and I have had no flesh in many days, and we require sustenance."

She handed Da-va-ro a knife. While she swiftly and efficiently began gutting the Kalkar bodies, Da-va-ro danced exuberantly about, reaching in to slice off bits of the corpse, popping them into his mouth, and chewing with evident enjoyment.

Victory reminded herself that other worlds have other customs, but her stomach churned in disgust. She took her pouch of Kalkar weapons and stepped away from the sheltering branches into the rain-freshened air. The Va-gas paid no attention to her departure.

She set out to find food, but her eyes strayed often to the sights around her. Her adventures so far had given her little opportunity to indulge in exploration for its own sake.

"And what good is it, for the effect Tu-al-sa imposed on me to send me to so many worlds, when I find myself beset with conflict and with so little chance for discovery?" she said to herself. The climate here seemed extraordinarily mild and even, save for the incursions of the storms of Zo-al, whoever that might be. The two species she had met so far seemed to get along with minimal clothing. The sky above glowed with an even light that radiated from all directions, rather than from a luminary body. Indeed, she could not see any sign of a sun. Having a chance at last to contemplate the horizon, she realized with a leap of the heart that she was in a hollow world, like Pellucidar, homeland of her childhood. No wonder she felt strangely at home here. The fantastically colored landscape rose gently on all sides, curving upward until the far side of the globe's interior was concealed by towering pastel-colored clouds and shimmering mists. In Pellucidar, a central sun illumined all with constant light, neither rising nor setting. Here, she saw no trace of any central body. The mystery of the gentle, all-pervasive glow piqued her curiosity. A part of her longed to set out for the nearby mountains in search of answers, but the Va-gas were her only clue to this world so far. She determined to stay with them until she had gained all the knowledge she could from them. She had so many questions!

Thinking this over, she had roamed some distance from the large tree where they had sheltered. She entered a grove of smaller and more delicate plants, more like ferns than trees, with many fronds and curved tips. Clusters of firm, maroon-colored berries clung to the undersides of these fern-trees. Victory sniffed at them, then, hoping Ren-ah-ree had not misinformed her about the edibility of local fruits, popped one into her mouth. It had a sweet, tangy flavor, and a chewy texture. Victory roamed around for a few minutes, gathering some nutlike objects she found in a clump of bushes. Nearby, a group of taller, sapling-like stems dangled round, tough-skinned fruits that she was able to pluck by bending the stems toward the ground. Experiencing no ill effects from her first taste of berries, she returned to the fern-trees to consume another handful.

Once hunger was assuaged, curiosity drove her back to the company of the Va-gas. As she hoped, they had finished their bloody repast. Although blood-smeared fingers and knives still showed traces of the meal, the remains had been neatly packed in leaves and tied with vines. Da-va-ro was employed in hacking out a pit in the soft soil beneath the tree. Some of the packages had been stacked with the rest of Ren-ah-ree's gear. Da-va-ro quickly buried the rest and covered them over with the soft, mossy, pinkish turf so neatly that it would not be obvious that the ground had been disturbed.

"We are fortunate now to have meat for many days," Ren-ah-ree said. "Especially since you will not partake. These wrappings will keep it fresh for a long time. What we cannot carry, we will cache here to use later—should we ever return."

She grinned ferociously. "It is fortunate for you, as well. To feed my young one, I might have had to take your flesh. Now that will not be necessary. Your foolishness in standing up to the Kalkars has been lucky for all—yourself included."

Victory took a seat on the soft, mossy ground and cracked nuts with the hilt of her knife. She offered some to the two Va-gas, but being satiated with meat, they declined.

"Where are you traveling?" she inquired.

Ren-ah-ree scowled. "Why should I tell you that?"

"I had hoped that I might travel with you," Victory said. "I know nothing of this world. Your knowledge could help me. At the same time, I see that you have enemies. I have helped you, and might do so again."

A look of cunning crossed Ren-ah-ree's broad face.

"If you want my trust, you must tell me the truth. What is this city Pel-u-see-dah, where you come from? Where is it?"

"First tell me where we are," Victory said. "What do you call this place?"

Ren-ah-ree looked at her as if she had lost her mind.

"This is Va-nah. All know that, even the smallest children!"

"All this is Va-nah?" Victory waved a hand to indicate the entire world.

"Yes! Va-nah is all this space, the plains where Va-gas live, the cities of U-ga and Kalkars, and the great Hoos where Zo-al dwells."

"Good. Then know that I come from far beyond Va-nah. Outside it, in another world."

Ren-ah-ree shook her head and laughed scornfully.

"Your words are deceitful, senseless. Beyond Va-nah, there is nothing! Unless it be Zo-al's realm. But even Zo-al lives within the rock. Beyond this space is only rock."

"You spoke of Zo-al before. What is Zo-al?"

"Almost I can believe you come from far away! You know not Va-nah! You know not Zo-al!" Ren-ah-ree scoffed.

"Tell me of Zo-al," Victory coaxed.

"Zo-al lives in the great Hoos. Lest you ask, 'What are the Hoos?' I will tell you what every child knows—they are the great round holes in the ground, where space falls away into nothingness. Zo-al is a great, invisible beast. He makes the light that comes and goes in the depths of the Hoos. And when he is angry, he sends the wind and rain as you saw, and the deadly balls of fire that fall from the sky and roll along the ground, burning all before them. All other enemies, we can fight with our spears, but even the Va-gas fear Zo-al, for we have no way to fight him. I do not believe you could pass through the realm of Zo-al unscathed."

"But I have passed through the realm of Zo-al," Victory said, raising her chin defiantly to match the expression of the Va-gas. "Not on this world, but on my own world. I come from a place like this one—a hollow world. And I passed through an enormous Hoo in my own land, through the realm of Zo-al. We traveled in a great metal flying ship that protected us from the fires of Zo-al."

Ren-ah-ree's frown of disbelief did not change. Victory searched for a way to explain. She picked up one of the tough fruits, about the size of a grapefruit, and held it up.

"Here, I will show you."

She plunged the knife into the rind, cutting the fruit open. She was pleased to see that the interior held seeds that were easily scooped out. She turned the resulting hollow toward Ren-ah-ree.

"You see this? This is like Va-nah, and like my world of Pellucidar. Within the flesh of this fruit, there is a hollow space, just as there is a hollow space within the rock of the world. We live in this space, as the seeds were held within. But the rock around us, like this flesh of the fruit, does not extend forever. It has an end. If you could pierce through the rock, you would find an end to it. Like this rind, there is a surface to Va-nah, and beyond that is not rock but empty space. And in this empty space are many, many worlds."

She held up another fruit in her other hand and caused it to circle the first.

Ren-ah-ree scoffed. "Your hand holds up this fruit. What would hold up these other worlds, if not the rock within in which we live?"

"Beyond Va-nah are invisible forces, like the wind. The force that holds the worlds in space is called gra-vi-tee."

The Va-gas shook her head. "Your words are meaningless."

Victory had never felt so frustrated. With all her knowledge of physics, she could not explain it in terms the Va-gas would understand. There were no words for the concepts she wanted to express. The English words simply failed to translate.

"Almost I might—might—have believed that another space like that of Va-nah could exist within the rock, beyond Zo-al's realm. But this? That the rock ends and then there is nothing? Either you try to trick me, or you have been tricked yourself by these empty words.

I hoped you could help me find my city, but you cannot. You don't even know where you are!"

Victory refused to give up.

"I am still learning about Va-nah. I can be a valuable ally. You saw that when we bested the Kalkars. Tell me of this city you search for. How do you know I cannot help until you ask?"

Ren-ah-ree seemed to be thinking it over. At last, she settled herself on her haunches on the soft moss, as a big dog might curl up to relax.

"So be it. You are but one, and you are far from home, wherever that home might be. If you try to harm me after you hear my story, my vengeance will be swift. But I will tell you that story. It will be good to know that one being will remember my journey, for truly I doubt I shall ever return—especially now that the Kalkars have seen me.

"I was born in the tribe of the No-vans, a mighty tribe. And I will tell you, since you seem to know nothing of our ways, that among my people, females are the wealth of the tribe. The men are the warriors. Battle is their life, and all who fall in battle become meat for the victors. Females are never eaten. We are protected and kept alive so we can give birth to meat and warriors. I never questioned this.

"At a young age, before I had borne a litter, I was with a group of other females who were captured by another tribe. I was taken by the Sar-vans. There I grew to maturity, and there I had my first litter. They were like all other young ones. Then came my second litter."

She bent her head as if to hide some emotion Victory could not guess.

"It was a small litter. Two males were born feeble and were taken for meat before they could walk. The third was—this one." She jerked her head toward Da-va-ro, who was playing quietly by himself in a corner. "He is hardy enough, but for his forelimbs. They were—different. Deformed, our leaders said. His fingers are not strong and tough for galloping. They more resemble yours—thin and weak. The other young ones mocked him and lay in wait for him, hoping to kill and eat him. I protected him, and then their mothers mocked me. They said he would not keep up when the tribe moved. If he fell behind, he would be eaten, lest his meat be lost to the tribe. I made him coverings out of tough hide, to wear when we were running, so that he could keep up. I carried him on my back when his forepaws hurt. It is shameful to protect a weakling. I was teased and tormented. Many times, they tried to take Da-va-ro while I slept."

"Wait! Hold on a minute," Victory said. Her mind was in a whirl. She was painfully aware that she had misjudged the Va-gas, dismissing Ren-ah-ree as a violent creature without feelings. At the same time, she felt horror at the way of life Ren-ah-ree had just described.

"I want to make sure I understand what you're saying. Your people actually kill and eat each other? Not just adults, but small children?"

Ren-ah-ree shrugged. "Often the children will kill each other, and eat each other too, if adults don't intervene and make sure the meat is fairly divided. If a young one is too weak to survive, what else can we do? We need flesh. It can't be wasted."

"So, it's not just Va-gas eating Kalkars and vice versa, but Va-gas eating Va-gas."

"Of course. Tribe fights tribe to gain their flesh. You have not mentioned the U-ga, but just like the Kalkars, the U-ga once kept Va-gas in captivity and bred us for food. Probably they still do, but we seldom see U-ga. They stay in their cities."

"But why?" Victory demanded. "Why can you not eat fruits and nuts, as I do? Or other animals?"

"There are only three other kinds of animals," Ren-ah-ree said. "All are poison to us. If we eat them, we die. Of course we eat the fruits. Da-va-ro and I have survived on fruits and berries since we left the tribe. But after only a few days, we become weak and tired. If we cannot get flesh, we will die and be eaten by others."

"This doesn't make sense," Victory said. She knew of societies in Earth's upper world where protein scarcity resulted in cannibalism, but only in certain circumstances, for a limited time. It was hard to picture a world where intelligent humanoids survived through cannibalism indefinitely.

"A biome with so few species is impossible," she said. But again, she heard her words become a meaningless blur of noise when she used terms with no equivalents in the language of Va-nah. She wondered if Va-nah had suffered an ecological crash of some kind, or even whether the humanoid population might have come from some other world. It was frustrating to discover so many intriguing mysteries in a world from which she might be snatched away at any moment, without a chance to solve them.

But for now, she had to focus on her immediate situation.

Ren-ah-ree had been watching her closely.

"You find our ways hard to understand," she said. "Is it not so in your city?"

"No, it is not! We have many plants to eat that supply us with the same nourishment as flesh. Some of my people live without eating meat. And we have many animals without human minds that we can eat for food, without killing each other."

"And yet you will not take me to that city, that I, too, may live without killing for flesh."

"I can't," Victory said. "Believe me, I would return there if I could, and take you with me. I have been taken from my home, and I don't know how to get back there."

Ren-ah-ree rapped her forepaws on the ground. Her eyes flashed with intensity.

"How did this happen?" she said. "Was there a glowing purple light? A warrior woman with ebon wings?"

Astonished, Victory leaned toward the Va-gas.

"Yes! Well, not exactly. There was a device that controlled an invisible force—" She shook her head. It would be impossible to explain the Gridley Wave device to most humans of Earth, let alone this stranger from another world. "But yes, a purple vortex appeared." She shook her head once more as the word "vortex" again failed to translate. "A purple cloud, a wind, that swirled around." She motioned with her hands. "It created a kind of opening in the sky, and I found myself swept away by it, as the air that runs away sweeps you when Zo-al is angry. It carried me to another world, after which I was swept from place to place by some other, unknown force, until I found myself here. I saw no winged woman when I first traveled through the swirling cloud, but later I saw one such as you describe. And during our confrontation, again I was snatched away to another place."

Ren-ah-ree was nodding her head in vigorous excitement.

"The purple wind! Like the one surrounding the winged woman and that which surrounds you."

"You can see the purple wind around me right now?" Victory asked, wondering if Va-gas eyes could perceive a part of the spectrum that humans could not.

"Yes. That was what made me think of leaving my tribe. I went to gather fruits, away from the other females to escape their constant tormenting. A winged woman appeared in the sky surrounded by a purple glow, as you did, but unlike you, she did not fall. The purple wind blew from the winged woman onto me, and then, at the moment she vanished, it swept me away, with Da-va-ro on my back. I found myself in a strange place, underground it seemed. I saw others, two-legged people. I thought I might have been taken to a U-ga city, but they were strange and not like U-ga. They looked more similar to you.

"I do not know how much time passed there. I grew hungry. I tried to speak with the strangers, but they could not understand me. Then I found myself back on the hillside, the other females still within earshot, as if nothing had happened. And at that moment, I thought to myself that there are other people, other places in Va-nah, and I decided we would try to find such a place. Maybe it would be better than living with the Sar-vans."

"This city you seek," Victory said, "do you know how to find it?"

Some of Ren-ah-ree's excitement faded. "I do not. But I believe it exists. There is a saying among Va-gas, 'News comes from the females.' Because we do not go to war, we have much time to talk among ourselves and exchange stories. Whoever has new stories is liked best, at least for a time. Females of different tribes often mingle. When we are captured by warriors of another tribe, we are taken to their huts and live with them. And so news spreads from tribe to tribe. I heard a tale once, when I was young, of a U-ga woman who had fallen from the sky and lived with the No-vans for a time, but she escaped before she became meat. With her, there was another, who said he came from another world, as you claimed. This was considered a very funny story, and we laughed at it very much. We thought the U-ga must have feared so much for his life that he lost his mind and said many things that were not so. But when I saw you fall, I wondered."

"Not long ago, more females of another tribe were captured. And there was much talk from them of a secret city where some Va-gas had traveled, a city where U-ga did not eat Va-gas anymore. A city where flesh grew like fruits in big pots. The Sar-vans thought this was a very funny story. But after I was carried away by the purple wind, I thought that anything might be possible. So I am going to seek this city. I know how cities are found. The U-ga build in the mountains, at the edges of the great Hoos. Within the lip of one of the Hoos, the way to the city will be found. So I have heard. We are warned to avoid those places, because that is where the U-ga capture us, and also because Zo-al dwells in the depths of the Hoos. But I will defy Zo-al's wrath to find the hidden city."

"Then let me come with you," Victory said. "I can fight for you. If we can find the city, I may be able to make a device—like these, but more powerful—" she waved one of the Kalkar guns, "and with it I might control the purple wind. Then I could take you to my city, to Pellucidar where there is food for all."

Ren-ah-ree scowled as she pondered Victory's words. "When I first saw you, I thought you an enemy," she said. "I saw the glow of the purple wind hanging about you. I thought you had come to snatch me away again. But if you also were taken by the purple wind, we have the same enemy."

Gradually, her scowl changed to a fierce smile. "I have decided. We will go together. We will fight together. If we succeed, we will eat together—and if you are lucky, we will eat flesh that is not yours."

Victory felt almost certain Ren-ah-ree was joking, but it was hard to be sure. Still, her spirits lifted at the thought that the Va-gas might lead her to a place with the technology to make metal and weapons. In such a place, she might actually be able to fulfill her boast to Ren-ah-ree, and rebuild the uncertainty gun she had lost when swept away from Pellucidar. Then she could try to employ the principles of the Gridley Wave and its quantum energies to connect again with Jason Gridley, and possibly even find her way home.

"Now we are full-fed," Ren-ah-ree said. "Next we will sleep. Then we will run to the mountains to find the city."

The two Va-gas curled up in the moss. Victory stepped out from the shelter of the trees to have a look at the Kalkar garments she had put outside. The stains of blood had been washed away in the storm, and the fabric had dried in the sun. Victory rolled them up and used them for a pillow. She lay back, reflecting that she'd been able to provide much better for herself in Va-nah than in most of the "angles"—the Mahar Queen Tu-al-sa's word—through which she had been tumbled.

Watching idly through half-closed eyes, she observed that Da-va-ro was not asleep. He had picked up the fruits with which Victory had attempted to explain cosmology to Ren-ah-ree. He held them up and moved them through space in swooping gestures, talking to himself all the while in whispered words she couldn't quite catch. Ren-ah-ree might have rejected Victory's teaching, but it had kindled the young one's imagination, and now he pictured worlds spinning in space to a tale of his own invention.

Victory noticed that his supposedly deformed fingers easily grasped and manipulated the fruits. They were far more deft and flexible than the tough paw-like digits of the adult Va-gas. Victory was intrigued. While Da-va-ro's hands might be a disability for the life his tribe now lived, they could be a favorable mutation that might lead to a technological leap for the Va-gas as a species. She wished she could count on having time to explore and assist his abilities.

The little Va-gas glanced up and saw that she was watching him. Quickly, he made a rude face at her and turned his back on her. But she saw that he still clasped the fruits as he slept. Soon, Victory slept too.

She woke before the Va-gas, and used the time to pick more fruits and nuts and pack them in the pouch that carried the salvaged Kalkar guns. She returned in time to help the Va-gas load their supplies onto Ren-ah-ree's back. Victory persuaded the Va-gas to let her tether the flying gear to the straps of Ren-ah-ree's harness, pointing out that it weighed almost nothing. Victory had not yet examined it in detail, and she was reluctant to leave it behind without learning its secrets.

They moved swiftly up the mountainside. Da-va-ro frolicked alongside.

Victory nudged Ren-ah-ree to get her attention.

"Here on the mountains, his difference is not a disadvantage," she said. "He moves as quickly as we do, and he can easily use his forelimbs to grasp and climb, as I do."

"But Va-gas don't live in the mountains," Ren-ah-ree said.

"You are here now. Things can change."

Ren-ah-ree snorted irritably, but Victory thought her eyes dwelled more thoughtfully on her young one.

They climbed higher and higher. For Victory, the journey had a dreamlike quality. There was no night or day. Va-nah's illumination came from everywhere and nowhere, glowing through the ever-changing clouds and mists in shades of lavender, rose, and gold. They slept and ate when they had need, and then moved on in what seemed like an unending afternoon.

But their ascent was no picnic. The rests were brief. Ren-ah-ree turned often to look behind them.

"The storm was good—maybe it washed away our tracks. But I fear Kalkars seeking revenge. They are ruthless and do not take defeat lightly."

From the height they had reached, they could look out over vast distances below. They could even see, far out on the plains, moving masses that might have been troops of Va-gas on the march. Once, below them, they saw dark flying shapes that might have been winged Kalkars or U-ga. Ren-ah-ree quickly took cover, and they did not resume their journey for some time, and after much scrutiny of the skies above and the sweep of land below.

Victory cut her own rest short to work with the Kalkar devices. She found the guns easy enough to use, and startled the Va-gas out of their naps when she learned to activate the firing button. Ren-ah-ree cast the weapon aside as useless, after finding that her powerful, leathery digits would not fit within the trigger guard. But Da-va-ro was fascinated by the guns, and Victory was impressed again with the agility and potential skill in his digits. The young Va-gas sulked and made faces at her when she would not allow him to try firing the gun. Victory did not dare take the gun apart to learn how many charges were left, or how they worked. They might find themselves in sore need of its defense, and she could not afford to let Da-va-ro waste shots in play.

Victory experimented with slipping her arms into the flying harness, and scrutinized the controls until she had some idea how they might work, but Ren-ah-ree showed great agitation at the idea that Victory should try to activate their power. The Va-gas' greatest fear was to attract the attention of more Kalkars, or the mysterious U-ga she also feared.

"Stick to the ground," she demanded. "Flying people are nothing but trouble. Do not cast yourself into empty air and lure them to us."

Victory complied for the time being, but it went against the grain to deny herself a chance to learn. The next time Ren-ah-ree paused to sleep, Victory donned the gear and made a cautious hop into the air. She hovered for a moment close to the ground, and then, as she manipulated the controls and stroked the air with her wings, soared upward twenty or thirty feet. She wheeled about madly, like a kite in a gusty wind, as she experimented. While at Oxford, she had taken the controls of a friend's glider a few times, after persuading him to take her up. The feeling of guiding her flight came back to her—like riding a bicycle, she thought, but this was a very special and tricky kind of cycle! She caught an updraft and circled serenely, loving the feeling of ease and height. Va-nah's vistas, curving majestically around her on all sides until the mountains and vales disappeared into the endless mists, were a glorious sight.

She quickly returned focus to her goal: reconnaissance. She was eager to know how far it might be to the crater Ren-ah-ree claimed they would find. Riding the rising air, she crested the next ridge, and saw a deep cleft in the ground ahead, within which the vast rocky rim of a crater showed plainly. Victory had never been sure that Ren-ah-ree knew where she was going, but now it seemed clear that the Va-gas was right! Their destination was in sight.

Eagerly, she turned to share the news, only to find her eye drawn to movement on the mountainside far below. It was a furtive stirring among the grasses, out of sync with the lazy rhythm of the breeze. Something—more than one something—was creeping up the slope toward them. She prepared to dive, but it was too late. She heard distant shouting as one of the pursuers burst out of hiding and pointed at her.

She plunged earthward, hastening the dive with powerful beats of her wings. She landed too fast, with a thud and rattle of stones that roused the Va-gas to instant alarm.

"Kalkars are tracking us," Victory cried. "Move!"

Taking in the sight of Victory's wings, and grasping the situation at once, Ren-ah-ree bared her teeth in a grimace of anger.

"I told you not to fly," she growled. "Now our enemies have seen us!"

"But we never would have seen them if I hadn't spotted them from the air," Victory said, as they sprang at once into a run uphill. "And the good news is, this Hoo of yours is near at hand. Just over the next ridge, if we can beat them to it."

Ren-ah-ree put forth her full strength in great, ground-covering bounds. Victory found that with the wings still attached, she could keep up, skimming just above the Va-gas and stretching her wings to the utmost.

But the pace up the steep slope was too much for Da-va-ro. He fell behind.

"Get on my back," Ren-ah-ree panted. He scrambled up, with a boost from Victory. But his extra weight slowed Ren-ah-ree considerably.

"Stop for a minute," Victory said.

"Can't stop! Kalkars will kill us!"

"I have a better idea! Stop!"

Ren-ah-ree might not have complied, but her flanks were heaving, and exhaustion was persuasive.

Victory dropped to the ground for a brief moment, just long enough to help Da-va-ro wrestle his arms into the other winged harness. Even in such danger, he grinned with delight. Perhaps too much delight, Victory thought. She took another precious minute to tether the young Va-gas with a strap to his mother's back harness, so he couldn't fly off out of control. The flotation sac took the weight off Ren-ah-ree's back, and while Da-va-ro's arms were too short to fully extend the wings, he soon got the hang of rowing against the air to provide some forward impetus.

Now they moved swiftly indeed, and Victory's hope soared, as it seemed they would outdistance their pursuers. They toiled up the summit of the slope with heart-bursting effort for Ren-ah-ree and Victory, and glee for Da-va-ro, who was thoroughly enjoying himself. A struggle among boulders at the top, and then they were scrambling desperately down a precipitous slope on the other side, toward the rim of the crater.

At its edge, they halted, peering down into darkness. Night never came to Va-nah. Its blackness existed only within the Hoos.

"Stay put," Victory said. "I'll fly down and see if I can find a path."

Ren-ah-ree stamped her feet, glancing anxiously up the slope behind them.

"Hurry!" she said.

A cold shudder of fear went through Victory as she forced herself over the edge and down into the darkness. Perhaps it was not fear alone that chilled her, she thought, but the cold current of air that swirled within the crater. Here there was no warm wind to support her wings. The cold seemed to draw her down. She had to beat hard with her pinions to keep from sinking into the depths.

As she descended, a sudden flare of white light blinded her. It took anxious moments to readjust to the darkness, moments in which she could see nothing at all. Cautiously daring another look, she realized the light was distant, showing as a crescent deep in the crater. It was only visible from the correct angle. A wild hypothesis came to mind: was she seeing all the way into the so-called realm of Zo-al? Then, she had an even wilder yet more plausible idea. Perhaps this Hoo, like the polar passage from Pellucidar to the outer world, penetrated all the way to the surface of Va-nah, and the light she saw was the light of Va-nah's sun! The intermittent solar radiation could be the explanation for many things, including ferocious storms like the one they had experienced. Not for the first time, her desire for exploration and discovery warred with the needs of the moment.

Victory clenched her fists in frustration at the stupidity of sentient beings squandering their time on pointless warfare when the universe with all its secrets lay before them. The gesture inadvertently depressed controls on her flying gear, and she dropped precipitously. Arresting her fall after only a few feet, and trying to reswallow her stomach, she found herself staring at a ledge clinging to the curve of the crater, twenty feet or so below its edge. She beat vigorously with her wings to lift herself back to the surface. Was it her imagination, or had the air currents reversed, now blowing outward from the depths and assisting her upward motion? She had no time to explore that possibility, either.

A cry of rage from the surface above hastened her flight. She shot into the outer air in time to see a six-man squad of winged Kalkars plunging toward them over the crest of the ridge. Ren-ah-ree stood at the lip of the crater with her spear raised, ready to defend herself. The Kalkars spread out to encircle the Va-gas, preparing to fire on her from above.

"Quick!" Victory commanded. "Over the edge! Try to climb down. There is a ledge not far below. It should catch you if you slip. I'll hold them off."

Ren-ah-ree frowned as if she would resist retreat, but when projectiles from the Kalkars' guns whined past her ears, it was clear she could do nothing to defend herself and Da-va-ro. She bounded over the boulders on the edge of the crater and plunged into shadow with Da-va-ro in tow. Victory tried to replicate her earlier crazy-kite flight pattern, while pulling her own weapons from her pouch. It wasn't hard to zigzag unpredictably, as she tried to control the wings while arming herself. She wondered how the Kalkars managed it. Their bullets whistled about her as she dodged.

She held them off with a couple of quick shots as she dove, then pulled up to hover just below the protection of the crater's edge. She had not been mistaken earlier. A powerful, chill blast blew up from the depths. It tossed her like a small plane in turbulence as she aimed to wing the pursuers. One of her godfather's favorite oaths burst from her lips as one shot went astray. Her next shot also missed the intended target of the Kalkar's wing, but struck the flier's hand and the adjacent controls. "Sorry, mister," she muttered. "Next time you might try not attempting to *kill* me." Trailing blood, the man dropped out of sight.

Victory turned to battle her way downward and catch up with her allies. The two Va-gas remained tethered together by the length of a strap. Da-va-ro whimpered in fear, but his agile fingers found cracks in the rock to which he could cling. Ren-ah-ree had greater difficulty. Her body, though muscular and powerful, was not well formed for climbing. Victory hovered alongside, hoping to assist them if they fell, and wishing she had a flashlight. She hoped the flying gear still strapped to Da-va-ro's back might hold him up or at least slow his descent should he lose his grip.

The winds were rising, and it grew more and more difficult to control the wings. Earlier, she had struggled to fight the downward pull of the abyss. Now, she fought to descend rather than being hurled up out of the crater by the rush of wind from below. She felt as if the wings would be torn from her arms, or her arms would be torn from her body. With a blinding flash of light, what looked like a ball of fire whirled past her toward the surface. She briefly felt its scorching heat, and heard the cries of the Va-gas, as she spread her wings in a vain attempt to shelter them.

While she was still recovering her vision, the remaining five of the Kalkar flight squad dropped over the rim of the crater in renewed pursuit. More practiced in flight than she, they banked around her and dove toward the Va-gas climbing below her. Another flash of light showed Victory that Ren-ah-ree and Da-va-ro had almost reached the ledge. Yet, while still using all their limbs to climb, they were defenseless against the renewed onslaught. Victory had no stomach for killing in a conflict she still did not understand, but she could not watch idly while her companions died. She set her teeth and determined to aim better.

Firing on the Kalkars from above, she punctured the gasbag on the back of the nearest. Catapulted into erratic flight like a leaky balloon, he bounced off the wall of the crater and was carried upward and away by the rising storm.

Ren-ah-ree had gained the ledge, but she and Da-va-ro were barely clinging to their perch as the storm winds tore at them. The disabled Kalkar's gun had fallen at their feet, and Ren-ah-ree tried, in desperation, to aim the despised weapon at the remaining enemies, but her three-digit hands could not manage the controls. Casting it aside, the Va-gas prepared to fend off the attackers with her spear alone, but they were too wily to come within stabbing range.

Victory tried to wing another of the fliers, but her desperate squeezing of the firing button had no result. She had expended her last charge. Diving, she brought the butt of the gun down on the Kalkar's head with all her force. Half-stunned, he wobbled in flight and missed his aim. Ren-ah-ree cast her spear, impaling him, but he carried her weapon with him into the abyss. Ren-ah-ree boldly faced her enemies with nothing but a knife.

Da-va-ro, who had been shoved behind his mother for protection, reached past her to seize the discarded gun. With his hands, once judged defective by his tribe, he proved able to aim the weapon, reach the trigger, and fire. His first shot flew wild, but a second effort hit the gloating Kalkar who was poised to slay the Va-gas, and sent him tumbling away, to crash against the wall of the crater. Victory turned to face the attack of the remaining members of the flying squad, but they were nowhere to be seen.

"Cowards!" Ren-ah-ree shouted triumphantly. "They dare not face three warriors!"

Victory descended to join them on the ledge with difficulty, for the rising winds threatened to drag her away. Together, backs pressed to the wall, the three of them inched along the ledge in search of shelter. Suddenly, Ren-ah-ree, who went first, stumbled and nearly fell into an opening in the rock. Da-va-ro dashed ahead of her, into the opening, heedless of their calls for caution. When he had gone a few feet into the darkness, a light appeared within, illuminating the way ahead.

"Come," Ren-ah-ree shouted. "Here is shelter! Enter quickly!" She hastened after Da-va-ro, delirious with joy. "The marvelous lights must surely mark the way to a city!"

Victory, too, felt her heart leap with hope. Such high technology might indeed be a sign of a possible refuge where she could rebuild her uncertainty gun. Home might be within reach.

A stone just in front of her feet shattered, stinging her with rock fragments and stopping her before she could follow the others to safety. She whirled to see that the last of the Kalkars had returned. They hovered before the opening to the tunnel, ready to fire again on the fleeing Va-gas, who had nowhere to hide.

Victory leaped back out of the tunnel, into the air again. The full force of the wind struck her. She tumbled and for a moment expected to be smashed against the rocks. She struck out in midair with hands and feet, connecting with one of the fliers. As she steadied herself in flight, it was he who crashed into the wall.

Victory heard Ren-ah-ree call out to her from the mouth of the tunnel. The Va-gas had turned back for her, as she had on the day they met.

"Come to safety!" Ren-ah-ree shouted. "I will guard you! I will not leave you!"

But this time, Victory could not accept her help.

"Protect the little one," she cried. "He must live to fight again."

The Kalkar righted himself and turned to come back at her, as his companion in arms descended upon her from above. She braced herself to face them, armed as she had been at first, with no weapons but courage and her bare hands. Another ball of lightning hurtled up from the depths, lighting the scene with a lurid glare. Victory threw up her arms to protect her face as the fireball exploded with terrific force and a deafening crash of thunder, ripping both Kalkars to oblivion.

Disoriented and tumbling, Victory nearly missed the ledge, to be swallowed up by the storm. She felt a strong grasp seize her, as Ren-ah-ree leaned out from the tunnel opening to pull her to safety. She alighted on the ledge, and their eyes met, but Victory could not hear what the Va-gas said to her. She thought her ears were still ringing from the thunderclap, but then recognized the sound as the same discordant twang that preceded a fall out of present time and space, back into the void.

Her limbs tingled. Ren-ah-ree's words were distorted in Victory's ears as the quantum link that allowed translation began to dissolve. She felt Ren-ah-ree's grasp slip away as the scene faded from her eyes.

Ren-ah-ree's words, finally making sense to her, were the last thing she carried with her into the void: "Goodbye, my friend."

QUANTUM INTERLUDE
WHERE ANGELS FEAR...

Ruins of the Mahar city of Mintra, Pellucidar, circa 1950

THE YOUNG MAN STOOD irresolutely in the cave opening, the perpetual noonday sun of the hollow world at the Earth's core hot against his back.

"Jason!" cried a querulous voice from the shadowed interior. "Jason Gridley! Why are you dawdling there in the doorway when I need you in here?"

He ducked through the opening and stood blinking across the dim chamber at the little old man hunched over a table piled high with strange instruments.

"Abner?"

"Yes, yes, come here." The old man turned his face up to squint at him in the flickering light of half a dozen haphazardly placed candles. "But, hold on. You're not—"

"No, Abner, I'm not Jason. My father's gone missing, don't you remember? That's why we're here."

"I do beg your pardon, my boy. Of course, I remember. I haven't lost all of my marbles quite yet, you know. It's only this blasted candlelight. My eyes are accustomed to proper electric illumination, as we now enjoy back in civilized Sari, and for a moment you looked just like . . ." Abner Perry cocked his head to one side. "You've shaved off that ridiculous beard of yours, haven't you? Are you deliberately trying to deceive me?"

Janson Gridley, son of Jason and of Jana, the Red Flower of Zoram, rubbed self-consciously at his smooth chin. "No, sir," he said. "I just thought that, well, Victory seemed to prefer—"

"No need to explain, lad," Perry said in softer tones. "And have

371

no fear. We will find your father and young Victory ere long." He pointed to a small, boxy machine in the center of the jumble of equipment. "In point of fact, I have been receiving some very odd signals through the Gridley Wave for the past while. Nothing intelligible as yet, but I feel certain I have heard snatches of human speech. It's very promising!"

He hopped to his feet and wandered around the cluttered room, peering here and there in frustration through the dim light. "Now where have my ether plates disappeared to? Do sit down, Janson." He motioned the young man to take his place at the table. "I must go to the supply tent and I do not wish to leave the apparatus unattended. I shan't be a moment."

The young man slumped into the chair with a sigh as the old inventor hastened from the room.

He was staring aimlessly at the collection of tubes and tangled wires, his thoughts far from the little cave, when the transceiver burst into life with a swell of hissing static.

"Hello?" came a distant voice. "Can anyone hear . . ." The static rose again and washed away the rest of the utterance.

Janson leaned forward in excitement, his hand fumbling for the microphone through the chaos of the table top. Distant or not, he knew that voice!

"Victory? Victory, is that you? It's me—it's Janson! Where are you?"

". . . barely hear you," came the hissing reply. "Did you say Janson? Janson, you have to listen to me. I've figured it out! There are worlds upon worlds, Janson—ours is not the only universe! You have to tell Abner . . ." Another wave of the weird interference washed over the urgent voice. Janson held his breath, bending low over the transceiver. Thirty seconds later the voice returned amid choppy waves of static: "There is a field surrounding . . . when traveling between the outer crust and . . . aurora effect at the North Pole . . . guessing the iron mole also passed through a . . . incredible to believe, I know . . . multiple realities!" The static rose in intensity once more, then abruptly the device fell silent.

"Victory!" Janson was clutching the microphone so tightly that his fingers ached. "Are you with my father? Tell me how to find you!"

A few seconds later the faint voice was back, borne on hissing waves and even weaker now: "Abner will know . . . follow the signal . . . ." Silence.

"*Victory!*"

"Come, come! What is all the commotion, my boy?" Perry came bustling back into the chamber, thin arms laden with metal instruments. "Talking to oneself is a sign of failing intelligence, you know."

"Abner!" cried Janson, leaping up from the table. "It was Victory! We spoke with each other, but only for a minute or two."

"Victory, you say?" The old man looked about in confusion before his eyes alighted on the Gridley Wave set. "I see! Well, what did she have to say for herself, lad?"

Janson repeated Victory's words as faithfully as he could recall them. "Unfortunately," he concluded, "the rest was lost to some kind of fluctuating interference."

"Oho." Perry dropped into the seat, already deep in thought. "But that's marvelous. Gad! That's just what we needed to know. Don't you see?" He peered up at the young man's puzzled face. "Why, I'm disappointed in you, Jason."

"It's *Janson*."

Perry clucked his tongue dismissively. "It's this preoccupation with minutiae that prevents you from seeing the big picture." He tuned a dial on the Gridley Wave set and examined an adjoining meter, then nodded with satisfaction as the needle came to rest at a particular tick mark. "As I was saying, a simple carrier wave modulated with the original frequency should do the trick."

Janson's face lit up. "You mean we can find out where she is?"

"Well, of course. Isn't that what I just said?" He cast about among the pieces of apparatus he had dumped onto the already crowded table. "Here, assist me in calibrating this theodolite." He made a few measurements, then pulled a book of star charts from the outer world from a shelf beneath the table, and began riffling through the pages. "Ah, here we are. The coordinates of origin are in the direction of NGC 7006."

"NGC?" Janson repeated. "A globular cluster?"

"Quite so, my boy."

Janson's heart sank. "Abner, how on earth—or *in* it—do we bring her back from the other side of the galaxy?"

The old man shrugged his thin shoulders. "I have no idea. Oh, don't look so crestfallen, Anson. We can always dispatch someone to visit her."

"Visit her? How?"

"I have been speaking over the wireless with young Moritz about his ideas of energy-matter transmission. It strikes me that his theories are not incompatible with what we found on this ancient Mahar tablet." He gestured to a corner of gray stone peeking out from beneath the pile of instrumentation. "The difference being that the Mahars evidently knew how to put into practice what remains a mere pipe dream to Moritz. I'll have to work out the mathematics, of course, and construct the appropriate mechanism, and then we should be up and running."

Janson at once appointed himself the old inventor's assistant, remaining faithfully by his side as Perry alternately prayed to the Almighty for the success of their work and swore at the equipment with such an inspired and profane facility that the younger man was left in awe. They made an unusual pair, Perry clad in the khaki jacket, breeches, and stout shoes he favored, while Janson dealt more practically with the heat of Pellucidar's everlasting day in his loincloth of antelope fur and a pair of rough sandals fashioned from the hide of the rhinoceros-like *sadok*.

Time beneath the stationary sun of the inner world is a subjective prospect and Janson had no idea how long the project took. He only knew that he had practically reached the end of his patience by the time Perry finally leaned back from his table with a sigh of satisfaction and announced that his work was complete.

"Now it should be a simple matter of converting a living being into energy and effecting its transmission along the carrier wave." The old man's face turned thoughtful. "It will likely be a one-way trip for our voyager, however, and I daresay we shall have great difficulty locating someone either courageous or foolhardy enough to volunteer . . ."

But Janson was grinning broadly. "Oh, that's where you're wrong, Abner."

The Swords of Eternity super-arc concludes in
Victory Harben: Fires of Halos
by Christopher Paul Carey

ABOUT THE AUTHORS

JOHN CARTER
OF MARS®
GODS OF THE FORGOTTEN

GEARY GRAVEL is the author of the Philip K. Dick Award finalist *The Alchemists*, as well as the novels *The Pathfinders*, *A Key for the Nonesuch*, and *Return of the Breakneck Boys*. He has also written several novelizations, including *Hook*, based on the Steven Spielberg film, and *Batman: Mask of the Phantasm*, based on the animated movie. He lives in western Massachusetts, where he worked for decades as a Sign Language Interpreter for the Deaf.

VICTORY HARBEN™
STORMWINDS OF VA-NAH™

ANN TONSOR ZEDDIES first encountered the ERB Universe as a child, when an old professor who lived down the street allowed her to choose a volume from his shelves. She chose *Tarzan of the Apes*. Later, she read the adventures of John Carter aloud to her young son. She is the author of six science fiction novels, two of which were Philip K. Dick Award nominees. Her short fiction includes stories in *The Ultimate Silver Surfer* and *Magic in the Mirrorstone*. She lives in Michigan with her husband, near the shores of an inland sea.

EDGAR RICE BURROUGHS: MASTER OF ADVENTURE

The creator of the immortal characters Tarzan of the Apes and John Carter of Mars, EDGAR RICE BURROUGHS is one of the world's most popular authors. Mr. Burroughs' timeless tales of heroes and heroines transport readers from the jungles of Africa and the dead sea bottoms of Barsoom to the miles-high forests of Amtor and the savage inner world of Pellucidar, and even to alien civilizations beyond the farthest star. Mr. Burroughs' books are estimated to have sold hundreds of millions of copies, and they have spawned 60 films and 250 television episodes.

About Edgar Rice Burroughs, Inc.

Founded in 1923 by Edgar Rice Burroughs, one of the first authors to incorporate himself, EDGAR RICE BURROUGHS, INC., holds numerous trademarks and the rights to all literary works of the author still protected by copyright, including stories of Tarzan of the Apes and John Carter of Mars. The company oversees authorized adaptations of his literary works in film, television, radio, publishing, theatrical stage productions, licensing, and merchandising. Edgar Rice Burroughs, Inc., continues to manage and license the vast archive of Mr. Burroughs' literary works, fictional characters, and corresponding artworks that has grown for over a century. The company is still owned by the Burroughs family and remains headquartered in Tarzana, California, the town named after the Tarzana Ranch Mr. Burroughs purchased there in 1919 that led to the town's future development.

In 2015, under the leadership of President James Sullos, the company relaunched its publishing division, which was founded by Mr. Burroughs in 1931. With the publication of new authorized editions of Mr. Burroughs' works and brand-new novels and stories by today's talented authors, the company continues its long tradition of bringing tales of wonder and imagination featuring the Master of Adventure's many iconic characters and exotic worlds to an eager reading public.

Visit **EdgarRiceBurroughs.com** for more information.

EDGAR RICE BURROUGHS AUTHORIZED LIBRARY™

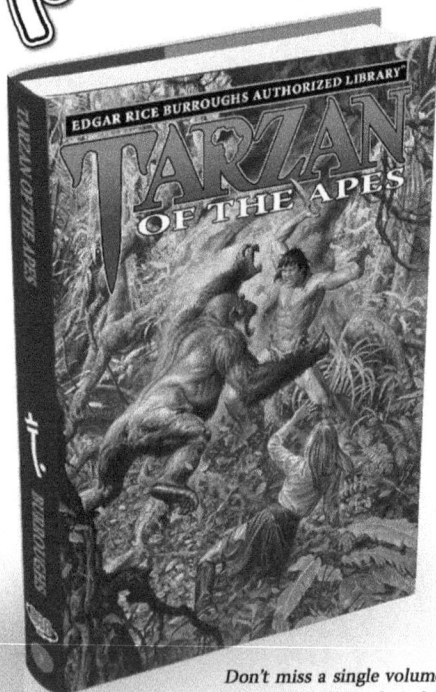

COLLECT EVERY VOLUME!

For the first time ever, the Edgar Rice Burroughs Authorized Library presents the complete literary works of the Master of Adventure in handsome uniform editions. Published by the company founded by Burroughs himself in 1923, each volume of the Authorized Library is packed with extras and rarities not to be found in any other edition. From cover art and frontispieces by legendary artist Joe Jusko to forewords and afterwords by today's authorities and luminaries to a treasure trove of bonus materials mined from the company's extensive archives in Tarzana, California, the Edgar Rice Burroughs Authorized Library will take you on a journey of wonder and imagination you will never forget.

Don't miss a single volume! Sign up for email updates at ERBurroughs.com to keep apprised of all 80-plus editions of the Authorized Library as they become available.

Spine titles (left to right):
1. TARZAN OF THE APES
2. THE RETURN OF TARZAN
3. THE BEASTS OF TARZAN
4. THE SON OF TARZAN
5. TARZAN AND THE JEWELS OF OPAR
6. JUNGLE TALES OF TARZAN
7. TARZAN THE UNTAMED
8. TARZAN THE TERRIBLE
9. TARZAN AND THE GOLDEN LION
10. TARZAN AND THE ANT MEN
11. TARZAN, LORD OF THE JUNGLE
12. TARZAN AND THE LOST EMPIRE
13. TARZAN AT THE EARTH'S CORE
14. TARZAN THE INVINCIBLE
15. TARZAN TRIUMPHANT
16. TARZAN AND THE CITY OF GOLD
17. TARZAN AND THE LION MEN
18. TARZAN AND THE LEOPARD MEN
19. TARZAN'S QUEST
20. TARZAN THE MAGNIFICENT
21. TARZAN AND THE FORBIDDEN CITY
22. TARZAN AND THE FOREIGN LEGION
23. TARZAN AND THE MADMAN
24. TARZAN AND THE CASTAWAYS

THE JOURNEY BEGINS AT ERBURROUGHS.COM

ERB INC.

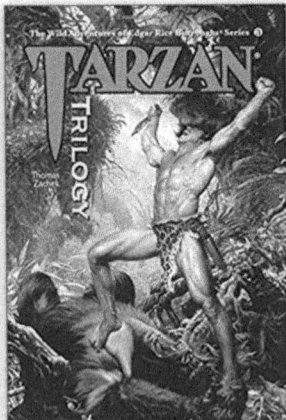

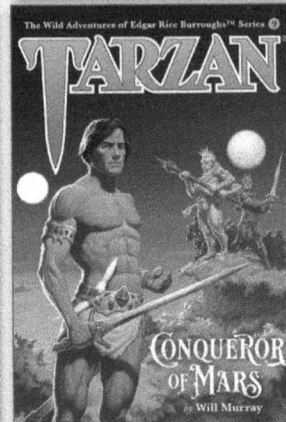

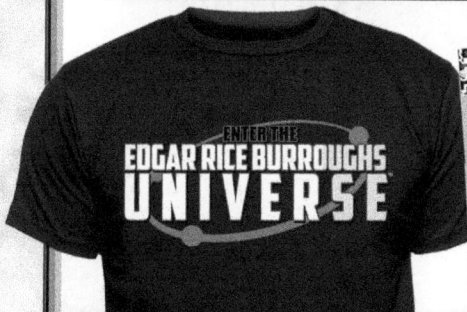

Lightning Source UK Ltd.
Milton Keynes UK
UKHW011529140921
390567UK00001B/289

9 781945 462337